ALREADY DEAD

ALSO BY DENIS JOHNSON

Fiction

Poetry

Denis Johnson

ALREADY

a california gothic

DEAD

HarperCollins*Publishers*

Some passages on pp. 417–418 are quoted without citation from Pedro Meseguer, S.J. *The Secret of Dreams*. Westminster, MD: The Newman Press, 1961.

HarperCollins books may be purchased for educational, business, or sales promotional use. For information please write: Special Markets Department, HarperCollins Publishers, Inc., 10 East 53rd Street, New York, NY 10022.

FIRST EDITION

Designed by Elina D. Nudelman

Library of Congress Cataloging-in-Publication Data

Johnson, Denis.
    Already dead : a California gothic / Denis Johnson. — 1st ed.
        p.   cm.
    ISBN 0-06-018737-9
    I. Title.
PS3560.03745A56   1997
813'.54—dc21   97-1528

97 98 99 00 01 ❖/RRD 10 9 8 7 6 5 4 3

for Cindy Lee

IT IS A PLEASURE TO THANK THE CHARLES ENGELHARD FOUNDATION AND THE LANNAN FOUNDATION FOR GIFTS THAT MADE THIS WRITING POSSIBLE; AND A PARTICULAR PLEASURE TO THANK THE POET BILL KNOTT, FROM WHOSE GENIUS SPRINGS THE PLOT OF THIS TALE.

In nightmares, which are no more than intensifications of some worry through anxiety, the terrible expectation is always fulfilled: the bull catches you, the knife reaches you, the axe whistles about your ears—but at this point, when you have given yourself up for dead, you wake up. (Though I once actually felt the cold steel of a sword thrust into me.)

—PEDRO MESEGUER, S.J.
THE SECRET OF DREAMS

Book One

August 7, 1990

V an Ness felt a gladness and wonder as he drove past the
small isolated towns along U.S. 101 in Northern
California, a certain interest, a yearning, because he sensed they were
places a person could disappear into. They felt like little naps you
might never wake up from—you might throw a tire and hike to a gas
station and stumble unexpectedly onto the rest of your life, the people who would finally mean something to you, a woman, an immortal friend, a saving fellowship in the religion of some obscure church.
But such a thing as a small detour into deep and permanent changes,
at the time, anyway, that he was travelling down the coast from
Seattle into Mendocino County, wasn't even to be dreamt of in Van
Ness's world.

The side trip he took off 101 into Humboldt County only proved
it. He deserted his route at Redway, went five miles west to Briceland
and from there a half dozen miles to the Mattole River and past an
invisible town (he saw only a one-room school in the corner of a
field) called Ettersburg, and then switched back and forth along
mountainous terrain another few miles to a dirt road that cut
through the King Range National Forest.

Bucking slowly in his Volvo down the steep zigzag track among dusty redwoods, Van Ness glimpsed the sky above the sea but not the sea. He stopped for two minutes at an elbow of the road overlooking the decline and ate a pack of cheese-flavored crackers and whisked the crumbs from his long mustache—handlebars arcing down into a monstrous Fu Manchu and serving, along with thick rimless spectacles, almost to obliterate any personality from his face. The crackers were the last of his food. He tossed the wrapper onto the floorboard and drove on.

Vaguely he wanted to accomplish some small cleansing of himself in this remote area known as "The Lost Coast," wanted to fast beside the Pacific and lie on his back all night within hearing of the ocean's detonations and look up at a meteor storm: between ten and thirty-five stars were expected to fall every minute that night, according to the weather report on his radio.

But when he reached the shores of the Pacific, he realized he'd only managed to find the back way into a place called Shelter Cove, a vast failed housing development on the isolated coast, hundreds of tiny empty lots set among asphalt streets with green signs on poles—CLAM AVENUE, BEACH DRIVE, and so on—shaken and speckled by the sandy wind. Half a dozen actual homes fronted the beach, and a few overturned runabouts, and a delicatessen, but really almost nobody had ever lived here. The sea burned in its heartless blueness while overhead flew helicopters filled, according to news flashes on his radio, with National Guardsmen and agents of the federal government conducting a massive raid on the marijuana patches in the unpeopled hills he'd just driven through. Van Ness bought his lunch in the deli and complained silently to himself about the weak coffee and the gull droppings on the picnic table. The only person he talked to was a pretty woman who swore at him because, as he walked past her table to the trash can, she dropped her sunglasses, and he stepped on them. The glasses were unsalvageable. He gave her fifteen dollars, although she claimed they'd cost twice that. Van Ness was back on the main highway again just a few hours after leaving it. He'd circled back to the town of Redway, the point where he'd turned off. The whole pointless excursion had a way of sealing his mind even further against any notion that great changes might beset him unexpectedly. And yet later he encountered the woman, Winona Fairchild, again, more than once; and eventually these encounters forced him to acknowledge the reality of fate, and the truth inherent in things of the imagination.

A California Highway Patrolman pulled him over on a stretch of 101 he had to travel before he would reach Leggett and turn west again toward the coast. Van Ness knew he'd been speeding; he did it habitually, compulsively. He carried a passenger at the time, a teenaged girl dressed after the style of Lithuanian peasants, in a long skirt, bright scarf, and sharply pointed purple shoes, her name a poetic creation possibly designating a flavor or a scent, like Rainbow Day or Temple Jasmine, but it had escaped his memory even as she'd said it. Except for the introductions, she and Van Ness hadn't traded ten words since he'd picked her up hitchhiking by the Texaco in Redway, at which time he'd said to her, "Welcome, Fantasy Lady."

Now he wished he hadn't said it. When the young patrolman stooped down beside the driver's window to peer within and ask for the license, the hippie girl leaned toward him over Van Ness's lap: "Is it about another ten miles to Leggett?"

"Yes, ma'am, little over eight miles," the patrolman said.

"He's really scaring me," she revealed suddenly.

"Who?" the patrolman said.

"This man," she said. "He made remarks. He touched my thigh."

"When?" asked Van Ness. "When I was reaching to the radio? That was an accident."

The policeman concentrated intensely, irrelevantly, on Van Ness's license. "Are you friends, you two people?"

Van Ness said, "No," and the girl said, "I was hitching."

"Go stand beside my car," the patrolman told the young woman.

Van Ness turned off the ignition. "I feel sick about this," he told the officer as they watched the girl walk, slightly pigeon-toed, toward the spinning lights of the squad car in her purple shoes. "I really feel confused. I didn't do a thing. Look, I know I'm no Casanova."

"Were you watching your rate of speed?"

"Yes, yes—I mean," Van Ness agreed, "I was definitely speeding, yes, sure. But this? No."

"I have to write up a ticket," the patrolman said. "Then I have to see about her. Then I have to see about you. If all you did was talk dirty and touch her thigh, I couldn't care less."

"I didn't talk dirty."

"If you *grabbed*, if you left a bruise or *mark*—"

"I didn't. I wouldn't."

"I'll talk to her."

"She's crazy."

"I meet very few who aren't," the patrolman assured him. "Not in this job."

"Okay."

"You probably are too," the officer said.

"Yes," Van Ness said.

As he waited for the officer to interview his victim, Van Ness felt the pent-up needs, sorrows, rages, in the cars speeding past them through Humboldt County, the passions walled up behind transparent windows.

Nothing came of it all, and he was on his way within a few minutes. He hadn't even been cited for excessive speed. The patrolman relieved him of his passenger, and Van Ness drove alone through Leggett and then over the hills on California 1 until he reached the coast again. Now he was in Mendocino County.

For eighty miles or so he followed the Coast Highway without stopping, testing his tires on the innumerable curves and wishing he had a sports car. Occasionally a house row or hamlet popped up and was gone, nothing substantial or even really provable aside from the towns of Fort Bragg and Mendocino. The terrain reminded him of Ireland, or of his idea of that country, which he'd never visited: the open fields strange and blue-gray in the oblique illumination, fields that everyone called palomino when the sunlight bleached them, but in a clutch of horses shading among evergreens at a pasture's edge he saw two palominos much more uniformly pale. Coastal moisture kept the grasses vital through the droughts; the potentiality of rebirth visible in the—

A right angle in the highway had him slamming on his brakes. Suddenly he was in Point Arena. He reacted with shock to the echo of his own car's engine off the buildings. Just before the place, three blocks ahead, where the town abruptly ceased as if coming up against a window onto the fields, Van Ness turned right and continued toward the harbor only because he enjoyed the look of things in that direction. Van had known many such communities, some that had included shabby houseboats. He liked the seafarers and the little clubs of progeny they brought with them from harbor to harbor. The land descended through a flat wandering valley, once perhaps some great diluvial watercourse, but not so much as a creek remained of it that he could see. Still the line of trailers and junk heaps might have been floated and abandoned here by a flood. Not a soul in sight, and the ocean was enormous. Before he turned back to the highway he sat in the idling car a minute looking down at it all. Here were homes, a large half-built restaurant, a fine new pier, boats at anchor. Everything waited to be touched, explored—fingered, broken.

Van Ness's lethargic pilgrimage—he was meandering south ostensibly to look for work in the marinas of the L.A. basin, though actually he had other plans—broke off at the southwestern corner of Mendocino County in Gualala, a town once named among the California coast's top ten ugliest communities. But Gualala wasn't so awful, not to his eye, merely aimless, its stores and motels strung along the oceanside cliffs in complete unconsciousness of the beauty they inhabited, of the hills above them massed with redwoods and the waves beating themselves to pieces in the mist below.

Frankenstein, an old friend from the merchant marine, lived a mile back in the complicated terrain above Gualala, on a long ridge accommodating another north-south road and another string of buildings, these more residential and much more widely scattered—a second, elevated Gualala. Frankenstein's was a small house on half an acre with a distant view, maybe a view of the ocean, it was hard to say: with the clouds lying down on the Pacific today, there seemed to be nothing left of California but the sky.

Nobody came to the door when Van Ness drove between the redwood slabs that marked the drive and alongside heaps of junk and stacks of unidentifiable salvage, the accumulations of a clearly eccentric personality—nobody answered when Van Ness went to the door and knocked, though Frank himself was visible through the picture window, sitting next to the dark mouth of his fireplace with his legs stretched far out in front of him, a long man, six feet, nine inches tall.

"It'll be dark out here pretty soon," Van Ness called through the windowpane, "but I won't leave."

In a minute the giant stood in the doorway looking down at him. "I don't answer anymore. There's never anybody there."

"I'm here."

"I'll give you the benefit of the doubt."

Already Van Ness wished he hadn't come. His friend had been

released only recently from a drug or psychiatric ward. Over the last few years he'd suffered setbacks and disarrangements.

Inside, Van felt even more uneasy. Frank had evidently torn apart his living room with a heavy tool, a crowbar, possibly, working in his surroundings a lot of zany perforations from which insulation puffed like yellow smoke. Much of the flooring had been ripped away down to the plywood.

Before he sat back down, the host yanked a plug from the wall socket, saying, "I was just listening to the radio. Did you hear? We're sending one zillion deranged Marines to the Gulf."

"I heard they were considering it."

"Considering no longer. It's an accomplished thing. This is a war, man."

"Isn't it a little early to say?"

"The *Pequod* is there right now."

"Right now?" The *Pequod* was their nickname for the *Peabody*, the merchant vessel they'd served on together some years before, a small freighter making ports in the Arabian Gulf and the Indian Ocean.

"Oh yeah, right now. Benhurtz cabled his wife, and she called me last week. Just after Iraq crossed the border."

"Just before you hit the unit."

"I was very fucked up, but I understood the conversation. Benhurtz is on the *Pequod*. *Pequod*'s on the Gulf. They're worried Iraq's going to pop mines out around there, dive-bomb the shipping, et cetera."

"It's hard to believe we were ever there."

"We could be there now. Smack up against a war."

"Do I sit down?" Van Ness wondered.

"Hey, take my chair," Frankenstein said, jumping up.

Van Ness dragged a chair away from what must have been the dining table and set it beside the cold hearth. Candy wrappers filled the fireplace, and the splintered lengths of oaken floorboards.

"The fog is here," Frank said, moving closer to the window.

"It was sunny all the way down the coast."

"We had twenty-one straight days of fog last month. Usually it licks up this high and then the morning backs it down a few yards. But last month it stayed."

"How many days have you been back?"

"I wasn't counting."

"Six."

"Okay," the giant said, "six." He turned and took a can of lighter fluid from the mantel and started squirting down the wood in his fireplace. He lit a cigarette and, discarding the match, set the kindling ablaze. The front of him turned orange and the room filled with purple shadows. "I was only *there* for three days," he said.

They'd been shipmates for nearly a decade. Van Ness had left the merchant marine after ten years. A "career move," a phrase covering a plenitude of small failures. Frankenstein had been drummed out a bit earlier for striking an officer. Van Ness had been a harbormaster in Florida, sold boats on Lake Champlain and most recently on Puget Sound. Frankenstein had taken up a trade and still owned, but did not operate, a plumbing business.

"During that whole time, I was in here with Yvonne," Frank said, "that entire twenty-one days of fog. Every morning we looked out that window and saw nothing but the truth—formless uniformity, the fullness of emptiness. Wow, it made my dick hard! We couldn't stop fucking! Then the thermodynamics altered off the coast, and the whole monkey dance began again, the universe: relations, progressions, transactions. The designation they give that is fair weather. They say it's clear. They call it good." As he spoke he was opening the front door, grabbing chunks of wood from a stack just outside and throwing them on the blaze. He sat down breathing hard, knocking over his ashtray, puffing on his cigarette, coughing. "Makes weird noises, don't it?" he said of the fire. "Whines and squeaks, clanks and moans. You should've been here two weeks ago. Unprecedented acoustics." He cleared his throat raggedly and spat at the flames. "Our happy little thing went sour."

"Whose thing?"

"Her real name isn't Yvonne. She invented a new name to devalue the memory of her parents, castrate her father."

"Weren't you doing therapy with her?"

"That's what was so beautiful, that combination—lover, therapist, goddess. Primal foe."

He'd struck the fellow, a recently commissioned ensign, a single blow with a closed fist; and squatted for thirty-six hours in the gangway outside the infirmary waiting to learn whether the ensign would live or die. They hadn't confined him because he'd been well liked by the captain and considered too large for the brig.

"She was victorious," he said, "in trying to destroy me with lingerie."

"She split," Van said. "Is that illegal? What's her crime?"

"What's her crime, right. The theft of sacred objects."

They'd had no problem dumping him from the service, because he'd lied about his height in the first place; had wilted somehow for the measuring. No formal hearing had been required. It had simply been a matter of correcting the figures and having him cashiered as unacceptably tall.

Frankenstein had been the *Peabody*'s resident intellectual, at least belowdecks—maybe an officer or two had been more widely read; maybe the officer he'd struck—studying, reciting, often getting passionate about things that didn't matter to most people. The others had always given space to the tall man, a natural leader because of his size, intelligence, and sweetness.

"I came here," Van Ness said, trying to speak carefully, "because I thought you might have something further to teach me."

"Teach you? Did I ever teach you? We read a couple books. Then what?"

"I don't know—what?"

"Do you think we're educated men? I haven't spoken to a college professor in my life. I could have done UCLA on a basketball thing, but I just skated on by. What did we really understand of Wittgenstein?"

"I know what we liked about him—"

"That he rejected his whole order of thought, yeah, and started fresh halfway through his life."

"His independence even from his own truths—"

"But we didn't understand those truths. On the *Pequod* we were just two assholes who collected big words. Everybody knew we were full of shit but us."

Van Ness was astonished. "That's very sad."

"No. It has no value one way or the other."

"I'm sick," Van told him.

"Sick?"

Van Ness said, "I'm not well."

"Not well . . . That sounds even worse."

"It is."

"That sounds like 'a lengthy illness.'"

"That's right."

"'Has died after a lengthy illness.'"

Van Ness put his face in his hands.

"Dying, huh? That's a very animal thing to do."

"Is that all you can think of to say to me?"

"All? No. I can bullshit till Christmas. I can spew reams, man."

Frankenstein looked nervous, bopping his foot, rubbing his fingertips rapidly with his thumb, chewing his lip. Van Ness recognized these as Frank's signs of anger. Intimidated by his own size, he denied himself any wilder expressions.

There was nothing here for Van, but he couldn't stop himself, not after five hundred miles spent rehearsing these thoughts. "Maybe we were posing, sure. But you opened the door for me. Wittgenstein, Spinoza—"

"Nietzsche."

"Yeah."

"Yeah? And why not Hobbes, and Locke? Why not Marx?"

"I don't know."

"Because they were pointed toward the depersonalized robot zombie Earth we now inhabit. I'm pointed toward the personal, the subjective, the much more deeply real. And I've gone on travelling in that direction. You—you cry, you weep, you want a theory to eat like a pill and make it all go away."

"You misunderstand me. Fuck you."

"If you're dying, then what you really have to do, man, what you're really gonna have to do most deeply now, is go ahead and die. Just animal right on out. Nice knowing you."

Van Ness said nothing for a few minutes while the giant chain-lit another Camel and smoked it away with a series of little convulsions, going into and out of the firelight repeatedly to flick the ash.

"I've had those golf clubs for years. I took a nine iron to the walls because I heard the mothers inside there scurrying around and whispering. Part of this, yeah," Frankenstein said, "was psychotic bullshit. But there are actual people involved, too, taking advantage, you know, of the chemical dementia. I wanted to split their heads open. I know who they are, some of them. They're shooting some kind of mist, some kind of spray, into the windows at night. I can hear it leaking into the car, man, when I'm driving. Oh yeah! Oh yeah! I can feel it on my skin. I yanked the guts out from under the hot tub, let the water out, turned the bastard upside down—okay. Nothing there. I took that nine iron and smashed through the floorboard in the panel truck, the Chevy, and I got one, man! I stabbed its face to shit with a screwdriver, blood all over my hands, my shirt, it was like a waterfall. Got up the next morning, the blood was gone. Not a trace. They washed it all off me while I was asleep. And they're shooting microscopic darts at me."

He paused to light up.

"I'm not a golfer," Van Ness said.

"Ninety percent of this is psycho bullshit, I realize. But ten percent of it is real." Frank pointed a finger at Van Ness's throat. "And that's the ten percent we have to watch out for."

The burning redwood hummed steadily. The fire was in its middle age. Rocking back and forth to dip his cigarette ash with his large hand, Frank seemed to enter and exit the changing torchlight of a primitive incarnation, in one of the smoky grotto shelters he liked to claim had been forgotten by his mind but imprinted on his spirit.

Frank had always preached a personal creed fixed, in a scholarly way, to the migrations of the human soul. Maybe, Van thought now, he was right, maybe Frank's own soul had checked out, simply left a TV babbling somewhere in this big, ruined hotel.

And yet two decades before, Frank had been the one to lead Van, the twenty-two-year-old, into the light of philosophy, the one to guard him while he grew.

Among the sailors belowdecks Van Ness had been seen as the large man's personal creation, a kind of pet—thus the nickname: Van Ness had had to struggle to remember, when asking for his friend's number from Directory Assistance, that Frankenstein's true name was Wilhelm Frankheimer.

Frank asked, "What have you got?"

"You don't understand, do you?"

"What's your disease?"

"Shit, man. Call it radiation poisoning."

"You haven't got anything. You're not dying."

Van told him, "I'll be dead within forty-eight hours."

"A short ride."

"Still: I could easily outlive you."

Driving south back into Gualala's town proper, Van Ness encountered a straight stretch on the coast route and pressed the accelerator pedal down all the way. And found himself, what with the fog and his headlights, driving into a wall of brilliance. He had no idea how far out in front of his windshield the pavement stretched before it hooked left or right and his own trajectory hung out over twenty-five fathoms of air. Within a quarter mile the machine was topping out at around 105, he believed, although the speedometer's needle came unmoored and whipped back and forth deliriously between 120 and nothing, and the Volvo itself shivered rhythmically awhile, then shuddered so hard he had to clench his teeth, and soon it shook like a crow's nest in a bad gale, threatening to break loose and fling itself to pieces in midair. Van eased his grip on the wheel until he was not quite touching it, warming his hands on the fires of out-of-control; then something in him—not his will—slapped his hands back onto the steering and pointed him at a legal velocity down the middle of the fog.

Van made it a habit to be friendly wherever he went; while he contemplated a late supper in the bar of a cliffside restaurant later that night, he bought a drink for a man who was also a visitor to the area, a wild-pig hunter. They'd started out by kidding the barmaid together and then got to talking. "Make it a double," Van urged the man. "I can't drink myself. I've got pancreatitis."

"Oh, any old thing," the hunter told him when Van asked about his line of work. "I've done a lot of logging lately."

"Where's that? Here in California?"

"Del Norte County mostly, yeah. Everywhere, practically."

The man's hunting companion, another bearded, bulky woodsman, came in and joined them. He'd just driven down from their campsite, and he complained about the fog and the curves, and the cliffs.

The first one bought his friend a drink and for Van a club soda. "You got—what? Your pancreas, something?"

"Pancreatic cancer, actually."

"Oh."

The men paused, sipping their drinks.

"Shit," the other burst out. "I'd be double-time paranoid behind something like that. Fatal, right?"

"Nothing's certain. I could still easily outlive you."

"Man"—the logger searched for words. "It's like—a big blue *light*."

"Really," Van said.

"Yeah."

"Listen. As far as cliffs: my sister's husband," the first man now told them, "went to welder's school in Santa Rosa down here. One day he was driving on the coast, on those cliffs north of Jenner. Have you seen that place? Five or six hundred feet straight down, no shoulder—you'd have time to shit your pants and change into clean ones before you hit. He was driving along behind this black Corvette. Corvette downshifts, Corvette accelerates, Corvette sails half a thousand feet down to the Pacific Ocean. Right over the edge. Turned out the guy had just bought the car that morning, brand-new Corvette. Some jilted kid. The brake lights," he said, "never winked."

His partner asked, "What year Corvette?"

"A year that don't concern us," the first man said impatiently. "A year you probably never heard of."

The chemistry between them was suddenly familiar to Van Ness. Their connection gave off a sour smoke, like bad wiring. He sensed they'd served time in prison together, or belowdecks.

Wilhelm Frankheimer felt easier when his old shipmate cut the visit short and left him. He had some coal soaking out by the forge, and he wanted to get to it.

He'd come by the forge as he had the rock saw and the panel truck and a few other large items, just inheriting them from people he'd once plumbed for, who'd gotten too old or too dead to use them.

As a child he'd wanted to be a blacksmith and had pictured himself slaving in the mighty light from a smithy's mouth. But this one wasn't much bigger than a backyard barbecue grill. You could almost mistake it for one, except for its stovepipe and the hand-cranked blower attached to the side like an oversized schoolroom pencil sharpener. He'd had the forge for years, but hadn't set it up until he'd come home, this last time, from the priests of reason. Working with steel had quickly become a pointless and happy obsession. He'd fashioned a simple knife and a couple of lopsided horseshoes, but for the most part he didn't make anything, simply heated steel, pounded steel—affected, worked, and changed steel just for the small glory in it, sometimes burning up the pieces by blowing the fire too hot and watching the metal spray stars until it was gone. *Products, forms*—he couldn't have cared less. This was the time of molten things. He'd entered a private and personal Iron Age, submerging himself in the elemental depths.

The day was nearly gone by the time he headed out back to the shop, a dirt-floored gardener's hut built by the people he'd bought his house from.

The fog was bad tonight. If he hadn't known precisely where the shed stood he couldn't have found it.

In the backyard Frankenstein held still a minute and listened to the faint yawping of the seals on Shipwreck Rock, a sound like that of numerous unlubricated things—pistons, pulleys, hinges—drifting up to him nearly two miles on the wind. Some of those sounds were in fact words. Some of the entities out there on that rock were not seals. And not the legendary wraiths of the drowned fishers howling without rescue these last eighty-seven years. Nor the lumberjacks, helpless on the stormy shore, who wept to hear them one midnight in 1903 while the fleet of seventeen barks went down, driven on a gale from Bodega Bay and ground up on these promontories with hardly a stick of kindling to show next day for all their lives and works. Actually, no, these entities belonged to *him* . . .

Carefully he listened. Not a word tonight. They were asleep in his veins.

As soon as he'd stepped inside his shop and turned on the light, Frankenstein felt his burdens lifting. At the forge he picked through yesterday's ashes, throwing aside the gnarled clinkers, keeping the pieces that had burned down to coal-coke. He scraped a space over the ash-grate in the tiny hearth and poured onto it three handfuls of wood pellets and doused them with kerosene. But something heavy lay inside him . . . Where did the weary heart come from? He struck the match, set the pellets ablaze. He didn't like having to start the fire again, that was the source of this small sadness. You get tired of these endless beginnings.

He and Van Ness should have broken off contact years ago. True enough, they were both alone, but in completely different ways, and they didn't deserve each other. Van, you're sort of a demon, he thought, scraping yesterday's coal-coke back toward the center of the hearth and over the burning wood pellets, using a metal trowel. He heaped onto his fire a few scoops of wet coal from the bucket of soak water, and raked them into a ring around its center in order to cook the sulfur out of them slowly.

Yes, the object was to remove the clinkers and the sulfur because anything that does not burn terribly, producing great heat, just worthlessly absorbs it. Only the steel must be allowed to take heat. White heat . . . He stripped down to a pair of cutoff shorts and work boots and put on a pair of skiing goggles tinted amber, then cranked the blower mindlessly until the coal burned with a coppery brightness.

He was making a fireplace tool of some sort, he didn't know what exactly, an improvised and probably useless fireplace tool. He jammed the end of a meterlong stretch of rebar into the fire's sunny heart . . . The fire had a heart and a mouth and a song . . . he cranked the blower till the conflagration blazed white.

Frankenstein took the three-pound hammer from the wall, found the hand-sized area on the anvil that rang the clearest and gave the most bounce to the hammer's head—the anvil's "sweet spot." Everything has two meanings, he thought, our simplest, smallest words branching off into the storms and whirlpools of sex, warfare, worship. Therefore the words do not work. He breathed shallow while the wet coal at the fire's edges coked up, the sulfur cooking out of it and filling the shop with lung-stinging fumes. "Coked up"—the verbal thing there made him wonder if he wasn't just doing this to be *doing coke*, if the part of him that literalized all words, the undeciphering, dreaming part of him, believed he was in here getting high. Several nights of sick dreaming had preceded his relapse. Various dreams but they all happened in the same place, a city he must have visited once and couldn't remember anymore, depopulated now, vast and silent stadiums, motionless streets. The man in the dream was no longer himself; it was some other fool, some other drugged maniac, and he, Frankenstein, watched the rest of it from a place beyond, like a moviegoer—a dreamgoer. He'd never before had a dream and failed to be in it.

Van Ness, now—Van had always showed a quality like that: a figure outside the scene, watching even himself. When he entered the frame, he was dangerous. No such thing as speculation for Van; all aimless bullshit had to be actualized.

As his therapist, a healer, a shaman, Yvonne had been dealing with the dream part of him. Yanking me in a Jungian way . . . She had the husk of me open—Jesus, it's not beautiful now, the memory of it is nauseating, it's obscene—

So, Van, you're going to kill yourself. Good. Everybody's agony twists in me, but yours hurts more than most. The only person whose suffering I don't touch somewhere on the searing surface of it is Yvonne. I thought it was because we were special, our connection blessed, banishing pain. But there was never any pain in her to start with. Her center's a pinpoint, a microscopic star, burning without any life at Absolute Zero. She sucked it out of me, the stuff I get back by inhaling the fires of this forge—the heat. She took my heat. Traded it to the devil for some bauble.

An ache had coiled itself around his arm from wrist to shoulder. His perspiration dripped, hissing, onto the hot steel. What were these things in his hands? The anvil rang as he pounded the orange tip of the reinforcing bar, the kind used in concrete construction, flattening it. What kind of fireplace tool was this? Maybe another knife. A sword. The anvil's cries were feminine, operatic.

Was there somewhere another noise? he stilled himself, head hanging, the hammer dangling from his fist—the beating of mighty wings? The future tattering his walls with its beak. Something flared beyond this room, headlights, possibly, stroking the fog. Although many of these sparks and vibes signaled nothing, and most meant less and less as he evened out after those many days and nights spent flying in the talons of a wondrous beast, some sounds were real, some were seeds, blossoming into events.

This one, for instance, quickly placed: somebody from the barefoot welfare life was in his driveway. That toylike Volkswagen rattle. VW vans from the sixties survived in this county inexplicably, like frail kites in an attic. The noise of the little engine stopped.

He stood at the door of his shop holding the hammer tightly in his right fist, reaching with his left hand to cut the overhead light.

A small voice cried Help! when the light went out.

"What do you want?" he asked loudly, and in the dark moved away from where he'd just let himself be heard.

"I can't see—and so I want to see!" A woman—one with a foreign accent. "Please light your door for me or I can't take one step or I'm going to fall."

By the uncharted logic of his wars, anybody openly approaching had to be neutral, and he flipped the switch again.

"Thank you, yes!" Who was this turning up out of the foggy dark? She came at him at a kind of diagonal, like a little dog. "I was just driving by," she said, "and I saw you. I saw you glowing."

He recognized her now. The Iron Curtain chick—immigrant from the tortured lands. Skinny, devoutly New Tribe—ethereal, yes. She had a beautiful face. She wore a white turban on her head.

Once or twice, but not lately, he'd dealt with her. The van she'd driven up in would be the Sheep Queen's.

She looked a little wrecked, her mascara descending in streaks. Maybe she'd come from a party, left suddenly after a disastrous scene. Mussed and tearful. She was appealing like that. He wanted to participate in her fugitive chemistry.

"Oh my God," she said, "you're beautiful! Sweating, half naked, torn clothing!"

"Yeah? Maybe I should tear your clothes, too." He hadn't wanted anybody since Yvonne.

It was not unprecedented for women to walk up to him like this, right out of the void—his size and power, his rippling beauty. Van Ness had explained it years ago: they were drawn to him exactly as they were drawn to horses standing in the sun.

"It stinks inside here. This is a bad pollution," she said, although she was smiling.

"It's sulfur smoke." He sensed no need for delay. "I think I'll rinse off in the hot tub," he said, and took off his shorts. He was wearing only his big work boots now, his Wolverines.

"There's no fat," she said. "Your physique is perfect."

Her clinical tone was a disappointment. "Why are you here?"

"I heard it's no more Yvonne. You're lonesome."

She took a step in his direction, and he thought he might as well lift her up and hold her against him so they were face-to-face.

"Are these silk?" he asked, fingering the waist of her baggy slacks.

Wagging her feet, she kicked off her thongs. "They're silk from India," she said, and kissed him very softly. Her second kiss was ardent, needy. He tasted lemon and tequila.

"Yeah," he said, "your name's Melissa. I kind of remember us getting it on one time last winter, at the hot springs."

"And now again!"

Melissa lived with the Sheep Queen close to the Garcia River and was known to be screwing Nelson Fairchild, an alcoholic pot-grower, very rich. She probably did drive by this house every day, back and forth from the sunken barnyard where the Sheep Queen kept her bleating ragged flock.

She clutched him tightly around the neck, hanging two feet above the dirt floor, onto which he tossed her Indian silk pantaloons after stripping them from her legs. He let her keep the white T-shirt and turban.

"Your light in here makes a dome in the fog. It's soft." She kissed him again. "I want to float inside."

The Sheep Queen made a practice of rescuing these types and taking them in and looking after them until they died or went completely crazy. Well, he was going to jane this psychotic skinny waif. She probably had two dozen diseases but we're none of us born to perfection. In order to get hard he had to think of Yvonne. He pictured her naked in the lotus position. It was pornographic when she did that. Arousing not because it was obscene, but because he himself was obscene. He moved Melissa up and down on himself and right away she started, it seemed, to climax repeatedly. For his part he sensed with despair that he wouldn't come, no matter how long they kept at it. But this activity made him happy, he could stand here all night and offer pleasure to this other human being, this creature of form and flesh crying like an anvil. Not, however, in this atmosphere. The forge's draft had failed and the place was thick with sulfurous clouds and heat. His eyes burned with the fumes. Melissa was crying out but also coughing. She leaned back in his embrace. Tears ran down her cheeks. "We're screwing in hell! We're screwing in hell!" she screamed. But Frankenstein was thinking of Yvonne. Why didn't she love him anymore? Why did he love her more than ever?

He carried Melissa outside into the dampness and dark. "I can breathe!" she said, and did so several times deeply. She put her face against his chest, and he felt her lick some sweat from his nipple. She offered her opinion: "It tastes like madness." He put her down. She yipped when her feet touched the dewy lawn, and then she stood trembling in the yellow light from the shop's doorway.

He stepped back inside for a second and brought her her pants all bunched up. "Matter of fact," he said, "the hot tub isn't functioning."

"Oh? Does it have a hole?"

"I thought some enemies of mine were hiding inside it."

"Oh, those crazy old enemies," she said as she got on her pants, bending over and diminishing in the bit of light, looking like small ivory.

"What's that accent? Where are you from?"

"I'm Austrian."

"Like Hitler."

"Yes. And many great poets and philosophers."

"Wittgenstein?"

"I don't know their names."

She put on her thongs, kissed him, and left right away. For that he was grateful.

Before dawn the fire in the forge had died, and Frank lay in his small bedroom sleepless, or worse, lay dreaming that he couldn't sleep. He listened carefully to the walls . . . Nothing. Tonight he had fashioned, from six pounds of rebar, a small flat three-ounce paperweight.

Two visitors in one day, each of them arguably more batshit than himself. The German, or whatever she was, was goofy. But he liked her, and maybe he'd see her again if he didn't perish first of cocaine or Yvonne. As for Van Ness: just another ghost in another dream. And uglier than ever with his magnified eyes and that Kung Fu mustache like jungle vines. Frank felt sure that Van Ness had materialized here in the role of a demon—but not, thank goodness, one of mine, he thought. This time it's somebody else who's conjured him. I was fed up years ago, weary and sick of the power the world gives us to create entities like Van Ness.

His own demons whispered from behind the walls and underneath the floorboards. They had a special slyness, and their cowardice was devastating. Van Ness bore quite other markings. He might have been bodied forth out of some Eastern parable or Buddhist fairy tale, in particular one that Frank now recalled concerning a pilgrim and seeker in the North Country. Tired of his travels, this man sat one day in the shade of a tree in the heat of the afternoon to meditate on the changing emptiness of life. The air tasted good in his throat, but after a while he was thirsty, and he couldn't drink the air. He wished he had a cool drink. Immediately a big urn full of fruit nectar appeared on the ground in front of him—because this tree he'd stopped to rest beneath happened to be the legendary Wishing Tree. He took a long, delicious drink, and then he felt his hunger and thought how good some food would taste. Instantly, he had a plate of wheat cakes in his lap. He ate and drank his fill. What a great spot I've come to! he thought. It occurred to him this would be exactly the right place for a little home. And there it was, sunlight pouring down around it, a cottage made of white stones. Now, he thought, if only I had a wife . . . A completely beautiful woman strolled up, sat down beside him, and took his hands in both of hers. They made love and then nestled in the grass together, he with his head in her lap. As the man started to drift off to sleep he suddenly wondered with alarm if these wishes weren't being granted, perhaps, by some sort of devil. Sure enough, a terrifying devil, red as anger, huge and stinking of rot, appeared before him. And right in front of his wife and his gorgeous home, the monster tore him to pieces and ate him.

August 8–10, 1990

My wife is a lovely woman, and we've built one of this area's most beautiful homes.

It's a new house, of true adobe brick, with redwood interiors, solar heating, a fireplace, two bedrooms, all on forty acres. Certainly no mansion but perfect for a childless couple providing they love each other. But we don't.

Winona loves California. Winona loves her westward, golden dream. And I love Melissa.

Melissa: your eyes: the gravities and winds across those skies . . .

I saw Melissa drifting up the rutted drive. Her music was sad. But as I saw her walking in her alien softness, squinting under the indelible blue sky, I vowed again as I had at my first glimpse of her that for this woman I would throw everything away. All of you: if you make it necessary, I will.

"How'd you get up from town?"

"By begging rides."

"No. Melissa—you can't *do* that. Someday somebody's going to kidnap you."

"And what will they do to me?"

"Things," I said.

"The things you like to do."

She was a nature's child of the drug-demented sort, always living without power or running water and dressing from the rummage sales, but just for me she sometimes wore dark eye shadow and painted her lips a pale disheveled pink. Just for me she'd put on long blazing rags and fake jewels and high-heeled sandals and no panties and we'd whiz in my convertible to someplace up the coast where you could get a freezing margarita by the sea. We'd get smashed and kiss on the open wooden decks of these restaurants while the sun went down and the whole world blushed and trembled. Do you get it? Do you think I could do that with Winona? Thoughtful, muscular, artistic Winona? No—with her I stayed up through the first nights of our romance talking about Europe, and we said everything there was to say about Europe, where I'd never been. Later I did visit there, and it was a fantastic, an inspiring region. But I like Melissa even better than Europe.

Let me tell you about this girl. Her eyes are brown and wet. Her mouth twists from the effort of hiding her bad teeth when she smiles. But when she's drunk she laughs widely and her gold bridge-work flashes. Bartenders like to lean forward to light her cigarettes and in the match-glow examine her as closely as a lover would. It's all exactly there. The punished child in the stolen makeup. Eyes that are never going to look at anyone again. And then she leans back, receding into that wonderful posture, her left hand in her lap. Sometimes she wilts, and sits hunched over a drink drumming her fingers on the bar, and then she looks like a whore. She's capable of sneering. A woman this vulnerable and perverse is usually taking time out from being tortured to death slowly by a man who looks exactly like her father. Things come to me in images. I see the image of a man strangling an orchid. Oh, flowers!

Up and down the Coast Highway you drift, orchids and azaleas, your petals smeared underfoot.

She was looking too hard at the busboy—blue-eyed, ponytailed, shirt open wide under his strong Adam's apple. His music was Asian flute and hollow sticks knocked together. Ah, she probably knew him. He'd had her, probably, on the wood table of his shack with orange crates full of garbage stinking by the windows, had her on the sand at Schooner Gulch in a chilly wind, he'd torn at her gooseflesh with his beautiful teeth.

"What's the matter?" she asked me.

"Did you screw that guy? No"—I ran over her sudden, fearful laughter—"but you're going to. Before your life is over you'll have every last one." The tequila was mixing badly, my brain glinted like a knife, I wanted to make a famous speech now, to tell her how much I hated her for being a woman, for being able to open up and *receive*, but all that came out was, "The whole *world* will be inside you, you're like the *ocean*—"

And then I'm driving fast in the open, yellow Porsche, head clearing in the blasting atmosphere, searching my heart for apologetic words while beside me Melissa cries, "Burst apart, explode, fly, galactic, starburst, asunder! . . . "

For three generations my family has belonged to Northern California, living in the shadow of its ways—nature's big moves, the colossal, twisted gestures of cypresses along the bluffs—bluffs, there's something about that word that rings right, you can hear the grunts of God shoving these massive cliffs into place.

And to this natural grandness the best, the finest people are drawn, people just trying to touch life with awareness and kindness.

But it's also a land of interminable rains, baffling droughts, and, in July and August, the thick, cloying fog banks. For twenty-one successive days they clung to the North Coast this summer, like . . . like the American Dream plowed up against the freezing sea. Now we mean to set up oil rigs out there and dig our dreams from under the ocean's bed, our black, dripping dreams, so that we'll remain at liberty to drive our dream-deals faster and faster along these tight roads. I myself drive not only the secondhand Porsche but also an open jeep with a high-speed rear end, both very fast. Or I did. Winona's got the jeep now.

We do what we have to do in order to make it all come true. A few years back a man in our area paid a seedy character to kill his wife so that he could collect her insurance and live with his mistress. The supposed assassin, it turned out, was an undercover agent. The husband was charged with conspiracy and spent three years in prison.

After a few months his mistress forgot him. During the third year his wife paid him several visits. They're back together now.

Melissa's been my mistress since October. She's Austrian, this beautiful hippie. I believe she's anorexic; she's like a bird; when we make love I try to break her bones. I met her at the high school play last year. It was a piece of shit, and I was embarrassed to see my wife, Winona, involved in it. Winona worked backstage. Melissa sat right under the lip of the stage, on the floor, with the smallest children. I watched her all night.

I want to lock eyes with Melissa, my passion, while casually destroying Winona—I want to drop Winona crumpled beside the plates of our feasting.

Winona's music is the big, symphonic kind—maybe Vivaldi, *The Four Seasons.* Any one of them, or all four. She's small, somewhat chunky, but on her it's becoming. Her face we call cute, darling. She's snuggly.

In the middle of a pasture on our property, Winona keeps a ramshackle studio where she makes her sculptures. Her works stand in the sunny pasture, in that coastal clarity made stunning by the ocean's nearness, big wooden totems of a modernesque unintelligibility, also unpleasing iron shapes—crescents stuck to parallelograms, et cetera—eight, ten, a dozen feet tall. Winona's strong. She cuts the wood with a big chainsaw and hefts the iron into position for the welding all by herself. Welding's dangerous. High voltage. Even a simple mistake can fry you. I imagine coming home to find Winona standing there with her clothes burned off, a crisp black self-portrait among her other statues. I like to think about it. I imagine ways of making it happen.

And she views me the same way. She loves our forty acres. She'd do anything to keep it—increase it—divorce me? Without a blink. I think she'd shoot me. She'd trade her talent, what little there is of it, anyway, and probably her immortal soul.

Our land overlooks the distant Pacific, and below us, all the way to the ocean, stretches fifteen square miles of timber, mostly redwood. That forest belongs to my father.

If you ask anybody in these parts, I'm sure they'll tell you without hesitation that my father is an awful man, a terrible person, and they're right, he's done harm to anyone who ever befriended, needed, or trusted him, and if there's anything wrong with me, then I serve as an example of the warpage worked, a map of the fissures cracked open and shaped uncloseable, by a childhood spent loving such a person. Right—I know—the world has its horrors, mine among the privileged, American kind. But let my statement stand: I blame my father for myself.

Father, for his part, was messed up by Grandmother, an Italian woman of mountainous and steadily mounting stature, well over three hundred pounds by the time she died, with the resulting embarrassment of extra pallbearers at her funeral, a banshee from Palermo. She couldn't stand being married off to a Welshman, the only British rancher around, one of the area's first sheepers. Couldn't stand being removed from the Sonoma wine country out here to the coast. She died when I was four and my brother Bill was seven; we share vivid memories of her, in our little eyes she was a nightmare of alpine blubberiness, and vaguely I recall our grandfather, her poor husband, an immigrant from Cardiff, who was dead at fifty-five—a bit earlier than she, but ten years her junior—his British steel battered down by her angers, griefs, and nights of wild religion. My father was the son of that tremendous coupling, and he served to convey its stresses perfectly—the Italian passions choked off in that stiff British neck. It made him mean. His eyes twinkled when he caused disappointment, when he sowed doubt, when he reaped scorn. Uneducated in the ways of domestic life himself, marooned on the shores of parenthood without any equipment, his manner of teaching us, my brother Bill and me, was to ask mysterious questions as a way of indicating we'd made some mistake or other: "Would you like to see that horse bloat up? and lie down? and turn over and die by morning?" Then we knew we'd erred in the feeding or some such, but he'd never tell us exactly how, not until we begged. "How far you think your brains would splash under a tree like that?"—would indicate unsafe behavior in felling timber; "Do you have an idea you'd like your leg broke?"—maybe we were waiting in the wrong spot while a load of logs went on the truck. But in that case where on this earth *should* I be, Father? Where do you want me, what should I do? Anything, but only tell me. I don't know what you want! Speak! A child, I'm miserable admitting it, a child stands like a priest under his father's sky. Why do you fate me to fail you?

"Burst apart, explode, fly, galactic, starburst, asunder!" Melissa liked to shout American words while we drove too fast in the

Porsche, a creamy yellow 356 roadster, a third of a century old. But on the rare Coast straightaway it easily broke a hundred. I could get a word in only on the tightest curves, when the engine quieted.

"I'm sorry," I told her. Then a brief straightaway. A Porsche is not a cream puff car. It's angry, full of wrenching torque. A curve: "I know you wouldn't screw that guy." I meant the busboy I'd accused her of. "Okay, you would, we both know it. But my job is to love you anyway. That's my task."

"It doesn't matter."

"It matters to me. I'm going to show you how much it matters. Show you something I've never shown anyone."

"I'm getting carsick again." We'd entered a series of zigzag hairpins taking us down toward a creek that passed under the highway and out to sea.

I didn't keep to the road, but turned off abruptly just before the culvert.

"Why are we turning here? It says no trespassing."

"I'm checking things out."

"Checking for trespassers? Is this your land?"

"Shut up, please. Watch for the plates."

A pickup with a camper shell lowered itself down around the hairpin switchbacks, passed our position, and started climbing up the other side of the gulch. It kept to the highway. They hadn't seen us turn.

Melissa said, "Plates?"

"The plates! The plates! The license plates! Were they Oregon? They were blue. Could have been California. How many in the car? I saw two. Did you see two?"

"I see someone bringing me a license on a plate. To eat!"

"Were there dogs in the back?"

"English is impossible!"

"Those men are following me. They've got dogs."

"I didn't see. Listen to me. English words are like prisms. Empty, nothing inside, and still they make rainbows."

She was crazy about words and figures of speech, the result of having had to learn a second tongue.

The skinny gulch the creek cut through made a little evening over us. The surf, out of sight, muted by two big hills, merely grunted and thumped. I was woozy with drink. Still I was frightened in a rubbery way. I calmed myself by contemplating the water and thinking this Buddhist thought: that the river is everywhere at once, at each part of itself, although it gives the illusion of moving and we think of its journey as having a beginning and an end. Many of our most powerful dreams begin on an empty road, beside a river, which indicates the great depth of the dreaming.

Melissa snuggled close, awkwardly bridging the gearshift between our seats.

"Everything about you is extremely tiny," I said, kissing her tiny nose, mouth, fingers. I tasted margarita salt.

"Who wants to follow you?"

"I could name a few."

"Why?"

"Because my life is a mess."

Melissa wore an old high-fashion ladies' hat, a kind of white turban thing that kept her hair from whipping at her eyes and protected her beautiful ears from the chilly wind. When we drove with the top down she always bundled herself up in a fluffy white terrycloth robe I kept for her behind the seats. In this coast-cruising outfit she looked not quite recuperated from brain surgery. I kissed her some more, dreaming that my miracles would heal her.

Her eyes were sideways and wide open, looking at my watch. "What is the time, please?"

"It's four-forty in the afternoon."

"We're drunk before supper again. It's marvelous! I'll be asleep at eight. I'll wake up at three this morning and walk out naked into the stars."

"When was the last time you saw the stars at the Sheep Queen's? There's always that mist off the Garcia," I said, starting the car.

Maybe they *had* been following me. People were, they truly were. Anyway, now I was following them. And I would let them get away.

If you drive back inland along almost any of the hill roads, as I did along Shipwreck Road three times a week, you pass out of the fog into a dusty silence filled with tall second-growth redwoods. They make a windbreak for the crumbling old ranches, and they stand over the abandoned lumber camps that brought down their mothers and fathers, the original giants, and they shade and hide the twisted dregs of the old communes—once the best, the finest people, lured here by the piping of a lovely song and then held by drugs or religion, isolated minds bending around tightly to feed on themselves.

Those ghostly hippies, do you think I feel sorry for them? No. They came here and did what they dreamed of. The lovely song becomes a shape, and strides forth.

Melissa and I came into the town of Point Arena on the particular day I'm thinking of, and I turned off the Coast Highway and climbed into the hills.

I'm thinking about the day I took her to see my marijuana garden, an indiscretion that added to my fears a thousandfold.

I took us far back on Shipwreck Road, miles past where the pavement ended, the Porsche sliding on the gravel curves, hauling a small hurricane of dust. Our tongues tasted of dirt, but back away from the sea the day was far too hot to put the top up. Melissa closed her eyes and left her face empty and hard, stroked by feathery shadows.

When we parked, the trees, which had seemed to be rushing to this place alongside of us, stopped immensely. I cut the motor: the silence played one true, clear note. Beside me Melissa opened her eyes.

From this ridge we looked down into a canyon a quarter mile deep and half a mile across, and saw the peaks beyond Napa Valley, a hundred miles away.

"Do you know where we are?" I said.

"It's quiet. I feel like we've driven to under the ocean."

"This is where I grow my pot."

I was trusting her with a great secret, but she was just drunk.

That's what touched me so electrically, so sadly: she didn't partake of our dramas. Really, I never saw her more clearly portrayed than in the light of my first glimpse of her at the local high school play: sitting on the floor, in the shadows, up front with the smallest children, while an arm's length away frightened adolescents strutted the stage and shouted dialogue.

Is that why I went wild over her? Because once I saw her truly? Is devotion as simple as that?

I left her and climbed down off the ridge. First I walked. I stumbled as the canyonside steepened. I sat down and slid on my butt. I stopped now and then, just to make the climb last. Far below me the slope gentled and vegetation flooded the bottom of the world, mostly evergreen on the shady south, and, on the north side, oak and the relatives of oak, their shadows pasted on the platinum grasses. Here and there the blighted chinkapins were resurrecting themselves in this season, dead at the tops from some previous devastation, but living up out of their tragedies somewhat on the order of certain majestic, crippled alcoholic women. And the assembled redwoods, really just youngsters, less than a century old, but already a hundred feet tall, drinking in everything audible, giving none of it back . . . I felt about these trees that in their mindful silence they were inventing a new, an unexampled bliss, to which I'd be admitted when I shed my scruples.

At the moments most precarious for my sanity I'm lost somewhere on these back roads, teetering on these cliffs, witnessing this grandness and longing to match it with the grandest gestures, acts equally solitary and monstrous, things I can never confess. Is it possible for you to understand?—to imagine?—coming around a curve onto a cliff and looking over the dry evergreens and silent dusty arroyos as far as your eye will go, and seeing a stream that cuts through the bottom of the chasm so far below that you can't hear it, and finding five black buzzards who stand, trembling, in the middle of the air? The wildness of this terrain creates and explains me as much as anything I've inherited or been taught. The shape of this land affords brash designs—no, demands extravagant pretensions. I've visited cathedrals in Milan, also Sicily, filled with this same sacredness and yet this same cosmic dementia: very dramatic, very biblical, very strange.

By now I'd come down a hundred fifty feet from the roadside above. The canyon's face curved south here for a space before hooking back north. The exposure was southern, hot and windless, but the route to the garden led into and out of a cool, shady draw made damp by a rivulet trickling through it. Here we kept our spring box, a hundred-gallon cedar vat that filled with water and dribbled it out through a thin black plastic irrigation line.

I made my way across the slippery draw, braking my downward slide now by grabbing at the fat, comical leaves of bloomless rhododendrons, following the black line around the draw's western edge out of the shade, and then along a row of twenty-seven marijuana plants that grew on a wide ledge—tall, lush, expensive bushes, pungent in the summer sun. They got hot light fourteen hours a day this time of year. The energizing principle of pot cultivation is ecstasy: the object is to get the flowering tips of the female plant to produce as much as possible of the intoxicating drug tetrahydrocannabinol. The plants' sticky resin contains the drug, and the leaves and flowers exude the resin as protection from the rays of the sun. To keep a garden you need water, hot sun, dry air. Beyond that you need only female plants of a hardy, exotic stock, which will be harvested just before they go to seed. And you need a garden spot that's not only exposed to plenty of sun, but also protected, in our Fascist era, from aerial observation. This canyon presented certain hazards to helicopter flight, downdrafts and updrafts, that made it hard to get close. Three years running we'd harvested our plants without trouble from the authorities, an astonishing record of success.

These days it's likely your plants will be found. Half-trained yokels, cowboys with Uzi machine guns, hired with state money, will likely jump out of hovering choppers and rip up your crop. Unless you're standing right there at the time, they can't arrest you; certainly the state can't prosecute with any expectation of winning. But still they take the plants, and they can hope the faceless grower goes broke. If you've dared to garden in your own soil, the revenue people, federal and state, will treat it as an undeclared cash crop, tax and penalize and hound you, eventually confiscate your property. Our plot grew at the edge of a full section, one square mile, owned by a man named Wyeth who'd been dead for years. His family hadn't gotten around to doing anything with the land. It borders an area of vast timber holdings. A survey some years ago cut a few yards off Wyeth's section, and he lost his spring to the Georgia Pacific Lumber Company, at least on the map. But the lines of ownership don't move back and forth quite that easily, and our garden grew in a legal blur.

I checked our plants. The water line was functioning. The ground at their feet was wet. They opened their leafy arms, as a grade-school rhyme once had it, to pray. Not twenty feet distant, buzzards balanced in the thermal currents. Nothing to it, step outward in faith and tread the air.

In my dreams of flying, the power of flight emanates from my heart. I had many such dreams last year, while touring Italy. Even when awake, I felt much lighter than that world over there—Europe is ancient, the culture has tremendous mass. Milan: greatness and sunlight and the wild eyebrows of the citizenry . . . I was travelling with Winona; important to remember this now, with Melissa hovering like an angel above me on the ridge, out of sight . . . Winona and I walked into the massive duomo there, a church as tall as a modern skyscraper but centuries old and only a single vaulting story within. Inside it I felt smaller than ever, farther than ever from heaven. The upper reaches lost themselves in a haze of incense. Looking up I relinquished my lightness, was suddenly plunging, drowning with the iron freight of desires, frustrations, selfish hopes. Oh, holy atmosphere, marbled with sweet smoke: with how much yearning are we gifted? Of how much capable? The church's dome was as deep as a California canyon. These buzzards hanging in the air, one wingbeat beyond the lip of Signal Ridge, would have been at home there; in fact I believe I felt their presence or that of something like them, sensed observant birds of prey balanced high up in the gigantic dimness.

The faith is gone from those places, the heart-power of flight, this I believe. But come to California. Come to these canyons if you want to be driven by sacredness into the air. If you dream of the true, clear silences, if you want those silences to sing—come to California.

I didn't get out to the garden often, but my growing-partner, Clarence, was down in Los Angeles that month, if I remember right, robbing poker games or attending a transvestite wedding, nothing, certainly, that wasn't completely unholy. During his absence I looked in on our investment every two or three days, making sure the water flowed. Right now I stood on the cliff with my head poking up from our little jungle. I trimmed the plants, putting their dead leaves in my shirt pocket. Stroked the jagged fingers of their little hands. The upper leaves felt not just sticky but slaked with a substance entirely other, not earthly, not mine, as if my mother would snatch at my hand now saying, "Don't touch that!" Almost all twenty-seven were doing nicely, all but one. Transplanting sprouts in the spring, nervous about it because we hadn't been to this place for months and it had seemed foreign and dangerous, fated, even, I'd jayed the roots of this one, bent them upward; it had never recovered. I yanked it, and now we had twenty-six. Each one of these things might be worth seven thousand dollars or more.

My partner, Clarence, is a surfer. He does everything with a vacant look. Between harvest and planting, after he's sold the dope in L.A., he travels all over the Western Hemisphere, walking the waves of the world with a big foot of fiberglass. He glides in toward the beaches of Nicaragua, of El Salvador, without a clue. The Left, the Right, class struggle, agrarian revolt—Clarence just wants to feel the softness of the sand. When he comes back from these winter trips Clarence looks uncharacteristically alive, so darkly tanned that his eyes seem to glow in his face with the mania of sainthood.

Clarence is a dozen years older than the local surfers, but out of perverseness he speaks the surfers' dialect. "I could heard that, dude," he says, and other such unsearchable stuff.

Usually, according to our arrangement, Clarence is the one to stay near the plants. I supervise things, I will take care of any legal problems, I make the contacts for sale down south, I handle all the money; and I can be trusted because if I let him down, if I rip him off, he'll hurt me. Clarence was a gunner's mate in the U.S. Navy and somehow managed to see ground combat in Lebanon. He actually killed people up close, and got medals for it.

At the time I'm thinking of I often wished I could hire him to get rid of my former friend Harry Lally. Terminate, assassinate the guy. But that was a plan with too many indicators pointing back to me.

For Winona I dreamed of a job-related mishap. She used a chainsaw after all. It wasn't a plan so much as a vision, a guilty one, but one that I enjoyed, that thrilled me as much as fantasies of pirate ships and Peter Pan had thrilled me as a child: Winona lying beside a patch of shiny red grass with something, an arm or an ankle, unfortunately detached. Tough luck! —but now my life is cured. Melissa and I hide from our consciences awhile, pouring insurance money—half a million on Winona's life, just as on mine—down our gullets and into the tanks of my fast cars, and then we live out our days on my splendid property, growing pot in these hills and waiting to inherit my father's timber.

Half a million! In this fantasy I don't have to kill Harry Lally. I just scrape a hundred thousand off my stack and he goes away happy.

Harry Lally wants money from me and would certainly hire people to get it. I believe in fact that they're already in his employ and closing fast, two of them, two ugly men who claim to be loggers from Del Norte County and have asked about me, by name, in Jay Haymaker's hardware store, two slow, muscular, flannel-encrusted mountain men. Here to hunt the wild pig, they explain—that's why they travel with an arsenal and three dogs. They claim to be old friends of mine. They'd like, they say, chuckling in the hardware store beside Jay Haymaker's antique daguerreotype of five gunslingers hanging dead from the rafters of a barn (underneath his sign reading OUR CREDIT POLICY), to take me up into the hills with them. I don't want to go!

I inhaled the sharp green stench of the shoot I'd plucked. The crop was quality. If everything continued like this, Clarence and I would soon be rich. The hills before me loped inland to where Italian families still grow grapes and crush out wine. I could see, all the way from here, the vapors of life swirling over the Sonoma vineyards where my grandmother had been raised. A place very much like the Sicilian hills overlooking Palermo, and the inland wine country of her father's birth.

I took Harry Lally's money to Palermo. Gave it to a solemn Italian attorney wearing heavy black spectacles and beset by a general heaviness, which I took to be the great weight of his personal wealth; and as I added to his riches by about a hundred thousand of Harry Lally's dollars, this attorney gave me a satchel with four kilos of cocaine inside it. Then we had prosciutto ham with honeydew melon, spaghetti, sturgeon, and coffee, which we served ourselves from large metal urns with spigots as in any Tenderloin cafeteria, and hot milk from similar urns. I stuffed myself. All was well, we were devouring this lunch downstairs at the Palme Grande, where Winona and I had taken rooms and in whose mezzanine the Mafia had slaughtered several of each other a few years before, toppling corpses down the wide sweeping staircase. I sensed the mighty stones of a traditional lawlessness, ancient, impenetrable, walling me safely in.

But two days later, at the airport in Rome, I sensed no such thing. I felt empty, I felt alone, and I chickened out. No airport guard, no travel clerk, no janitor, waitress, or ticket-taker seemed incidentally placed. They were all after me, scratching at their guns. All right! Shoot! Shoot! But for God's sake don't embarrass me in front of my wife, don't expose me, don't chisel open the crust I've built around myself and air the filth, the nauseating truth, beneath. Winona didn't tumble. Never had a clue, didn't turn and say, as in her favorite films, Hitchcock—I don't like them, everybody's too happy and ordinary, James Stewart, Cary Grant, I only like *Notorious*, and then only until we find out Ingrid Bergman isn't really bad—say, "Darling, you're trembling, what's the matter?" as my liver went sinking down through the mush of me.

You can't get rid of an anonymous package in a European airport. The bomb squad won't have it. They treat any such object as a disaster until it's proven innocent. Even the trash cans won't accommodate anything bigger than a wad of Kleenex. I had to sit on the toilet for half an hour, ripping open forty plastic packets, dissolving and flushing a fortune in cocaine.

As soon as I stepped onto American soil and cleared Customs I couldn't understand, or even recall the force of, my vertigo in the Roman airport. I turned up in Harry Lally's living room baffled, empty-handed except for the Sicilian attorney's Japanese-made satchel, the lining of which I'd ruined by washing it out with toilet water. My failure stretched the fibers of our friendship. Okay, I don't need to be flip: I can admit that first by my avarice, and then by a compounding cowardice, I earned myself a mortal enemy. And now I'm in a war.

And now the two hunters, and their dogs—clearly part of Harry Lally's program for extracting reimbursement. He wants his cash. I don't have cash. These men have been sent to get all I have that's quickly convertible to cash—these twenty-six plants.

And I would say: take them! Take my watch, my rings, my fishing gear, my shoes and socks! But the *plants* aren't *mine*. They belong equally to Clarence, the decorated killer.

I sat on a hump of earth and cradled the withered slip, moping and shrigging this deadborn of its fronds and looking out over the canyon. At sunset the redwoods take on a coppery light. The leaves of the chinkapins are extinguished. The bigness of evening walks up the western slopes shivering, trailing a cool damp smell. Dusk comes earliest to these canyons, right out of the fissures in the earth. Shapes fade. The tide of the realm of dreams steals higher and higher up into my life. The wetness of nightmares this far inland . . . What a jerk! Feeling cornered, strangled, in the midst of this great peace! Only the greediest simpleton could have served himself this mess.

Now I'm terrified to hear the rasp, rising and dying, of tires on the gravel above. I've been an idiot. Anybody from around here knows the yellow Porsche. They all suspect I have a garden. Clarence would destroy me if I ever signaled, to use his demented combat parlance, his military phrasing, our position. Could be Harry Lally's boys. Yes, "Harry Lally's boys"—my life now spoken out of the side of the mouth in a gangster drawl.

The dust of a vehicle showed around to the north, where Shipwreck Road switched back. They'd passed on.

"Melissa!" I screamed.

I was always afraid she'd vanish when my back was turned, off in some strange, fast car to a new affair.

Her voice drifted down from above me. "I don't want to smoke any of your drugs because I'm already completely, wonderfully drunk!"

I climbed up slowly, clinging to the occasional manzanita root, trying not to leave a trail of torn vegetation. When I stopped to rest, blotting the dusty sweat from my face with a bandanna, I heard her singing something in German, a folk song, maybe a fairy tale, something from very far away, where she lived always.

"Who was in that car? Who was in that car?" I cried breathlessly as I climbed up over the rim of the draw.

And there she was, my love: Melissa, sideways in the open door of the convertible, skirt blown up over her wan, destructible legs so that I wanted to weep. Everything. If these idiots force me I will trade it all for this woman.

"Look at me," I ordered her.

She stared at me with a question, a smile, and a sweetness in the hesitation of her eyes.

"Don't you see I'm going crazy?"

Nights are cold but we drive with the top down for the oxygen. The cypresses on the cliffs high over the sea, dragged sideways by the wind over centuries into permanent blurs, whizzes, smears, seem to be part of a comic strip as we, drunk and dangerous, scream past in the heartstopping blue twilight. Offshore, the small lights of fishing-boats float in the dark: if you let them they'll start symbolizing everything. I slow way down to light the reefer I've rolled, sucking in the smoke along with the damp clean ocean air. Melissa shakes her head. I jam the pedal.

Making love to Melissa is a dangerous blessing. It's almost all I ever want to do. But when we've been on a party like today's we generally forget to sleep together. I just drive her back to Acorn Road, to the woolly barnyard where she lives in her shocking trailer, and let it go at that. Anyway you won't too often catch me entering that little home of hers. She takes in stray cats, the place is just a litter box.

She's organic. I described her as drug-demented, but she eats only untreated vegetables and gets high only on natural herbs and plants, which include most wines and certain very expensive brands of scotch whiskey and tequila; sometimes also marijuana, when it's baked into pastries—she refuses to take smoke into her lungs. She says she once had cancer of the liver but cured it with her mind.

I took her to the bottom of Acorn Road. The river mist met us less than halfway down. Not visible, but everywhere. "Good night, I'm going to sleep in my clothes," she said, "and I hope I dream I'm not drunk," and didn't even kiss me.

When she'd gone into the trailer, one of the rounded, aluminum ones, a Silver Stream, I laid my head, which was suddenly full of sorrows, against the steering wheel. The night wind stirred through the treetops on the ridges. The distant commotion got the sheep bleating—a word that just doesn't invoke the aged, human grief in their voices. Across the drive the owner of this property—the Sheep Queen, a Mediterranean-looking woman in her fifties, a nice enough person, but perfectly crazy—sat eating dinner in the kitchen of her ranch-style home, feeding bites from her plate to a big dog that loomed over her, standing up, as it were, with its forepaws on the table.

It's sad to love a woman who won't love back—it tears at a man—to love a woman who gives herself to others and uses his good intentions and sets his meaning aside. But I have a feeling that this stupid torment is the nearest thing going, for me, to what life is all about. I don't just sense it dimly. The feeling is overpowering that this is the closest I can get to the truth behind the cloud.

Dreaming of one woman, I drive home to another.

Actually Winona wasn't here lately. The ranch lay dark, the oaks like cut-outs against the smeary stars.

And actually Winona lived here alone. We'd been separated many months, beginning just a few weeks after the house was finished. But as Winona didn't have a lover, at least nobody anybody knew of, I wasn't in the way, I came and went, and in her absence I tended the stables, though I rarely crossed her threshold and this would be the first night I'd slept here all summer. She'd been travelling lately up and down the coast, visiting people she didn't, in my opinion, actually know well enough to be visiting. On some kind of pilgrimage: Going Through Changes we call it in our region, where the Haight-Ashbury dialect flourishes unevolved.

I parked the Porsche out of sight in the stables because I expected, sooner or later, a visit from Harry Lally's boys. I hadn't set foot in my own apartment since I'd heard they were in town. Eventually they'd locate me here. But I'd see them a mile off and be down the hill, walking into the forest—my father's forest, where my brother lives—long before they reached the house. They'd never know for sure that I'd even been here, unless they searched through all the outbuildings and found the car.

I come and go, but this is decidedly not my home anymore. None of my stuff is here. In the bedroom Winona sleeps in a single bed now. My office, a shed out by the barn, has been put to a better use, she says. As a matter of fact spiders live in it.

There was a note from her, three weeks old, run through a nail on the house's front door. *Red's got worms—feed store has the stuff—give him a full syringe*—and I tore it off and put it to my lips and inhaled, trying to catch a whiff of the woman I'd married. A woman I'd loved then. But that woman was gone. A man told me—this in the Gualala Hotel bar one night—that if I were only older, I'd have seen by now that people pass through ages, and I'd have learned that when they've changed and been lost, you find them again somewhere in the next age. But later that night this same man got mean under the liquor and had to be restrained. He lunged at me, raving—the meaty arms of salmonmongers and the greasy hands of big-rig operators yanking him back. *Eyes fixed*, he gave meaning to that old phrase in his truly psychotic, really animal state. His eyeballs scorched and chilled me across space. He raised blisters and goose bumps, even through the window, as I stomped off the hotel's wooden porch into the dark. So much for the wisdom of our counselors. That madman wasn't going to help me find Winona, not in her current age or any other. Don't ask me who this woman is, walking around in my wife's body with a decisive air.

I woke up in the bed I didn't belong in, woke up smelling my wife, but it wasn't the same smell I remembered. I stood by the railing upstairs and marked how much the place had changed since the last time I'd spent a night here. My hands shook this morning. I'd slept in my clothes. My foreignness overwhelmed me. Only the thought of leaving right away held any cheer. I decided to take Winona's old pickup and get coffee in town.

The ridge road parallels the coast for dozens of miles, wagging down into draws and crossing creeks and climbing out again. This isn't the Coast Highway, but a much narrower route, better suited to my kind of car and my kind of driving, but not so well to Winona's looming Dodge. No shoulder, the trees crowd right against it. Ordinary, happy people live along here in nice houses you can't see from the road. Often they report me for speeding past. I sense them back in those woods tending to their animals and their gardens. For them the darker alleys of thought have been clearly marked at the entrances. Everything's fine, maybe a little guano has to be cleaned from the left boot, something dropped by one of their innumerable geese. Sun-shot California mist in the morning. A stirring of wind chimes, their cats rolling on their sides and stretching in the ripe greenness while New Age Muzak, what I call Electronic Obvious, sprinkles down over everything. My good neighbors. When I hear my good neighbors at the drugstore talking about pamphlets from the Government Printing Office, pamphlets about horticulture, free pamphlets—I want to kill them. I suppose we all feel that way some-times. We all who? Ah, we who probably should be hunted down and jailed I suppose.

But today no chats in the pharmacy. Today I stop at the feed store for one bale each of oat hay and alfalfa. Since she was a child my wife Winona has kept a red horse named Red. Red is more than twenty-five years old now. He does nothing but conjugate hay and consult with the large-animal vet about his stomach ailments. And hadn't there been a note? Something about medicine? In my shirt pocket I found it: Red had worms.

I ran into one of Winona's friends. "Hel-*lo*." It was Yvonne.

"Yvonne! Hi! I'm getting some stuff," I said, talking more than I wanted, as I always do to people I don't like.

"Nelson, how are you?"

"Fine! Great! Getting some birdseed?" I said for no reason at all.

She held up a small cardboard box. "These are white rats."

In our part of the world people may do, say, or become whatever they feel like without apologizing. And tomorrow its opposite.

"White ones, are they?"

"I haven't seen you since you and Winona split up. How is that working for you?"

"Working?"

"How is that working for you?"

"How is the breakdown proceeding? How is the malfunction functioning? Briefly, I'm confused and sad and pissed off."

"The restructuring of the relationship," she said, not without humor.

She reached out and squeezed my hand. Imagining herself some kind of healer probably.

"Well, see you."

"See you."

I went inside without looking back.

"Yvonne bought two rats," the lady behind the counter told me.

"Why do you sell rats?"

"She buys small animals but never buys cages. Does she let them go?"

"Who knows. Who cares?"

"Some people feed hamsters and things to snakes."

"And is that why you have hamsters and things at a feed store?"

"Well, I don't know. It's not my store."

"It's not my store either."

"Didn't I see you selling fruit the other day?"

"Anything's possible."

"You were drunk, and you were selling fruit."

"I was just helping the guy out. We got to talking and I—you know."

"I always get my fruit at the fruit stand. It's better than the store. Cheaper."

"I don't want to talk about fruit, actually."

Or anything else with you, Feed Store Lady. I'd known her for years—long red hair and glazed blue eyes, possessor of a marshmallowy intellect. Chipper, coping, as in the early stages of some unbelievable catastrophe. She'd emigrated from Los Angeles so long ago that by now she'd be an imbecile in its streets. She barely managed among a few bales of hay. "I need wormer," I told her.

"Oh," she said sympathetically, "Red's sick?"

Sick? The animal's been teetering at the grave's edge for years. His mistress gives him enemas regularly, cooing. His master's in the feed store with the staggers and jags, standing before you as the fibers of his reality tear loose. "The wormer's for me," I said. She laughed. We in California show anger and pleasure the same way, by a little

California laugh. You need an ear for the difference. And things aren't "good," and things are never "bad"—no, in this lush eternity by the sea we measure our moments by two other words. Everything on the spectrum of undesirability, from minor annoyance to universal tragedy, is *okay*. Anything better to any degree, all the way up to a colossal lottery jackpot or the return of Jesus—that's *neat*.

"This'll get those critters," she said, handing me Red's medicine in a little white sack. "Can you get the hay on board yourself?"

"You bet." Another most useful rural California phrase.

Outside I saw the two strangers who'd been looking for me, probably to kill me, and that was okay. Then they passed by in their big camper. They headed south, they didn't find me, not this time. And that was neat.

Not a half hour later I was having a sort of breakfast five miles north, in Anchor Bay. It wasn't that pleasant. Too much cinnamon in the apple pie, and now the cook had spilled chemical cleanser on the griddle and we were all asphyxiating swiftly here in the Full Sails Cafe.

The patrolman from Point Arena, a new man to our part of the coast, had already been making me nervous, sitting in full uniform at the counter and spying on the restaurant's gangly brunette waitress, looking bored and hopeful of making an arrest. "I really would like to get a date with you," he told the waitress.

"What do you mean?" she said.

"Go to the movies or something."

"You mean the movies in Point Arena?"

"Or the submarine races."

"I've heard of them," she said.

"We could rent a video."

"I don't mind videos."

"How about nasty ones?"

She didn't say anything.

"You want to rent a nasty video?"

"Okay," she said.

"Do you like cops? Do you like uniforms?"

"I don't know," she said. "Yeah. Most of the time."

"I'll get a show about a cop."

"You don't waste too many words, do you?"

"Maybe I'll just skip the video completely."

"There goes our entertainment."

"Maybe we could rehearse our own video, and I could play the cop."

"Well," she said, "you have the uniform, obviously."

"Maybe I could be the hero, sort of."

"Then who would be the criminal?"

"Well, I could be the criminal too."

"I guess you'd have to be."

"A rapist."

"I wouldn't have it any other way."

Right then I lost interest in their talk because the two hunters turned up outside. They pulled their rig in next to Winona's, and one of them went into the Anchor Bay store. They'd come here by coincidence, couldn't have known Winona's old pickup by sight, but I died. Their truck was a long-bed Chevy Silverado.

I paid up as quickly as I could, and on the way out I said hello to the cop, whose name was, I thought, Navarone. He nodded. "What time do you have there?" I said, just to be seen talking with him.

"Ten-fifteen," he said. "Why? There's a clock on the wall."

"Oh, that clock," I said.

Naturally I'd seen him around. He was a big-city boy who just didn't get it and was stepping on everybody's feet up here, enforcing the petty ordinances but failing to track down loose livestock.

I caught the two hunters outside as the driver fired up their stupid Silverado. I could hear the dogs scratching and yelping in the camper shell. The passenger had just gotten back in the car with his purchase.

I shouted: "You men!" I pointed toward the cafe. "I've made you known to the police!"

There wasn't much to see of them, except that both seemed big and strong and neither wore a cap. Hunters, it seemed to me, should be wearing bright red caps so as not to be shot by their friends.

They pulled away carefully, hardly glancing back at me.

For a minute I wondered if I hadn't made a completely silly mistake. I stood there feeling embarrassed and thinking, Who is anyone, excuse me but who are we all supposed to *be*? and looking back in through the cafe's big window.

And I suddenly experienced the gladness of seeing people walled off behind glass: the cop and the waitress, now without voices . . . each heart quivering in its gossamer of falsehood. His swagger was sorrowful. He had a look of dawning pain, as if he'd just finished telling a story that trailed away with the words, "I was happy then . . . "

I drove back to Winona's with the tottering hay bales, also the horse goop, making sure I wasn't followed by anybody who could murder me. If anybody wanted to. Wild pig, wild pig—maybe they only wanted game pork after all. Of course they hadn't done anything sinister except lie about knowing me. But when you think about it, that's sinister enough.

Gualala had been covered in clouds, but the ridge was clear, the house burned whitely in the sunshine. I hadn't finished my breakfast. The sight of those two had sent me scurrying here. I sat out on the deck behind the house—hidden from anybody coming up the drive—with a liter of wine and a skinny cigarette rolled out of last season's *sinsemilla*.

From the height of this ridge I looked this morning down on the cloud bank. I saw nothing of the sea, only this fluffy oblivion under the blue sky. To the westward no land, no peaks, nothing higher than my property. I might have been standing seven miles above everything. Actually the elevation is about 2,200 feet. Higher ridges lie to the east of us. We're six miles back from the ocean.

I deeply enjoy spending time here alone, looking out over the Northern California morning, drinking Northern California zinfandel and blowing on a Northern California reefer. To my left I see our pond, nearly three acres of blue-green water, and below me the fuzzy sea of my father's treetops, all that timber, and all the land it stands on, going down into the clouds. To the right, to the north, glimmers a tiny orange dome: the temple of a Tibetan Buddhist monastery far up in the hills. On the highest ridge east of here you can see two brilliant white structures, quite similar in shape to the Tibetan one and even, when you think of it, related to it in the tilt, so to speak, of their thrust: a U.S. Air Force radar station, stroking the aether with receptors.

I used to sit out here while my wife talked to me, with my mind five miles out to sea.

Winona became hateful shortly after beginning a friendship with Yvonne. Her "cute" quality took on a piggish cast. By a subtle slanting her cuteness became oinky. She didn't gain weight. But her vision became near and small and the space between her eyes narrowed in self-absorption. She added to her vocabulary a contemptuous snorting sound and used it on me ceaselessly, claiming she wasn't aware of it.

Her pal Yvonne is very New Age. Into channeling, crystals, wycca, et cetera. She holds "sessions": seances, basically, in which she claims to be inhabited by various nonmaterial entities ready to solve petty romantic problems and answer worries about the future. Channeling is just the new Ouija board, but the people involved are grown-ups, and usually money changes hands. Basically Yvonne's a professional sorceress. Flat green, jail-green eyes. Flaring nostrils. To me she looks like a witch, but not because of a warty beak—in fact she has a lovely face altogether. Yet when I think of her face, what comes to mind is something quite different, unappealing, maybe even disturbing. The Slavic cheekbones, broad nose, flared nostrils look, in my memory, like those I saw on gargoyles on Italian churches. In Palermo, for instance, where my life's dark night fell. Her face and theirs blur together, gazing down on my most stupid moves. Sure, Yvonne's probably harmless. But I hate her. I've got her mixed up in my mind with bad things.

I sit out here and think convulsively until I'm numbed by dope and confused by my own brain—think about my business woes, my wife, my mistress, my region and my region's demands and allowances. My idiot brother. My ugly father. Free will? Personal decisions? It's not that simple, not at all. What am I but the knot, the gnarled dark intersection, of all these strands? They keep me from acting, and they tug at me to act. Stand fast, and I'll be torn. But if I want to move, then all of these things must break, they all have to be ripped apart, and that's the end of me just as much as the end of them.

What if there were such people as Yvonne pretends to be, sons and daughters of men trafficking with mysterious powers, ready to fix things backstage, in the darkness behind the scenes? The witches who ended up with Carla Frizelli's crucifix—I'd like to talk to them. Milt Sharkey claimed witches stole it, this token from the Coast Silky's claws. You know the silky, a creature of fancy with a divided life, like a were-man or werewolf, but of an aquatic order: a seal in the ocean who takes the form of a man and crawls ashore by night, dripping and ashamed and bent to the corruption of the unaccursed.

The Coast Silky is said to have been an actual man, one of the

Denis Johnson ▪ 44

sailors from the seventeen boats that went to pieces in the storm of 1903, only this man didn't drown like the others. The strife of waves carried him far out past Shipwreck Rock, where he clung to some logging flotsam, slowly freezing until he bumped against a big bull seal and with his skinning knife opened it from jaw to crotch and clothed himself in its bloody warmth, and in the next night's darkness washed to shore still alive; and thereafter hunted and wore the seals and believed himself one of them. Sometimes he'd shake off the psychosis, traipse the dark fog in his fisher's rags seeking some way back into the company of humans, some place to begin again. Many times he was witnessed by loggers and trappers, seen weeping in the light from a camp-cabin window. As the story has it, he befriended a young girl, Carla Frizelli. But soon word got out that Carla Frizelli frolicked by night with a creature of the sea. Laughter and dread formed itself around her. The local doctor said she'd been deflowered in some unspeakable way, and one Sunday at Saint Alphonse, in Point Arena, the priest cursed her from the pulpit. She was jailed for a while in Ukiah and focused on briefly by the San Francisco papers. She disappeared suddenly. Nobody heard of either of them again, not the girl of the woods or her alien lover. But her crucifix washed ashore, knotted around a briny whip of kelp. Milton Sharkey found it on Bowling Ball Beach. For years it dangled from a hook in his shed. I myself saw it more than once. The sea had leached the plating away and turned Jesus green. Milt was a boy when he found it, an old man when I saw it, and now he must be dead or in a home, I don't know which. The shed still stands, the hook's there too, but not the crucifix. The rumor is it fell into the hands of local witches, who work with it in their ceremonies of blasphemy and invocation. And that's easily possible. Lot of those gals around here. Yes, I'd even turn for help to people of their sort, if they weren't actually just a lot of drug-addicted tramps with runic tattoos, if they truly had a line on spells and curses.

Believe me, you wish for things like that when you've built a twisted life of lies—your own deformed universe. But wishes aren't horses—wishes aren't witches. In order to get on in this underworld you've got to practice *bushido*, the warrior's way, the samurai's inner art, the art of being already dead. Bury your self and go to war. You won't find anybody to work magic for you. The best you can hope for is to hire a mercenary killer.

My partner, Clarence. When his face is dusty he doesn't notice, doesn't wipe away the little smear. Sucks the dripping coffee from his mustache after he takes a sip. Stands around in huge psychedelic short pants just barely kept aloft by his hips, and talks of auto parts, teenage women, offshore currents. Across his torso, from his crotch to his shoulders, he carries seven scars from bullet wounds he received charging into a terrorist ambush in Beirut on the same morning the two hundred U.S. Marines were killed by a car bomb. He doesn't see that moment in the urban desert, when the forces of his life drove him beyond the comprehensible pale, when the ties were shredded and their tensile strength exploded into murderous action—he slaughtered six terrorist guerillas, was highly decorated— as anything more than twenty seconds of goofy adrenaline burnoff. If it came to it he could certainly deal with Harry Lally's hirelings and also, probably, eat their dogs. But I'm devising another plan, a horrible plan. A plan that makes me very sad for all of us.

The pig-men came hunting me that afternoon at Winona's ranch—their camper moving fast down the drive, bouncing heavily, spewing a wake of dust behind it. I wasn't surprised. This wouldn't have been the last place on their list.

I was already out of sight, having leapt off the deck and then behind the heavily treed embankment. Peeking up over the dropoff I watched them bail out of the truck, leaving both doors open and the engine running, and make for the house. Their music was the type from mixed-up Italian westerns, the shiver of snake rattles and the flurries, outbursts, of whacked guitar strings. No try at stealth—the dogs lost their minds anyway as soon as they heard the truck's doors open. The men were as big as they'd seemed, one just a little taller and thinner, the two marching now side by side with their shoulders swivelling, arms swinging, hands scooping the air. They didn't knock. Fortunately for the door they tried the lock before wrecking it—in these parts, doors are rarely locked. In the clarity of this air I might have heard their feet stomping through the house if the floor had been wood, but it was ceramic tile, solid and without vibration.

I crouched thirty feet away from the back deck and monitored their silence, which seemed to drift and turn like a gigantic whale through the rooms, while their dogs' chatter came faintly over the roof. I didn't have any shoes on. I'd been sitting on the porch in my white sweat socks. Silence . . . silence . . . Then cupboards began opening and closing in the kitchen. I didn't want this! Tears burned inside me, but nothing came up. Corrosive tears, they were giving me an ulcer.

Somewhere in the house was a gun—I'd left it with Winona—a .357 magnum, the original Smith & Wesson issue, with a serial number in the low four thousands, a collector's item I didn't know the sure location of and certainly wouldn't have threatened these types with in any case. I liked to think of myself as something of a cool guy or even perhaps a cowpoke with my .357 and my 356—my Smith & Wesson and my Porsche—and my adobe rancho. But right here and now I washed my hands of all three of them.

My brother's cabin lay over a mile from my house, a good half of which I'd have to spend lurching from tree to tree in my stocking feet until I found his drive. It was all downhill or I wouldn't have tried it. I just prayed they wouldn't let loose the dogs.

The truth was I'd never hiked through these woods before. This wonderful scenery and its atmosphere was something to witness, something to inhale. I didn't like being immersed in it however, stirring up its dust and scraping against its bark and getting its gravel in my socks. All this was fine for my brother, Bill, because he'd given up on civilization. As for me, I was ailing, hungover, had no business rambling under the boughs. I'd been meaning to check myself into one of those places where they feed you grains and herbs and help you moderate the drinking. But the captains of moderation, what happened to them all? These days they want you to stop drinking entirely. Okay then!—let them drink this fear. Taste it coming up from the stomach through the sinuses. Let them try it, it's like being hung upside-down and everything rushing the wrong way until the blood drips out your ears. I need tranquilization. Those men up there touching stuff, walking into all the rooms, they counted among the many, many things impossible to face. And I'd hidden the Porsche, but left my jogging shoes in plain sight beside the kitchen table. They'd find dishes in the sink, and upstairs the slept-in—tossed-in, sweated-in—bed. If the men had brains they'd let the dogs nose around and strike my trail. But I doubted the men had brains.

Now I came on a deer path and followed it with less trouble downward. On this walk things that happened played like sparks over the bits of dreams I'd had last night. Stepping on a thorn brought back a dream of catching a large insect. I tore off its wings and stepped on it, and it lashed out, but helplessly, at my foot with a large stinger. Hadn't I been dreaming, in fact, of this place, and these trees? Before long I entered the fog. The woods were cool and stopped with a cottony silence. Soothing, protective. The ever-changing here and now presented itself in small discreet chambers materializing out of bright mists. I'm speaking of the actual walk, not the walk I dreamed.

I found Bill's drive, the winding two-rut road lined with seventeen junked cars, which he believed to be antiques. Most of his delusions were pitiful. The only interesting madness he'd exhibited had been years back, when he visited the nearby reservation and disrobed and begged the Indians to crucify him. He was on LSD.

Here, on the gentler slopes, the big trees can keep their hold—even a few old-growth redwoods, already standing here the day Julius Caesar was born and now nearly two hundred feet tall and thirty feet around. I might have been wandering through a region of vaulting aboriginal monuments lifted up by a dead race. Nobody worships them now. Unattended they accomplish their vast meditations. Their indiscernible deaths. Their tremendous, crashing funerals. Then the interminable wasting down until, underfoot, not earth, but a quiet rusty bread. Bill keeps his cabin at the western edge of an untouched several acres of old growth. When the fog burns away he looks down from his back porch onto the ocean, a sunny postcard full of distant black rocks splashed with foam. Yet from his front door he steps right into the prehistoric. Big silence. Big redwoods. Ferny dusk beneath. Forests once sheltered half our race, but now very few humans live in such places, towered over by slow and ancient lives. I believe the effect on my brother has been nearly miraculous. These kind-hearted monsters have wooed him away from madness into a beautiful, if easily perturbable, mildness. Now he's just a quiet man who gets too excited when he drinks anything with caffeine in it. Once or twice a year I come to see him, and each time I wonder why I don't just join him forever in this healing place. My father owns it, but it is my brother's forest.

Among the practitioners of oneiromancy, the forest stands for the unconscious, symbolizes the very place containing all we see when we're asleep. And the same for the ocean. My brother keeps the forest on one hand and the ocean on the other, dwells between two entrances to the deep dark source of dreams. The forest is a place of danger, magic, and happy endings. All night the dreamer travels in this region and doesn't realize he's asleep. The differences between the logic of that world and the logic of this waking one are vast. But they *feel* the same. And isn't that how we recognize logic, by the way it feels? Whatever Descartes may say, his first fact rests only on a feather, this *feeling*, the same one we have as we wander through forests that don't exist, forests that are just as primary in that world, entirely as real, as thinking-thus-being is in this one. I passed the junked carcasses with which my brother lines his road, old cars with their histories misting up through their broken windshields, powerful in their deaths, sinister and candid and, to me, frightening. Dust thickening over the stains of messy kids and backseat lovers, engines oxidized to brittle red lumps. Candid I mean in the absence of any dissemblance in their smashed faces, like dying dogs. If this sweaty hike were dreamed the waker wouldn't have to ask: these wrecks mean exactly themselves, they mean that everything wastes away, that even steel will be putrefied, they mean that youths coupling in the depths will dissolve. But who cares? Translating dreams in advance, well, then why have them? Why sleep?

I rounded a bend and there was my brother, bearded and blond, standing beside an International Harvester Scout, dripping water from a coffee can onto its hood.

Bill saw me watching him.

I could very nearly witness the lurching of his brain. He needed words. He'd forgotten they existed. He had to energize his atmospheres and let words form, like clouds, inside him.

"I'm washing the birdshit off this vehicle," he said.

He wouldn't get it done, not without a cloth or a brush. No. He was just fooling around because nothing was necessary here.

"It looks like you don't have shoes on," he said.

"This is an emergency visit."

"Hey," he said, "hey."

"Nobody's dead, no."

Nobody meant our father. Our father wasn't dead.

"Hey, okay," Bill said.

"I just had to get here fast."

We stood not twenty feet from his door, but he failed to ask me in. Didn't want me in his one-room house because he thought I'd peek at the letters he was writing. During his manic runs he corresponds voluminously, in a trembling scrawl—with whom I don't exactly know, but he does in fact mail his letters out, usually in big batches, sometimes, though rarely, to one of our fellow Gualalanians, who then shows them all around town just for laughs. His cabin's well made, with a back deck, a gable over the front door, a small tidy porch. I followed him as far as the creek that ran beside it, where he got down on his muddy knees to fill his coffee can again. Young acacia trees nosed in under the taller creekside alders. Acacias bloom golden and abundant in the spring, but the variety propagates ruthlessly and has to be contained. A couple of severed deer heads hung down on bailing twine from the branches, with asterisks for eyes, exactly as the cartoonists show them. "I believe that's a doe," I said of one.

"I'm a poacher," he admitted, "but in or out of season I don't take doe."

This was his life. He killed and butchered deer, packed the bloody meat back and forth between here and our father's freezer. An elemental calling. "If a couple of people came down here after me," I asked him, "would you shoot them for me—make them dead and make their eyes like that?"

"No, no. No, Nellie," he said, using the hated childhood diminutive. "I wouldn't violate anything around here."

"You killed those deer."

"But I don't do war. War is a diseased game."

"I'm a target for certain unpleasantness."

"In fact you yourself are a diseased game. Too much exposure to radar. You shouldn't be here."

"This time it's my intention to stay for a while. I'd like to hide here."

"Stay at the Tides. Or the Hotel."

"I've rented five rooms in six days."

"Go hide in your pot patch."

"I can't."

"All you need is a sleeping bag! Be a man, will you?"

"It's my plants they're after. It's a money thing."

"They'd never find the place."

"I got drunk and told Melissa where it was."

"Melissa!"

Bill disapproved of everything outside this forest. But for my mistress he had special contempt. Well, I guess we both judged her incapable of any real loyalty.

"I've got to have a place to hide and think. I've got to take care of this mess fast. Before they get around to her."

"She couldn't give them detailed directions, could she?"

"In general. She could tell them generally, and they'd find it. They have dogs."

"They?"

I nodded.

He was suspicious. "Is this a real they?"

"Yes."

"Or a chemical they?"

"They're real. They were just at the house."

"But maybe your reaction is chemical."

"No, I have good reason to be afraid."

"Or maybe partly chemical."

"Once in a while a joint. A bong hit. Recreational use."

"Maybe you don't cure it right."

"Too much alcohol of course. I really should moderate."

"Green dope and tequila! Plus whatever the radar's doing to you."

Now I made a scene, I'm afraid, shouting, "They're coming for me! They're coming for me here or there and sooner or later! They're getting paid for it! These are hit men, hit men, hit men!"

"Okay, okay, okay." I'd unbalanced things now, set the energies whirling. He was angry but he didn't know how to be angry. "You mentioned dogs?"

"And I'll mention more dogs! Their slimy noses in the dirt, jammed against my personal essence!"

"Not police dogs, I hope."

"The smell of *me*."

"This isn't the cops, I hope. Did you do something bad?"

"What happened to the time when brother helped brother and no questions asked? What happened to those times?"

We were standing beside his jeep again by now. He put his can of water on the hood, laid his hands on my shoulders, looked into my eyes. He meant, by this, to signal that those times regrettably were gone.

I'm always astonished by his hands. He's grown on the ends of his arms the very hands we were always so afraid of. Thick fingers, wrinkled knuckles, emphatic grip. They're precisely our father's. Our father wasn't dead yet, but we'd both already inherited more than we could stand from the old man. We were weighted with it, dragged down struggling, anchored impossibly in our father. Not just by his hands. And not just by things passed on in the chromosomes, but by learned habits and sorrows that gave us an inner understanding of him and made it hard to hate him as much as we wanted to.

Mother left Father—we all left Father—when I was five. Mother never remarried, spent her days recovering from him and raising Bill and me in a succession of rented houses either side of Point Arena until I went away to high school. But it was a long time, nearly twelve years, before she managed to divorce him, and he never remarried, didn't even date publicly until a year after the divorce—because that was, coincidentally, a week or so after the death of his business partner, whose wife Father had been screwing for decades. He bought her a house, Mrs. Willis Winslow was her name, but for a long time he didn't change their arrangement. Until very recently they lived apart. She managed his motels. They got together in clean, anonymous rooms periodically. I can't help thinking they were even more excited then, cuckolding his spirit and memory, than they'd been when betraying Willis Winslow in the flesh. And people wonder why my brother and I are nuts! Or perhaps they don't. Maybe I'm the last one left wondering.

And now my brother grips me with the old man's hands. Wraps me in arms a lot like Dad's. I can't breathe. I won't inhale—what if he smells like our father?

"My life is strange," I told him.

"I don't like it when you cry."

"I'm not making it out there, Bill."

"No. Nobody is."

"What do I do now? What do I do?"

This got him going. "Hey! I've taken stock, I've made an assessment, I've done the thing sitting out here counting my fingers and toes and actions. And I got the truth on one side and my lies on the other, the nutty stuff and the stuff that's real, and we've convened, me and the trees and the spirits, and I got it calculated that the only thing I ever did right was buy that oak flooring for the cabin when they tore up the bowling alley in Point Arena. That's it, the oak flooring."

"It's very nice."

"I can't advise, is what I'm saying."

"I understood you."

"I mean everything else is on the failure and insanity side."

"But what a floor! Something to envy."

"Go ahead," he said.

"A floor to make you commit sins."

"Go right ahead and be like that," he said.

After Mother left, Father fought the divorce like mad. A misaimed Roman Catholic determination. But he failed because she took nothing, wanted nothing but out. What happens when a man like that fails? He goes right on. He starts fighting the scourge of divorce among his offspring—by willing everything to Winona and threatening to do the same when Bill gets hitched, which he will of course not. Bill's nuts, but he understands that if Winona divorces me, my life is a pauper's. Why would he do the same—pick out a bride to take everything from him?

"I'm asking you one last time: will you help me?"

"I'll drive you back home."

"They're up there waiting! They ran in and I ran out, don't you get it?"

"They won't be there. If they come back, you can run down here again."

"At night? What if it's at night? Why don't I just stay awhile?"

"Essentially this isn't your kind of place. Not essentially."

"Two days."

"Not spiritually."

"Oh. Are we going to do that one?"

"In a very deep way I don't want you here. In a deep way you're destructive."

"Of what destructive? What do you mean?"

"It would take centuries to get the harmony and balance back."

"I happen to agree. I believe that too. What I don't believe is that you are in any way aware of these things, that you feel these things, that you'd be affected by any disruption there. It's like knowing you're being struck by gamma rays."

"I am being struck by gamma rays."

But once I'd entered into this kind of argument with Bill I was finished. Just to acknowledge his concern with the inaudible thrumming of the planets and the trees was to throw in the towel. No, my life is a soup of corruption, emanating a sickly voltage. The trees know it, he knows, I know. We can pretend to be not yet convinced—to be waiting for the verdict of science—but we know.

Brother Bill. He gave me the sideways attention of the slightly crazy, his posture tentative and tilted, his left side bathed in radiation from another universe. Pouring a quart of water onto a car. It was thrilling, the confusion of sorrows that moved like a cyclone through my lungs, it took my breath away: my brother—I was more perfectly alienated from this person than from, say, Harry Lally, who wanted me dead, or from my unrecognizable wife.

My brother drove me back home. In his completely funky International without a fourth gear or reverse. Astonishing that he could have got it running, or that he'd ever finished building his cabin—my brother, who'd stopped taking his medication long ago, if he'd ever started—or that he could actually drive the thing, that he even knew which half of the road was his. My brother, the one who'd raced, in a driving rainstorm, all the way to the reservation to be crucified. Once also he tried to climb into the Buddhist monastery and got his sleeves tangled up in the barbed wire on top of the fence. The monks—who look like regular people, I've seen them, in down-filled vests and loose athletic apparel—clipped him down from where he was hanging and sent him away. Pretty much as he'd sent me away now from his own sanctuary, and in the same spirit.

Bill knew all the ruts and managed to haul us up out of his world without breaking an axle. He knew the trees and the taste of the water, he killed the animals and ate them. He belonged in these woods. I guessed I didn't. But in this place he was getting much better, and meanwhile outside of it I was getting a lot worse.

Two miles before Winona's place we came around a curve and right up against the entrance to the Tibetan Buddhist monastery. Usually I'm anticipating it and it doesn't surprise me, but today we both had our minds on other things. When you're not expecting it, it's like a fatal accident and then heaven.

California!

Suddenly and often in this strange land, there opens before the dreamer the Golden Gate. In this case the Tibetan Buddhist temple with its raging copper dome, five stories high, and the hundred-foot-tall pagoda, gilded with actual gold, standing up through the mist above the green pasture—better than one square mile of pasture, and all of it surrounded by chain-link and sparkling concertina wire. This is not a dream, illusion, or metaphor. This is California. There really is such a place. It is not a mistake of the imagination, it doesn't disappear like a mirage or back away like a rainbow.

Anything, anything, anything!—that's what California offers.

This day, the one I've been thinking about, when I woke at Winona's, when the men came after me and I visited my brother, was also the day the drought broke and we got two inches of rain.

It had been dry all spring and all summer. The Spanish moss turned brittle, broke away from the boughs and lay on the roads like ash. Meanwhile dust hung over the world like smoke from a gigantic fire. "Brown heat," Bill said as if noticing it for the first time. And this may, after all, have been his first trip above the mist in months.

"Look," I begged him when he dropped me off at Winona's ranch, "don't tell Clarence about this."

He and Clarence were buddies and pals, of a sort. They worked on cars together.

"Clarence?" he said. "Clarence isn't like you think."

"We have differing interpretations of Clarence. Only one of us can be right."

We dropped the subject and didn't bother fumbling around for another. When I got out of the car and rapped on its hood, he put it in gear and headed down the tiny road rapidly until he went around a curve. I heard him making a turnaround in a wide spot, and here he came again past the gate peering ahead intrepidly, speeding off toward wherever. And there I stood in front of my troubles without anybody to help me, not even my brother.

I noticed right away that the bogus sportsmen had strung a filament of fishing line waist-high between the gateposts, a trick to find out if a car had entered—more use to me, once I'd ducked under it, than to them: flanking me as ably as any moat.

Just the same that night I was crazy with fear, cowering inside the house with all the lights out, maybe drinking. Not a fear of men. They'd only check their trip wire, they wouldn't come all the way in. They couldn't reasonably expect me ever to return anyway. In fact I was only here because I couldn't have stood another minute in the car with my brother, who smelled bad, who smelled like shit, who smelled crazy. To think of him as healed was exaggeration; he'd merely gentled down to a precarious strangeness. Anyway, no, that night the fear was of the earth and the moon. Of the abeyance in the air that signaled a storm. Of the silence, of the silver light, of the wolf spiders' webs I could suddenly see in the meadow, the reflecting dew strung on every strand. Now the spider is a stranger in its nest, the wren confused by these miracles. In this perfection of lifeless things, this steely inanimate loveliness, everything alive is sordid, unwholesome. To live is evil, the word itself is evil spelled backwards. What a relief when the breeze picked up, stirring pockets of warm air, bringing noises in through the screen doors and windows—I heard things, and then one set of sounds was real—an engine, and a car's headlights passed along the ridge road. They didn't slow down.

I'm remembering now that it was after midnight when the shower began. But first we had the moon and the mist. The big ones blow past from the north, well offshore, and then twist back around to lash at us from the south, driving the coastal fog up into the inland heights. And yet the warm front, giving way before the coastal cool, keeps the heavens clear until just seconds before the rain falls. So we get the mist over the ground and the piquant irrelevancies of a moonlit sky and slashing meteors above.

And then it rained. I went out to the deck to take the hammock down just as the first drops started, tremendous things, exotic, glittering, cold. I had a sense of them crashing into the dust on my skin. The breeze had an animal smell. The empty hammock rocked. There was jazz in the little race to get it untied, a happy feeling in getting there just in time. The feeling of a poetic moment, a mingling of California and nostalgia—on the air a forbidden, a religious scent, an intuition of the summers of other people's lives,—airy summers, pleasant people, unfettered lives—of the land from which I was exiled. A moment of tenderness, the smell of rain overpowering, as thick and unbreathable as smoke, and almost sentimental, not just the atmosphere's pregnancy and ripeness, but the strains of grief rising up from somewhere—from within. The simplicity of certain pleasures bursts in my heart. I'm weeping, and asking a ludicrous question: will my life ever be like this?

For a few seconds everything was brushed with just a single quick stroke of moonshine. The deck chairs and spool tables and potted succulents stood out like negatives. Then I lost the moon. Vagueness came up over the ridge in billows. I'd had PG&E put a streetlamp at the head of the driveway, it cost less than seven dollars a month, and they took care of the thing. Its glow a quarter-mile off seemed unattainable, seemed imaginary. A large creature, an owl probably, in this atmosphere it looked white, swept up from under the edge of the hill behind me and passed directly over my head. I could hear its wingstrokes like desperate breaths. I followed around to the front of the house and watched it moving off toward the front gate and the streetlight, where its shadow opened out from behind it like a tunnel through the lamp-lit fog. The tunnel closed to nothing as the bird passed over the source, and now there was only the iridescent mist. Everything looked so much like the cover of a science-fiction comic book it hardly seemed possible to be inside it and not to be able to turn a page, impossible to be breathing the weather and the mix of rain and dust and sea-damp and tasting a little of my own sweat, washed to the corners of my mouth with the rain.

And then suddenly another tunnel opened in the light, the tunnel of a man, a ghost treading the backlit moonwater, drifting through the increasing storm.

I tried to convince myself it was the owl coming back, making another pass. Even if I'd been able to believe it my skin knew different, tightening all over me so that my scalp prickled and my scrotum actually shrank. But I didn't run, didn't even take a step, just stood there with my arms around the bundled hammock and waited, getting rained on.

The figure coming up the driveway was clearly a thing too sorrowful to be alive, it was a black absence, the ash of grief, a lost, wounded soul, but was now clearly, as it came even with me, heading right for the pond, a man walking. He got within ten yards of me. I could almost see his face. Still he seemed unconnected with our earth, had nothing to do at the moment with our violent dramas, not even with the taste of rain on the wind changing to a drink, not even with the strands of it thrown against the side of the barn and the sheds as he passed. There was something special about his stroll, as if he were exploring a place once thought familiar but now completely new— like a youth on his first day of hooky, for whom simply walking inside this stolen holiday is exotic and monstrous, and everything— this is what it is about hooky, and about this figure's emanations— everything is original because it's been chosen. Yes, he gave the impression of being somebody who'd rejected the routine forced on him and decided just to walk on the surface of the world, a pilgrim. We see them by the roadside, particularly on the coast, solitary unburdened travellers. They're probably crazy, that's true, but we have no way of knowing. Enlightened ones may live everywhere among us, looking like functional failures. This might have been the ghost of one of those.

There was nothing troubling about this presence; this apparition was emphatic but not desperate, also unhurried but not at leisure. It was passing along the edge of my life and I felt no fear. Only a hunger—I ached to discover what gift he'd been given. Because clearly he carried some treasure in his heart, some powerful token from the true universe. Nothing got in his way, the shrivelled clumps of fern in the pasture, the hunks of log and metal, the haggish sculptures—he'd withdrawn any investment in these things, they weren't quite contemporary with his purpose. He never looked right or left. His every step had the quality of a stirring finish, of bursting through the tape. He walked right into the pond. At the edge of the bank he spread his arms like wings and took a great step out into the air. In the banshee squall his landing in the water was inaudible, not quite real. And then I got it—I was witnessing somebody in his ultimate moment. For him, the planet, and its ponds and such, didn't count. A deep preoccupation was making him invulnerable to the elements. He would stride on the floor of the water for its whole width, two hundred feet, and burst onto the facing bank like a military vehicle and head straight on, dismembering the pitiful trees, I was convinced of it. I didn't realize, until I took a deep, damp lungful, that I'd stopped breathing. Now I dropped the hammock at my feet. I was soaked. The rain ran off the ends of my fingers. And it whipped across the surface of the pond in sheets, covering any trace of him. But I could see him better, now that he was gone—I was seeing the person I can't be. The one who marches to the bottom of the depths, who beats his bullshit ruminations into a sword and hacks at life's entanglements until he's free. He'd come bursting up out of the water in just a minute, like a baptismal figure . . .

I realized as the minute and then another passed that I was crazy, this guy was drowning, anybody would, it's the natural result of breathing underwater. I shouted!—but naturally he didn't hear. He was gone. He was now without action, he'd passed into the underworld of drowned souls—who would he rescue there? . . . No, *I* had to be *him*, I had to rescue him, call him back from the dead. I had to be the person I couldn't be. I swear to you that this was the level of my thoughts and feelings, I was inhabiting the realm of the gods and heroes, this person had truly inspired me. I ran inside the front door and cut on the porch lamps, which lit up the yard and the dirt walk and hardly fingered the edge of the pond; raced back out into a scene completely changed by their illumination—the rain around the bulb, the crinkling and rustling of it on the pond as I plunged toward the water—this night!—wings, sorrows, iridescences, wounds, exile, the owl, the mist, the moon, dew's light-emitting diodes on the webs— the blow to my guts as the water went over me. I could feel my eyes punched against their orbits, a seizure, a response of some electric force that shot strength out even to the ends of my fingers, even into my fingernails, as I splashed in a half panic, struggling for my own life now, no longer god, hero, not even human, more the mindless rac- coon stalked by the dog of death, plunging out into anything. I couldn't stay afloat. I kicked off my shoes and tore off my sweater, sinking below the surface as I wrestled it over my head. I came up again. My limbs were going numb in the chilly water and I was sur- prised that it was happening so quickly. I forgot what I was here for. In one direction I saw nothing but the porch lamps, the other way lay an acre of water in a world of darkness, sizzling in the rain. I was afraid.

Then he surfaced just ahead of me, modestly, without thunder—so unlike me, so much wiser, not struggling at all, unconscious and beautiful. I grabbed his sleeve and pulled him easily to the shallows, but dragging him up out of the water was murder. The world became terrible and slow. I fell backward. All I had out of the water was his arm. The rest of him drifted like a log. He seemed past saving. I even thought, winded, nauseous with fatigue, of giving up, letting him float away. But I pulled him up the bank an inch at a time, resting between inches, until we were both stretched out in the mud. I'm saving this person!—but I'm so drained I can only lie beside him, just as helpless, the only difference being that I'm breathing and he's not. All I can think of is turning him over and putting my lips on his. All I want to do is breathe into his death. But I can't move. If I don't, I myself will drown in the flood. I can see it rushing down at me, stu- pendous, wobbling globes. I turned onto my belly, got my hands and knees beneath me and crawled over to look down at his face—he had a long mustache, and a pair of eyeglasses snagged on his left ear. Mud dripped from my face onto his but there was no response, no breath, no pain or trouble there. He was dead! Complete! Mysterious forever! I'd heard of pinching the nostrils shut, tilting back the head, clearing the passages of obstructions, but heard about them it seemed in a foreign language I had to decipher now, in the act. Water ran out of his mouth when I turned his head to the side. I rolled him halfway over and he vomited into the mud—alive! Over on his back once more and I put my wide-open mouth over his. The fear ran out of me again and I entered another clear space in which I felt the rain washing us both until we were beautiful. We breathed. He tasted like vomit, but good, like my own when I'm very sick with wine and I know this purging is the cure.

R ight around midnight the beeper on his hip blew, and Officer Navarro had to leave his TV movie to go out on a call, an estranged husband with a gun. The wife was a sweet sort of middle-aged dyke, that was Officer Navarro's take on the thing, who claimed she and her friend had heard something unusual out back while lounging in the hot tub. The husband, a sixties veteran, she explained, had made threats, was known to go armed, dealt drugs. Her friend was a tall beautiful blonde named Yvonne. Navarro knew her slightly, and she gave him the creeps, or anyway the situation did. The house lay at the edge of Point Arena, at the end of a cul-de-sac, and the deck with the bubbling hot tub looked back over dark empty pastures toward the Ranchero, which was, if he understood this right, an Indian reservation but somehow not a federal one. The girls didn't see fit to mention the guy's guns till they'd been standing there a good five minutes. "Would you cut the lights, please, and lay down inside?" he asked them. That gave them a thrill.

Now he was scouting the backyard, and the long flashlight, which he didn't want to turn on, trembled in his sweaty grip.

He thought he heard something out there himself. Cows maybe, moaning. The fog had cleared down here, it seemed to be rolling on up to the ridge, and with the shine of moonlight dissolving surfaces he could barely make out around a thousand shapes in the tall grass, but they weren't the shapes of cattle. And he couldn't use the lamp. No way he could light things up in the vicinity of a guy possibly in a mood to throw rounds at something. This was your typical bullshit. In East L.A. he'd have four cars backing him and a chopper making daylight all over and the SWAT commander on the phone to the lieutenant, angling to be called in. It only made him lonelier and more scared to think about it right now. These are the sons of bitches who'll pull the trigger on a cop, it's a pissed-off-husband statement intended for the wife, like smashing something made of glass, a bottle or a window. And he felt like glass out here. And he didn't like the wind. Usually there wasn't any wind. Weird breeze, the moon brooding over it, you can't do this stuff when you feel like you're made of glass. For something like this in L.A. they'd have news teams taping it and the block roped off and the whole neighborhood jostling against the sawhorses. But here, just the wind and the empty feeling of the Ranchero inland and the big blackness out to sea.

Officer Navarro hated to retreat, but he'd made a mistake coming out here. He backed up against the house, went inside after two taps on the French doors and then clomped through the silent living room, where parallelograms of moonlight gleamed on the hardwood floors. "Ladies," he called, "I'm gonna bring my wheels around back. I'll try not to scuff the lawn."

"Okay," he heard somebody say softly. They were hiding in a back room.

Out front he started up his car and headed it around the house into the yard, lit up the search beam and headlights, and left the vehicle quickly, half-diving but feeling idiotic because, after all, it was merely a small-town thing and nobody'd been fired on—in fact he only had the wife's word there was a weapon out there. It's the trunk thing, she says he keeps it in the trunk, I see big-time dealer ordnance, RPG's and such. And the Vietnam aura, all that, a lot of these guys haven't given up feeling like killers because nobody ever let them off the hook for it.

At least in this desolate place his outsides matched his insides. But what had brought him here eighteen months ago? What was he doing up here where the sea and the wind made all this noise? Life had turned lonely after the third divorce. He'd felt his future wearing out and had left LAPD, applied to CHP, dialing up his dream, making it a thing. Was turned down—why? Did the Highway Patrol expect he'd been contaminated by LAPD? Then he'd tried the local constabularies, last stop before rent-a-cop; sent résumés to several small towns on the coast, was offered a job by every one, and moved up to Point Arena from East L.A., where things had been tense and mean in a way he now remembered fondly. In East L.A. he'd spent his shifts making his way among foreigners and perpetrators and the more-or-less mentally maimed, the slum dwellers rattling loose, who, when he restored them to order, shrilly accused him of trampling over the rights of "ordinary citizens," and then shut up. Most of them had never met an ordinary citizen, never even seen one this side of their greasy TV screens. Navarro hadn't known too many either, sleeping in the day and working that area at night. But here in Point Arena he engaged with actual ordinary people every day, and they were beginning to terrify him. They never squawked about their rights, they just kept quiet or even appeared quite friendly while he issued them tickets or ordered them to leash their dogs on the beach or rattled his truncheon at their drunken teenagers and kicked out their teenage beachside fires. But behind the acquiescence skulked a buddy system of ordinary folks and their ordinary resentments—a network, a spiderweb, practically, of ordinariness. Everybody he dealt with was somebody's cousin. The youngster he prodded with a nightstick tonight was bound to be the one bagging his groceries tomorrow, the mayor's nephew, the judge's godson. There was a different way of handling things in a small town, and Officer Navarro didn't know what it was. He just knew he wasn't popular here.

This person in the field here would probably turn out to be his chiropractor. Navarro hoped so, he'd need his services after all this humping around. Navarro crawled softly, as much to avoid grass stains on his knees as to keep quiet. Suddenly he understood there was truly somebody else in this darkness. He could feel the man moving, flanking him, inadvertently he hoped, before he heard any movement or saw the bit of T-shirt flash briefly going through the headlights. Navarro jerked upright, said, "Freeze!" and moved to his left quickly. The figure didn't stop or fire but ran.

Navarro followed the footsteps into the dark, limping along as he buttoned the flap on his holster, then letting the adrenaline run his legs over the rough ground, caring for nothing, taking great breaths of air, feeling brilliant, weightless, gaining on the white shirt.

As soon as he got his hands on the shoulders he knew it was a kid and tried to go easy, taking much of the fall on his own knees and elbows and, he knew, getting grass stains on them after all.

The kid's breath went out of him in a whump. A young sound, kind of dreadful. A girl? He felt the kid's chest. Thank God, no tits.

They'd run a fast two-twenty here, but the juice was still jolting through. He felt great. He had the kid wrapped in a headlock and felt him shaking, heard him wheezing, panting.

"What the hell are you *doing?*"

No answer but sobs.

Navarro let him up. He kept hold of the kid's arm. But he didn't feel like putting a light in his face. He could see well enough.

"How old are you, kid?"

No answer. Navarro unbuttoned his light now and put the glare on him.

"You get a good look at them naked ladies?"

The boy's lips trembled wildly.

"Anybody with you?"

"They—no, nobody."

"Your friends made a quicker exit, didn't they?"

The boy was thin. Navarro had his arm in a come-along hold, and it felt like it might break.

He let go. "Scat," he said.

The boy stood there.

"Don't come back," Navarro said.

The boy took a few steps into the dark. "I'm sorry," he said.

"Don't apologize. Change your conduct," Navarro told the boy, who was gone.

Back in the house, in the living room, where he stood talking to the two women with all the lights blazing, he told them the field had proved empty save for cattle. "It could be you're getting spied on by kids. Maybe you should put up one of those lattice partitions."

The two women stood hugging themselves, one in a Japanese robe and one in black terrycloth. "We were just absorbing a little of this rare energy," the tall one said—Yvonne.

He gave her a military smile. "This an energetic neighborhood?"

"There's a storm on the way."

"Really?" Not a drop of rain had fallen in seven months.

"Don't you feel it?"

He did feel something.

He took a description of the husband's car and promised to make a tour of the neighborhood. He took the husband's last address and assured the two ladies he'd be looking in on the man. "But it doesn't sound like a crime's been committed," he felt obliged to point out.

The homeowner, Barbara James, still legally Mrs. Shank, complained softly, with tears in her eyes. "Regular people are getting buried alive by laws. Meanwhile maniacs roam free."

The women walked him out to his car. It looked eerie now, parked here in the backyard.

"G'night, Officer Navarro," Barbara said.

"John," he suggested.

"G'night, John."

Yvonne said, "You might have to protect me from my latest ex one day. He's dialing into some mysterious frequencies. Frankheimer."

"Don't know him."

"By sight I think you would."

"What does he look like?"

"He'd be the only one out there behind my house."

"But I mean, help me out. How tall, please?"

"About seven feet."

"I'm sorry?"

"Better get one of those zoo guns. One of those guns for tranquilizing elephants."

He laughed. "I've seen him around."

They said good night again and Navarro went out to the squad car, on the windshield of which he found a brief and kind of pointless note—he assumed it referred to Yvonne and had come from one of the peeping children. Did he look like a scholar? Why did everybody send him notes and letters? Driving away he thought to himself that Yvonne wasn't such a bad sort. She was certainly a fine specimen. He didn't know what it was about her. When he'd walked in she'd said, "Hel-*lo*"—personality forcefully projected, a sense of being met halfway, a sense that you matter. Sunny. Truly winning. But in retrospect, truly phony. Giving one impression in the flesh, completely different when called to mind.

He'd heard her mentioned around. She had a reputation for unsavory weirdness. What was it, mistreating small animals, acquiring occult paraphernalia, books—I thought I saw her walking by the road late at night. But I was off duty—the badge was off—I didn't even slow down. She looked like a widow. Mourning. Somebody claimed to have spied her one night standing naked on a bluff over the sea. Absolute bullshit. Not for free. You'd have to pay to see that type naked. Though it was dark and he was supposed to be steering the car, he glanced one more time at the note in a child's hand—

The lesbo is a Witch

—before jamming it into the ashtray. The atmosphere in this neighborhood seemed unusually warm and strangely hushed. Something thumped on the hood, and then several more times on the roof—and before he'd travelled two more blocks he was driving through a downpour of such ferocity that he could hardly see ahead of him.

It stormed steadily as he eased the squad car down the main street and parked beneath the windows of his home: he'd rented a place over the video store, and at first it had seemed ideal—not far from the ocean, looking out on this quaint little stretch of Route 1 through Point Arena—but since then it had shown itself to be just the kind of spot he always ended up in, solitary and cold. Rather than get wet finding his way up to it, he sat for hours in the car looking out at the blurred drumming California street. Or maybe it just seemed like hours. He cracked the window an inch, rested his torch and stick on the dash and settled back and dozed.

He found himself under black skies, out on a battlefield looting the uniforms of slain clowns. The woman Yvonne was on the periphery of things. He could smell her, and it was erotic. He woke up still seeing her strange face.

Toward dawn the weather let up and he uncurled himself stiffly from the front seat and stood on the sidewalk in a town that seemed fresh and hopeful, its chastity in a way renewed. It made him hungry for breakfast. But nothing was open yet. Despoiled of any alternative, he climbed the stairs toward his home above the movies.

Van Ness woke up with a sore throat, sore tongue, sore mucous membranes up through his ears.

Somebody was having a fuzzy conversation. He seemed to be part of it.

"Are you all right? What a stupid question. I've got your glasses, let me—"

So he could hear. And he could almost see. Otherwise his lack of information was complete.

"What's your name?"

Even down to that. His tongue was swollen. He made a noise with his voice. That was a mistake. It went dark. I've shut my eyes, he thought.

Then he came to and everything seemed white—daytime, morning?

The guy gave him something in a cup. Van drank it. It was tea.

He wasn't unconscious, but not paying attention. He felt the warmth of spilled tea with pleasure on his swollen hands.

He watched the man at the kitchen table in his green bathrobe, now punching buttons on a telephone. Zealously he accomplished this, ecstatically. "Do I have the main library? Reference?" he said. "Well, no then, the information desk. Information?" He was leaning into it. The man was on the phone. "I wish to know," he said, "how far ahead of the hunters, usually, the hunting dogs will go. By what distance usually, *usually*, does the dog precede its master in the wild? On the average. It's a matter of life and death."

He wore a baseball cap with an emblem on the crown, the bill of which he worried incessantly with his free hand, like a baseline coach. "I'd like you to direct me, also, if possible, toward some literature that would discuss the smelling powers of these animals. These hunting dogs. Or dogs in general. The whole odor thing."

Van woke up again later. Daylight still, and still the man sat at the kitchen table, but he was silent. He appeared to be playing solitaire.

He looked over at Van. "How old are you?"

The man was willowy, pale, with thin hands, and eyes that were large and feminine and wounded. His ears jutted out because he wore his baseball cap pulled down tight on his head. He looked to be in his late thirties. Maybe younger, but eaten-at.

"Forty-two," Van told him with an amazing croaking sound.

"Born in forty-eight? Forty-nine? A child of both halves of the century. Do you remember a song—from the sixties, I think—whose refrain went like, *Sometimes . . . the hunter . . . gets captured . . . by the game . . . ?*"

Van did not reply.

*   *   *

Around sunset, Van Ness sat at the kitchen table with a blanket around his shoulders, spooning up clear broth out of a heavy bowl. Through the window he saw the man he assumed to be his host, still in his bathrobe, his white feet, in zoris, showing beneath its hem, walking flat-footed in the pasture as if it were wet out there, and carrying a black bucket. He poured its contents at the feet of a fat ugly horse. He took his cap off, fanning at flies while the horse bowed its head over the food. All around the pasture grandly proportioned assemblages of gray timber and junk farming equipment scattered their shadows. He took their intent to be artistic.

Van found the kitchen a pleasant place. The house's design was solar-efficient; the late sun reached him now, and it was warm. This was a small home with a big loft upstairs and also perhaps a single room—he saw a door at the top of the landing. Down here just the living room and kitchen and a door to, he presumed, a study or a little den. He'd been sleeping in the living room, in a Hide-A-Bed contraption.

He'd done it. He'd killed himself. And here he was. He was probably dead in that universe, but in this one right next door he persisted; his consciousness had simply moved over into this other, potential world in which he did not die. Right. You go down through one hole and come up out of another. Death just moves you to another square. Now he could be sure all beings were immortal. He couldn't kill, he couldn't die. They'd been telling us that life was an illusion, but they lied. The illusion was death.

Van's host stood inside the front door kicking his thongs off and then strode barefoot to the kitchen, nodding in the direction of the pasture and the horse. "Our equine amigo."

Van sipped at his broth, which tasted like chicken. It seemed to make him hungrier. Maybe some cereal would go down.

"I'm Nelson Fairchild," the man said. "And I'm going to pour myself some wine. Will you tell me your name?"

"Van Ness. First name Carl."

"And you won't be saying much more," Fairchild predicted, referring to the terrible sound Van was making words with. "Now," he said, "I'm going to offer you a glass so you can toast with me. Drink it or not, whatever you feel like." Fairchild held the liter bottle tightly with both hands as he poured. He raised his glass high: "The first person ever to be born in space!"

He sat down at the table, and Van watched him drink. Fairchild was younger than he'd thought, more like twenty-five than thirty-five. A young dude with an old man's fear in his eyes—fear was the driving wheel. There was a form of security in knowing a person's prime mover. The young man's hands were steady now. He lifted and spread the deck of cards from his solitaire game, stripped one gently from the fan, slapped it down: "The Suicide King."

Funny how the pictures were always right side up. Yes, he got it—the King of Hearts, stabbing himself, for some reason, in the side of the head. The Suicide King.

Fairchild said, "You're silent. Stunned by the coincidence."

"I'm tired."

"You don't believe in destiny?"

Van swallowed with some pain, happy to answer. "The concept is almost always misused." Anxious to answer, even with his throat all torn up.

"The one real road, the signs at the turnings?"

"I make the road. I draw the map. Nothing just happens to me." He swallowed, trying not to grimace. "I'm the one happening."

"How can you say that? I just pulled you back from death. You've been lying there virtually not happening for ten, twelve hours. For over fourteen hours," Fairchild said, checking the clock on his electric coffeemaker.

Van stood up and turned over the table.

"React," he said amid the noise of breakage and the sound of fragments singing over the Spanish tile.

Fairchild said nothing, righting the table and kneeling to scoop up two or three pieces of china pointlessly. Van could see he experienced his anger from the outside in, first in his skin. In twenty minutes the guy's guts would start burning and he'd freeze it out with a shot of his wine.

"My point still holds," Fairchild said finally, setting down on the bare table one dripping shard.

"Theoretically it holds. But life isn't a theory, not mine anyway. I have to live it."

Fairchild seemed to make up his mind not to clean up the rest of this mess just at the moment. He sat back down.

"You're exactly the person I thought you were," Fairchild said.

"Meaning who?"

"You're a true man of action."

"Not a man of action," Van said, swallowing hard after every three or four words, but feeling compelled to speak, dizzy with the necessity of speaking. "I'm a man of will. But I can't believe in my will, can't feel it, unless I act from it."

"Act from it, no matter what."

"No matter what."

"Overriding everything."

"That's right, everything."

"Then you act in boldness."

"Can I be given a little cereal?"

"A man of true courage."

"Just feed me. I won't hurt your table."

It wasn't night yet but as Fairchild walked among the rooms on the lower floor, speechifying—Van assumed for his, Van's, benefit—he turned on all the lights, every last one. "When I saw you heading into the pond! Unforgettable. I'm telling you, you banished the storm. We would all hope to accomplish a moment like that in our lives. You accomplished it in mine . . ." At one point he put a record on the stereo, a Sonny Rollins thing. Van tried to let it soothe him while the madman talked: "Last month I went down to the main San Francisco library. They know me personally, I'm famous, my obsessive queries. I drove down there I don't know when—three weeks ago. I won't go south of here again, not on that Coast Highway. The cliffs beckon. If you were really trying to kill yourself in our pond, I know the desire. But when I'd turned inland after Jenner, I was safe. You head through the Russian River valley, then you're in the other California—sunshine, vineyards, windmills, small motels . . ." He went on without the benefit of Van's attention until the music ended and then he made a segue, lurching, into talk about some movie . . . No, he wasn't telling about the movie as much as the experience of having gone to the thing, of being in a theater, darkness—"big people. Gargantuan busts, I mean their heads and shoulders, not their titties. Although also titties. Now: something quite out of my experience happened in there, Mr. Van Ness. A panic got hold of the people in the theater."

Fairchild had gone pale; the work of speaking and remembering had pinched the blood out of his flesh, perhaps concentrated it all in his brain; his energies didn't make him lively, Van thought—just incredibly tense, his fibers humming to the point where levitation seemed imminent. A deep vibration jiggled the cups and saucers on the table.

"The floor," he said, "*rumbled*. There were rapid footsteps down the aisles, a lot of people moving all in a bunch, and all with the same thing in mind, whatever it was, and I had the sense that some *group* was playing a prank. Something made you feel that it was all rehearsed, like a fraternity stunt, and I expected these people to kidnap a freshman and carry him out on their shoulders or something like that. Then I thought, but there are *dozens* of them. The rows were emptying in waves, starting at the back, and we, those of us down front, we turned around to see that everybody was leaving fast, through every available exit." Fairchild himself was in motion now, looking around for something in the kitchen. "Now let me tell you," he said, rummaging abstractedly in the refrigerator, delighted with this memory, "nobody screamed, nobody yelled. Nobody loosed even a *tiny* exclamation, Mr. Van Ness. There was only a little muttering as people wondered what was going on and then decided not to stay to find out. The only sounds were the tremendous rumbling of everybody's feet, and the actors on the screen continuing their dialogue. Mute, terrorized people pouring out of the place! By this time we in the very front were able to guess what was happening, but we were also able to feel sort of removed and safe from whatever was scaring them so much up there in the back—a crazed *killer*, whatever. So the people in the first three rows didn't run. We just waited. An usher, a young woman, entered from the lobby and we heard her talking to somebody, but she didn't make an announcement until one of us up front yelled, 'Tell us what's happening!' Then she starts screaming, 'It was just a shoebox! A man with a shoebox! There isn't any bomb!' All this while, the giant . . . *heads* of actors are conversing up on the wall—moving pictures, talking pictures, without any power of illusion left to them. But do you know what? We sat down, those of us who'd stayed around, and in a couple of minutes we were completely consumed again by the drama, which wasn't a very compelling one to begin with anyway. Cereal, cereal, cereal," he said, "it's all we seem to have." Van watched him dump flakes into a bowl.

"Afterwards I recognized a famous man, a television star, standing there in the lobby with a red and orange sack of popcorn in his hand."

Van had no idea how to respond to this stuff. The sun was lowering into the clouds, a deep rosy light filling the kitchen window, Nelson Fairchild staring out. Tears shone in his eyes. He rode a roller coaster, all right. The emotional Tilt-A-Whirl. Van watched him fashion a face out of all this sadness before he turned full on and started laying fresh places at the table. "And you're feeling all right?" Fairchild asked him. "I've never saved anyone's life before. You're okay?"

Van said, "Thanks," only because he pitied the man.

"Did you walk here?"

"My car's by the road up there. It's out of sight I think."

"Is there somebody who should be called?"

"No."

"Nobody?"

Van felt a panic of his own beginning to stir. "Listen. You didn't call the paramedics? Or the cops?"

"No."

"Nobody knows I'm here."

"No," Fairchild said, "and that's how it should be. You're here, you're a secret, I'm giving you cereal. Your appetite's back. You look better."

"Just assure me you're harmless, and we're fine."

"We're all pretty harmless aren't we? Until we're cornered?"

"That's not reassuring."

"But I thought you wanted to die."

"Maybe so. But by my own hand."

Fairchild closed his eyes, maybe, Van thought, with exasperation. "The point I was making earlier is this—that each person who went to the movies that day believed each of the *others* capable of killing *all* of us. And aren't they exactly right?"

Fairchild was back at the refrigerator, from which he turned now with an odd, pompous air, upholding a carton of milk. "Who knows what a murderer looks like?"

He stood next to Van's chair. He leaned too close. "Lately I think I'm ready to become one." Van smelled the rot of wine on his breath. The hat's emblem read IGNORE PREVIOUS HAT.

Van relaxed. "I see. You're just fucking with me."

"Hermann Göring," Fairchild said, pouring milk over his cereal with unsteady hands, "was found at the end dressed in a Japanese kimono and stoned on opium, wearing lipstick and eye shadow and playing with a model concrete railroad in his living room—that's how crazy you have to be to kill as many people as Hermann Göring did. This is how crazy you have to be to kill *one*. As crazy as me. Allow me:" He tipped the carton and loosed a quavering ribbon of milk over Van's bowl.

As soon as he put a spoonful to his lips Van realized what a hunger he had. But the flakes were hard on his throat. He waited for them to wilt in the bowl.

Fairchild said, "Of course I'm simplifying. It may be that in a case like Hermann Göring's that's how crazy you get *from* killing that many people, and this is how crazy you have to be to *start*."

"Your guess is as good as mine."

"One murder probably leads to another."

"I wouldn't know."

"Why don't we find out?"

"I don't get the meaning."

"Would you like to find out?"

"Find what out?"

"I'd like you to kill somebody for me. I'd make it worth your while."

"You'd make it worth my while?" Van said. "What the fuck is 'worth my while'?"

"Money, whatever."

So he'd done it. He'd killed himself. And he'd surfaced into this. All right. It was the next thing happening, and that was that. "Money doesn't work for me," he said.

"What would?"

Van Ness hadn't touched a drop of wine, but the room was accelerating anyway. "I'll do it. Sure."

"What would work for you?"

The chickenshit. He was going to ride right past it. "I said I'll do it."

Fairchild stood up and said, "Louise." He put his thumb and finger to his eyes and pressed. Visibly composed a speech in his mind and then launched into it, crunching the phrases in the collision of emotions. "In the place where Louise works there is a lady called the Singapore Lady. The Singapore Lady was once a wild young woman married by common law to a carpenter there in San Francisco. She was the terror of the neighborhood. But the carpenter wasn't afraid of her; he came home late, he catted around. He didn't care if the Singapore Lady knew. Mistake! She stabbed him in the eye, and he died. Then, with his own saw she sawed him into thirteen pieces. She put the pieces of her husband in a big trunk and had it shipped to a fictitious address in Singapore. Well, during its journey the stink of the corpse became profound and somebody opened the trunk to find green arms and legs and green other parts, including the one-eyed staring head. The woman was quickly arrested—why? Because she'd put her return address on the trunk. Louise says they call her the Singapore Lady because for the last twenty years she's been wrapping empty packages, addressing them to Singapore, and handing them over to the counselors and guards at the prison to be mailed.

"Louise is my mother. On the day I went to San Francisco she had three months to go before retirement. I wanted to go see her while she was still working in order to avoid the possibility of a longer visit."

Van had eaten most of his cereal. He pushed the bowl away and sat back. "Ignore Previous Hat, huh?"

Fairchild said, "I'm thinking of inviting you to be my accomplice in a murder."

"I said okay," Van said.

"Actually, my henchman."

Van said nothing.

"Does one murder lead to another? I think it does, because I'm suddenly, now, already thinking in terms of killing two more. Maybe three. Or at least one more. Harry Lally."

Night had come and turned the windows to mirrors. Fairchild had a habit of studying his image, moving closer, peering right at the reflected mouth as it spoke. "You do this murder. Maybe you should kill everybody who troubles me! Anyway you do this murder. Then you come back here—well, no, definitely not back here—but somewhere; you go somewhere. And finish committing suicide."

But the guy had a psychotic charm. He entertained. "Have you been diagnosed?"

Among his windows Fairchild kept silent a minute, untwisting cords from their stays and loosing scrolls of rattan down over the glass. "You don't know the situation. Anybody would go crazy."

"No—I think you're fine. But I was wondering what the professionals had to say."

"You wonder why I'd want to get someone killed. I won't just answer 'why not.' But the question implies that a person would have good reasons, and that's a lie. There are pressures, yes. But nothing to justify it." He sat down.

Van thought Fairchild was about to take his hand—something about his hesitation, his gravity—but he didn't.

"I am in trouble with my criminal associates. I owe a vast sum of money. My wife's insurance would take care of that if she died. I can't get money otherwise—nobody will give me any, particularly not Father, and anyway the words to ask him have been closed inside the fist of hate for decades now. It would be easier for me to let them kill me, or go to Clarence and say, 'Listen to me please; I want you to grease Winona; snuff the bitch.' Or something a little more subtle but with the same meaning.

"You had no right to spill my table," he added suddenly. "You broke my things. These things are mine."

"Clarence is who?"

"The only guy I know who's actually really killed people."

"This is about money? Divorce her and sell the house."

"If you go out the door and look west," Fairchild said, "you'll see all I stand to lose by divorcing her. All that land and all that timber. From here to the ocean."

"It's hers?"

"It's my father's, and he's willed my share of it to her. My Catholic dad. To keep us married."

"Why not disappear? Pick up and boogie?"

"Or why not kill myself?"

"Why not?"

"The ultimate disappearance. The ultimate boogie."

Van laughed. It hurt, and he stopped himself. "How old are you?"

"I turned twenty-nine three weeks ago."

"And who do you want killed?"

"My wife, Winona Fairchild."

"Yeah . . . that name."

"Winona."

"I think I met her."

"You met her?"

"Yes, I met her. In Shelter Cove."

"That's no place to meet anyone."

"I met her there anyway."

Fairchild jerked at the pocket of his bathrobe. Produced his deck of cards. Laid himself out a hand of . . . Klondike, if Van knew his solitaire. It was dramatic, really kind of striking, Van thought, the way he fought through pain by clinging to something, anything, of *interest*. "*Bushido*," Fairchild said now—Van had known him a single afternoon but already could tell when a lecture, like a whale, was surfacing—"do you know the word? *Bushido* means 'the way of the warrior,' a Japanese samurai concept. The idea is, the samurai achieves total detachment by seeing himself as already dead. I invite the would-be suicide to adopt this concept."

Again Van laughed, again it tore at his throat. "Coincidences are gonna drive us crazy."

"You should have seen yourself going down!"

"All right," Van said. "All this is getting to me. I mean I'm thinking about something, and two minutes later—two seconds, even—you're saying it."

"A dangerous chemistry develops between us."

"You're not a simple guy, are you? A simple guy would leave what troubles him."

Fairchild sprayed the cards into the kitchen sink. They arced from his fingertips as if enchanted. He did possess a flair. "I have called for a new deck often. But I have never changed my game."

Van enjoyed topping him. "For the third time: I will kill this person for you."

Thompson drove the truck, and Falls talked: "I was working on some stuff, just jotting down notes, et cetera—things to work out when I had a chance to sit down. Some of the things he came out with about eighteen months later, man"—Falls was talking about Jerry Jeff Walker, the country-western composer—"not the words, but a little of the ideas and the rhythms, they were exactly and precisely what I was doing, man. Or would have done, was about to do. And he must've been working on those things right when I was, if they came out eighteen months later. I have a special quality for him, man. I feel we're in synch."

This interested Thompson not at all, the synch or lack of it between Bart Falls, whom he considered to be nothing but a pitiful recidivist, and Jerry Jeff Walker the swaggering barroom minstrel. Thompson liked California jazz. Chet Baker. Art Pepper. People who really lived it. Tom Waits, if you had to have words and concepts. "Look, I think we passed it," he said.

"No, I'm watching close. No redwood gate."

"It's gray."

"It's gray redwood. That's what happens. Redwood turns gray."

"I'll go another mile."

Thompson took them around a tight curve in the road and into what appeared to be another world.

Disneyland. Shangri-la. It knocked the breath right out of him. "You're shitting me," he said to Falls.

"Well—stop the car," Falls had to tell him.

Thompson braked and they looked over a colossal ornate Japanese-looking building with a copper dome, and beyond it a tower, a pagoda, shining like gold.

Thompson stared. A thrill of gratitude travelled his bones. "Hah!" he said, nodding his head several times. He knew his excitement sometimes made him look stupid. But everything had been going wrong, and they'd both been feeling like losers. Now this—this was like finding Egypt.

"Look at the fence," Falls said. It was fifteen-foot-high chain link topped by loops of concertina wire. From what they could see, there must have been miles of it surrounding the grounds.

"They're keeping something sweet in there, I absolutely guarantee you, something very sweet," Falls said.

That morning Thompson and Falls had awakened in the serenity of their camp just inside Sonoma County. It was a state-run campground but nobody else was staying in it, possibly because the rates were high, fourteen dollars a night. The fog was doing its snake dance up from the Gualala River. Falls, propped on one elbow and frisking himself for cigarettes with his free hand, suddenly paused. A feeling had him lightly by the throat. He lay back in the musty bag and listened to a distant rumbling more deliberate than the river's.

"I could get used to the sound of that train."

He watched while Thompson, fully dressed and freshly shaved, hunted for something in his Alice pack.

"Used to get right up beside the trains going by in Fresno," Falls said, digging out a smoke from his shirt pocket, where they seemed to have suddenly materialized, and holding it out toward the coals. "Down by the community wading pool. The bigger boys would jump after those things. Everybody's mom said it would wrench our arms right off if we ever tried it. They also said you'd be sucked under by the wind if you got too close to a train."

He reached over and gave the coffeepot a jiggle. "I think it was Fresno." He shoved the pot down among the campfire's warm ashes.

"That's not a train. That's a helicopter."

"A helicopter?" Falls said.

Thompson tossed his pack aside. "I think I'm out of toilet paper."

"So? Use theirs."

"Get my bowels moving about and making sense."

"Theirs is perfectly good."

"It's just like jail. All state paper is the same."

It did sound like a chopper after all. As soon as the noise faded, Falls heard the dogs bumping around and whining inside the camper.

Falls considered himself to be making breakfast, though Thompson would probably claim he was just sticking last night's supper back on the fire. "Somebody left the top off this chili," he said, and, "We were in town. We should've gotten eggs."

"I keep thinking I'm gonna fish," Thompson said, so Falls stopped listening. He crawled out of the bag and tiptoed across the damp earth in his socks to let the dogs out of the truck. They bolted past him through the door as soon as he had it open, the three of them all balled up like one animal, bringing with them a canine stench and whipping his ribs on either side with their tails.

When he tuned back in, Thompson was saying, "She's full-blooded Norwegian. Her birthday's the day after mine. She was born in Kenya, South Africa, but she spent most of her life in Fargo, South Dakota. Does this sound like a confused past?"

"Somebody's definitely confused." Women bored Falls even more than fish. He pissed for a long time on a bush and then went over and checked the chili. "This stuff's all crusty now."

"Too bad."

"It dried up because the top was off, is probably what, mainly. And another thing: let's get out of here."

"Out of here?"

"I don't wanna do any more time."

Thompson looked at him with the face of a baffled child.

"You said this wouldn't be a snatch," Falls reminded him.

"No I didn't."

"Yes you did."

"I didn't say one way or the other."

"You said it'd be a little visit. This is not a little visit. We're gonna have to take him right off the street."

"Why?"

"It's no big coincidence we're losing him. He's dodging us. We're made. He made us."

"We're 'made'? We're *made*." Thompson started humming the theme to James Bond.

"We've been here too long."

"Who made us? God made us."

"We're seen and known."

Thompson split the chili onto two paper plates and started eating his. In a minute he said, "Fuck everything and run, huh?"

"Yeah, more or less."

"Fuck Everything And Run—F-E-A-R." Thompson was delighted with this.

"I'm trying to reach a decision, and you're just playing the conversation game."

"What is making you so uncomfortable? What's the worst thing that's happening to you right now?"

"Start with this idea of bringing three worthless dogs along on this thing. That wasn't necessarily smart." Falls sailed his plate away and like some multiheaded harpy the dogs charged from out of the brush and dismembered it.

"We might be glad we brought them. I mean, I don't know."

"If we let those critters loose on a trail we'd be all day getting them back. They're incompetent."

"We're hunters. We brought dogs."

"One hundred percent bullshit."

"Wait." Thompson gestured back and forth with his hand between the two of them. "I know what this is about, okay? I know."

Falls sighed and marched over the embankment to the river. He knelt by the clear water and rinsed the saucepan, scrubbing it with gravel that rasped loudly against the steel.

He heard the campfire snapping on damp fuel and went back and found Thompson feeding it wet green twigs, filling the camp with brown smoke. "I want to dry the pan," he told Thompson, "but I can't breathe all that smoke. That's why I'm sitting on your side of the fire, okay?"

"I told you—I understand, I know, I'm hip," Thompson said as Falls crouched down next to him and held the pan out over the meager flames.

"*Hunters* get guides, man. *Hunters* bring their kill to the butcher, they put meat in the local locker. You and me are just dicking around in an obvious way."

"We're campers then, Bart. That much is true fact. And, okay—we might have to snatch the guy. Probably we will. Or maybe we'll get lucky. That's possible too."

"And in the case of real bad luck—the joint."

"Right. Of course. That's always the thing. But you just do the thing in spite of the thing."

Falls didn't think he could feel any more jammed up: the dogs, the job, various concerns. "This should've taken fifteen minutes."

"Whining! Tearful! You know what you're doing, man? You're hurting me. I hurt, I feel jack-shitted, when we're on the line and I look over and you're there picking your nose and dreaming, because you know what you're doing man? You're backing out. Do you realize that?"

"No! I'm just—I thought we were open for discussion."

"If you're out," Thompson said, "you're out on your own. Take the rig, take the worthless frigging dogs, good-bye. But you'd be leaving me here with no resources and a job to do, because I ain't out. I'm here. That's what you're discussing."

"No—I meant both of us should leave," he said.

"I'm not going anywhere."

"Okay."

Thompson said, "You got any toilet paper?"

"I use theirs!" Falls shouted. "I got the same ass I had in Chico, and Folsom, and Quentin!"

"I wouldn't know."

"I've just had a chance to think about this situation, that's the shot here," Falls insisted.

He lay down with his head on his pack and sighed with sorrow. "I got the doldrums."

Denis Johnson ▪ *80*

"Tough shit."

"You're boring me."

Thompson said, "I feel a real breakthrough coming on."

Falls sat up.

"I like those breakthroughs."

Falls said, "Let's snatch him, then."

"It's daylight."

"I like that."

"Well, yeah."

"It's sexy."

"It is."

That night, after they'd made miserable losers of themselves, been eluded again and even been confronted by the man, Thompson celebrated by getting drunk on Seagram's Seven, kicking one of the dogs and chasing the other two around with a stick, standing by the fire with his pants around his ankles, pissing in the flames. "If this was an electric heater, I'd be dead right now," he told Falls.

He lectured Falls with the apparent idea of delivering Falls to himself. "You know why you're so tough? I got you dicked. You want to make yourself strong enough to kill your father back when you were a little boy."

Falls was angry. Not nearly as drunk. "When I was little, huh?"

"That if you were up against your father now, comparatively the size and strength he was back then—he'd be a giant, but you'd be strong enough to kill him, tough enough, you see what I'm saying, to prevent his abuse. The project of your life is retroactive. It's empty. It's total bullshit."

"Maybe. But there's nothing wrong with it."

"How many people have you killed?"

"In my life? Two."

"Counting prison."

"Four."

"And you say there's nothing wrong?"

Falls had served his first sentence for killing his father.

"You come out with this shit about once a year," he told Thompson. "It seems like you don't even know me, don't even think about me at all, then all of a sudden here's the weighty analysis."

"Excuse me there? Who's analysing who at the moment?"

Eventually Thompson apologized to the dogs and gave them bits of sausage off a pizza he'd brought from town. "Whoops," he said later, dropping half of it in the fire. The dogs cowered under a bush. One of them made a small high intermittent whistling noise that Falls spent a quarter of an hour tracing to the animal.

"He's worried about something," he told Thompson. "Maybe this strange-feeling weather, I don't know. Do you feel it?"

Thompson felt not much of anything by now, but he noticed the rain when it started and he stumbled wordlessly toward the truck. Falls made it to the cab first, leaving the doghouse-camper to his inebriated psychotherapist. Later, when the rain was particularly hard on the roof, Falls went around to the back of the vehicle, tiptoeing in the downpour as it filled the woods with a kind of African music, all percussion, and a cold breath that moved around slowly. He tried the camper's door, but Thompson had locked it from the inside.

"Tommy," he called, "Tommy."

The camper stirred. Thompson's voice was muffled. "Back off about a million miles."

"Brother, I got another one," Bart called . . . He waited a while and then said, "Well, I'm just getting sopped out here."

In the cab again he sat till the storm blew off east, some forty-five minutes, upright and dazed and gripping the wheel. In the eventual quiet he suddenly came to himself and quickly, shaking ink down into his ballpoint, filled another page in his notebook.

When Thompson came out to slake his drunk-thirst, Falls had built up the fire and sat beside its altering light with his notebook open in his lap. "Okay, man."

"Jesus, lemme get some water."

"Are you sober enough for this?"

"I just hope I'm drunk enough." For thirty seconds or better Thompson attached himself like an infant to the gurgling canteen.

Falls bowed his head above his notebook. "This isn't about me. This is more really about you."

> You'll ride them highways like the rivers
> naked warriors rode of yore,
> making camp alongside mesquite
> whispering secrets on the shore,
> 'cept you'll be dropping change at truckstops—

stomping cigarettes on the floor.
And you'll know how sad the waitress
gets when she flops down at night
looking at the nighttime talk shows,
heads of laughter, heads of light.
You'd tell her but you just can't say it right.
Rain slips in your truck's old doorframe
where it bent that time you wrecked,
you don't light up because she'd see it,
but right now she don't suspect,
she couldn't guess a desperado
loves her in the parking lot,
sitting here inside this pickup
bleeding like he just got shot.

"I gotta say, Falls . . . Your stuff ain't that shitty."

"It's almost pretty good, you mean."

"Yeah. You really should make a tune for some of that claptrap maybe."

"Yeah? The tunes are the hard part."

"Well, one thing," Thompson said, "the rain sure dosed that fog. Beat it down to the bottom of the river."

Falls turned his palms over in the firelight and then back up so they cupped shadows, held up the night's entire darkness, in fact, as he looked at his hands, a murderer's hands.

Thompson got down in himself and stared at the flames. "About, what was it, maybe seventy-six cars wrecked at one time on Interstate Five, in the fog. A real bitch mother of a fog. It was one of those Sacramento-foothill things, not average like you get down around the ocean here. Fog thick enough you could fuck it. Tooley fog. I say just pull over and sleep till the sun burns it up the next day. I don't know why people would drive in it. Seventy-six people looking for excitement."

V an Ness felt no hesitation. But as it turned out, something forced him to put off his project with the psycho,
Fairchild: Van Ness's mother died.

The news didn't hurt him. But it surprised him. He'd never heard a
word from her doctors. A lawyer got him on the phone at his motel—
"Is this Carl Van Ness, son of Elaine?"—and by that time she was
already in the ground. The lawyer had contacted the folks at Van's
old boatyard in Seattle, with whom he'd left his address because he
was owed commissions. "—son of Elaine?" He knew by those words
alone that he was an orphan.

He was the only child, and had to go to Monterey County south of
San Francisco to take care of her affairs. She'd left him her little
house, but he had no use for it. He ended up spending nearly three
weeks there.

Many afternoons he drove over to Salinas, in the Central Valley, to
take in movies he didn't really want to see: to sit for a while in front of
out-of-focus scenes from lives that weren't actual and then walk out
into shopping centers surrounded by a vast agricultural enterprise.
Sometimes he followed Route 1 through Castroville, the Artichoke
Center of the World, or drove around Monterey Bay to Santa Cruz

and took rides on various not too thrilling amusements along the boardwalk there. He had nothing to do with himself but these pointless things. His mother had perished of something he didn't understand, something to do with electrolytes and the balance of hormones, anyway something that had shut her up for once, the poor, miserable woman, and he'd inherited some money, and the house in Carmel-by-the-Sea. Carmel wasn't his kind of place. The clouds moved too swiftly in off the Pacific and managed to look gray and crimson both at once. The fields to the east were burned blond and crested relentlessly by small sports cars. In the town itself he drifted alongside the shop windows, blown by a careless loneliness past arrays of gifts he'd never have wanted for himself. Subtle incense. Liniments—tennis, horses, all that.

He was better suited to the bay's northern shore—seedy, sandy Santa Cruz. He liked eating out of the cheap beachside stands and trying his luck at the boardwalk games where surely they tried every way they possibly could to gyp him. He felt comfortable among the beatnik survivors and carnival types, people with self-created histories and fictitious names, tainted and used-up people. In septic barrooms he hung out drinking only black coffee and, when asked the reason, explained that he had pancreatic cancer. Or fatal hepatitis. Or things like Tangiers syndrome, which he made up. And when people offered sympathy he told them, "I could easily outlive you."

He stood for hours at the shooting galleries, always his favorite thing, blasting away at ducks and jungle animals who lurched happily into his sights and disappeared and then turned up again, identically reincarnated. Now he saw why, as a boy, he'd felt called to such places. It amused him to identify these contraptions as important teachers and this completely mechanised region as the birthplace of his life's philosophy: everything happens again and again . . .

At one point he joined a handful of tourists looking at least partly amused by a monkey dancing on a long chain. The animal wore the stock getup, the bellboy's uniform minus the pants, performed somersaults absentmindedly, flipping himself as easily as the onlookers' coins, which he gathered up with a brisk professional aloofness. When they weren't tossed he approached people one at a time with his startlingly pale simian palm outstretched.

But the instant his gaze fell on Van Ness, the little acrobat charged at him viciously. Van had seen the surprising menace and then the baffling rage pass over the monkey's face, and was already backpedalling swiftly so that the beast, now nothing more than that, a wild, killing animal, savaged its own belly by running up against the end of its chain. Van walked away fast, shaking his head for the bene-fit of anybody looking at him—and they all were. A hundred feet from the scene he turned to see the monkey clinging to the side of a litter barrel, still staring at him, its mouth wide open, hissing from down in its throat. With surprising strength it hoisted the large receptacle and banged it down on the ground over and over, never taking its eyes from Van's face even across this distance. The crowd stayed back. The monkey's master crept up on him cautiously, gath-ering up the chain hand over hand. He looked as confused as any-body there.

This run-in seemed just a silly part of his fate, a maverick detail in the general design. He'd ended one life a suicide and planned to spend the next a murderer, but things like this, stinging outbreaks, ambushes—he thought of the woman he'd picked up hitchhiking who'd nearly accused him of rape—things like this still had the power to hurt his feelings. And now he couldn't believe it. He was weeping. He bent over and tried to make it look like a bout of cough-ing. An angry monkey, an angry monkey was making him cry. No, no—it was Elaine Van Ness, his mother. She'd lived alone, had raised herbs in her weedy garden, stolen books from the local library, col-lected miniature ceramic cats. And now something had happened and all of that had stopped. Her loneliness, how had she borne it when he himself couldn't stand even the thought of it? Her son . . . he hadn't felt like her son since some time in childhood. Waiting for her to come home from work on schooldays, watching TV shows meant for younger children and eating the peanut butter and crack-ers she'd left out for him on a plate under a pastel paper napkin. They'd lived in an apartment near Baltimore, just the two of them. Later he'd taken to starting her car in the basement parking garage and driving it around down there. On the smooth concrete the tires squealed, even at a snail's pace. Eventually he'd smashed one of the headlights against a concrete pillar. His mother had forgiven him. Today he'd have described himself as once again unsupervised and piloting a stolen machine. Quickly, with the heel of his hand, he erased the tears from his face, and then stood up straighter, clearing his throat several times.

As he recovered from this inexplicable fit of mourning, he looked up and noticed a woman watching him. A small blonde by the entrance to the Haunted House. She'd just tossed a big head of cotton candy into the trash and now she wiped her hands on a napkin, holding them far out in front of her as if temporarily disowning them. She stared, and then turned away—it annoyed him to be a small panel in the tapestry, it annoyed him to be brief.

Van Ness was sure he recognized her. She passed under the boardwalk's arch onto the sandy lane of shops and stalls, Pacific Street, and Van followed her for a while with a sense of how she brushed through the thickets of aromas and things like that coming out of other lives, sunlight banging down off a wall, cool dark hovering behind windows, the entangling essence of one person after another at the center of every little scene she passed. He could feel how she let them stroke her—he'd been doing it himself for days now around here. Irrelevant bastards. Nobody to be introduced to. It annoyed him to be one of them.

He'd seen this person before in similar surroundings. Shelter Cove, the seaside deli—Mrs. Fairchild. This was Winona Fairchild. The woman he was supposed to kill.

She stopped at a shop selling neon signs and the plastic busts of clowns, openmouthed surplus Bozos from squirt-gun shooting arcades. She spoke to no one, studying their painted faces. She made things like that herself. Van had seen her sculptures. Her husband had seemed proud of her work.

Fairchild planned to knock her out with pills. After some hours, Van would smother her with a pillow. He himself had slept in the bed where she'd die.

Fairchild would spend these moments of terrible genesis in a public place, some miserable tavern it was likely, where he'd be visible. The coroner would blame pills and booze, always an unpredictable mix.

Van reflected that you never knew with these delirium-tremens types. The extremity of Fairchild's delusions, the abandon of his folly. He intended to move in with his mistress—whom he'd described for Van, and Van had been amused—and position himself to lead a life in most respects more conventional. He wouldn't know conventional if it walked up and spat in his face.

Van observed the wife. No question who it was. He hadn't quite placed her at first because on this breezy day she'd tied her hair back in a long blond ponytail, that was all. In her tattered jeans and sweatshirt, black high-top sneakers, she looked like anybody else around here, but for Van she stood forth magnificently. The day burned in glory, the sun slashing into dark doorways, the woman surely more beautiful than she'd ever been, more virginal and serene in her role as sacrifice, unconscious target, dead clown. It pissed him off. She'd never been so beautiful. He'd never been so angry. And he realized he'd been feeling it for days—the tapestry laid out, a tale told in panels, by design—for days feeling the tragedy and loveliness of fate. First his own. And now hers.

August 11–September 5, 1990

A s caretaker at Winona's place my final act was to give
Red, the horse, his wormer. I'd been putting it off, but
Winona had called. She'd started home. Odyssey over. Although,
come to think of it, it's in setting out for home that the odyssey, the
Greek one anyway, the one full of monsters and gods—in turning
homeward that the odyssey really begins. And it ends in poignant
strangeness, among staring alien eyes, the foolishly gazing faces of the
wanderer's beloved people melted, thickened, elongated by time.
Maybe you, too, Winona!—maybe you'll find nobody you know at
the journey's end. You'll stand in just this spot, inhaling the dregs of
night mist evaporating from the world, perhaps, and shudder to realize you've never smelled anything like it, and you never touched any
of this, you never made these sculptures, it's all garbage now, thanks
to your mistakes, most of them innocent, and thanks to my father's
stubbornness and to certain bad conjunctions, like that of myself and
Van Ness, the killer I conjured out of a storm. Thanks to these things
you may soon be dead—the ultimate stranger! In the meantime, I'll
cure your horse. I couldn't face you if I sluffed it off.

The horse was something of an epic traveller himself, having
started in Vermont and crossed to Oberlin, Ohio, with Winona dur-

ing her undergrad days. Where he languished without her while she travelled on to Berkeley for graduate school—she and I met there, in fact, during my freshman, and only, year as a big-time university scholar. That June we left school together, Winona with a master's in fine arts and I with a lot of bitterness. She sent out to Ohio for Red, and here he stands, fatter and fatter on the fields of lotusland.

"And we should come like ghosts to trouble joy," say Ulysses' men among the lotus-eaters, in the poem I believe by Tennyson. And this is how I came to old Red this morning, materializing slowly, bearing unpleasantness. Coexistence was our game, but today I intervened. Finally I felt ready to deal with a sick horse, walked directly out of the house from the last dream in a good night's sleep, a dream of flying so inspirational I found myself already standing beside the bed as I woke up, tasting victory and looking for fresh tasks. In it I piloted a one-man jet and then actually became the jet, rocketing straight upward, screaming and dangerous, but friendly too. Why should a bad man be visited by beautiful dreams? I suppose because the dream is unconscious, knows nothing of good and bad. But Red's unconscious too, and he knows. Red has never liked me. I approached this morning holding out a big carrot bright as a flame, keeping the plastic syringe out of sight by my side. There's no needle involved. You simply jam the thing in his mouth and squirt a bunch of paste onto his tongue. Gunk the consistency of peanut butter, but no snack for intestinal worms. Once it's stuck to his tongue he can't spit it out, down it goes. Simple in theory. But then again. Red's a horse, yes, but he's no idiot. He doesn't eat poison, even if it's prescribed. Let him get a whiff of that stuff and his lips are sealed, he doesn't know you. In fact he flattens his ears and claims boldly not to be a horse at all—

Carl Van Ness, what did you dream about, down under the water? The bastard, he refused to say. Not that he'd soon befriend anybody ripping him from that incredibly comfortable sleep, his drowning. It took him two days to decide to wake up. When I walked him around the grounds on the second morning, the tall sculptures coming forward out of the mist surprised him. But he'd been looking out the window right at them all the previous afternoon.

I executed a classic switch on poor Red, substituting the syringe for the carrot as it passed between his lips, jamming the plunger and gagging the old boy with his wormer. One more thing he'd hate me for. The perpetual sad boredom blasted right off from his face and his tongue performed all sorts of tricks in his mouth, but the only way through this experience was to swallow his medicine. As for the carrot, I almost tossed it outside the fence. Sometimes I feel like being cruel. These dumb animals frighten me, so complete, and so prophetic in their completeness, arcing from infancy to old age during the short time we know them, promising us the same. But I gave him the carrot, fed it between his lips like a log into the pulp mill.

The idea was to pull a similar substitution on Winona.

Carl Van Ness had understood the mechanics all right, but I wanted to make him understand everything.

I tried to explain why I'd fallen for Melissa. "I'm not fated to be burned up in the fires of ecstatic adoration. That's who I am, but I landed in the wrong century. In the days of saints they had heavenly entities—virginal, right? and immaculate, right?—but today I settle for somebody transparent and uncomplicated. Somebody you can see through."

Van Ness really had nothing to say on this or almost any other subject. "Sounds like a dose of push-push fever" was his sole remark.

I talked to him on every subject anyway. I'd always wished for a confidant, someone I could open up to about all this. Clarence was my partner but forget Clarence. Melissa on some levels could be spoken to, but never *talked* to.

I was walking him over the property, letting him get his legs back that second day among us. We toured the sunny acres and stood at the edge of the steep woods and their soothing amber light and muted ocean-sound, and I showed him a sacred spot, believed by the man my father had bought the property from to be an ancient Pomo Indian burial mound. I'd never excavated it because allegedly spirits camped here. Farther on, in an open place among very old madrones, crackly garlic plants still marked the garden spot of the area's original homesteaders, and we could see also where wild pigs had rooted, just the night before, under oak trees where for hundreds of years various clans of migrating Pomos had stopped to gather the same food—acorns. The pigs hadn't lived here way back then; they're descended from escaped domestic animals. We toured the boundaries and ended up staring, I stared, anyway, at the muddy swatch torn out of the pondside grasses where two nights earlier I'd dragged him from the water. And at that moment he'd been dead. Here he'd been a corpse, now he walked past the same spot alive, gazing through from another universe, or so I gathered he believed. But he hardly glanced at the spot. I told him I was going to name the pond Loch Ness. Did he think it was funny? I couldn't tell.

"You said you'd pay me to kill her," Van said.

"I don't mean I'll pay *you*. *You* have to go on and finish drowning—and do it in somebody else's pond, please. But I'll give ten grand to anybody you say."

We sat on two oaken stumps side by side. Last year I'd sold most of the younger hardwood, a hundred thousand board feet, to a timber outfit. They'd chopped it all up and peddled it for firewood. I know—I know. But I'd been desperate for cash.

Sitting there on the stump, Van Ness put his hands on his knees and looked tired and confused. He wore mustaches like two horse's tails, and round rimless glasses, very thick. These accessories nearly took away his face.

He said, "I want you to pay for Wilhelm Frankheimer's rehab."

"Rehab?"

"He's a coke fiend. You know him?"

"I know him."

"It'll run you more than ten grand."

"I'll pay for his care."

"Not until he wants it, though."

Certainly I knew Frankheimer. In fact Frankheimer had done the plumbing for the house, and he'd also put the roof on top. I saw him once at a beautiful moment—watched him balance his hammer on a stack of cedar shingles one day, step carefully to the structure's edge, and stand there two stories up in his giantism, loosing a glittering archway of piss down through the light. Evidently they were great buddies, Frankheimer and Van Ness, or had been once.

I took Van (as he liked to be called) back into the house because he did seem weary. Also I had something I wanted him to see. But I was nervous about it and so I began to hold forth and hog the whole show—it's a terrible habit I have. I knew he'd like Nietzsche, if he hadn't already heard of him, so I read to him from a book on Winona's shelf. It turned out he'd not only heard of the arrogant German, he could quote him endlessly and really get you squirming with boredom. I indulged him as long as I could stand it, after all he was my guest, and then I said, "I want to show you how I've arranged things."

I went up to the bathroom to get it while he sat in the living room on the couch. From the loft above he looked small and isolated. He did appear capable of almost any crime. He seemed possessed by a curious inactivity, settled there alone on the edge of the cushion, a tentativeness conveying complete disbelief in everything in sight. You can do anything, in a world you don't believe in.

In a minute I sat down next to him on the couch and put a plastic bottle of capsules on the coffee table before us. "These are Winona's Nembutal capsules," I said. "Pretty potent." From my pocket I produced another bottle.

"More Nembutal," he said, reading the label on the second bottle.

"Why don't you take one? One won't hurt you."

"I'd rather not."

"What if I offered you a thousand dollars to take one?"

"I don't think so."

"Two thousand."

"So these aren't Nembutal."

"You knew right away. You're a natural-born plotter."

"What's in them?"

"Nembutal on the outside, horse dope on the inside. Zielene. Two of these will knock out a thousand-pound horse."

"Will it kill her?"

"No. It'll just put her out. Nothing will wake her. Tie a plastic bag around her head and go off for half an hour. Come back later and remove the evidence."

He put his hands on his knees in that old-man way of his and scowled through his thick lenses and down over his dangling mustaches at the two little bottles there on the coffee table.

"I'd rather just smother her with a pillow."

The electrifying thing about all this was that each of us had come to the other out of nowhere. Nothing contradictory surrounded us, no evidence that we weren't capable of anything—no familiar context full of obstacles, no deflating local histories. As a prophet gets laughed at in his hometown, so also the big-time conspirator. But a stranger could be God. If we kept on talking like this it would all actually come about.

"Then, afterward, you have to finish killing yourself," I said.

"You won't have to remind me."

"If you have trouble going through with it, I'll do it."

"You're too nice to me, Mr. Fairchild."

"I would have to, you see that. I couldn't let you live. One way or another you're sealing your fate. In a sense you're dead as soon as you kill her."

Van Ness pursed his lips, seemed to be kissing that thought as it hung in front of him. "That's poetic."

At the Wharton School in Monterey County, a prep school, one of the best (which I bored right through, though I hardly dented college), I read Hermann Hesse's Demian and dreamed of a friendship like the one between Max Demian and Emil Sinclair, a bond that frees a person from other bonds and leads him into a new dimension.

From the little he told me I gathered that Van Ness had started out looking for that friend, too, and for that life worth staying on for, that religion, that woman, that vocation. The tall plumber, Frankheimer, may have served for a while in that regard. Once upon a time he'd accomplished a painful transit through a sort of incarnation where he'd been capable of friendship, arriving eventually at his present unapproachable state, this coked-up condition, everybody knew about it, that made him pitiful and dangerous both. And once upon a time Van had depended heavily on Frankheimer's kinship, and on Demian as a guiding light, an affirmation and a model. But now he'd outgrown it in what he thought of as a cold and Nietzschean way. Outgrown all models, all reasons, outgrown life itself.

Now Van Ness claimed already to have died, more than once, in various other universes. Who can refute that? Is there any proof otherwise? Imagine a slight revision in Nietzsche's myth of eternal return: not that at history's end all matter collapses back to the center, Big-Bangs, and starts again identically; but that it starts again with one infinitesimal difference in the action of a single molecule—every time, and an endless number of times. When you die, your consciousness blanks out, but it resumes eons later, when the history of molecules has been revised enough to preclude your death due to those particular circumstances: the bullet hits your brain in this world, but in a later one merely tickles your earlobe. You die in one universe and yet in another go on without a hitch. You don't mark the intervening ages—subjectively you experience nothing other than *almost* having died. But in fact you've edged into another kingdom, ruled by another king, engaging other potentialities.

If this were true, the person who understood it would have conquered death. Would be invulnerable. Would be the Superman.

There's a dizzying thrill in a philosophy that can only be tested by suicide—and then never proven, only tested again by another attempt. And the person embarked on that series of tests, treading that trail of lives as if from boulder to boulder across the river of time—no, out into the burning ocean of eternity—what a mutant! Some new genesis, like a pale, poisonous daisy.

The terrible drought had broken only briefly, that single night of rain soaking us with less than two inches, but the winds seemed benevolent afterward, often trundling high, white clouds along the very shores of outer space, and mixing the airs so that the coastal weather stayed in general crisp and sunny. People called it an early autumn.

Van Ness disappeared the minute he left Winona's ranch. He'd been registered at the Tides Motel, but now no more, and I suddenly really didn't expect to see him again. He'd succeeded in scaring me more than I'd scared him, and maybe that's all he wanted. But he sent me a postcard from the town of Carmel, explaining that his mother had died and promising to return on Tuesday, September 4. *Then we'll see*, he wrote. *We'll see if our eyes are open.*

Still, the reality of our plot was fading. Maybe he just wanted to keep the fear alive by saying hello.

Meanwhile I learned, also, that the phony loggers in the black Silverado pickup had been camping across the Gualala River but lately hadn't been seen there. Things were easy. Winona settled in after her coastal wandering and the ugly horse Red was no longer my responsibility. As soon as Clarence came back from L.A. I'd have the pot cultivation off my hands. And Winona mentioned that Harry Lally's wife had boarded her horse at the Say-When Ranch, where the equestrian set held their gymkhanas, and gone off for three weeks in Brazil with her gangster husband. It seemed these autumn breezes had carried away all the heat and fog around me, leaving my days sweet and vacant.

I had more time to spend with Melissa, but she had less for me. I'd never suspected her of anything like fidelity, certainly, but since the day we'd started up I'd believed I was the only steady one. Now I didn't know, I sensed another presence in her thoughts, and I didn't ask for the truth because I feared that's what I'd get.

A week after I left Winona's I woke up in my own apartment, a rickety box in a fourplex, but mine, an apartment holding more garbage than furniture, but all of it gloriously mine, for the first time in many days. Nobody after me, and coffee in my very own cup. Maybe the weather had anticipated this happiness, this treading through trash in what was supposed to be my living room thinking that I should wash the plastic floor, that I should pull the bedsheets from the windows, popping tacks, which I'd sweep out of here immediately along with all this other crap, mostly wine bottles and paper plates, and put up hopeful, restful curtains.

But such spacious freedoms can't be infinite. What we gather together has a way of unravelling. That morning I visited Melissa, but she acted nervous and, if possible, more foreign. As if she were hiding something from me. And when I refused to stop talking with a phony British accent, she kicked me out of her little trailer. She'd actually swept the place, and I'd have been willing to hang out longer.

But I felt alien vibrations as we made love in her narrow bed, our knees and elbows banging the trailer's walls, and when I came, I ejaculated a paranoid essence.

"Did I mention, dahling, that my teddibly beloved wife is back in town?"

"I told you, please don't talk that way."

"Okay. Okay."

"It isn't funny, not to me. I'm trying to learn American. Get out."

"I'm leaving," I said.

For a few minutes I sulked, sweating beside her in the bed, our skins sticking together wherever we touched.

Usually she let me open up, use different personas. One was a version of my grandfather, the Welshman, revised somewhat during my years in ritzy prep school and then put away. Usually I made her laugh—I spoke in Granddad's voice, walked with his bowed legs, expressed his smugness, his gruff eccentricity and the ubiquitous terror wriggling underneath it. I hadn't known him long, but having seen him a little as a very small child I had no trouble tracing some of his mannerisms through my father and finding them in myself. My brother Bill, in profile, especially when the late sun lights his blue eyes, looks exactly like Granddad. It's breathtaking, the persistence of that man's invisible force, that soul, blazing up decades later in another face. Anyway lately I'd let my Britisher out, and it was hard to get him back in. I'd seen this man in my dreams a lot lately, angry dreams where he attacked, sometimes brutalized, soft Italian film stars, white Italian statues, even a church door of the type I'd admired in Milan. It doesn't take a high-paid shrink to explain that the two faces of that alliance are still at war, that the feelings once knotted up in the marriage of my paternal grandparents still whirl in my own guts, that the judging Anglo half of me blames the passionate Italian for all my troubles, and that my going around imitating him isn't just a stupid laugh, but a sure sign that the strong British male is dominating, that he's going to do the horrible things made necessary by the woman inside, the crazy Italian female part of me who's disarranged my life.

"Did you forget how to put your pants on? It's over the legs."

"Right, I'm sorry."

"You're just holding them in your hands!"

"I'm sorry. It's been chaos. People have truly been after me, but it's going to be better now. Those two loggers, you saw them, in the Silverado—they weren't loggers—"

"With the dogs? Such happy dogs!"

"Their happiness really doesn't interest me, honey."

"They came here yesterday. They paid a courtesy call."

"Who? The dogs? The men? Yesterday?"

"The dogs *with* the men. They want to ask me about you but I said, I don't know."

"Oh my God. *Yesterday?*"

"Yes, it's as I said, yesterday! They ask if you have some marijuana growing."

"I'm having an attack. I'm going to vomit."

"I said I don't know. Nothing, nothing."

"And they accepted that?"

"The man said, very well, okay, see you, we'll be in the neighborhood, we know your address. I said that's obvious!"

"Oh, yeah? And what did he say to that?"

"He told me that this is just a courtesy call, and next time no. It won't be."

"No, sweetie, it won't. Do you remember where my pot patch is?"

"Sure. I wasn't so drunk."

I put my face in my hands and expected, from the wild churning in my solar plexus, to explode with horrible sobs. Instead it suddenly occurred to me that the timing here might be not too inconvenient. "Actually," I said, "if we lose the plants before Clarence turns up, he'll never know how it all came about. He won't necessarily blame me. Harry gets the plants, I get off the hook. Clarence gets the shaft, but that's better than eternity in the grave for me."

"Clarence the surfer? I saw him last night."

"I'll cut out your tongue!"

"In the Safeway I saw him buy bread, and beef jerky, and magazines. And for that you want to cut my tongue?"

"Forgive me," I said.

Take it all around, life showed every troubling sign of having sunk to its usual clammy depth. Clarence! I'd have to get honest with him, fill him in truthfully, face his disappointment.

I'd just dragged my jogging shoes onto my feet when she asked me, "What are you thinking?"

I was always flattered when she asked after my thoughts. I always gave her the truth.

"I'm thinking how nice it would be for us if most of the people I'm supposed to love would drop dead."

Wilhelm Frankheimer sat on a stump beyond the sheep pen, bending far over toward the ground, going to almost acrobatic extremes to attack small scurrying ants with an old saw blade while Melissa moaned and sighed and sometimes laughed inside the trailer. Frankheimer was still naked.

After a while, Fairchild came out and drove away.

It sounded to Frank as if the little heap, a rickety Porsche, stood in need of potent ministrations. But it got Fairchild up the hill and out of sight and that was all Frankheimer cared about. He strolled back inside.

Melissa sat on the bed's edge shivering. The whole business turned him on.

He stood in front of her until she took him in her mouth. In seconds, he came—he'd been screwing her for half an hour and hadn't even been all the way erect; now the low-rent quality of the moment gave him ecstasy.

She turned her head, leaned sideways, and spat sadly onto the floor. It made him feel like marrying her. This underfed wench he could usually take or leave. Women did, he seemed always to forget, have moments like stilettos. No telling when you'd be stabbed.

"Why did you make me hide?"

"I told you to *leave*!" she said. "Not to hide!"

"Where am I gonna leave to, with no pants on?"

"Obviously to no-place. And then you come back inside and make me suck your cock!"

"Why did you make me hide?"

"Because," she said, "he's important to me. Now do you want to lie down with me? He won't come back. Do you want something cold to drink?"

Frankheimer reached down under the bed, feeling around close to the wall. "I just came back in here for my clothes."

He was standing there buttoning his trousers and looking at Melissa's very white features, her small, pretty mouth, when it hit him again—the astonishing persistence of the Yvonne problem. That hurt kept swimming up. He looked at his reflection melting in the cheap mirror and declared out loud: "Maybe I just need sincerity. I think that's all I need."

All of a sudden, he understood that he was going to shoot up.

He happened to be carrying some crank, a quarter ounce of pebbly amphetamine he'd agreed to deliver to Harry Lally—but not to Harry Lally in Brazil. He could feel the bulge in his right-hand pocket. He'd really never cared for the stuff but it had a habit of presenting itself at certain moments. He consoled himself that he'd probably been intending this anyway. He'd been carrying his outfit around for days.

Melissa watched him, scowling. "Rape me, spy on my boyfriend, now you're going to shoot cocaine."

"I'm not doing coke. This is crank, not coke."

"It's all poison."

"Frank's on crank," he said.

"So long. So long to your mind."

"Would you lend me some money?"

"Good-bye and good luck to your brain."

"I could use a little cash."

"Do I look like I have some? Or even any?"

"Just a thought."

Frank rummaged in her kitchen drawers and then bent the neck of one of her spoons to mix up in. The needle was barbed. He had to file it sharp on a matchbook cover. He liked the fascinated look on Melissa's face.

For a minute he sat with one leg draped over the other, holding the syringe between two fingers like a cigarette.

She was goofy and told him her goofy fears. "Nelson is going to do something about his wife."

"Who's Nelson?"

"Him. Nelson Fairchild. Don't you recognize him, didn't you work for him?"

"I laid the roof on his house."

"There, you see?"

"I did the plumbing, too."

"He's going to do something bad. You see?"

"All I see is you don't speak English."

"He's going to murder his wife."

"Nelson Fairchild?"

"Nelson! Yes!"

He stuck a vein, introduced the crank and walked a half mile up to the ridge and four miles down to Point Arena feeling electric and friendly. When he got to town his legs just kept going.

Some kids in a Chevy van picked him up walking south along the cliffs. Ragged Metallica echoed out of their stereo's speakers, but the black ocean contradicted all rock-and-roll. A bit farther down the coast the cloud cover dissolved, and he stepped from the van onto the sunlit sidewalk of Anchor Bay, two rows of buildings laid out on either side of the highway, which became the town's main street for the distance of one city block. He'd built half these structures. He remembered measuring and cutting the wood for the counter in the Full Sails Cafe, the counter at which he sat now, spreading his hands out on its surface in front of him and feeling they were magnificent things and smiling at the waitress. He grabbed a napkin from the dispenser and wiped at his nose as a way of covering up his convulsive happiness.

The waitress said, "Catching a cold?"

"Oh . . ." He paused to consider the question. "Not necessarily."

He remembered he wasn't hungry and hit the sidewalk outside, the thud of his feet on the pavement running up through his head and the screen door slamming with a thrilling rightness.

Across the street were the Laundromat and service station. A spiky-haired young boy stood by the gas pumps with his mouth open and his hands in his pockets. Frank believed he recognized the lad.

He crossed the street, adjusting and readjusting his sunshades, and raised his hand in greeting.

"I was sorry to hear about your dad."

"My dad? What about him?"

"Well, that he died, little friend."

"My dad?"

"I knew him well," Frank said. "He had a great tan."

"My dad is right there. That's him. He's alive." The boy pointed toward two men talking by the grease pit.

"Well, hell then, shit then. Who died? Somebody's dad, I thought."

"Not mine."

He didn't like this. Second thoughts started eating him and the clouds began to look like fists and the shadows like deep gashes.

Half-remembered things, words he hadn't quite heard, details that hadn't quite registered, suddenly swarmed over his consciousness. The connections proliferating, lighting up, formed a grid that fell down over his understanding like a net. He shook it off.

"Going to school, kid?"

The kid wouldn't talk to him, and walked over toward his father instead.

Frank took a few paces to stand by himself at the edge of the street, taking note of everything around him. The cars, the people, any distraction at all. But random facts now coalesced in a geometry of crushing significance. Remarks, events, all of which had seemed by chance, suddenly became evidence. Things he'd heard, whispers. Words he was about to remember became tendrilous heads like those of sprouts, their mouths open. But nothing came out. They didn't communicate telepathically. It was much more intimate than that.

He turned to the window behind him and looked through it. He saw the Point Arena cop doing the bad Laundromat thing, moving and folding clothes—bad because it's all yours, all falling apart, like the universe—and it occurred to him that now was the time to go public with all this, time at last to seek justice through the system.

To the west, assuming they had Laundromats in Japan, it was seven thousand miles to the next nearest coin-operated cleaning machine. Four dozen miles north to the Laundromat in Fort Bragg, fifty miles south to the one in Jenner, several others twenty-six miles due inland in Ukiah—over twice that far by the roads. A long ways to a wash, any way you wanted to go. It irked Officer Navarro that he had to drive down here to Anchor Bay, nine miles from Point Arena, every time his socks smelled. Certainly he'd travel that far for a steak, a show, two minutes with any reasonably pleasant woman, but there was nothing to do in Anchor Bay—twelve buildings and a commercial campground set between Gualala and Point Arena, with a spectacular view of the Pacific—except sit in the one bar and have a few, then drive with an illegally high alcohol blood level back to Point Arena. And he really shouldn't do that. He was off duty and wearing plain clothes at the moment, but everybody seemed to know him.

Navarro fed dimes into the automatic dryer and made up his mind to nurse a beer at the Full Sails.

Just as he left the Laundromat, half expecting to end up publicly drunk, the tallest man in the county—Frankenmayer?—approached him and held up a hand the size of a baseball mitt.

"Can I get a minute, friend?"

He'd seen this guy around—from a quarter mile off, you saw him—but this was the first time up close. The man created a shadow. He was a walking eclipse of the sun.

"Sure thing," Navarro said, and, keeping in mind his public-relations crisis, made certain to smile.

"People are doing things to me."

"I'm not sure what you mean."

"That's the simplest way of putting a complicated thing. The other night I heard something out back and I found one of my hoses cut."

"A hose?"

"A water hose, yeah. I think I know who's doing it but I can't prove it."

"I wouldn't get too worked up about it."

"That's just the latest example. People are watching me, cutting into my phone lines little by little, tampering with stuff, spraying mist through the windows. They had my car rigged to spray mist. Now listen," the big man said, suddenly smiling, almost jovial, "I know how it sounds. But if you staked out my place for forty-eight hours, you'd make the biggest arrest of your life. You'd change history. I shit you not. The history of the world."

"People are pranking on your car?"

"I'm talking to you. Are you listening?"

"If there's been actual damage, then you're talking about vandalism, which is illegal."

"They've got very tiny devices attached that spray mist out at you. This mist fucks with your meridians. It upsets the physical metabolism in a very dangerous way."

"Meridians?"

"Do you know anything about acupuncture? The I-Ching? Ancient Chinese philosophies?"

There was a way of sliding around a thing like this. You had to regard it as encased in glass. "I'm not sure I have your name right," Navarro said.

"Frankheimer."

"Could you show me these devices, Mr. Frankheimer? Something that doesn't belong in your car, that sprays mist like you say?"

"I tore all that shit out, man. The mirrors, everything. I don't get in that fucking car. Why do you think I walked down here?"

This guy was massive. Massive. "I don't see where a crime has been committed," Navarro said.

"You mean it's no crime to yank on a man's mind? To cut a person's hoses? Assault him with chemical mists? I'm telling you, they're stretching me out about yay tight. This is tension"—showing the cables of muscle in his forearms. Jutting his chin and turning it, like a man shaving, to display the tendons in his neck—"this is tension." It was only prudent to map out the moves for restraining this remarkable specimen should that become necessary. Shit, Navarro thought, I'll shoot him in the knee. Nothing less would do it.

"What was your name again, please?"

"Wilhelm Frankheimer."

"Wilhelm. I gotta tell you. Do you have anything physical to show me? Something that's been damaged? Because it's all sounding very unreal."

"Just stake the place out," Frankheimer insisted.

"Again, I'd have to say we're dealing with suspicions here. Probably not too rational ones."

Frankheimer executed an abrupt shift in his focus. "Now there's something for you, Officer." He swung his head around slowly, following the progress of a pale convertible sports car as it passed.

"I'll stick with General Motors," Navarro said.

"That's Nelson Fairchild. I just got a message that that guy is plotting something nefarious. Do you know what he's doing right now?"

"He's going to the store."

"He's picking up the *Barron's* financial weekly for his dad, I bet."

"I gotta do something similar, Wilhelm—errands and such. We're always available if something specific turns up. Until then—"

"Was it *his* dad who died? Was it old Fairchild?"

Navarro flashed him a false smile. "Nobody dead around here lately."

The tall man raised up one finger in front of Navarro's face. "By way of a simple farewell: don't get your lips frozen on me. And don't run over my foot."

"Great," Navarro said, and started across the street thinking that anybody who hung out in a Laundromat deserved exactly this.

The kid he'd caught peeping the other night was also on the scene. He stood over by the gas station, his gaze avoiding Navarro's, trying to look as if the man with him, obviously his dad, was no acquaintance at all. Navarro decided to let him shape his own zone, and crossed to the cafe without looking back.

He thought he'd better not start with the Coors. Better get a piece of pie, check out the cafe's fragile-looking waitress, avoid having to arrest himself later. It was warm inside, and the place smelled good. The waitress was a little older than he'd thought. Or at least not too well made-up.

He'd talked to her before and had felt, at that time, that he was getting somewhere. In fact she'd practically agreed to host an orgy. "How's the pie?" he asked her.

"I wouldn't lie about it," she said. "I don't own the place."

He hadn't stopped in again, so he guessed she'd put them back at square one. But she smiled halfway when she set down his pie and coffee.

She had a tattoo on her right hand, a tiny peace symbol. And it looked like one nostril was pierced, though she didn't have a ring in it. In L.A., cops didn't date such women.

Here they did. Here he was opening up to aberrations, transforming under the unrelieved stress of these absurd people and their New Age ideas, which seemed less and less outlandish beside the genuine psycho driveling of the Wilhelm type, not to mention the pounding surf, squawking seals, laughing crows, and the aliveness of all these monster trees. In L.A., it—these people, this scene—would all fit, all of it and much, much more, into the category of senseless Martian crap, this category a kind of fishbowl in which almost everything swam except you and a few other cops. You had to cut yourself off in L.A., stay outside the glass. But here the majority of these thousands of lives are only big, slow trees. Slow isn't even right, the concept probably hasn't got a word, it's just that the aliveness of these millions of cedars and redwoods is hardly happening. So you find yourself dropping your defenses, opening up, breathing things in.

He sat at the counter jabbing with a fork at his apple pie. When the waitress came down to his end of things with the coffeepot, he lifted his hand to detain her wordlessly while he wiped his lips with his napkin and swallowed. She was svelte. Okay, bony. But definitely beautiful. "What's your name?"

"Mo. But everybody calls me Maureen." She laughed wildly. "I'm sorry!" she said quickly. "Cops make me nervous. I mean, it's the other way around, they call me Mo."

Her smile hit him right in the gut. She definitely had the face. He'd always been a face man, come to think of it. "Mo," he repeated.

"And you're Officer Navarro."

"But everybody calls me Off."

"No. But really."

"John."

"Okay, John. Cops make me nervous, John."

She left him and went to take care of a young couple way over by the window, the only other customers.

And of course every once in a while you breathe something of these people into you, their kinky exhalations. You don't breathe in anybody in L.A. Breathe? Breathe people in? Christ. He was starting to think like them. Which only proved he was breathing them in, a concept which, itself, he had breathed in. It was a vague deal, but then too he sensed that if he had to shoot somebody around here in the line of duty, if he killed one of these types, he'd stop turning into one of them.

What about the big man and his lurching accusations? What had he said? Anything real? Maybe drawing attention to himself, maybe trying to get himself some help or just his way of saying, Stop me before I do something too uncontrolled? Sometimes the twisted ones accused everybody else of doing what they really, in their hearts, wanted to do themselves. These berserkers were infants in big bodies, that's what the condition chiefly consisted of. Imagine a six-month-old with manual dexterity and an arsenal. He'd get his bottle all right. Then the SWAT people, and everybody dead and nobody knows why.

"Mo—"

She brought over the coffeepot.

But he covered his cup with his hand and said, "Remember when we talked before?"

She didn't answer. Because they were virtually alone she was, he could see it, reluctant to be flirtatious now.

"I'd still like to see you sometime. Tonight, even."

She wouldn't quite look at him, not directly.

"What do you think about that?" he said.

"I don't know," she said, and suddenly her loneliness stank all over the room.

He told himself: let's get out of here.

"Save my seat," he said to her. "I gotta move my clothes around across the street."

He left a five by his plate. Because he wasn't coming back.

"Wait a minute," she said when he had his hand on the doorknob. He could feel his shoulders hunching and knew she could see it—he'd be looking yanked back, stopped against his will. "You left too much," she said.

"No—keep the change."

"This is a five."

"I'll be back in a second."

"It doesn't seem like you will."

He had to go back and break it.

"If you'd really like to get together sometime," she said.

"Sure," he agreed, revolted with himself.

"I get off at nine."

"Okay. Yeah. Fine."

The look in her eyes was friendly and not that stupid. "You sure you're up for it?"

"I said so, didn't I?"

"You look like you're under arrest."

Navarro got back up the coast with his laundry before 5 P.M. to check in with Merton, nominally his boss but no one's boss, really, before Merton headed home or wherever he headed each day at five. Navarro in truth didn't mind the drive between Anchor Bay and Point Arena, a stretch of coast that opened into breezy emerald meadows where an occasional bunch of cows or horses just stood still, apparently thinking. Here the coast jutted westward, farther westward, he'd been told, than any other part of California, and well out into the clouds and fog of the ocean's weather systems. Point Arena was generally sunless, damp, depressed, a scrawny community gathered around a fishing harbor whose pier had been wrecked by a great wave some years back and only very recently rebuilt. Now the revival was on, however: other renovations had started along the main street, and Navarro only hoped they crept up the hill a couple blocks to include his own territory. The police station didn't quite rate the designation—it was a moveable structure meant for use as a temporary classroom in overburdened schools. Certainly it was big enough for the two-man department, but it felt wrong. In a work-space this size they needed dividers, which they'd had briefly but which had been commandeered—by the school, as a matter of fact— and which would have given it less this air of a hovel crouched in a universe of chaos. Everything was everywhere, and the three desks, his, Merton's, and the part-time clerk's, seemed to be rising on a tide of stuff, mostly paper: fliers, notices, findings of the county and state attorneys, things that should have been taken out and burned.

Merton greeted him only by raising his eyes while lowering his head to drip Skoal snuff out of his mouth into a Styrofoam cup.

Judging by Merton's silence, nothing was happening today. The office closed at five, and after that the two men could be summoned by beepers—Navarro would take the calls tonight.

In fact he'd had it in mind to ask Merton to switch with him because he felt he might get lucky with Mo, the tall waitress, but now he decided against it because, in the event he was wrong about his luck, he didn't want to be loitering around and lamenting the fact.

He paused at the file cabinet to check the mail, which had obvi-ously lain all day in its wire basket undisturbed. Jenny, the part-time clerk, did not actually open mail for fear of creating confusion. Merton didn't open mail either, but as today's included a stack of half a dozen brown envelopes bearing a familiar, earnest scrawl, he might have been expected to. Merton enjoyed these little communi-cations—the first one Navarro opened started right out *PS: Now I am*

Already Dead ▪ 107

mad as shit kicking in Hell . . . Their correspondent wrote and sealed and stamped them on different days, but dropped them in the box all at once like this, in a batch. Two or three times before they'd come, and Merton always got a kick out of reading them out loud. Today's sampling looked basically illegible.

"Anything up?"

"Nah," said Officer Merton. "Another perfect day."

Merton was a large battered handsome man on whom a police uniform looked like something he'd wear doing yard work. He kept his boots next to his desk and worked in his stocking feet. Good clean white socks. Nothing untoward there. In fact to a degree they offset the effect of the snuff, and the spitting. He'd been employed by the Sheriff's Department in Ukiah for one year, in the county jail; then he'd been out of work for quite a long time before moving over here for this job. In Navarro's opinion his colleague showed a flair for law enforcement though he lacked experience in basic police procedure. The truth was he navigated the local waters more skillfully than Navarro could ever hope to. Merton had found great success in viewing Point Arena as a large jail—there were good and bad prisoners, some serving sentences and some not yet proven guilty, and he anticipated nothing much to do unless called upon to crush a mass disturbance. "What?" he often said into the phone, "I'm not going out for that. I just had my feet up and was reading the newspaper. Dogs are supposed to bark. And if your neighbor calls me tomorrow and says his dog's been poisoned," he might add, "I won't go out for that either."

Without a word right now, though, Merton pulled on his boots, stood slowly, winked, touched a few things on his desk in a secret, superstitious way, hefted his Styrofoam spittoon and then pitched it into the wastebasket, gathering himself to leave the building as usual with great informality, even haste. Navarro suspected him of some arcane habit or vice. He pictured Merton in a smoky den gambling with Chinese guys.

Opening another of the day's brown envelopes, Navarro noticed that it was addressed to him by name. He discovered they all were.

Last May, the second of his three ex-wives had written to him, sounding strange and sentimental—he'd wondered if she'd lost her looks or fallen prey to booze. Otherwise, these collected lunatic ravings were the closest he'd come to receiving any personal mail. He got lots of ads, that was about it, and he wished he could take a cut on the money people made selling him off to mailing lists, mostly for companies offering high-tech law-enforcement gadgets. All the cops were buying plastic Glock automatics now. He wouldn't have minded owning a ten-millimeter himself, 649 foot-pounds of knock-down power in every one of fifteen shots, and all that. To what purpose? Well, for the hell of it. *I have activated brain power,* the second letter began without salutation or heading—

I have activated brain power to 85% brain capacity and using every inch, every drop so help me GOD in anti-beaming these rays as mentioned, but had to move at 4.14 PM to here behind the hill which contains zinc, zirconium compounds, and combinations not to be revealed despite CIA efforts, including almost getting that girl to intercourse with me, under the alieas or alien name of Miran. 4.14 PM on March 12, 1985, this is the day fateful indeed that I gave up the battle but it remains to be seen if only temporary as a disguise or strategy or, in the end, really. If you examine any leading author on electric, magnetic, physics, thermodynamics, also related to evolution, solar, exc. You find that positive and negative equals out. Not so as mystic authors tell us, even the Bible if original translation could be released by CIA from the library of Congress and Smithsonian Institution, but which would destroy their ruthless, magnificent plan to CRATE A FALSE UNIVERSE. Therefore mathematicalmystically it turns out the two domes do NOT cancel or neutralize out and what is breaking my heart is the tragedy of this and its effect on anything metal, even trace elements, in our brain, our endocrine, our everything. But wait. The mind is bigger than that. Ultimately we are safe. But how absurd and it bends me low to be the only one to say, look, just turn off the radar and see! Paradise in ten seconds! As soon as the beams stop, and a few of us activated up to 85% brain capacity like me, not to mention many over that, not too many but say 1200 on planet earth. We're tired! I am anyway. Let us heal the sick and teach you to activate to high and even higher than that, so you can do it. Then you get UNIVERSAL HARMONY, and I mean ten seconds! Put an injunction on them at 1.21 PM and ten seconds later, Paradise in ten seconds. I cannot stress how good that would be. No exageration. And I'm tired, my whole head gets overheated and burning, THERMONUCLEAR I might as well say from the pity of it. And it's stupid. You turn left off the ridge rd. where the picture of a boat used to be. I hope you stop off for coffee. Drive two miles down dirt rd. there. That is if I just don't put an end to it by joining the army and turning over my capacity and teach them how to jump the radar beams for the purpose of destruction instead of harmony like I am now, God be praised.

Not to offend anyone but I choose you for reasons not to be revealed in this letter, which is being read by satellite and analyzed in Pentagon, exc. They won't kill me but it's just for your sake. I think it's all through computers and radar but who knows with these unscrupulous men twisted by their own MENTAL-DESTRUCTIVE MACHINES, they might drain your brake fluid or something to fake a wreck. Rays, or off the coast road—your just as dead either way, so tread lightly with prayer on your lips and understanding of GOD ALMIGHTY and infinite love. I Am sorry to involve you. I am sorry to involve you "but"! Remember the goodness you feel is not God's goodness it is actually God. And so your feeling God. And remember STOP THE RADAR and best wishes.

W. Fairchild

Navarro bent to stash the envelopes in the "Federal" file, where letters from W. Fairchild were kept because they sometimes came close to constituting threats against the Air Force radar station atop Arena Ridge. He didn't like Merton reading them out loud and making fun. Navarro agreed you had to keep your distance, but he respected crazy people. He more than just sometimes felt a little crazy himself.

Navarro had visited the radar station once, just driving around. Kind of an imaginary place, a hot, windless island surrounded by an absolutely stationary sea of silver stratus cloud. Nobody had challenged him, in fact he'd seen not a soul that day, and he'd wondered if the radars actually operated—that is until he'd pulled up near the forty-foot-tall twin domes and heard static spitting from his radio, although it was switched off . . .

The "Federal" file stayed pretty thin—mostly these crackpot pleas and a few others tattling on tax evaders and campsite vandals in the national forests. Vague bureaucratic nightmares had made these messages a harbor here, some incompletely imagined disaster that had everyone destroyed for failing, when Congress demanded, to produce one of these letters. *PS—*

PS just to mention as proof they don't know their stuff microwaves made me a eunuch before 1985 (brain capacity doesn't count) but they still sent Miran, an alieas or alien name for an implanted agent of surprising disguise (real name Yvonne) who said I'm lost, please, help, and tried to intercourse with me (which they told her just get him alone and broadcast mentally, his brain capacity will pick up mentally what you're beaming.) Pretty stupid, huh? Just to show you they have no protection from their own mental-destructive beams, can't think straight till they get the compounds analyzed in this and a few other hills not to be revealed. No way, not by me!

Sincerely, W. Fairchild.

Navarro's hamstrings burned. For some minutes he'd been crouching before the file cabinet's open bottom drawer with these letters in his hand. He stood up to make sure that Merton's car was gone from its parking space out front. He took the letters to his desk and sat down.

AUG 8

Since coming behind or also down this hill which contains zinc, zirconium compounds, and other precious compounds (or trace elements compounds, not to be revealed) at 4.14 PM March 12, 1985, where spirits can be interacted, God is king, and operating at 85% brain capacity without anti-beaming, I am definitely resting, getting ready, and my final decision is YES. I will network up with those of such capacity to mentally anti-beam as long as the fight is necessary, UNTIL THE DOMES GO SILENT. Then wouldn't they be beautiful things? The round white knees of some giant sunbathing up there is what I saw when I thought of them quiet.

Officer Navarro! Sorry I had to choose you in this capacity "but." Do you think I get so thrilled being the only one anti-beaming on this planet literally until my ears are smoking? AND I smell my hair burning? AND I have been exhausting even further in the task on top of that, which has me screaming in the woods until you can feel the sap going whop-whop-whop inside of all trees, which is to sort out screwed up acid nonsense of those years back from true visions made available after activating up to 85% brain capacity in late February 1985.

Then at 4:14 PM on March 12 I moved behind zinc-zirconium-not-to-be-revealed-compounds protecting me in this hill, and God have mercy but the struggle is just exchanged for the next one, which is exhausting me further as I say, to separate the true from the false. Now at last I can make the spectacular announcement (please broadcast over police frequency in designated code remember always) ten days and two hours ago on July 29, 1990, I boxed in black mental powers ALL THOUGHTS, VISIONS, MESSAGES, HALLUCINATIONS that I received of any kind at any time before 4:14 March 12 1985 and will hold it in unused percent of brain capacity, where it can never do harm to our fragile loving spirits on this earth again. I would say Halleluah but dear people of the planet the tears are falling down like rain, that struggle I am sorry to say is just a minor one compared to the energy-drain unless I can network up with others of high brain capacity. Sometimes I wish I was dead. Is this hill preventing anything and everything from getting out, just like its compounds protect me from the beams? Therefore please in addition to aforementioned broadcast send out in designated code on police frequency the following message: ALL OF INCREASED CAPACITY NETWORK UP THE TERRIBLE STRUGGLE BEGINS ON JANUARY 15, 1991 BUT GOD IS WITH US. Repeat daily.

P.S. Fear not, it's all for the best.

AUG 8 IN THE PM

PS: Now I am as mad as shit kicking in Hell, buddy boy. Not at you, but I forgot what's going on! Networking is for the purpose of anti-beaming radar domes. But I forgot to stress you must get an injunction to stop the beams at the source so that those of us with 75% brain capacity or higher (I changed the number due to the enormous danger of the situation bearing down on planet earth like an enormous asteroid, planet-size . . .). Could be as many as 2000 of those. If we are free from anti-beam duties and terrible energy-drain we can heal the sick, teach others to activate up to high capacity—all within ten seconds of shut-off on those radars. Please read the Bible.

Sincerely.

P.S. Something important, a woman of surprising disguise was sent to mentally attempt intercourse with me, alieas or alien name Miran, code unknown, origin unknown, on a date not to be revealed. Real name Yvonne. May still be in area. Current alieas or alien name unknown. In my loneliness result of protection from radar, preventing me from connecting mentally, zinc-zirconium compounds and others not to be revealed basically a blessing and a curse, I don't know. But I'm getting vibes that she's still in area. Still practicing witchcraft.

AUG 9

I believe there is now a situation I can't straighten out. I am attempting to work on it mentally but it's torture, I think the suffering and exhaustion may be letting in some laser rays or things I can't deal with, only lie down and let them cut me up in AGONY, TOTAL AGONY. This torment has got me about ready to JOIN THE ARMY. My brother came down behind this hill. He was implanted long ago, it's not his fault. But he speaks in code. Please as your HIGHEST PRIORITY interview with recording device and decode by reverse playback over police frequency at designated code. Bible does not work to decode this one, but don't let that stop you from reading the Bible and prayers on your lips. WHAT CAN I SAY. Too bad, you were chosen? I know, I know. Just all will be well and fear not, that is all.

PS I have mentally boxed in a black box all messages, thoughts, hallucinations from before March 12, 1985. But the information that my brother was implanted (Nelson Fairchild, Jr.) comes from both eras of from before said date and also SINCE then. So don't be confused.

Sincerely, W. Fairchild

AUG 10 IN THE PM

Dear Sir

What is really fooling them is completely organic surroundings around here. They figure the beams have to penetrate. They forgot two things: zinc, zirconium compounds, and certain compounds, mainly trace elements not to be revealed, not even to you. (not your fault, it's all mental, you're not activated up yet) Then there is the question of floorboards in my house, which started out organic but absorbed beams in Pt. Arena (alieas, alien) bowly alley, reversing molecular structure to nonOrganic radarium. This keeps anything from getting up from under. I don't care if they tap in mentally on you and get that one, there's nothing they can do really.

PS. The Bible is mistranslated but all you have to do is touch it. It's still there, gets decoded even on the way to your head. God's power. Ultimately we are safe. Just HANG IN THERE BUDDY. You're all I've got, your mission the fate of planet. But don't get nervous.

P.S. If it gets bad go inside Pt. Arena (alieas, alien) movie theater. That has been absorbing rays a long time. Molecular structure of organic materials reversed to make radarium. Bring others, espec. women and children, if DIAMOND GRIDS or anything like lasers appear in the sky.

PS. Advise you to pick out survivors in advance of January 15, 1991, as per coded messages coming fast and furious. For some its just in one ear and out the other, but for you, pick who you want and shelter in Pt. Arena (alieas, alien) movie theater. I forgot to tell you that if DIAMOND GRIDS or laserlike things appear in the sky it's probably too bad. Your fried. So be alert and get in there 1/14/91. How do you like this weather we're having? Very nice. All peace is available in this eternal present.

Sincerely, W. Fairchild

PS.—This is being read by satellite and analyzed at the Pentagon by CIA, FBI, exc. I don't code it because they just put it in their decoders anyway. If we remain simple and true they cannot help but defeat themselves. UNSCRUPULOUS, SATANIC, INSANE, EVIL. There's no fighting that. Remain simple and true. Fear not. Resist not evil. All will be well. Infinite love. God says so. STOP THE RADAR. God says so.

W. Fairchild

Dear Sir

Up till now I have been too tired anti-beaming to explain about implants. It's hard to explain. How did they get even the idea of a third lifeform? How did they discover processes for structural disintegration-reintegration? Was it through study of RADARIUM post-WWII? A lot of radarium turned up then. But in fact I cannot use my powers to see behind this hill protecting me by GOD'S STAR-BURSTING GRACE into their dastardly minds to tell you. Anyway—

Anyway they continue in pentagon, CIA, FBI, exc. (some presidents know, most don't, and others get assassinated) to continue to pose nuclear threat as a ruse. Had you fooled, huh?

Third lifeform SPERMS destroy and reintegrate inside the womb (don't worry, this doesn't happen every day, it costs 17–19 trillion U/S money for each attempt, which is successful one in a million. That's why my brother may be one of the only ones and may explain why I'm involved. Or were we just chosen? Like you?) (Again I can't see.) When the implant population reaches critical mass, LOOK OUT. But look at me. Do I look worried? Sometimes I'm not sure if I should be taped, reverse-played over police frequency at designated code. Oh God in Heaven I hope and pray please NO! But if you suspect me at all then you must do so in the name of all that is holy and spiritual and standing between our human hearts and the complete total DESTRUCTION OF THE UNIVERSE. Take the left turn where there used to be a picture of a boat. The sign still says HILD and the rest is broke off. 2mi down dirt rd. to cabin with RADARIUM floors. Peace and tranquillity all your blessed days.

AUG 11 (CONT. LATER LATER)

All will be well. The goodness that you feel is not God's goodness, it is actually God. So you are feeling God right now. Thanking you for your broadcasts, which I cannot pick up mentally living now since 1985 (March 12, 4:14 PM) under protection of subteranean compounds in this hill, mostly zinc, zirconium-compounds, and others mostly trace elements (not to be revealed). I have been resting mentally. Peace in the valley. Spirits, deer, hilarious rodents with a small capacity but telepathic and humorous, squirrels, woodchucks, chimpmunks, all warming in the sun. What a pitiful sharp joke it is because my very protection cuts me off in loneliness. But it must be that the networking has begun, the miracle is at hand, I just wish I could lead the way. But it's my fate, IMPRISONED, MISUNDER-STOOD, FORGOTTEN, half the time I'm screaming until the trees fall over and some other times I cry until the TEARS MAKE MUD AROUND MY FEET. Now possibly soon from happiness, lonely happiness but happiness. Thank you for your broadcasts, Officer Navarro! I am sorry I chose you but now you know. All was always going to be well.

All was always going to be well.

Sincerely, W. Fairchild

I nevitable" and "dreaded" . . . "Bloodshrinking" . . . What other words describe our visits with our mothers and fathers? How I look forward to visiting their graves.

Each Monday *Barron's* financial weekly came in at the Anchor Bay store. I usually delayed till Tuesday, sometimes Wednesday, but in the months since he'd taken to his bed I had never completely avoided picking it up for my father and paying him this horrible regular visit.

I drove over directly from the store that afternoon, Tuesday, September 4, a week after I'd left Winona's and six days after Winona's return—the day Carl Van Ness would show us all what he was made of. *We'll see if our eyes are open.* Maybe I believed his note. Maybe I was looking for an alibi for murder. But few folks hereabouts would imagine Nelson Fairchild, Sr., as an alibi for anything.

I'd come from an unhappy interview with Clarence—vaguely unhappy, not violently. Yes, he'd come back to town and found me and I'd told him about Harry Lally's henchmen. He didn't thump me—in fact he raised my spirits, but not before making it clear that he hadn't cultivated the marijuana just to ransom me from my fate, which he called "the just punishment of a fuck-up." I had a little bit of hope, just a feeling, that he wouldn't abandon me to those killers. He wanted time to ponder this mess, but he didn't know how to say, "Let me think." He was a doer, not a thinker.

Oh well, the day had been a long one, that was all—Melissa resonating strangely, then giving me the horrible news that my pursuers were back on the scene, and after that I'm afraid I told her too much. Also possibly we had Carl Van Ness bumping up on the horizon, and because I thought he might already be in town I'd gone to Winona's ranch while she was out and—done something; a little thing I'd probably later regret. Could thirty minutes with Father make the day any longer?

The old man lived north of Gualala, on an acre looking out at the Pacific from the highway's west side. Two stories, three bedrooms, a two-car garage and a workshop, like the home of almost every other sixty-two-year-old person in Mendocino County.

The door from the garage stood open, so I knocked while stepping through it into the kitchen, and Donna Winslow asked me if I would like some tea.

"Thank you, no," I said, "but what about a glass of wine?"

I generally found Donna here in the wifely regions, with her stretch pants and long-sleeved yellow dish gloves and her failure to connect, in certain important ways, with her surroundings. Willful failure. Cheaper by a long shot than tranquilizers. But it made her seem a little scary, even if her face was pale and kind. Eva Braun might have turned out like that. "We've got some open," she said of the wine, "is that okay?"

"Open's fine. Poured is better."

Father had refused to let her move in before the stroke and after that had probably just failed to prevent her. I thought it was fine that she lived here. Particularly I admired her ability to survive without cheap conversation. She never bothered me with that stuff.

I stood there sipping red table wine from a too-small glass while she climbed the stairs to tell him the elder son had turned up with his *Barron's*. I don't just bring it here each week; I also read it to him. It is the strangest thing I do.

I heard Donna's voice from above. But not his. Maybe he'd snuffed it, and I'd be spared.

His partner, Willis Winslow, had suffered a run of strokes and been laid up for months when my father started sleeping with his wife. The story they tell now is that Father hefted Donna across his shoulders and carried her upstairs to the master bedroom one night right out from under Willis Winslow's helpless gaze, and had her every night after that while Winslow wasted away in a downstairs room, listening.

Now Father lies in bed as Willis Winslow once did, attended by the same woman. She's too old, I would imagine, to be cuckolding him. But I hope she is.

And the same woman he carried up the stairs is coming down now alone.

"He's kind of dozing, Nelson."

"Should I disappear?"

"No, he said to come on up. Then he drifted off."

"I'll come back later."

"You could go up and just give him the paper, maybe."

"Okay," I said forlornly.

"You want a refill?"

"I'll take the bottle."

She'd done a tremendous job on the house, over which formerly his office had run amok, inroaded generously by his shop. She'd pushed everything back, all the tools and ropes and greasy broken automotive parts and fatly unrolling blueprints and escaped and antique correspondence. His rusty file cabinets had disappeared, all but one, the drawers of which she managed to keep closed and the top of which was free of anything but two white daisies in a vase. In his living room she'd put up flowery curtains that matched the Pacific, also hangings of woven rope from Mexico, and, on the walls of the staircase, which I climbed now, but slower and slower, my ankles in a sense shattered, dragging the devices he'd laid years ago to trap his children—let me never reach the top!—she'd nailed up pictures bright as windows.

Don't ask me why I'm here. Because of a sickly fascination, I guess, but that's only one of the many feelings that stab at me now as I find him asleep in his small room at the top of the stairs. There he lies, out of it. And I'm as shocked as ever.

He once threatened to kill a man, a perfectly unsuspecting tourist, when he found this stranger sitting in his accustomed chair in the barroom of the Gualala Hotel. He's famous for having decked a county commissioner at a meeting of the Point Arena town council; also he assaulted the high school basketball coach right on the street when that fine citizen started dating our mother, and although that contest went against my father—he ended up flat on his ass—the coach quit calling, and Mom never had another date in these parts. All night once, with a shotgun across his knees and a two-gallon jug of gasoline beside him on the floor of his bulldozer, he waited quietly in his equipment lot—this a great many years ago now—to surprise whoever had been thieving from his construction supplies. Father did nothing when the man pulled up under the nearby trees in his pickup truck, he sat like stone while the man peeled away the tool-shed's padlock with a crowbar, waited until he'd gone inside before climbing down from his perch up in the monstrous vehicle. When the bandit tiptoed out of the shed with his arms full of tools, my father paralyzed him with the touch of the shotgun's barrel to his throat, and soaked him with the gas, all two gallons of it, pouring it down over his head. "I'll give you ten seconds' head start," he promised the man while producing his Zippo lighter. They both leapt into their pickup trucks, and Nelson Fairchild, Sr., hounded his victim all the way to the outskirts of Ukiah, where the poor burglar took himself, his skin eaten by the gasoline, to the hospital emergency services. Later he sued for thousands. My father would have had to pay him, too, if the man's lawyers hadn't bungled it. Father's never been sneaky when it comes to revenge. He's rumored to have had people murdered, but I doubt it. I think he'd have done the killing himself, openly, publicly if possible, and then brazened it out in court surrounded by unbeatable attorneys.

Always the same image arises when I think of him—a face quivering on the border between irony and disgust—so I think of him as always the same. Not till recent months had I ever seen him with his eyes closed. But he slept a lot these days. There was no irony now in his face, just a bland, pasty innocence ratified by a cowlick. They'd moved in one of those hospital beds that rise and flatten with a button—they'd made a puppet out of him, even if he controlled, to a degree, his own strings.

I wasn't about to wake him. Maybe he needed his sleep. Anyway just getting to his room had licked me. I was beat, might as well have swum up here through blood. I poured my glass full and raised the window just a handsbreadth and inhaled. Without the fog to dilute it, the sunshine put everything on a slow bake, but this near the shore the air felt cool and smelled of voyages. Faint thunder drifted up this way, the flailings and snoring of the Pacific. It came through the window and woke my father.

He opened his eyes. He spoke immediately: "Let's make every little thing illegal, and put all of ourselves in prison."

"Hey, dig it, why not?"

"I'd like to get the sombitches"—he pushed himself up on his elbows, forgetting his automatic bed—"I'd like to get the sombitches down under my boot for just ten minutes, and then I'd stomp an explanation out of their sorry faces. Just why is it that a motel, a good aesthetic-looking structure designed by any hippie or any faggot, they can choose whoever they want, cannot rest by the edge of the cliff, a badly needed motel? When rooms are up around two hundred dollars a night on this coast? So the sea can remain beautiful, they say. Beautiful with bars across it. Beautiful if you can pay two hundred dollars a night and wait a month for the reservation. Don't they realize where beauty is? Do you happen to realize where yourself?"

"I think you want me to say beauty is in the bank. In the faces on the money."

That shut him up. He wrote me off. I could see it in his eyes. But if I'd had to I could have seen it in his ears or hands or hair. I could have looked at one fingernail and told you I'd once again squirted away my chance to be his son. He always gave me a chance and then always, within minutes, saw me fail. I was used to the process. It gave me a sick thrill, if you want me to be frank.

Part of his silence owed to his disease, whatever it was. He woke with a bang but petered out fast. He wouldn't say what disease he had. The doctors knew, and they'd told him. But he felt they lied just for fun, if for no better reason—projecting his own relentless untruthfulness onto others. His dishonesty wasn't weakness: it shaped his faith, helped constitute his creed. He believed strongly in the efficacy of lying. He valued falsehood as a tool. The truth he feared as uncontrollable once you let it out. But he knew the difference between the two.

"Well, it's Higgins and Tom Aiken"—two environmentalist lawyers—"my personal Rawhead and Bloodybones. If half their rat-shit buddies weren't on the Coastal Commission I could subdivide down to square meters and build clear up into the clouds. They figure to stall. Get the game called for darkness. They think I'll roll over dead. Not hardly! Hand me that phone."

"It's damn near six P.M., Dad." I always get western in his presence.

"Dial me a number."

I put the receiver into his tiny clawing grasp and punched the buttons he wanted. "Give me a minute, please," he said, covering the mouthpiece.

Banished inside of sixty seconds? I may have achieved some record there. I left him to his shenanigans and went down the hall to the toilet. The one-man barbaric horde, he's in yet another war. Everybody knows he's a crook. Big deal! Who cares? My father not only knows the difference between right and wrong, but he's also willing to live with it, and let others draw their own conclusions about him. Not me.

Not me—I'm the Mole Person, hiding from the truth in any hole, here, for instance, in my father's upstairs bathroom, on the shady side of the house, half-dark and quiet and cool as its tiles. A small chamber, but with me in here it holds magnificent structures of natural growths, the big fat systemic organism of my deceits. Maneuvering through my lies was like hopping faster than the eye could follow from branch to branch across the roof of a jungle, a jungle cultivated to cover up earlier lies, the whole business lacing back delicately to find its mother-root in my first lie, completely forgotten now, and never to be discovered by anybody else, the lie to cover my first little crime, also forgotten—no, I swear I didn't take the cookies—or, more probably, a whole childhood fashioned to avoid the question of the cookies in the first place, my every move, to this day, warped around the absence of getting caught, the void where there should have been my arrest and trial and punishment: a new route to school planned in order to avoid the boy who owned the stolen cookies, and a reason invented to explain the new route to whoever might ask, and evidence concocted to demonstrate that the reason isn't a lie—I need the exercise, I'm going out for track and field—and then a career of track-and-field events and long practice in a sport that doesn't interest me, and a new personality shaped, a false persona who thrives on track and field, who loves running (But I do love running. Don't I? Or else why spend so much time doing it?) and hurdling over the intricacies of his falsehoods toward this day, Tuesday, September 4, when I'm ready to commit murder to deal with my mistakes without actually correcting them because . . . because I don't want to correct them. I can't survive the correcting of them. I just want them erased.

My father would never have understood these things. Even now, if he'd found himself in my place, he'd have crawled out of bed and somehow gotten, he and his sawed-down Winchester shotgun, up the hill above Anchor Bay to put a third eye in Harry Lally's forehead.

He called from his sickbed, "Somebody hang this thing up! Hang this sombitch up for me, damnit!"

Donna was standing at the turn of the stairs as I headed toward his room. "Yes?" she said. "Yes?"

"Tell her to get lost," he said as I entered. Donna must have heard this, because she didn't appear. I put the phone on the table for him, and he said, "I'd hate for them to win the last goddamn battle."

I pulled up a chair and unfolded the paper, the *Barron's*.

He said, "Didn't it come yesterday?"

"I don't know when it came. I picked it up today."

"You know how you talk to me, you little pissant? Like all the other little pissants on earth now. Like I'm old and fizzled out in the brain."

"I don't think you're fizzled in the brain."

"You repeat my words, like these are the *key* words . . . It's hard to explain. Read."

While he rested and caught his breath, I read out loud about this and that, the conclusions to be drawn from certain upswings and the stance most profitable given the tenor of the times (all of it obviated by the week's events in Kuwait, and nothing that would help my kind of money trouble certainly), glancing up once in a while at my sick father with his zero face. His eyes were open, but I don't know if he was listening to this stuff any better than I was.

"How's Winona?"

"I haven't seen her. We've talked on the phone. She got back."

"Why hasn't she stopped by to see me?"

"Because she doesn't like to see you like this. It nauseates everybody as a matter of fact."

"Did she file the divorce?"

"She did. I don't have the money to fight it."

"I've written her a letter."

"Concerning what?"

"I'm yanking her up and kicking her legs out from under."

"What do you mean?"

"I've straightened her mind out on a few things, is all. She'll see what it means to discount me. And you, meanwhile, you've been seen drunk in public with that gypsy runt."

"I have?"

"Your hedge-whore."

"Melissa."

"Do you dispute the appellation?"

"Hedge-whore, no. You're very colorful." You who have lain with them endlessly.

"By God, I won't see my line carried down through that bitch's scabby sluice!"

"No danger of that."

"*You* say! Because *she* says! *She* ain't fixed. She's deceiving you."

"Is this new information? Or the same old misogynist paranoia?"

"I base my suspicions out of experience. A woman without guile in her thoughts has guile aplenty beating right down in her bones. You poor elongated day-old infant! She's got your brain sucked down to your pecker and the blood squoze out in that tight little kennel of hers." He mumbled the last of this. He'd lost interest in my follies since the shadow of the death-bird's wing had covered him. The carrying forward of his line, that was his passion now, that and somehow controlling his sons and his dough and his land from beyond the grave. I doubt he cared, really, which particular wench or wattle mothered his grandchildren, so long as somebody did.

"Father, I want to talk to you again about the timber."

"The timber stays. I've seen to that. It's deeded in now. Nobody harvests them redwoods."

"Ten thousand acres! For God's sake, let us just thin them! A forty percent reduction wouldn't change the profile!"

"You can take the windfall out with horses. There's plenty in there, and it's all redwood, don't matter if it's been on the ground awhile. But I don't want no fifty mile of skid road cut through there, or no timber cut neither. The day I bought my first woodlot I swore an oath: that someday I'd own ten thousand acres of trees that would stand forever."

"Is it this?—no, let me ask this, I want to understand—is it maybe that you want to take it all with you? Is your secret myth this Celtic thing that you have to preserve your own land to live on in the after-world or something? Your own patch of earth in Valhalla?"

"Valhalla? That's not Celtic. And I'm a Welshman, anyway! And I don't explain it to you because you're idiotic! Deprived of oxygen, I'm sure, back in the womb of that harlot who spawned you. Just be aware that I've sworn an oath. And my word's good."

"I'm aware." I stood by the window again listening to the sea and hoping he'd sleep now and never wake. I didn't understand how somebody who wanted to string the world's loveliest coastline with the cheapest possible motels could also be passionate about a bunch of redwoods. And it hurt me that I didn't understand, because this was my father.

I didn't want to clear-cut. But we could live in comfort forever off a periodic thinning, my brother and I—Winona too, and Melissa—once we'd built the roads.

"The Hospice people called me again."

"Hospice? You mean—"

"The morbid pissants, the voyeurs of death, yes, them's the very sombitches I mean."

They'd been after him for a while to let them ease his death. Fat chance! If anything was going to be hard, it would be this old man's dying.

"Close that window, will you son?"

I pulled it shut.

He said, "I'm sorry I yelled at you."

"Which time? When have you not yelled at me?"

"I hate to see my own boy kill a jug before sundown."

"Then don't watch."

"You've got a purple mustache, you look like a child. No, don't sass back at me. Read. Read. Read."

I read to him from the opinion pages, amazed and depressed that I let this runt boss me. My height comes from Mother. He can't be taller than five-eight. Today he looks half his original size, only a miniature of the mean giant of my childhood. And all the time he gets tinier. He brings to mind the Mole People who also terrified me back then. They were in a movie, on TV. Big, strong mutants living in subterranean darkness. But even so much as a dash of sunshine wrecked a Mole Person. Dragged out of their tunnels they became shrivelled, lifeless, went from Mole People to Prune People in no time at all. I think they scared me because they hinted at some sort of truth about our shy, secret selves. Now even Father seemed like one of them, groping around, seared by a tremendous light from another world. I'm telling you. Everywhere I go the people seem to be staggering, fatally irradiated. There's a dose out there for me. I can't duck it forever. The old man, Christ would you look at him, was proof enough of that. For he'd once established himself in my sight as a figure to blot the sun, the world's entire sky, and now he'd ushered forth something that would shrink and extinguish even somebody like himself. He sinks to the sand before a great lonely sea—naked and old—something vast is dawning, and nothing he's built can shelter him from its revelations. I guess I'm reading but I don't hear a word of my voice, I'm only aware of my father and a feeling: me, my father, and a feeling.

Had I kept on reading? Or had I just stopped?

"Dad?"

Twilight was turning the pages gray in my hands.

"Dad? Are you sleeping?"

Father? Are you dead?

I watched him breathe. Someday soon somebody, maybe the woman who loved him now, would be sitting here like this when his last breath spiralled up out of his throat toward the rafters, parting the lips of a corpse.

I laid the paper on his nightstand and left the room.

The woman who loved him was waiting downstairs, sitting on a stool in the kitchen, beside the counter, raising and lowering a teabag in a little cup. I gave her the empty wine bottle, and she said, "How's your dad?"

Or someday soon somebody, maybe one of his sons, would come downstairs like this and in answer to that question say, "Donna . . ." and right away she'd know.

Meanwhile the old man would probably be up there pretending to be still alive. If there's one thing he's been desperately hiding, it's the terminal nature of his sickness. This love of lying, I don't share it. I hate my lies, they oppress me. But I did inherit one of the tenets of his strange faith: I believe in boldness. Believe that boldness makes things happen, makes the unlikely possible. Therefore, don't hedge. Bet your stack. Wager half on a long shot, you lose. But you win if you wager all.

"He's sleeping."

"That's good."

"Good for the Coastal Commission," I said, and she smiled.

Outside I put the top up on the Porsche. I was shivering.

I have the belief in boldness. What I generally lack is the boldness itself.

Because boldness doesn't feel bold. It feels scared, not brave. The explorer feels more and more lost, the prophet hears himself unintelligibly blaspheming.

Naturally I'm thinking about the dare I've taken with Carl Van Ness. But we are, at this point, just—still, at this point—just hypothetical, surely. With Van Ness out of town the reality seems to have diminished. What we've done up to this point is possibly only a rehearsal. I started the Porsche and, as the sound covered my voice, realized that I was talking to myself out loud, saying, "That we'll do it seems still likely but with, how shall I put it, an *ethereal* likelihood . . ."

But how can I talk of boldness, when it's Van who's taking the dare?

Well, yes, because, as we know, I'm a liar, mine the kind of dishonesty that can cherish two beliefs at once, opposing ones. I can act the coward while telling myself I'm testing the limits of boldness by the same puzzling mechanism whereby we sometimes know, for instance, that it's Tuesday, September 4, and that we have an appointment Tuesday, and yet fail to understand the appointment is therefore for *today*.

On the other hand, making it happen is making it happen. If I shoot the gun, am I somehow a coward because I don't happen to be the actual bullet?

Van does his part, I do mine. We're a lethal combo. And if Van Ness is back, and means what he says—then that's it. Because my part's done already.

This afternoon, while Winona helped a friend break a horse at the Say-When Ranch, I traded her bottle of Nembutal for the Zielene.

She'll have come home tired from the stables, turned in early with two little red capsules. She'll be out. And I'm out too. I have stepped out in boldness. Boldness. Out into dreams made real.

Each move I made now was one I'd invented months ago and played along in my head many times. How drab the real thing felt! Driving the mile into Gualala's little strip of shops and restaurants just made me tired. The light and aromas from the pizzeria next door to the big old wooden hotel bored me, and a certain not totally unfamiliar neurotic symptom developed as I pulled in beside the hotel, the conviction that something oily had got all over my steering wheel. Inside the reeking barroom I made straight for the toilet, wiping my hands on my pants over and over. A dozen or so people drifted down the loud canyon of certain hilarities, lifting their steins or whatever. The Gualala Hotel has stood across the road from the Pacific for close to a century, and for some decades of that period stood miraculously, on the brink of falling flat on its face, but in recent years through a jag of remodellings has managed to recast itself as no longer a place where men might spit on the floors in the hallways; but men still do spit on the floor in the bar. Going into the bathroom I had the experience you have at least once a night in such a place, that of ramming up against somebody, some derelict mastur-bator, coming out of the stall. "Pardon," I meant to say, and meant to step back, but my jaw went tight, the words jammed, and I leaned forward. I tasted murder in my throat, I shoved past, staring at his eyes—the same rage showed in his face, it all flared unbelievably. It was Carl Van Ness. He shouldered me aside. He stumbled away. We couldn't stop staring at each other. He never glanced anywhere else as he straightened himself and left the bar. I was breathing hard, my chest full of a lion's roar. *Then we'll see if our eyes are open.* His were. It was abundant in his eyes: he'd been to Winona's house. He'd done something terrible.

Van Ness thought himself a traveller through eternity, and whatever he did to negate himself—suicide, murder—it's all fuel for the journey, so why not? And to the mystifying question "why mur-der?" isn't "why not?" just as good as a whole constellation of answers? But I have a theory why he agreed: I just bring out the killer in people, that's all. Spend a little time with me, I'll work on you like Dr. Jekyll's potion—the man a few months back, for instance, in this very bar here among, I wouldn't doubt, these same rough drinkers, the character who started out lecturing me in a peaceable way on the stages of womanhood, the progressions of marriage, and so on. But after thirty minutes inside my aura the man got hostile. As if some-body had flipped a switch and turned out the spark in his mind. What a darkness, nothing more than that. Only, I swear it, the pin-point reflections of the jukebox in his eyes, and images from the oversized TV screen. Nothing from inside, just a lot of light bouncing off. The scene ends there in my memory, with him in his animal state being restrained while I beat it with I hope dignified haste. But how can you be dignified when you've just shown yourself and everybody else this puzzling trick you have of stirring up the preconscious evil muck at the bottom of one of mankind, some guy you never saw before—clink!—somebody you were toasting ten minutes before?

And here I am in the same Gualala Hotel bar and the same thing has just happened with another man, with Van Ness—and I realize it's all that's been happening between the two of us since the moment I watched him drown himself.

I went on with the plan, though now that it had started, going on with it seemed almost impossible. I yanked at the pay phone by the bathroom, forced a coin on it, pressed Winona's phone number . . . *Hello,* her voice machine said in its laboring parrot-cum-gramophone falsetto, *I can't,* it explained, *talk in person right now* . . . "Winona, it's Nelson, eight P.M. Tuesday. I wanted to pick up my fishing rod. I'll just stop up tonight and grab it"—this errand my excuse for appearing there.

I hung up the phone, got through the press of idiots, put my elbows on the bar. Immediately the tavern's breath soothed me. I expect always to be a small child in this place. That I can see over the tables surprises me briefly. In here I spent the most comfortable moments of my sonship, when Father was tipsy and told me stories and tossed me quarters, and I knew, at least, how to sit in a chair without disappointing him.

I ordered a glass of Carte Blanche, absolutely the world's cheapest sherry.

Till well after 1:00 A.M. I sat at a little table in front of the forty-inch TV screen, sipping drinks and watching baseball and rerun comedies and news bulletins—the world was falling apart around me as well as inside; the president was emphatic that he wanted a war with Iraq, if fuzzy as to *why*, precisely, and refugees poured into Jordan, and the New York Mets left the field with their heads down—but I'd gone crazy and didn't care who won or who lost, not in baseball, not in warfare.

And then around half past one I stood up, not the least bit drunk, and went to find out whether or not I'd committed a murder.

Aren't they always saying, "I'll never know how I got through the next few minutes, hardly remember," et cetera? The hell with them. They don't know what they're talking about. I remember the exact length of my fingernails, the sherry's sweetness, the bill I paid with—a five, face up, our beloved Abraham Lincoln—the give in the wooden floorboards under my shoes walking out, the wet smell of the air and the shine of moisture on my car, and two finger streaks in the dust that made an ideogram, unintelligible and scary, on the Porsche's dashboard; and I remember driving in the moonless dark and passing through the streetlamp's glow at the head of Winona's drive as through the spongy boundary at the end of the universe, remember realizing, at the moment I stepped from the car in front of her house, that it would almost certainly rain tonight, remember feeling the laces flap on one of my Invader-brand jogging shoes, remember pausing to deal with it, remember deciding not to. The kitchen light burned. Otherwise the place was shrouded. Winona's customized jeep, formerly mine, a Japanese jeep, a Subaru, waited by the walk. Out in the dark, Red bumped against his stall and snickered. I felt my left hand go out, palm up, in a gesture I often make in conversation. I was talking to nobody: I've come home to look for my wife, don't know what I expect. Maybe I'll warn her she's about to be murdered. I don't really want to go through with this. I'll give Harry Lally the pot plants, Clarence will break some of my bones, that'll be okay, then they'll heal, that'll be neat. No need for anyone to die.

—All the while humming with excitement in the center of my heart, because I've stumbled onto an explanation, correct me if I'm wrong, for the tendency of our race to grope toward tragedy: in order to ponder the imponderable—war, murder, our power to mutilate the planet—in order to concentrate our thoughts on these matters, we have to *plan* them. We have to be mapping out, not merely contemplating, the unthinkable. Or we can't think about it at all. And I reflected, forgiving my own delirious pun, that designs just lead naturally to executions.

I put my head inside the door as any nosy neighbor might. I called: "Dear?"

No answer.

I willed this. Yes. But I'm not sure that's why it's happening. I think I willed it in order to ponder it more deeply. I'm not a doer, I'm a dreamer. Ask anyone! This isn't me!

Had Van Ness stood here in this room?

Did something of his aura linger by the couch where I'd told him about the plan and read to him from *Thus Spake Zarathustra*? Nietzsche's wisdom on sleep was somewhat on the order of this: to sleep well, stay awake. Winona would have done right to have read that!

When I'd showed Van Ness the Zielene and Nembutal, I'd read to him from Nietzsche on sleep—"Avoid all those," Nietzsche's Wise Man warns convulsively, "avoid all those who sleep badly and are awake at night."

"I might apply that to you," I'd pointed out to him.

"And vice versa," he'd said.

Yes, yes, yes, I agreed with him tonight, half-aloud, running my finger along the spines of books . . . Oh yes. We should have avoided each other.

We'd talked about things other than sleep—he'd quoted at some length from *Zarathustra*—but what we'd read I couldn't quite—fumbling among the shelves beside the couch for the book, which wasn't there, scattering books to the floor in a spasm of irritation—couldn't quite recall.

Where was my book of Nietzsche? Winona never would have touched it.

Had Van Ness come here, and found my wife comatose, and put the pillow over her face? And held it there for a long time, until she was dead, and then gone on to violate something—please be sensitive to this, it's not absurd, please *feel* this corrupt truth—and then descended the stairs to violate something delicate and precious by stealing my Nietzsche?

I called out: "Winona?"

I looked around the living room. Nothing seemed disturbed. In the kitchen half a cup of coffee on the table and a scattering of mail, junk mail, and off by itself an envelope with a folded card jutting from it, a Hallmark card presenting the portrait of a little girl cuddling a dog. Inside on the left-hand page a printed cursive read "Just Thinking of You" and on the facing page in my own father's weak hand:

Since you don't have the care or interest it would take to pay me a visit, here's a letter for you. I mean to cut your name from my will and testament. Everything goes to my boys but they can't hack up the redwoods. Meeting my lawyers next week. You might as well clear out of that house, it's Junior's. And don't come sniffling around here at this late date. Once I say a thing it's solid.

I'd hardly begun to make sense of this communication before another one caught my eye—a postcard, the same kind Van Ness had mailed me—"Greetings from Santa Cruz," where the ferris wheel meets the ocean and seems ready to glide into that gigantic blueness.

I turned the card over. The message read *Now we'll see*. No postmark. He'd carried this card here in his pocket, and laid it down with his hand.

The spasm that wrenched me knowing that he'd actually entered this house set loose a spray of images inside me, bits and pieces blown above the forest, the forest of dreams—I'd walked in a dream through these rooms, but their walls had given onto other places, a ramshackle barn full of strangers who claimed I should know them, and I lied, saying that I did, and in that place this very tabletop had upheld a pile of fruit. It was impossibly strong, nauseating, violently so, the sense that I was both remembering and experiencing this, that I could, if I just stood still and collected myself, predict the next thing to happen in this kitchen.

According to the plan, the point of my being here was to discover the body. But I hadn't considered that I'd actually have to *discover* the *body*. This was no theory. I was living it.

"Winona?"

The silence sank me. Told me that Van Ness had lived it too. And Winona had felt his hands on her throat—or, no, the pillow against her face—or dreamed a cloud had come down and drowned her. What had Winona dreamed? What had Van Ness felt? What is it like? Who are we really?

Had she known it was someone, a person, doing this to her? It seemed only right that even in a dream, even in total blackness, even in drugged dreams, we'd know the truth if we were dying.

A man walks into the house where his wife may lie murdered. And realizes that he's twisted his life so badly that only this, the worst thing he's ever done, could twist it back the other way.

"Winona!" I scream, and it echoes beyond the window, puny and garbled, down the arroyos and out to sea. I can't bring it back. The name just disintegrates over the waters and that's that. It's impossible to bring it back!

Through this feeling of helplessness suddenly burst a piercing nostalgia for the lost world of childhood. The way it came right up against the heart, that world, and against the face. No indoors or outdoors, only everything touching us, and the grown-ups lumbering past overhead like constellations. I can feel the big silence upstairs

Already Dead ▪ *131*

getting bigger. There's nobody there and I'm not going up to see. Because I can't move. I'm small and my hands and feet are too large. Tonight's music was the moans of Gyuto monks and their smashed cymbals and rattling broken instruments and the unearthly squalling of their horns. Madness at first, adrenaline nightmare, nothing to grip, zooming madness, voices, a hundred thousand feelings, grief and regret chief among them. I've plunged into the water and I'm sinking, sinking. Memories roll over me. Italy—Rome, above all, Rome— pigeons lit up in the sunlight—and I saw the buildings in their dirty greatness but I kept thinking Keats, Keats died around here someplace . . . In Italy I felt closest to Winona, particularly in the churches, where I felt the farthest from heaven. In the cathedral in Milan I looked upward through twenty leagues of failure to the beautiful dome above. A bomb going off couldn't have hurt that silence. Everywhere dripped the blood of stained-glass martyrs, too many of them, we'll never get them sorted out. When we toured the duomo's basement, a region that seemed to pre-date even its stones, something in the ripe, must-filled cloisters seemed to have gone out—not a light, but a time. And something about those skinny moldering rooms of deteriorating jewelry made the whole cathedral somewhere above our heads seem a lie, the pomp dissembling over the darker miracle worked in the streets, in the spermy churches of apartment flats, where lovers in their beds were getting high, or spilling toward the Sea of Love with eyes grown soft and blind in loused-up situations. Miracle!—your incense followed the blond American woman to Sicily, to the town of Monreale in the altitudes, and I, her husband, followed you. And felt myself erased by the cathedral . . . fading beside the flowers . . . This church in Monreale was smaller and more to the point. On the walls and ceilings, from the making of our wild, tearful earth to the martyrdom of Saint Paul, they've laid out Christian history in a billion tiny tiles . . . You have to drop money in a slot to get the lights to go on—as grand as all this is, it operates on the principle of the honky-tonk jukebox. The electric lights brighten and darken according to the random coins the faithful feed the meter box, and in the dome Christ's concave face, the world's second-largest mosaic portrait, lights up overhead, looks down awhile, blacks out again. It doesn't matter that the church's curators are niggardly. Nobody goes there who isn't crushed by its beauty. In those vast religious places, as here, now, in life's deepest abyss, we feel a plunging sexual vertigo. Is it any wonder that later, exploring secret passages in the church's eaves, when we came out onto a parapet and found ourselves staring at half of Sicily and the ocean and the sky, I suddenly wanted to make love, right there in the daylight, to Winona? She said no. But later said she wished she *had* let me take her, in that high place overlooking a Palermo that seemed dreamed, with underneath us the massive mosaic Christ going on and off, Christ blooming and failing—

All right. In my breast pocket, a phial of Nembutal—replacement for the phony stuff, the Zieline. I turned, walked steadily through the house and up the stairs to the open door of Winona's bedroom.

A man climbs the stairs toward the room where his wife lies motionless. His feet tread the vacancies of starlight . . . I flipped the switch at the top of the stairwell.

She lay on her right side, her back turned, her right arm flung behind her as if reaching toward me. Not Winona, but a corpse, a thing. Nothing worth looking at. I stepped into the room and stood beside the body but I was still alone.

I pushed open the double windows and looked out onto the dark pasture. No stars, no moon, no wind. Just the head's unbelievable racket.

Something, a leaf or an ash, drifts down in front of my vision. No. Have I just seen a night bird drop dead out of the sky?

It strikes me suddenly that birds must actually, sometimes, die in midair. I've never seen this truth before—that sometimes they must enter heaven having lifted themselves halfway there. It seems such a little thing to understand, but I start shaking. I'm afraid if I try to touch something I'll pass my shimmering hand through the mirage of my life.

I moved the chair from her desk and sat down beside the corpse and closed my eyes and looked at blindness. I would do anything to undo this.

I have made a mistake.

What could be more trivial and irrelevant than this true fact? A few plain words—over all of this the phrase came floating like a sports headline, FLYNN HURLS SEVENTH STRAIGHT, on the destruction of a maelstrom: steeples and living rooms and drowned puppies and little dolls, whole lives washing down out of sight, then a line of old news turning in the current: *I have made a mistake.*

I'm sorry, meaning, *I want another world*. Give me a different world.

I leaned over the bed and looked down at her for a moment, an incomprehensible moment, trembling, hollow, insane. Not a moment, but a life. Not a sentence to prison, but a prisoner's life, not a moment of slavery, but the life of a slave. Converging darknesses like black cotton clouds . . . I hadn't taken her life, but my own.

I have never done anything real. There is nothing to get back to. Everything I am is shit. Everything to do with me. Everything I've made. All I have.

I touch her arm. She *is* substantial—I look down at her face in profile. But this is nobody I know. I'd never seen her before. No mistaking it. I've thought often that this person, this Winona, couldn't possibly be my wife. Now I know.

I'm not going to do anything wrong. I can't have done anything wrong. I have not done anything wrong.

Before this moment I'd lived as a mind. Body, heart, soul, intellect, so we carve ourselves into parts. But the whole of us, what can it be? We'll never name it. Before this moment I'd depended on the head, on thinking my way out of trouble, and when there was no way out depended on the head to tilt and revolve and distort until it found a new, a transcendent perspective, or a cheap rationalization for my shames, I didn't care which.

Intellect rampant on a field of ice, now it plunged through and froze and sank down to the heart in its cage under the North Pole. Will you believe me please if I tell you that the nameless whole of me had arranged all of this—just to break my heart?

A man walks into the room where his wife lies murdered. And begins to realize that only this could have saved him. That this, the worst thing he could possibly have done, was his only hope.

And then something stuns him like a blow to the neck. What is it? The phone! It rings and rings . . .

He won't respond. Won't touch it. Won't, *ring*, won't, *ring*, won't— two more and the machine would answer.

But *she* answers. Turns over. Reclaims her outflung arm. Fumbles with the telephone. Clears the death from her throat with a rasping sound.

"Hello?" my dead wife says.

Then says my name: "Nelson?"

Then lies back on her pillow, lets loose of the receiver and says, "Dear?" . . . This time she's calling out the word. Groggy, sightless, calling out because she thinks I'm far away. Calling me dear because under the water of dreams she's forgotten that I don't live here, that we're not close.

Dear—it can mean cherished, beloved, close. It can mean expensive, hard-won.

A man arranges to have his wife killed. (These things actually happen, tragedy does sometimes turn one particular night in people's lives into a crashing metallic thing, and sometimes that this tragedy has been *willed* makes all of it majestic.) He walks into his former home because he's arranged to be the discoverer of the body. Then the telephone rings. Then the corpse answers it, holds the phone out to the murderer, and calls the murderer dear.

He fakes it, takes the phone, clutches it in his hand.

She's fallen instantly back to sleep. Out cold, not a muscle twitching. You can't see her breathe. You could easily think she was . . . but yes. You certainly could.

He puts the receiver against his ear.

The voice of his brother says, "I have terrible news."

A small fierce rain began. Van found himself standing in it beside the Volvo's open door, looking into the dark leather interior, completely distracted, his heart thudding with aftershocks. He'd looked right into the man's face: his eyes like tunnels and a wild animal lurking in a stench of fear way back in there.

The joke had cosmic dimensions. But who was the joker? The trickster. Van made a mental note to get hold of a tarot deck, he seemed to remember a jester or some similar figure among its symbols, and then he forgot all about it as he supported himself by hanging on to the car's open door and a wave of nausea and hilarity crashed over him.

Threads, only threads, nothing more than threads—the curtain between this life and the sweet core, he could nearly push through it, it was down to threads.

The physical sensations accompanying all this—blasting, shaking, wrenching—had a completely unexpected intensity: he'd do it again soon.

*   *   *

Already Dead ▪ *135*

N avarro was stark naked, Mo was, too; still he could feel the badge.

Mo's place lay above Anchor Bay, up the hill and overlooking the stores. It was damp and chilly out, but they had a fire going and a sleeping bag wrapped around them.

He liked her because she was happy. "Jolly," even. It remained to be seen, though, who Mo really was. Sometimes people pulled out a whole new personality after sex happened. He'd been known to do it himself, and in fact he felt this might be one of those times. He was drug-out and lonely around here, starve-hearted. It was too easy in that frame of mind to start yanking on her like a security blanket. The worst thing about being a cop was the fear of disgusting somebody if you acted like a scared child. You get naked, and that's when you really start to feel the burden of the invisible badge.

They'd finished making love and were just lying around, halfway watching a porno flick. "Black women don't do it for me, usually," he said. "She's okay though."

"Are you against black people?"

"Me? Hell no. I'm more against Mexicans, if you want to know the truth."

"Isn't Navarro a Mexican name?"

"A lot of Americans have foreign-type names."

"I'm wondering. Why'd you decide to be a cop?"

"*Dragnet*," he said. "They show the reruns every day in L.A."

They watched two couples humping in the same bed and listened to their soft, unconvincing cries.

"Brunettes turn me on," he said.

"I'm glad to hear that."

"I could do without all these dicks, though."

"The dicks aren't there for you, hon. They're there for me."

"I know where there's a real one."

"So do I."

Her thinness worked better when she had all her clothes on, but he really didn't mind either way. She had the laughter and the sweetness of a fat girl. "I like your muscles," she said.

"They come in handy."

"Did you ever beat on anybody? Are you that kind of cop?"

"Not around here," he said.

"What about down in L.A.?"

"I was never accused of excessive force."

"What does that mean?"

"I thumped a few, yeah."

"But that's illegal."

"A couple per week, probably. Thump 'em if they jiggle . . . I'm not talking about attempted murder. Just a shot with the truncheon. It's kind of like punctuation. Makes it so you're understood."

He drew her closer and then with one mind they decided to open the sleeping bag and let the fire's dry warmth play over their sweaty bodies. He turned his attention to the TV, to camouflage the sweetness he was feeling.

"Everybody does what they have to do. Sometimes you've gotta stab your sister and get sent to Quentin and get kicked to shit by the guards and raped by guys with diseases, you know, and shut down in the hole for sixty days and nights. And if that don't do it, the poor sonofabitch'll just have to go get some more for himself somewhere, because this is what I believe, everything you get laid on you you asked for it, because you want it, because you need it."

"You just don't ask for it right out loud in your mind," she said, "yeah."

"But most of us don't get half the hits we need. One life won't hold that much horror-show, sometimes I think."

"That's what the next lives are for. And the ones you had before."

He got up on one elbow and jostled the coals with the poker. "I think we're leading into some nonsense here," he said.

"Then what are you saying?"

"I'm just improvising," he said, "to be polite."

"Oh."

"I don't like to screw somebody and then just lay there quiet."

"Oh."

"Like I'm sulking or I don't like you or something."

"I'm sorry. Did I fuck up?"

"No. No. No."

"Oh."

"All that's happening is I'm hanging around in your bed, because I like you."

She made an attractive circle of her mouth, opening it around a word that couldn't be spoken or something like that, a certain hesitation in the feelings before she said, "Oh. I like you, too"—liked him more than she wanted him to know, he could see that.

They lay quiet on her sleeping bag by the fireplace on the big dusty-smelling rug. Maybe he whiffed some cat piss there from a long time ago, he didn't care. He liked her too, and he felt serenaded by the mist outdoors sprinkling the trees and ticking down out of the boughs, low sighs from the fire, tinny sound from the porno movies, surf huffing and breathing below the cliffs way down across the highway. He was sadly content inside this smoky warmth, especially with the windows open a bit as they were, admitting cold fragrances on the wet wind, the little evergreen smell, the strange thin rotten smell of continually wet bark. It was generally kind of intimate, he found it all very sensuous.

They turned the sound off on the TV. She had a good stereo, and there was something playing now with just one acoustic guitar. He could hear the click of the flatpick and the instrumentalist's fingers squeaking across the strings. With the fire's hiss and the dampness down this close to the sea, you'd almost think it was drizzling.

He watched her while they made love. She lifted her legs up high on either side of him. It was beautiful, but everything she did that he liked—moaning a little, clutching his waist so tightly it almost hurt, holding him still against her when they were finished so he wouldn't get away too soon—he'd done it with somebody else before. He'd been around too much. He didn't get off like he used to—in fact sexually he got much more voltage out of watching triple-X rentals and jacking off. What really moved him about all this was her skin, and the way tonight it seemed almost to be raining.

He liked her belly better, somehow, than the bellies of young girls way back when, in high school and just after. He liked the still-soft but definitely older skin in the crook of her arm. It wasn't that the young ones had had less beauty, but he hadn't quite appreciated, hadn't tasted, hadn't savored. Now this woman was here and the others were gone. What a sadness, like watching things riff past with that half-happening feeling from the window of a train.

A man on the screen masturbated over an Asian woman's breasts and spewed jism while the woman raised her head from the pillow and watched, lapsing from fake wild passion into true interest, curiosity. Then she lit herself up again and started smiling furiously, signalling some unidentifiable emotion. Oriental women turned him on.

Mo lay in his arms, her head hurting his collarbone a little, and with one finger touched the sweat pool in the hollow of his chest. He smelled wood smoke in her hair.

They were all the way back to the caves again, when there was nothing to say. The blue shadows around them seemed friendly. The TV glittered like a sheet of ice. Everything was here.

"You can be quiet," she said. It was just the right thing to say.

"Do you feel like all this happened before?" he asked.

He came awake and heard himself asking, for no reason he could name, "What time is it?"

He heard her struggling out of the sleeping bag, and then the heels of her hands squeaking on the floor as she crept off the rug and found her watch.

"Just about two. About ten of."

He rubbed his face briskly. His beeper was going off. That's what had wakened him.

"It'll be the hotel," he said.

The drunks weren't happy to see him just when they wanted to get behind their wheels and crawl home. But often they misbehaved at last call, and he had to show.

"It's above the sink," she said, watching as he felt along the wall in the kitchen area for a lightswitch.

This time of night all calls were forwarded to the sheriff's dispatcher in Ukiah. He sat at her kitchen table with the phone and punched in, holding the receiver between his chin and shoulder and getting his socks on as he talked.

"Are you going?" she asked when he'd hung up.

"Yeah. Somebody croaked."

"Who?"

"A Mr. Fairchild Nelson."

"You mean Nelson Fairchild?"

"Yeah, some old guy."

"No, he's young."

"Well, he was old enough to go." He had his outfit on and was strapping on the holster, reaching for his beeper. "Can you turn those tapes in for me, honey?"

"They're triple-X!"

"Drop them in the box. Go real early in the morning."

"Well—"

"Because they're not rewound yet and I'm already gone," he said, making for the door, limping because one shoe wasn't all the way on.

He opened the door and stepped back. "Hey, it really is raining, actually."

"Yeah, it's gonna gust right in here if you don't shut the door." She knelt by the hearth and wrapped the sleeping bag around her shoulders.

"It's roaring right down."

She came and stood beside him at the open doorway, which was now suddenly a wall of wet. She took a breath to speak, but then just inhaled the rain's overpowering perfume.

Almost a year later, after it was all over, the drought of half a decade broken, the Iraquis decimated, his latest love affair a faded remnant—but before he'd quit in confusion the Point Arena Police—Officer Navarro sat one dusk on the wooden bench in the Anchor Bay laundromat while his clothes revolved, and he tried to sort through a mess of pages that he considered to be strong documentary evidence explaining events of recent history— the Fairchild thing, that whole tragic business. And anybody else would have agreed with him, outside of a court of law. But nobody else, as far as Navarro could tell, was interested.

Next to him on the bench lay the envelope he'd found the pages in, a white ten-by-thirteen mailer from the California Board of Franchise—the state tax people—the mailing label of which bore the name of Nelson Fairchild, Jr., now Xed-out and replaced by two names written, Navarro assumed, in Nelson Fairchild's hand:

TO:
Winona Fairchild
Carl Van Ness

For days he'd been combing through these unnumbered sheets, but he couldn't quite get them into a sensible sequence. Going by the first and last words of each page, he'd arranged them in several bunches, each of which seemed to be in order. He was aided in some sections not so much by the syntax as by the shape of the brown stain along the right-hand margins. And then what must have been the end page actually written in blood—as if Fairchild had dipped a quill in a vein to record his fading thoughts. But Navarro couldn't make a coherent whole out of all the separate parts . . . *the devastating force with which*, this one began midsentence,

the devastating force with which I am now this. Why do I think of lounges where black guys in mink coats softly worry the ice in their drinks? Films where the rotting corpse lifts up its hands? There are bars full of girls who do not want to be whores, they want to pick and choose, to fall, to find the shallows of love and be squandered. And who am I? Girls with tears in their eyes and bus station grime. Drove south some weeks ago to San Francisco, what was I running from, nothing escapable certainly. Getting down there I drove fast, on the Jenner cliffs I nearly took to the air, not a suicidal thing but something more in honor of my powerful car. Then soon—

Navarro had been in the habit of driving down here from Point Arena after work, nine miles, had done it almost daily, and for half a year, to see Mo. But that was over. And actually Mo didn't work across the street anymore. Still, he didn't feel like visiting the Full Sails, a place draped with cruel memories.

He blamed the spirit of this region for that. And for lots more. Certainly for the trouble with Mo. But above all for something coming loose in his own soul . . .

So he sat here with the handwritten pages he'd read and shuffled obsessively since discovering them he didn't know how many days ago—long enough, now, that he knew he wouldn't be reporting the find—in the Silverado with the camper shell and the two dead dogs inside it.

Then soon coming south into Marin County, first the bulky towers, sagging power lines, there's something elderly about them, and the last rural thing I saw was one farmer by the road, somebody who could have been my grandfather, except for this man's olive-drab oversuit, which is just what Grandfather would be wearing if he'd lived to see these modern, incomprehensible times: dressed like a mass murderer he stands in the vineyard facing the Frosty King near Novato as the fields at their edges crumble into clouds, a sign that says SEEK YE THE LORD and the smell of piss and shit from the dairy making lonelier the angles at which the planes of noon light lean . . . Everything gets kind of emerald down in Marin, and then the Golden Gate Bridge, and after that I just get tired. Frisco. Frisco. Frisco. They hate it when you call it Frisco. I can't abide our beautiful cities, not even our San Franciscos—the scourge of smells—joints with greasy doorknobs—air brakes coughing and whooping—gargoyles and doo-dads on all the buildings—down every sidewalk crawl little bits of trash. But that day I should have felt exalted. South of Market the porno-shop windows gleamed like the windows of cathedrals. Inside, a cartoon sexuality under fluorescent lights, videos of glories gone wrong (Yes I've been in them but I didn't find you, or anybody I ever wanted you to be).

And then Army Street with its flat-faced, secretive hotels, the pauper's breath of its doorways, stinky old men in the parks, unrepentant winos standing on the corners like figures in a parable. If only I could decipher them. No I don't want to. Ultimately all these old men turn out to be somebody's father. And how frighteningly old he's become, each one of them. Ultimately all these old-men thoughts turn out to be aimed at the matter of my own very ill probably dying dad (as he was that day, but now as *you* know all too well, no longer). And the faces, the faces, the faces: the murderous faces of children and the innocent faces of old men, the happy faces of the dead (Yes, and I want to tell you about that, I did actually see a dead person later that day). The planetary faces of gluttons. The faces of the rich sealed and locked. Also don't forget the day-old immigrants with their stupid clothes and suddenly useless life histories and their faces like broken toys. I should have seen the beauty in their stares. The religion. Instead I parked and bought a newspaper right away because you can't hide from them anywhere but in the movies.

Then I loitered with the newspaper at that restaurant where we saw the saxophonist, the breathy pissed-off one you probably don't remember but who astonished me, the tough broad, the tenor. That time we found her it was Jam Night or some such—a pickup group offers up an aimless jazz among cigarettes, our souls glinting and glimpsed in our plumes of smoke: our weird phony smiles, our bright exhalations—various semiamateurs trying out their moves, many of them talented but none like her. Remember how she extended her solos with reluctant widely spaced honks and quacks that made her seem disgusted? And I sensed in that a true cherishing of the art expressed as a loathing for her own attempts. And I've been back there once afterward with Melissa because I enjoyed it so much with you. Just as I've given Melissa poems I wrote for you and presents I bought for you. But in the morning it's not a den of jazz and smoke but a sort of washed-out student place with a lot of I presume unemployed younger Chinese from Stockton Street and Clay Street. I wondered if I'd see the sax woman, find her surfacing with her cigarettes and coffee into the day, and I hoped so because I was so happy with the way she would with distaste in the manner of a thirties cinema belle kiss another and then just one more despairing note from the thing. But of course she wasn't there, neither was the clarinet crying that it's hopeless, or the alcoholic muttering cornet—

Where was I? Oh yes: assaulted by San Francisco, looking for a film to hide in. I opened the paper, turned to the entertainment part, and when I read the double-page ads for new releases I felt a thrill in my soul, so many wonderful movies, the critics were amazed, according to the testimonials. Poets of the age! hack off your tongues. The impression dawned that we'd entered a dazzling era—this week, this single week, would glow in racial memory—and I shared it all, was in fact dazzled, you know how I respond to those ads and feel cheated later in the dark by all the fakery. But it doesn't matter. Nothing can help us anymore. There's no escaping the contradictions: but only here, at the movies—window looking out on the home from which I'm exiled—land where people look in one another's eyes feeling the words they say. That's what I wanted in life, still want, I want blue light on their breasts, wet sorrows, endnesses, endnesses, death after every satisfaction—

(Nobody was enough. Not Melissa. Not for long anyway. And never you, Winona. But you knew that. I just wanted to live as long as possible coursed through by that electric intoxication)—

I can't tell you how ordinary everything seemed at the fourplex movie house, or, I don't know, fiveplex—but this is important. Everybody moved, waited, ruminated, conversed—at the popcorn or the tickets or the advertisements or the bathrooms—the same as always when I paid my money for a courtroom drama, because I like the talking in those things, and headed through a little traffic jam near the drinking fountain. And I stepped into this group and almost tripped over the legs of a woman lying on the floor in their midst. A dead woman. Such revelations in the parted crowd!—I hadn't thought anything hidden here, certainly not this corpse of an elderly female with its blouse torn open and its gray-green face, not these two or three paramedics, one of them holding an IV jug up above the dead old woman's head, another bending to put a pair of those small hand-held flatirons against her breast and jolt her with charges from a small portable defibrillating machine. I caught a glimpse of worried faces, a middle-aged daughter and a son-in-law, I believed, and I turned away. Everybody had turned away. The lobby went on as usual. Out of a general, a profound, an aboriginal politeness, we went on in fact much more usually than usual.

Submitting to the same instincts I went into the bathroom and washed my hands . . .

Five minutes later, when I came out, the group around the woman had moved back a little. One paramedic was speaking to another while glancing at his watch, and the second, crouched there with a clipboard resting on his knee, wrote down the time.—Jan? Jan?—a third was saying to the victim, who sat up now looking at him with not much more than an animal in her eyes,—Can you hear me, Jan? Can you hear me?—They'd brought her back to life. Can you hear me, Winona? The dead woman was alive again.

And that's not all that happened in that theater that day. In fact I witnessed a panic in the darkness just minutes later. But I'm too tired to tell you about it. Enough to say I got my money's worth at the movies, and then I called Louise. Precisely as I used to walk to the pay phone when I was eleven and call her and say,—Mom? It's over. Come and get me—I dialled her number now. She met me at a tea-room, where I watched her eat Welsh rarebit. She works in a prison you know. She still loves Father I think. Also, maybe more so, the booze: on her cheeks and nose the trailing burst capillaries (I'll have them too before it's over) like faint grape stains. She's so fed up with herself she often pretends to be someone out of a book, copping monologues right out of Jane Austen, Dickens, Jack London . . . like me, a reader and a drinker. Especially fond of the introductory lines, when someone first appears on the stage. She probably puts on a whole new self—more real? or more false?—to go to work at the joint. Five days a week bossing lady criminals around, most of them nymphomaniacs, most of them abused a hundred ways since birth, most of them only half awake. I can't imagine what she does there but I sense without being able to explain why that these are the happiest and most worthwhile days of her life, I sense that she's helped people. Her blind hands groping to find their hands. Everybody lost together behind great cold walls.

Anyhow she's different. I don't know who she's turned into. In the laughing presence of the woman she used to be my father would throw me, his weightless toddler, toward the ceiling over and over, but always eventually too high, past any point of thrilling, and in anticipation of a crash I'd clench my whole body, as I did here and now in the tearoom, at teatime . . . The transience, the flight, the unbelievable rushing away of everything that looks so stationary, it's breathtaking, any old chair can stand there exactly like a chair in the field of my perception but nothing it's made of is where it was when I started one millisecond ago to perceive it. And so with this woman. Vague, vague! What happens to people, what happens to our mothers—our brothers and wives—what is being done, for God's sake, to the people we love?—No, this is nobody I've ever known. This one is sixty-five, still in many ways as energetic as she was at thirty. But she's got it all right, she's got it, that smell of defeat and confusion and rosewater and hovering angels. The florid atmospheres accompanying old women. They bring to mind the death of apple blossoms. The partial, nonessential deaths in orchards—fruit and flower but not the tree—the child who dies by growing up—the perpetual death of everything standing in this moment, all these items that pretend to hold still but are in fact, in fact, only known to us because of the unbelievable commotion, the chaos, of subatomic particles that are not particles at all, not matter, but energy, process, thought, conception, the enacting imagination of the thunderous intelligence that obviates the Great Void, the Void of Eternity—

Seeing a woman dead on the floor. Seeing her brought back to life. Why should a murderer be granted this privilege?

But anyway, excuse me, I'm not talking about her! I'm talking about *you*. About betrayal. About the fact—which I hid from you— the fact, the poignant hidden

Navarro looked around the Laundromat. His dryer had stopped turning, and he guessed the silence had summoned him.

Holding the pages in his lap he thought, aching physically, right in his heart: what could be lonelier than trying to communicate?

There were many more pages here. Navarro had read them all, more than once, and he would read them again. He could probably prove that this was Fairchild's handwriting, but without Fairchild he couldn't begin to prove anything else. And Fairchild was gone. The guy had sunk without a ripple, been missing for nearly a year.

Navarro couldn't quite remember Nelson Fairchild's face now, or much else about him except that Fairchild had been tall and very shaky. Navarro had met him just twice, first at the father's house—the night of the old man's death—and they'd hardly spoken either time. That first night the brother William had been there too, a woodsy, philosophical-looking guy with a beard and extremely pale blue eyes. Going only by their writing styles, Navarro would have guessed wrong as to which brother was which. Nelson junior had seemed a lot crazier than the author of this letter sounded, while William, the nutcase, had seemed much calmer than his wild communications. But nobody acted typical on the occasion of a death. It hurt a little to think back to that night, because he'd taken the call not two hours after he and Mo had made love for the first time. Then there'd been a storm. Not a long one, as he remembered. The wind had wrung the rain out of the clouds within minutes, and by the time he'd found the Fairchild place—overlooking the ocean, with the windows glowing warmly at 2 A.M., signalling tragedy—the squall had worn itself down and the drive over had mopped all the water off the squad car. He shut the Caprice's door and stood beside it a minute noticing how the gusts had softened to breezes. The weather had blown out to sea—he could hear it like a distant orchestra—and what was this, now: somebody else coming?

A cartoony little sports car pulled into the driveway with its head-lights jiggling the way a Porsche's will, and a lanky breathless citizen got out saying, "Good evening, how do you do," while pushing past.

Navarro followed him along a line of several other cars and into the house through the door of what turned out to be the kitchen, where an elderly man in crisp blue overalls sat at the wooden table, writing on a pad and puffing a cigarette. "Why wasn't I called!" the new arrival shouted at him.

The man kept one finger on his notebook and looked up and back and forth between the two of them, as if unsure which one had spoken. "Weren't you called?"

"Well, when did it happen? I mean, who was *here*?"

"Just Donna," the older man said, and then shouted, "Donna!" while vigorously stubbing out his smoke.

He reached into an orange kit bag on the floor beside him and took out a small bottle with a rubber diaphragm over its top, the sort for keeping injectable liquids sterile. He raised it up three inches before his face and, peering closely at its label, jotted some more notes on his pad.

Navarro was used to taking charge at the scenes of crimes and accidents. But as far as he could tell this was not one of those. He cleared his throat and removed his cap.

"Be right with you, Officer," the man said, and finished writing and set the bottle of medicine down.

"John Navarro, Point Arena Police. Would you be the physician?"

"Henry Schooner, M.D. Everybody calls me Doc. I requested your presence," the doctor said.

"And you must be family," Navarro asked the other.

"I'm sorry—how do you do, Officer. I'm Nelson Fairchild," the man said. And, after a breath, added, "Junior." He addressed the doctor: "Is my father really dead?"

"Yes," Schooner said. "Donna found him about eleven, when she thought he was calling for her. But by that time he was well gone."

"Well *gone*? What does that phrase mean?"

Schooner said, "It means cold. He was cold to the touch. Donna!" he called out again.

"Well *gone*," Fairchild said.

"What's in the bottle there?" Navarro asked.

"Morphine sulfate," Schooner told him.

"Was he in pain?"

"Considerable pain, for certain. He had colon cancer and refused surgery. But this is the only bottle he had, and it's full to the brim. Donna says she never administered any. He wouldn't take it."

Navarro figured this was Donna herself coming downstairs and into the kitchen, a woman in her late middle age, freshly groomed and dressed, gripping a hairbrush and gazing at the three of them with her comprehension running about ten percent. "Excuse me—

yes?" she said. She seemed at that moment to discover the hairbrush in her hand, and she laid it on the kitchen counter and looked at it. Navarro had seen hundreds of people in this state of mind in the middle of the night at the end of someone's life.

"Mrs. Fairchild, I'm John Navarro of the Point Arena Police."

"Winslow," she corrected him.

"Winslow?"

"Donna Winslow," she said.

Schooner said, "I was telling them how you found him, Donna."

"I heard Bill at the door and woke up and went upstairs," she said. "I thought it was Nelson calling me. But Nelson was gone."

"*Well* gone, in fact," Fairchild said, and then said, "Excuse me, boss," helping himself to one of the doctor's Camels. Navarro realized only at this point that Fairchild must be quite tipsy if not completely wrecked.

"Ms. Winslow, did you say somebody was at the door when you woke up?" Navarro asked her.

"I think Bill's around here someplace," she said.

"Bill," Navarro repeated.

"My brother," Fairchild said, and asked Donna, "Where is he?"

"He *was* out back," she said, "cutting up a doe." She looked around among the three of them, but they said nothing. "Otherwise it'll turn," she added with an apologetic air.

Navarro leaned over the kitchen sink to look out the window and down into the darkness one story below him, where a man in a raincoat entered and left the dim ellipsis of an electric lantern, butchering a deer. He had the carcass stretched out on boards between two sawhorses, with a heap of skin on the left and entrails on the right. Navarro believed he was making small sounds with his voice. "Hm! Hm! Yep!" For the joints he used a machete.

Now Navarro smelled sour wine—Nelson's breath, in fact. The tall man stood at his shoulder shouting down, "Bill! Will you get up here *right away* please? For Christ's sake."

"Would you excuse me now?" Donna asked. The men looked at her expectantly but she said no more, neither did she leave the room. She turned a chair sideways from the table, drew a paper sack toward her on the floor and put her feet flat on either side of it, reached in and began the process of snapping string beans, tossing the stems into the yellow trash can an arm's length away. For about thirty seconds they watched her, until she paused and asked, "Should I be doing this?"

Schooner put his hand out across the table, a friendly gesture that didn't quite reach. "If it comforts you."

"There'll be people around tomorrow, and they'll have to eat." She resumed snapping the beans.

The brother turned up at the kitchen door now, minus his raincoat, which hadn't kept blood from spattering his T-shirt. He pressed down the latch with an elbow and wrestled the screen door open with the toe of his boot. Navarro moved to hold it open for him. Nelson came a step forward as if to offer his brother a sentimental embrace, but stopped short; and so did William, with his gory hands upraised to keep from smearing things.

He said to Nelson, "I was on my way here. I felt it coming. I was seconds too late."

Navarro gave him a nod but got no acknowledgment. So this was the W. Fairchild whose letters, the latest addressed to Navarro personally, took up three-fourths of the "Federal" file at the Point Arena Police station. W. Fairchild stepped to the sink and turned the tap carefully with his pinky finger and started washing up.

Nelson stuck his face in his brother's face. "A doe, did you say? I thought you wouldn't shoot a doe."

"I didn't. It was dead by the road."

"Why wasn't I called right away?"

Bill turned off the water and looked confused and said, "Winona's was the last place we tried."

"Found me in the last place you looked?"

"It was the last place we thought of."

"The very last place!" Nelson seemed to be smirking. He started to laugh, blushing deeply at his own inappropriateness and then giggling all the harder, finally clamping his fingers across his mouth, but the laughter blew out his nose. "Fuck me! I'm so very sorry!" he said, coughing and snuffing back mucus and fumbling over to the sink, where he yanked at the handles and splashed cold water on his face for a full minute, gradually calming himself but giving out with an occasional hysterical-sounding bark. The others didn't know what to do but watch.

In a moment he asked his brother, "Am I getting this? You came here, found out Dad was dead, called the doctor, and went to collect a deer? A dead deer? Went to collect some roadkill?"

His brother was suddenly animated. "Look, asshole, we tried everywhere. I called the Sheep Queen and the bars and the pizza joint and anyplace that was open. I drove over to your apartment—that's what I was doing when I grabbed the doe. Doc told me it was down, I spotted it, it looked fine, so why not. It's edible meat."

"Is it? Then what the hell! Let's eat!"

"Nelson," Doc said, "I hit her coming over. So he went and got it. That's all. So settle down."

"Are you one of those people," Nelson asked the doctor, leaning over him, "who think they know what they're doing but really don't?"

His face was three inches from the doctor's. Schooner could only lower his own gaze. "Show some respect for the occasion," he mumbled, clearly embarrassed. "Show a little sensitivity."

Navarro couldn't stand it. "Maybe I'll have a look around," he announced, talking mainly to the woman. But she didn't get it. "Ms. Winslow? I'll need your permission, if you don't mind."

"That's fine," Donna said.

"It's just a good idea, when there's been a death, sometimes," Schooner assured her, standing up now from his seat.

"That's just fine," she repeated.

Navarro followed the doctor through the living room and up a staircase with a turn in it, then a few paces along a hallway and into a lightless bedroom that smelled of age and illness.

"The cancer started in his colon." Schooner turned on a bedside lamp. The corpse lay in a hospital bed with the blanket drawn up over its head. Schooner gripped the hem, flipped it down to expose the face for a second—Navarro was looking elsewhere, looking around the room—and covered it over again.

"Why am I here?" Navarro asked.

"Well, he was out of bed."

"At the time of death."

"Yessir, just here beside the bed, they tell me."

"And who put him back?"

"The son did—Bill. And Donna helped, as I understand it."

"Does that seem suspicious?"

"Nah. Your time comes wherever you are. He voided in the bed, but there was also urine on the floor. He was often incontinent," Schooner explained, "but he refused to be catheterized."

Navarro spoke with a certain gruffness that generally worked to cover the kind of confusion he was feeling right now: "I don't make the deduction here. I mean about urine and so on."

"He was pissing his bed, started for the john, and dropped dead on the floor. And finished pissing."

"He had colon cancer, right? You got a specific cause?"

"Something coronary, probably."

"Heart attack?"

"Nah, there wasn't enough heart left *to* attack. It just ran down and stopped, more likely."

"Well then, but—"

"He had about eleven holes in his pump."

"But what about the colon thing?"

"That too."

"So, cancer, heart—shouldn't he have been hospitalized?"

"*Should*'ve been, definitely. Should've been in CCU the last six months. Should've junked three yards of lower intestine. Should've been hooked to a gallon of painkiller."

"And you wanted me?"

"If he dies out of bed, yessir."

"Because you're not sure as to cause?"

"Because I had a lot of trouble on one of these many years back. So now if anybody under my care goes down while away from his or her bed—well."

"You don't just toss him in a casket and say adios—not unless I sign off on it."

"Right. Roger that, as you men say. But if you say so, I can have him in the funeral home in forty-five minutes."

"On the other hand, if I tell you to ship him to Ukiah for an autopsy, which might take—how long?"

"Which might take a week or more, and would certainly lather up the relatives—"

"Right. I'd take the heat."

"I guess taking the heat is partly what you're paid for."

"Almost entirely what I'm paid for, I've been thinking lately."

"Well, give yourself a raise," Schooner said.

"Yeah. Roger that."

Navarro wandered over to the window. It was wide open, and a little rain had wet the sill. He listened to the sea, realized he wasn't coming to a decision—wasn't even thinking, if the truth were known. "Well," he said, "let's hear what the wife thinks."

He stood staring at the bed as Schooner went out to stand at the top of the stairs and call down for Donna Winslow. By the small round depression in the bedclothes covering the corpse's head, Navarro figured that at this moment Nelson Fairchild's mouth was wide open. Navarro felt a brief, crashing vertigo. Nothing to do with corpses, because he'd seen plenty, but more to do with the force, the jolt, of suddenly remembering that just an hour ago he'd been making love with Mo.

He noticed the electric cord dangling beside the mechanical bed—the button that worked it up and down. He reached for it, held it in his hand, and would have indulged a sudden macabre impulse to make the corpse sit up and the shroud fall away from its face; but he heard the others on the stairs. He stepped away from the bed as the doctor came back with the woman of the house, Donna Winslow.

Donna Winslow took three steps into the room, looked at her lover's shape under the sheets, and sighed.

"Did he like the window open?" Navarro asked.

"Sometimes."

"Even in the rain?"

"I don't think the storm started till after . . . so no one noticed."

"Dr. Schooner says he was on the floor when you found him."

"Bill and I found him together. Something made Bill come," she said, "in the middle of the night."

"And this is his urine here, right?"

"Oh," she said, grabbing a box of tissues from the bedside table, kneeling—"oh, let me just"—and she sopped it up with a succession of wadded napkins, tossing them in a wicker wastebasket, while the two men stared down at her.

"Who put him back in bed?"

"We both did. Bill did mostly, I guess."

"Here—maybe we should adjourn to another room," Dr. Schooner suggested.

"In a minute." Navarro knelt by the bed and picked up a pillow from the floor beside it—bare, no slipcase. He asked the wife, "Would you have been the only one in the house around the time of"—he sought a word other than *death* but couldn't find one—"when his time came?"

"I was alone downstairs."

"Did you strip this pillow?"

"I don't think so," she said.

"Where's the pillowcase? Any idea?"

"The pillowcase?"

"Just curious."

"The hamper's in the bathroom. That'd be the logical place, I guess."

"Could Nelson have put it there? Did he have the strength?"

She came closer to the corpse and pulled back the sheet to bare the astonished death mask—blue-gray, openmouthed, with deep-sunk, wide-open, porcelain eyes—and said, "This is Nelson Fairchild, Sr. He could've done anything at just about any time. If he wanted to right now he could probably jump up and spit in your eye. There'd probably be no truer epitaph than that."

She didn't replace the blankets until Schooner cleared his throat and said, "Thank you, Donna."

"Let me just peek in the bathroom a second," Navarro said.

"Whatever you have to do, Officer," she said.

Schooner directed him across the hall, and he went into a small chamber and found the lightswitch and then the clothes hamper. Among the musty pyjamas and towels, all of which felt like artifacts because in them lingered the life that had just been lost, he found the pillowcase. Holding it up before the light, he examined a patch of half-dried saliva and mucus in the center of the white material, of a size and shape, he would have wagered, that nearly matched the corpse's open mouth. He bunched it up and threw it back into the dirty laundry.

When he came out, Donna Winslow was gone. But Schooner was still hanging around. "What's all this about a pillow?" he asked, following Navarro down the stairs.

Navarro shrugged. "Details, details."

"You want him cut up?"

"Do you?"

"I asked you first."

By now they were about to enter the kitchen, to which Donna Winslow had returned and where she now stood beside the table, pouring out cups of coffee for the two sons.

"I don't see where it's required in this case," Navarro suddenly concluded.

It stunned him that he had said it, because the statement ran straight up against his duty and training, which at a time like this required him to initiate all sorts of procedures. He was almost sure the man had been murdered.

What had him stalled was the added certainty that this had been a mercy killing. Probably perpetrated by this poor tired woman.

"I was seconds too late," the younger brother said. "Something's gonna be missing forever. At the end of time it's all gonna come up short!"

It occurred to Navarro that the younger brother could have done the killing. But everything he knew about people told him this one wouldn't hurt anybody intentionally.

"Would anyone like some coffee?" Donna said.

"No. Thanks. I'm going," Navarro said.

The older brother sighed and stared at his coffee, his hands circling the cup and his arms stretched out straight. Navarro could see that it was hitting him now, everything attending the death of a family member. Guilt. Relief. And a white curtain over the future.

To Donna Winslow he said, "I'm sorry to intrude on your grief. We're satisfied he passed on as a normal consequence of his illness."

"I'll call the mortuary in a minute," Schooner told them all. "Let me just see the officer to his car."

Outside, Schooner held the car's door as Navarro got in. He rapped with his knuckles on the roof, basically a nonspecific gesture, one that might have meant, *case closed*; but maybe not, because he failed to shut the door. "I guess you can see for yourself this is a colorful bunch."

Navarro said nothing, and hoped the doctor wouldn't say too much.

Schooner took several short breaths, as if suffering a spate of indigestion. "Look," he said finally, miserably, "it's my signature that goes on the death certificate. If this family gets a notion, they'll be in everybody's hair till Judgment Day."

Navarro coughed. Cleared his throat. "You bet."

"They think they're important. The old man's famous up and down this coast, a big property owner, sort of a semisociopath. I knew him well, and I can tell you that most of the rumors you'll hear about him are true."

"Who owns the property now that he's dead?"

"I couldn't say for sure. From what I know of him I'd guess most of his holdings go to his sons, the lunatic Fairchild boys. Donna wouldn't— I mean to say, I doubt if Donna . . . "

"She doesn't profit from his death."

"No," the doctor said.

The dawn seemed ready to light up. Navarro hadn't realized he'd been here that long. Perhaps it was an illusion created by the ocean's phosphorescence or something like that . . . He sat back in the seat, feeling tired in a cranky, unpleasant way. But all in all, this hadn't been so bad. He'd seen real killings, occasions where he'd reached the blood half a block before he met the person it was flowing from. "Well," he told the Doctor, "tag him and bag him, and let's all get some sleep."

"Fine."

One of the brothers had just come from the house. "Gotta go," Navarro said.

"All right, sir. I'll get him shipped out."

Navarro said goodbye and headed north, away from Gualala, toward Anchor Bay and toward Point Arena. In his rear view he saw the Porsche leave the drive and turn south.

Nobody had complained about the lack of an autopsy. Navarro could have promised the doctor they wouldn't hear a word from Donna Winslow . . . though now, today, he knew his reasons for believing that had been completely wrong.

Thinking back on it now, Navarro wished he'd found some excuse to show up at the funeral. No reason it should have occurred to him at the time, but if he'd come around the Catholic cemetery in Manchester that day he'd have seen the whole crew in one spot, the living and the dead.

He shuffled through Nelson Junior's letter, looking for the part about the funeral—if he remembered right it started on a page winding up the description of one of Fairchild's boring, pointless dreams, but finally for once a dream in which Fairchild had been feeling good, everybody had been joyful and content—

content and having fun, and I'm not annoying, I'm comic. It's happy, pleasant—some part of me must be that way. But I don't want to meet that part. Why should a man who's plotted murder dream happy moments?

I haven't been damned by dreams. Haven't had dreams that fall into the classes described in the Talmud, prophetic, oracular, therapeutic, spontaneous, provoked, and so on, or dreams where long-sought answers come, answers that disappear at dawn—Wait, it suddenly comes back to me that Mother was at the dream's periphery. I can see her but not her face, now let me think, basically she's dressed as she was at the cemetery, in fact I see now that this dream is a reprise or a revision of Father's funeral. Curious as hell that you never met her. I really don't think you recognized her when she turned up at the service and didn't say a word. Sorry, turned *up*? No, she was an apparition, she signaled that all the prophecies had been accomplished, her gown was blacker than if it had actually been black, if it had actually been a gown.

You, Winona, or anybody who happens to make such arrangements for me: I want a plot in the same graveyard, the Catholic cemetery south of Manchester, there by the sea, at the end of the world. Not because my family's in it but just because it's such a pleasant grove, with that long soft grass and the giant kneeling cypresses whose prayers have outlived all the griefs and crimes of the people beneath them, and the cliffs from which probably their souls plunged out after their funerals into the endless cycling of the water. Nice to anticipate getting buried in a place where you wouldn't mind, actually, residing in life.

Did you know Dad's was my very first funeral? We weren't invited to our grandparents'. Nothing for a child there anyhow, what's to experience, basically a static display around an open grave, almost like Christmas but with a coffin instead of a manger and a pile of dirt instead of straw, a kind of reverse Nativity scene composed mostly of people you haven't run into in a while—I guess, in the case of you and Mom, people you've never even met. But there was only one total stranger there—Father himself. He'd worked up something to amaze us all! He'd turned himself into a thing in a box, he'd accomplished the ultimate refusal. Of course we all knew he'd have arranged his own service, the cheapest one possible, practically nothing to it, and almost nobody welcome.

And what about William, did you get a load of William? All dressed up with that self-inflicted haircut and that suit from Hell? He looked like Stalin-Goes-to-Church, I mean you'd have thought he not Dad was the one worked up for the occasion by some unaesthetic mortician's helper. He did however appear calm. Let's give him that. Three nights before, he went quivering through the house insisting that he'd gotten some sort of telepathic summons from dying Father. Balanced beside the chasm of schizophrenic relapse, man, I thought he was going over. And what I wouldn't give to see him now and talk with him and hear him set the gibberish rolling out of his brain. I'd take him by the ears and kiss his mouth . . . Now I see he never grew. Nobody does. We stay children and only the pretending and the games and the dreams grow old. Billy. Billy. It hurts!

Well, at the funeral I couldn't have looked any less embalmed than Bill did I suppose. I started out that week blockading myself the usual way, with wine, but it didn't work right because of the increasing awfulness of the hangovers. Woke up the third day, Funeral Day, with my soul hollowed out.

Then the funeral, with Mom coming uninvited and the two wives looking at each other across the abyss of this guy, this black hole in our lives who never let any light out of the horizon of his immense gravity. Donna didn't throw her arms around my mother, but you saw as clearly as I that each respected the other's right to be there. It spoke well of our father that he'd chosen two women capable of trading respect—didn't it?

Father Tom orated monotonically, stoically, without shame. Priests! Once they had spine. Drove such as my father from the doors of the churches, held them off with shotguns on Sunday morning. Does gracious acceptance have them admitting every sinner nowadays, or is it apathy, hypocrisy? Donna hadn't called him to the deathbed. He'd dropped around the mortuary next morning and unctioned the corpse. So Father Tom with his birdlike face and perplexed eyes sprinkles a few verses over Dad while out there in the ocean Carla Frizelli drifts unforgiven, unconfessed. And then he left us, his coffin swaying on canvas belts over the void, lowered over chromed rollers onto cheap green felt by two drunkards in aluminum hard hats. I'd seen one of them in the Tastee-Cone just outside Point Arena once, talking trash with a little girl. She couldn't have been ten years old but she was puffing on a cigarette. Then they stepped back, the two diggers, so we could line up to toss down dirt onto my father.

No thief ever beat him, no enemy, no rival. His children he put in the same category as thieves. Detractors, partakers, leeches, swine. He withheld, defended against us with fire, tossed us slop. Well, give him this much: death didn't just walk up and inhale him. He wasn't exactly whisked away. He left claw marks on his life.

I guess you know Mother didn't talk with anybody at the funeral, not a word. But you don't know she didn't speak afterward either, not even to me. I stood beside her looking out over the ocean. I'd watched him shrink away. I'd learned how much bigger the sea could be. But she was getting it all at once—how endless the world is without him! I'd seen her like that once before, out back of the Blue Whale Motel where we lived for a while when I was seven, maybe eight, and back then, as now, I stood beside her a few minutes until she turned and wandered off along the cliffside. There is something ineradicable about a woman walking into the wind. Everyone remembers their mother at this most unmotherly moment, her hair behaving like a cloud. And seeing it at any time afterward returns us to that motherless feeling. I believe in beauty. Especially in these moments that make us children again.

Naturally the whole time between the death and the funeral had been crazy, spent phoning innumerable people and getting phoned by innumerable others—Beethoven's *Waldstein* Sonata (no. 21 in C Major, opus 53) the nervous urgent silent-movie *allegro con brio* part, I love that phrase, *con brio*, connoting brutishness—mainly I telephoned lawyers because I wasn't waiting around for any formal reading, I wanted it straight, had my father actually willed my entire share of his estate to my wife? Oh yeah. And had he died before he could change the document? You know the answer to that one. And what about the ten thousand goddamn acres? He'd put in what's known as a "timber clause," deeded it in, from now until forever the place would be a kind of zoo for big old trees. My wife and brother owned all of it now, all of it. Of course I co-owned half with my wife, but only until she divorced me. Unless—before she could arrange a will that prevented my owning it after her death—I brought about her death.

But you don't understand, Winona. I didn't want to kill you. Not anymore. Not since the moment I stood beside you thinking I'd done just that. And can I ask you now: were you actually sleeping? Anyway you don't understand that in the dark bedroom that night I wasn't gloating but wishing you back to life, realizing I didn't want you ever to suffer the moment of your death—still don't, still, I really don't—and coming to love you perfectly. I mean selflessly and with disinterest as only the completed unapproachable dead can be loved. Because that's what I thought you were. I'm even compelled by his death to love my father that way. Even though the stripes stay fresh, those wounds—I can feel them all over me, I can see them on Bill, almost spelling words, a thousand scars—he not only hurt us but with a certain careless cruelty taught us to carry on hurting ourselves after he stopped. And I love him.

You don't know about the last thing that happened that night, I mean the night Father died, and you won't believe me when I tell you, why should you believe me, I've always been a liar, but anyhow little Winona do you know this one stretch of the ridge road where it narrows and in April the beautiful purple trumpets called naked ladies bloom right along the edge for about a half a mile? I started crying so hard that right at that spot I was forced to let the car head off the asphalt. I must have crushed a hundred bloomless naked ladies as I pulled to the side of the road.

Before long I had to ask myself what the hell I thought I was doing there. It was so dark I couldn't see the dashboard, much less the world outside, if there was one, or had everything lapsed back to a formless pretime ungeometry with nothing in it but a lowing sound, small, far-off, agonized, as of something dying or being born? And what exactly *was* that sound?

Behind me the fog brightened and brightened, until the huge aurora suddenly burst and shrank to the size of two headlights. I waited for the vehicle to pass and pull the darkness closed behind it, but it didn't pass. Very near to my car, about a hundred feet behind me, it slowed down and pulled to the side of the road. Its headlights went off. Then nothing. It just sat there in the dark.

In a minute I believed I saw the brief glow in my rearview mirror of the other's dome light. But I couldn't make out any sound of the other's door opening or closing. I wasn't sure if I heard footsteps or not. I didn't turn around and look back. You know how the back roads at night unease me. It feels like hallowed ground. In Mendocino County so many beings seem to be awake when everybody should be sleeping, beings creating themselves, stirring and boiling and mumbling their prayers, sex-slayers and sacrificial maniacs, Jesus-wants-to-kill-you polygamists and Christian cannibals . . . Treefrog Jenny the castrator lived for years on the Boonville Road. And in West Point, you remember they found those seven skeletons in a single grave? And whoever dug that grave may still be living back here, may be awake tonight . . . Now I heard the footsteps coming. I jammed the pedal, cranked the starter, flooded the thing, had to wait there lame. On the other hand, I felt ridiculous. This could be some roadway Samaritan, this could even be some friend of mine, somebody coming to help the helpless. Or to destroy the voiceless. Because I knew I had no voice. Like one of those dreams where you can't scream. I could barely grip the key and turn it in the ignition.

Then the car wouldn't fire, and wouldn't fire, and wouldn't, and in a sort of happy torment I ground the starter till the battery gave out and then I let my heart break for every failure, for every bit of shit, and especially for us, for you and me. You see, I was on my way back to your place. I wanted to tell you what I'd just discovered about love—that in fact we need another word for it now, because this one we've maimed and crumpled, trotting it out to express our cheapest passions—all right, I admit they're not cheap, these passions, sometimes they exact an astonishing tribute—but they fade, they—look at it this way, they shoot up like miraculous fountains but dribble away into mud. And I wanted to promise you that these feelings, my lust for Melissa, my fever for the land, the timber, the money, they aren't love. But now I was broken down and sobbing in my bullshit machine with the future lovely flowers mashed beneath my wheels because I couldn't get to you. Now listen. Way down there's something I long for. I don't think for you it's possible to comprehend how I wish for this thing, how hungry I get sometimes for this thing I can taste on the wind, when the night carries a sweet teenage music, for a whole history that can't be mine, a tale of you and me: I'm baffled by school, I play the guitar, I work at the Texaco. I find you on your mother's porch. You wait for me while I'm in the Army. Sometimes I can feel it sliding by me like a twisted self in the house of mirrors, and I realize *that's* my life, and *I* am the distortion. There is the world, and here is the mirror. Here the car won't work and my father lies like granite in his bedroom and the wind scrapes against the grass and the moon goes down leaving such darkness I can't see my way to walk, and a stranger steps toward me on the road. And the rain that left everything so wet and cold hangs out over the sea in the night miles away with its ghostly tuba and faint horns, playing for the dance of the dead.

And who was the stranger made of shadow? Who came to my car

and put his hands through the window and touched my skin and said *what's the matter?*

The killer. Your killer. That is, the one who *should* have killed you.

—I wasn't even sure you owned a car, I said.

Please excuse me a second . . .

The old proprietor just interrupted me elbowing at the door with an armload of kindling and busted up my mood. You might recognize him darling, I'm staying at the little joint where we stopped a year ago last Christmas—or the one before that?—in the very same room, with the fireplace and the ratty bear rug and the stuffed trout on the wall. The same old boy still runs it, still lives and breathes, still refuses to take that cigarette out of his face, meanwhile frowns at my ascending amber tower of empties. The wheezy old moron. He dislikes me because I suggested that by the look of the pelt maybe his bear had been hunted down with ack-ack. I'm special that way, capable of making a lifelong enemy with one anemic

Navarro loosed more dimes into the dryer's slot.

The light outside was dying, and so he could see himself reflected in the window. He looked like a man in a Laundromat, but he felt like a man in a darkness, man standing in a tropical sports shirt and brown slacks way down at the bottom of a hole, his strongest identification now with another man who was probably dead and whose words floated slowly past on these pages. He hoped Fairchild hadn't died. He hoped . . . but he knew. And yet he couldn't have said for certain *what* he knew. In the blackening Laundromat glass Navarro saw the picture of a guy who would never know what had happened during a period roughly between the start of August and the end of September a year ago—particularly the first two weeks of September 1990—to a group of people Navarro couldn't even be sure about the composition of, but which included the Fairchild brothers and their father; also Winona Fairchild, and Carl Van Ness, and certainly the witch and "channeler," Yvonne. And possibly one other person who'd also been missing for a long time, an associate of both the Fairchild brothers, maybe a confederate or cohort—a local surfer by the name of Clarence Meadows.

Book Two

September 2-5, 1990

Around one in the afternoon a dozen or so miles short of the Bakersfield cutoff, just after making the long decline from Wheeler Ridge, Clarence Meadows took a ramp off Interstate 5 and headed into a Coco's Restaurant in the shadow of the hills for one of those prefab lunches. Lunch with the sheep, as he thought of it. He'd gotten a late start out of Long Beach and wouldn't make Gualala till midnight anyhow; another thirty minutes wouldn't matter. And the car's radio didn't work, and he wanted to get an update on the real bad news from Kuwait.

He bought a paper in the restaurant and sat at the counter drinking a Pepsi and looking things over: the hostages were leaving Iraq; U.S. troops still poured into Saudi Arabia.

As for Clarence, the whole idea of ground combat disgusted him. If they refused to make peace, let them use the atom bomb. That was honest warfare.

He laid the paper down and unveiled the squinting face of the man sitting two stools away, who must have been trying to read the back page. Their eyes met. "Here we go again," the fellow said.

"Another Sunday in paradise," Meadows agreed.

"No—I mean what's happening in the papers."

"I wish it was happening in the papers," Meadows corrected him, "but it's happening somewhere over there for real."

"You think we'll get all the way into it?"

"Yeah."

"A real war?"

"Yeah."

"For oil?"

"When it comes to the price of gas, we'll nuke the Vatican if we have to."

The fellow ran an unusual kind of salvage business. He bought old computers in bulk, he told Clarence, and broke them down and hauled the pieces to Southern California. "An obsolete computer's worth zip. But there's a hell of a market for some of the gizmos inside." Up in Montana he had three airplane hangars full of the stuff. "Hey. You should see my hat," the guy said, but then failed to explain why or to display anything in the way of a covering for his head. Clarence found the Montanan's manner soothing. There was a whiff of snake oil about him.

"You do just the opposite of what I do," Clarence said.

"You build them. You build computers?"

"No, I mean I buy junk in L.A. and put it back together up north. Classic cars."

"Where do you sell them?"

"Back down in L.A. It's really just a hobby."

"And what do you actually do for a living? Can I ask?"

"No," Clarence Meadows said.

Meadows was driving back north from L.A., having sold a car for Bill Fairchild and bought this junker and set up deals to sell the dope, his and Nelson Fairchild's, after it was harvested. Nominally the bartering was Nelson's thing, but Meadows happened to know a couple of music people in Long Beach, and he didn't see where the arrangement with Nelson was etched in steel.

Fifty or sixty miles north of the Bakersfield cutoff, Meadows pulled to the shoulder long enough to twist a piece of coat hanger around the brake's linkage, up near the firewall, because the pedal was rattling insanely. While he was down there under the dash he noticed two wires dangling, evidently chewed through by corrosion—he touched the ends together and heard the radio burp. He spliced them with a twist of his fingers, and now the speakers put out a flow of static that sounded promising.

When he raised his head back up to the level of the window, it mystified him to see something like a blurry cliff standing over the planet, bulging enormously in its middle, resembling nothing so much as a mushroom cloud and taking up the horizon's entire northeast quadrant.

What had happened, as he began to understand now, was that a colossal wind had lifted the desert half a mile into the air and kept it hovering there. The dust storm didn't seem to be moving. But he realized that it must actually be approaching fast. Quickly he rolled up the windows.

His main concern until this minute had been the running condition of the car, a Mercedes 190SL, a beautiful old thing but mistreated, with an unsteady carburetor and a tendency to blow oil out through the manifold seal. Now all of that seemed very secondary as the wind slammed across the road ahead and the car seemed to dive into darkness. Right away he was lost. He couldn't even see the pavement. Despite the tightly shut windows he tasted dust on his tongue. It itched in his nasal passages, and soon it made his eyeballs feel parched. He messed with the dials on the radio. Nothing reached his hearing but the faint voice of his engine and the fluttering of the wind, a very deep, suggestive sound. He let the car angle gradually to the right until the tires on that side commenced a steady shuddering. He didn't quite stop, but kept his left tires where he could feel the smooth pavement, the right-hand tires bumping through the dirt, and figured that this way he must be cutting straight along the shoulder, inching ahead so slowly the speedometer didn't register while the car's inside heated up and the dust and sweat turned the steering wheel all grimy. The drifting desert earth smelled old and untouched.

A white Cadillac materialized on his left and drifted past and faded away like a thought.

It seemed lucky now that he and Billy Fairchild had agreed in advance on a sports car. Otherwise he'd have brought his surfboard along, it would be sticking out the window at this moment, and he wouldn't be able to shut out the dust. As it was, he was packing a bowling ball and a trumpet and the accoutrements for other hobbies he'd suddenly been seized with a desire to develop because he'd been feeling very much at loose ends. He'd made the drive down just last week; within two days he'd sold the '38 Hudson he and Billy had restored, reinvesting the seven hundred profit in this wrung-out antique and performing temporary wonders on it to the degree, at least, that it was now rolling him north. This old Mercedes would be impossible to restore unless they got a line on parts. So what? Billy would be happy just contemplating it among his other pitiful monsters, not one of which he read as a failure.

In Clarence's vision Billy Fairchild, over the last couple of years, had taken on real stature because when it came to self-reliance, Billy was an actual instance. He had his episodes, but he'd learned for the most part to separate his spirit from the diseased part of him, the head, which produced the worthless thoughts. Every once in a while he jagged a few days on coffee and wrote letters to the president and screamed in the woods, but did it matter? Witch doctors behaved similarly. It was part of what made them valuable. Meadows felt he'd rather have a mad hermit defending him than a lawyer owned by credit-card companies. To find the people who've become truly sane, seek among those who've managed to do without sanity. The rest of us, Meadows thought, just brainlessly acquiesce.

Moving forward in first gear, Meadows decided he could travel on in this fashion indefinitely, groping ahead blind and strangled. Which was fine except that it too closely resembled life in general.

Again on his left, he passed two cars stopped in a kind of embrace, the huge intimacy of which he felt almost embarrassed to be witnessing. It didn't look too serious an accident. The cars' owners stood out on the median, one man scrutinizing the wrinkled bumper of his vehicle and the other craning, searching the little limit of visibility for . . . and then Meadows was past and the whole thing absorbed by the amber twilight, sucked up as by a sponge.

Off to the right he saw, occasionally, other things, a wavering milepost, a green unreadable highway sign, a stretch of faded fence. Fascinating the way each seemed to jump up solid, hover there, and then dematerialize like a smoke ring. Taken in sequence they seemed to want to say something, to act as the grammar of an emptiness that was trying to deliver some sort of coded hieroglyphic message.

As best he could figure, the squall had been boiling westward when he'd cut into its path, and somewhere in the middle of it he'd left the desert and crossed into the irrigated farming region of California's Central Valley. He started to see implements of modern cultivation, machines as big as houses only with giant, silly wheels and innumer-able claws. Visibility improved. The cloud was not so much night now, but rather fog, with startling bands of sunshine falling through it here and there. He swung past a row of three shabby orange biplanes, crop dusters tied down beside a field. The wind seemed no longer as loud. The storm had passed. But all these obscuring clouds of stuff it had unsettled would stay in the way perpetually.

Clarence shifted into second gear and picked up speed. He'd been two hours making the last dozen miles. Another twenty minutes and he could expect to reach the hospitality of the Regis Ranch, accord-ing to an advertisement shimmering in the dust, an electric sign that not only welcomed him but celebrated this as the nation's largest family-owned beef-cattle operation. He began to sense something other than dirt in the air. The storm had all but smothered a pun-gency which he'd often noticed in this region and which, now that he'd seen the billboard, he realized must come from the ranch's slaughterhouse. He'd been smelling the blood for miles.

The ranch had probably operated here for decades, but only in recent months had these billboards—and now a titanic yellow mar-quee pulsing above an exit ramp—sprung up to proclaim the place. Meadows took the ramp and pulled into the parking lot. The wind had died completely and the dust and afternoon sun brewed an exotic ocean of layered nectars, plum and violet and indigo, shot with streaks and cleaved by the shadows of hills.

The Regis ranching family, if that was in fact the family's name, had decided to found a regular oasis here, with a hotel and a restau-rant and several boutiques. And pumped it full of money, he gath-ered: things had a grand but tasteful feel, hand-hewn wood and adobe like cinnamon and a spaciousness that felt very western—elbow room all over inside, also a big, quiet feeling generated for the most part by a sense that nothing would ever happen here. Retail commerce had overlooked the Regis Ranch. The stink of distant butchering, just a whiff but still perceptible even indoors, might have had everything to do with that.

Meadows wondered if he could scare up some trouble in the bar, but it was huge and he found only the barman there, looking more forsaken than any of his customers would ever feel.

Suddenly aware of how played-out and grimy he was, Clarence went farther down the concourse to rinse the dust from his face in the men's room, which by its size and decor could easily have been the train station in a southwestern heaven. Blue tiles in sprays and arches gave it almost a pre-Columbian feel. Mostly it was adobe— russet, sound-absorbing, serene.

In there he found the computer-salvage guy, the Montanan, standing at attention before one of the urinals: unusual things, ceramic-tiled bowls something like the bidets Meadows had seen years before in Lebanese hotels. "You again!" the old gent said. Meadows only shrugged by way of a greeting. The Montanan had taken off his overshirt. Now he stepped over to his kit bag by the sinks to don a green silken one of a fancy western cut that seemed tailor-made for the immediate environment. After spending some time brushing his hair energetically in several directions, without any apparent idea what the hell he was doing, the old man seemed satisfied. "Remind me to buy you a drink one of these days," he said to Clarence. "And, also, I forgot to show you my hat. You'd get a kick out of it. You know," he confided, "I kind of like your style." Clarence wore distressed canvas deck shoes without socks, baggy madras shorts, and a UCLA sweatshirt with the sleeves torn off because it was too small in the shoulders, small enough altogether that a strip of his belly-flab showed beneath its hem; also a green BP baseball cap; and so what the Montanan might have meant by Clarence's style remained unclear. The door shut behind him and Meadows pondered the question as he stood alone before the squad of urinals, the sound of his piss jingling in a great and terrible and enchanted and holy silence.

At the sink he removed his BP cap to wash himself and confronted in the mirror a brown face with the line so sharp and the skin and hair so clean above it he looked scalped. He stood for a long time whapping the dust from the hat on the sink's edge.

Meadows had taken a parking space that put the nose of the Mercedes two feet from the side of the building. When he got back to the parking lot, he discovered a big lemon-colored station wagon blocking him from behind. Its driver had backed right up against the bumper of the Mercedes, possibly without having noticed the smaller car, and now the station wagon sat there with its rusty hood raised.

A young woman in a black dress stood beside it, reaching awkwardly into the driver's window with one hand and, Meadows guessed, turning the key in the ignition. But without any luck.

She stood up straight when he approached—a secondhand black

evening dress with, he now saw, red roses on it—but the awkwardness didn't disappear. It seemed her natural state. Her car was tilted too, with one front tire smaller than the others. "Hear that?" she asked Clarence. "It's just this gah-dam click-click-clicking—oh dear Jesus forgive me for swearing. First the battery won't keep a spark n'more. Got to jump her every time. Now this," she said, kicking the fender, and then laughed.

"Let me take a look."

"Ah! You're heaven-sent."

"You got me boxed up. I don't move till you do."

Meadows looked under the hood, surveying the engine for anything obvious before actually popping the distributor cap to see if she was getting a spark. The woman hovered around him saying, "I can't think why it won't start right up. Usually she'll sit an hour or more before the juice runs out totally. Maybe all this dust plugged something up, do you wonder?"

Meadows thought he saw a wire dangling down below the chassis from a junction that ran to the solenoid. Out of reach, unless he crawled under the car.

Looking around for a piece of cardboard or something to lie on, he came face to face with a child staring out the back window, a black-haired kid about four, a boy, a Latino maybe, though his mother, a blonde, looked and sounded from the North. Junk, belongings, bedding surrounded the kid. You could see these people lived back there. That was all right with Meadows, but it probably made for a weary childhood.

What the hell, he was a mess anyway—Meadows gave up and slid under the car on his back and took hold of the dangling wire. It was just a plug that had worked free from its joint. He shoved it back into place, crawled out from under the vehicle, and turned the ignition, reaching in through the window as the woman had done. It started up instantly.

"You're a godsend, I knew it!" the woman said.

"I'm a generalissimo of loose connections."

"What was it?"

"These prongs are loose in this socket." Meadows showed her where. "You have any electrician's tape?"

"Nope."

"Any tape at all?"

"Sorry."

"It'll rattle loose now and then—just keep an eye on it."

They all had an early supper in the restaurant where she'd just applied for work. Meadows invited them. He felt sorry for the kid and also wondered if the mother, on such short notice, could be persuaded. Her name was Carrie. He liked her in that wild dress with the cartoon roses and those bright red two-inch-heeled shoes and nylon stockings that seemed a little loose. Her hands, intricately weathered, but slender and graceful, with blunt nails crusted under by dirt, kind of got to him. Sweet eyes but definitely not feminine—everything about her a little big-boned and angular. Yet not coarse. Just strong, just ready. She had little hairs above her lip whitened by the sun.

"You following the crops?" It seemed to fit the evidence.

"I'm down for the lettuce. Then back up to Washington for the apples. But I'm applying for waitress jobs."

"You have a green card?"

"You got me, eh? Yeah, I'm from way up there. Born and raised in the Canadian Yukon."

"The restaurants hire you?"

"I'm a resident. No problem there. My old man's U.S."

"And the old man," Clarence asked, "is where?"

"Down the road. Nobody knows which road. We keep him in our prayers."

Carrie hadn't met with any luck here in the way of employment. The restaurant was big, with red tablecloths and good Mexican food, but it was mostly empty.

Meadows had lost any sense of a schedule. The concept of direction itself seemed to be on the fade. He didn't mind following them across the interstate to the Seven Flags, a generally cheaper truckers' kind of place, and waiting with the kid while Carrie went inside to ask for work. He and the boy leaned up against her station wagon and watched a series of peculiar-looking American people fill their tanks out front of the Big Chief convenience store. Meadows sensed a species change unless he was mistaken. The sheep had retired and here came the others, jamming at the trough. This was the low-rent side of the highway, evidently existing before the Regis Ranch had set out its lures. Hog Heaven. Porkville. Oinkopolis.

"Get a good look at that."

"What?" the little boy said.

"Whatever happens to you, kid—don't let it be that."

"I'm getting in back now."

"Do that. Yeah. Whatever."

Carrie's little boy, it now turned out, had established a small fort in the back of the station wagon from which he ran a complicated imaginary war. It cut across the lines of space-time so that some of it was science fiction and some of it was medieval Europe and some of it destroyed the wild American West.

"Did you see the dust storm?" he asked Clarence.

"Yeah. Did you?"

"I'm making a gray thing," the child said. "He can talk."

"Good."

"He shoots."

The child had modeling clay under his fingernails as his mother had soil under hers. Probably she'd been digging in some of this earth right here surrounding them. The Central Valley was all farmland thanks to the irrigation, but up from it jutted various dead formations, craggy desert hills of the kind you'd expect to see biblical figures driven to the top of and whipped without mercy. And these big interstates were scary. Certainly people had built them but they had this aura of deep geological truth, they seemed connected to infinity, gave you the feeling they'd erupted here like veins of—

But here in his stunning green cowboy blouse came the Montanan out of the Big Chief suddenly, gripping a six-pack with his thumb and finger as if with tongs. "Hey," the man said, and jiggled the brim of his baseball cap with his other hand. "Hey—get it?" Clarence felt like asking the guy if he wasn't perhaps a faggot. "Check it out," the man said, stepping forward and pointing at his own skull. Now Clarence registered the hat, with black hieroglyphs on it, or Greek writing. The Montanan stepped back. "See?" But no, Meadows didn't see—and then he got it—the hat's label did a trick of optical magic: the man took two more steps backward, and the outlines disappeared over this little distance, the hieroglyphs resolved, and the shapes became a message: EAT MORE PUSSY.

The Montanan leapt into his pickup truck and drove away, pulling along in his wake a utility trailer soon to be refilled, Meadows assumed, with priceless digital junk.

Meadows visited the Big Chief himself now and picked up a six of

Colt .45 and some cheap wine coolers, thinking it was funny the guy would come along and offer him such irrefutable advice, and just when he'd been trying to remember his purpose.

The little boy crawled out and sat on the car's back bumper. They shared a patch of silence which the kid traversed by leaning over and trying to drip spit on a bug.

"Looks like you got brand-new shoes there."

"Yeah. Somebody threw them away."

"They fit?"

"They fit if I wear four socks," the boy said.

"What's your name, little dude?"

"Clarence," he said.

"No shit? That's my name too."

"I know. It's my name too," the boy said.

He swapped a Colt .45 back and forth with this miniature Clarence. Before it was half done the boy said he felt dizzy and lay down in back with his head on his arm. He had big eyes with unusual, almost purple eyelids and looked very Third World, very lost, in his clean tennis shoes.

His mother returned, declared she disliked wine coolers but happened to be thirsty, and drank all three. She didn't embarrass herself however. Meadows watched her eyes, waiting for that flat look, but it didn't happen. At most she got a little sparkly and maybe even a bit more attractive.

She inspected his Mercedes and noticed the things behind the driver's seat.

"What's that?"

"It's a head, a severed head."

"No. Really."

"I was gonna shrink it, wear it around my neck."

"Is it a bowling ball? It's a bowling ball."

"Shit, really? Hell, I don't think I can shrink one of those."

"Come on, now."

"I guess I'll have to take up bowling."

"Are you a serious bowler?"

"I'm taking it up."

"Come on!"

"No, really, I got this one for free and I'm thinking what the hell, you know—"

Denis Johnson ▪ 174

"Well, let's see it, then."

He unzipped the zipper. "Take it. Go on."

"Lemme get my fingers in—"

"There's a bowling alley in every town, just about."

"Back off, now!"

"Give her a roll, honey."

He killed his beer while she bowled across the blacktop. The ball, a green spangled Brunswick, collided with the Big Chief's Dumpster and then rolled up beside the building among some old crates, where it looked very precious and original. Meadows wandered after it.

She called out to him, "And what have we got here? A machine gun? A pool cue I bet."

"Oh, I'm sorry," he corrected himself, coming back to her, "this is not a bowling ball. I'm terribly sorry. This is a golf ball. So this here's the dealy, the whacker. The club. You screw this thing together—"

"This is a golf club?"

"That's—yes. A seven iron. Yes, Ma'am."

She swiped at the bowling ball with the butt of the pool cue. "Got a tennis racket or some such?" she asked. She reached through the window again.

"Now this—ah, ah, ah—don't touch that," he said.

She tried to open the trumpet's case, and he said sharply: "Hey. Goddamn it, I'm serious."

"Oh," she said.

He enjoyed seeing the uncertainty in her eyes.

"I'm sorry. I—"

"I'm just kidding," he said.

"Oh . . . "

"At the proper moment I'll play you something sweet."

She smiled and looked away. He'd sunk the mood.

Not that it mattered, but he asked again just to be asking, "And what about the old man, now?"

"Like I say. King of the Road. Hasn't been heard of for a year."

He tried messing with her a little bit, and she jammed up against him so hungrily it pinned him to the car.

"Well," he said when they broke free, "you feel hot enough to take to church."

She was licking her tongue all over his teeth in a surprising way. He couldn't back up, and so he slid sideways.

"The Lord sent you to me."

"If you wanna try this again sometime when we're sober," he said, "you got a deal."

"We got a deal now. Don't you feel it? Don't you feel the deal?"

"No, I don't," he said.

She changed the subject suddenly, started describing some scene, some mushroom-picking thing in Oregon. "There was, like, boocoos of people there. Mostly Cambodians from—they said they shipped them in from Seattle or somewhere. Whenever I found a spot with the little suckers popping up, then the other little suckers come popping up too, nipping 'em and sacking 'em up quick as they could grow. The buyers all complained they were picking 'em too small. But they were on those little fungus bastards, I tell you, just as quick as piranha fish."

With her hands she made two such fish, rapidly chomping, a gesture that broke his heart about halfway.

She was reaching into the car's window again. "What's this say?"

"Where'd that come from?"

"What's it say?"

"This?" It was the cryptic baseball cap, actually a brand-new one, still creased. He guessed the Montanan had slipped an extra through the window.

"What's it say?"

"It's in an unknown tongue."

The saddest truth about this person wasn't the car full of junk or the fact that she was broke or her future life of grubbing for lettuce or onions or walnuts. The saddest truth was that, for her, he was the only thing happening for a thousand miles and maybe for a thousand years.

He said, "Fuck it. Let's do a motel."

"Sounds pretty good to me."

As the bullets opened up his body the Lebanon of dreams went black, and Meadows found himself awake in the California night. Alive. But he smelled carnage.

He placed himself now: here in the bed beside the woman, Carrie, and not too many miles from the Regis beef ranch and its slaughterhouse. The breeze must have shifted. He'd been smelling it in his sleep.

For years this nightmare had visited him, but less and less vividly, until now it returned with the shapelessness of a distant echo. And it no longer came to him every night, but these days only when urged by a little something, talking about it with someone, or, as tonight, feeling Carrie's fingers touch the scars and then sleeping beside her with those same fingers brushing his knee.

A few hours ago she'd reached across him in the bed and said, "Close your eyes, Clarence . . ."

"What for?"

"I'm gonna turn on the lamp."

When she could see, she said, "Oh, Lord God—looks like somebody went at you with a half-inch drill."

"I got shot."

"By who?"

"An ambush in Beirut. And I'll tell you what, I wasted all six of those fuckers. They're dead."

It had been six—no—almost seven years; and still that fact was the one, among all facts, that made him happiest.

But the dream had all the feelings, slowed down as if for savoring—or maybe they savored him—that during the actual events had been smeared sideways by motion and soaked in a wondrous deafness. Clarence dreamed of driving in the open jeep across Beirut with the sunrise burning over his shoulder. He didn't know what they were heading for but they were heading straight toward it. This was a general scramble of hysterical proportions, anyway some brief, giant thing had torn into the day like a can opener, and none of the rules applied at this point. He rode in back behind Tom Rule. He could name the others when awake but in the dream he looked only at the back of Tom Rule's head thinking, "The rules don't apply," while dark buildings tumbled past on either side. This was exactly as it had felt in actuality, including also the deep dread—it was all around them because of the all-hands scramble, the Condition Red that might mean a nuclear war—this dread accentuated by the fact that even all the Lebanese cowboys had abandoned their posts, and in the dream the jeep was blasting right on past each checkpoint, although in the real experience they'd had to stop while somebody jumped out and pulled aside the rubber strips of nails the cowboys always laid across the road, and then the jeep screamed through, scraping its antenna under each lifted gate. Somebody threw mud at Tom Rule's head.

Then the back of his head came off. The jeep stopped and Clarence got out and found himself standing at the edge of Lebanon in a gigantic desert watching Tom Rule flop back and forth in the jeep as it pulled away. In life he'd grabbed the big L-60 as more bullets hit the jeep. He'd shouted orders that he be left behind, and moved, *as if in a dream,* firing rapid bursts, toward the orange barrel-flashes and flowery sprays of ignited cordite erupting from the base of a hedge on a dirt knoll before a gutted building. In the dream he just walked empty-handed toward these innumerable little flares shouting numbers and foreign words—enraged because he thought if he could only make himself clear, he could change the situation—and in the dream, as he had in life, he felt each bullet hit him. In life the bullets hadn't mattered. But in the dream it terrified him to feel his body opening up and the air and dust touching parts inside that should always have been sealed off. At this point, in both the dream and the life, everything turned black: here was the border between the two worlds. Often he opened his eyes believing he'd just come awake, now, for the first time since he'd been shot. In fact, during the first couple of years, he'd invariably felt that way, and it was also during this period of the first minutes after waking each night, while he walked around the room in a small panic and then showered off the sweat, that one by one the little details returned to his mind. Standing by the jeep, he'd seen Tom Rule's right hand move. He was convinced that Tom had felt something and was trying to lift his hand to his head, which was no longer there. He remembered hefting the L-60, twenty-five pounds of incomprehensible metal—Where was the safety? Where was the trigger?—its feed box disengaging as he hit the wrong lever and the ammo stringing away like a broken necklace. From that point he was moving, and he experienced events as occurring not in time, but in terms of bullets and inches. He'd never been able to recall anything of the next twenty feet, which must have included many bullets. He remembered, after that, kicking the machine gun's ammo belt leftward in order to straighten it. Then he was on the ground crawling forward and firing steadily. By this time he'd certainly been hit but couldn't tell where, and didn't actually care—he just wanted the weapon beside him, pointing toward the ambushers, and the strength to pull the trigger, and that was all. By the time he'd gone through fifty rounds he'd been hit again, more than once, but the L-60 had chewed up the knoll and the wall behind it, and he wasn't sure he was getting any return fire. He draped the ammo belt over his left shoulder, counted to three, and then stood up. He found that he could move forward, and did so. He leaned into the bullets as into a hot wind.

The doctors had said if you bet your life at roulette five times straight and the wheel turned up your number all five spins—he'd been that lucky. Although the doctors had routed his digestive tract out of a nipple under his armpit, they'd promised him it was only a temporary thing, and they'd kept their promise.

A week later President Reagan came to the area to weep among the dead. He came to lift the spirits of the troops. Clarence had been scheduled to get his decoration, the Navy Cross, from the president on the *Nimitz*, but his wounds had kept him down. Clarence felt sure the president understood. The president had been shot once himself—with how many rounds Clarence didn't know exactly. Clarence had taken four slugs from Kalashnikovs, three of which had been slowed by his flak jacket and ended up in his intestines. The fourth had hit his left seventh rib, spun alongside his heart without touching it and torn around inside his right lung before flying up out of his shoulder—he'd heard it whisper a word as it came up past his ear. The jacket had stopped several .223 Armalite slugs, but one had come in high, just above the collarbone, skidded down the sternum, danced through his stomach, and lodged in the muscles of his back after barely nicking his liver. Five bullets altogether, and an additional small laceration where a .308, possibly one of his own ricochets, had nosed through the mesh of his flak jacket to break the skin. He'd stayed conscious long enough to empty the ammo belt and locate the six motionless cowboys in the ditch behind the knoll. They were skinny kids with red-checkered scarves around their heads like all the other cowboys. He pried loose a Kalashnikov from the hands of the nearest and put insurance in the right or left eye of each one of them.

People said of a killing, "It was him or you," without any understanding. Because that's who it is, at the moment of killing. It's both. It's either one. It doesn't make any difference.

Right now he sat up in the bed, swung around, put his feet on the floor. Stared down at them a long time. He thought maybe he'd get his pants on and walk over to the quick-stop there, the Big Chief or whatever it was, and get some coffee and talk a little with the clerk. Sometimes that sort of conversation could bring you back to level.

But the abattoir's odor . . . He smelled the ripe taint in the air as if it belonged to something that had followed him from that time back, a physical something, the meat that had let loose all these ghosts.

Carrie lay on her side with her back to him, one arm sticking out behind. He took hold of her fingers gently, so as not to wake her.

He didn't think he wanted to screw this woman again. Not after this evening's entertainment, no.

The Lord stuff had been just a phrase or two on her lips before they'd made love. Then afterward it was dark and they were lying there together and he touched the space between her thighs and she shuddered, moved away on the bed, sighed almost as if with exasperation. He'd only wanted to put his hand on her crotch.

"Clarence: I read the Bible. And this is wrong."

"What?"

"I ask you. Can't you just feel all that wrongness?"

In fact, he'd noticed no such thing.

"It burns a hole," she said, "right down through."

"Yeah? Well well."

Well well—he'd wondered if she could be persuaded. And so she could. But, he guessed, not without making it into something cosmic. Also rapturous, tragic, et cetera. Anything but casual. Not that casual existed when it came to this kind of business. Boring and silly, or dramatic and painful. Those were the existing categories.

That was the moment when she'd reached across him to cut on the light and got him thinking back to that morning in Beirut. He'd started messing with her again, turned on by the passion, his own wounds, darkness, raw smell of blood, all of that. Carrie responded for a minute, but then she brought it around again: "Clarence, it's the Lord dealing with me. I don't know what I was thinking. Look. My life ain't mine."

She sat sideways on the bed, letting her hair hang down between her knees, a regular portrait of dejection.

"I believe I'll start smoking again," he told her. "It gives me something to do when assholes are going crazy all around me."

"I had to lose my life in order save it."

"Hmm . . . I can't exactly decode your shit."

"Look," she said miserably, "I don't belong here, I belong to the Savior. In your fancy flesh-world I'm nothing but a ghost."

"I respect that. Really, most highly."

Denis Johnson ▪ 180

"Get down and pray with me."

Together they knelt by the bed, both of them naked, exactly, Meadows suddenly devised, as you should be naked to kneel down and pray. Carrie reached her hands out before her across the mussed sheets and knotted her fingers together tightly. So Clarence did that too. He felt a draft on his ass. "Dear Father in Heaven, Lord of all," she said.

"Could we do this in silence?" he asked.

She whispered, "Sure."

And before a minute had passed, the silence had turned into a charged beautiful moment, and Meadows cleared the spit from his throat and said, "Hey . . . why don't you put on your high heels."

She said, "Okay."

And then they made love.

"Don't expect me ever to do that again," she said immediately afterward, before she'd even caught her breath.

"You are one spun-out monkey," he said.

"Don't you see? This is just a flesh feast."

Flipping and flopping. As quick as they turned him on they switched him off. "I tell you this in a friendly way, Carrie. I liked you the second I met you. But you won't be seeing much more of me, because you're dizzy."

"I understand," she said.

Then he'd slept, and been visited by the dream. And now he was awake and trying to shake it.

He felt better as soon as he stood up. He walked into the front room. He'd splurged on this two-room suite, but it was either that or leave Carrie's little boy out in the car by himself. The kid slept now on the couch before the TV, which was running, and on whose screen a weather woman paced sideways from one end of the country to the other, pointing at geography with a stick and smiling falsely, bravely, as if the weather was hopeless. Meadows sat down naked in a cold vinyl chair. The news came on. Not much today. The president planned to make a speech. The pope was in Tanzania. And a hundred American hostages had made it home from Baghdad. Meanwhile, Meadows felt like a hostage himself. Maybe he should get back on the interstate. He wouldn't sleep any more tonight anyway. If this was the eleven o'clock news, and if he left before the end of it, then by dawn he'd have reached Gualala. And would no doubt start designing reasons to leave.

They'd probably get around to it, but they hadn't yet passed a law against coming and going. He could visit two days in Gualala and then head back south. He'd stay up there just long enough to make sure Nelson hadn't starved the garden, and spend some time down in the woods with Billy; with straight-out, mechanical problems and the tools for solving them. Billy was a healing influence, because he lived entirely out of his own stores. Self-reliance, it went deeper than mere independence—it meant, by Clarence's reckoning, complete balls-out freedom from any other fucker's will. People wouldn't have believed it about him, but Meadows was familiar with Emerson's essays. He revered them, but he hadn't read them lately. His stomach lurched when he considered the waste of the last few years.

It was a fact that occasionally something, some vague ripple, surged forward out of the past. And then you were dealing with despair.

Cath, his wife—ex-wife—had given him the Emerson book. He'd been fascinated with her when they'd met, because she read such things and seemed to live in two worlds at once—the world of her life, and the world of books in which she found her life explained. Eventually Meadows had seen that the two worlds came together somewhere inside of her and made for tremendous strength when it came to making large decisions, as, for instance, the decision to turn her back on her husband.

And occasionally what surged forward was panic—what is he doing floating around out here in his life without Cath? Seven good years, two on either side of his thirty-six-month naval tour. A couple terrible months off of some legal problems he'd had in San Luis Obispo, when an indoor pot-growing operation in the valley north of there had turned sour. He'd been accused of murdering his two part-ners and burning up their bodies in the greenhouse to conceal the crime—groundless charges, brought against him just for the nuisance of the thing, and dropped as soon as he'd bankrupted himself on attorneys. Cath knew he hadn't done it, but she left him anyway. It had been three years since they'd spoken to each other. He was ashamed right now that he'd let his mind go back to her. He tried to console himself that everybody had at least one. One unforgettable wife. One still-burning flame.

He shut the TV off and waited a few minutes in the dark before going back to the bed and laying himself down, as quietly as he could manage, next to Carrie.

He put his hand against the back of her thigh just to feel the warmth. But she was awake, and as soon as he touched her, said, "No."

He lay still, paralyzed in a way with solitary embarrassment, and reflected to himself that it wasn't working with people. So he moved instinctively in the direction of avoiding and silencing them. That's why he'd taken to travelling to foreign waters, to foreign beaches evoking a seamless sameness underneath all thought, taken to spending his winters in foreign places where the language eluded him.

That was supposed to be bad. You were supposed to find people and connect with them—and that was supposed to be good. But what could be worse than this, right here, tonight?

Yet a weight began to lighten in his heart. He had a feeling this was the last straw. Maybe, just by coincidence, for both of them. Possibly she too was facing with relief the prospect that this absurd game between the sexes had finally tapped itself out.

Maybe he should give it all up. Join a monastery. Or confess one or two things to the cops. Certainly he'd strayed far enough to merit a good long stretch in their custody. In either place he might finally come to value discipline, and then go on to make something of himself.

He'd always hated discipline, but he felt he'd met its essence in certain moments of his military training. Discipline consisted of keeping himself separate from whatever thoughts might be passing through his head. He needed that detachment now because he seemed to be reacting to the sadness of turning thirty, and still being at zero, with funky spasms and flashes of religious light. He'd set himself up for all this in ways that were now obvious: spending long days alone on this infinite-feeling highway with nothing to do but point the car and sit there and let his head trouble him with riddles, breaking the trip in odd empty places where he sat by the road to watch the desert or farmland drift around him like a sea, stopping off sometimes just south of Gilroy at a Holiday Inn tricked up to duplicate a Spanish mission, complete with a small chapel whose atmosphere worked on him, just as Karl Marx had predicted, like dope. Surfing was also a case in point. What had started out as an adrenaline thrill among teenagers constantly partying had turned into a cycle of lonely vigils in a huge blue medium that sometimes lifted and carried him—in the direction of all the beach parties and the sandy skin of young girls, yes, who smelled like marijuana and tasted like beer and salt; toward the high times and flickering fires on the beach, yes; but he never seemed to reach them anymore. He'd at first reached them relentlessly, spent the days racing over the ocean and the nights lying under the stars and seducing some of the world's loveliest seventeen-year-old females. But he was beginning to reinterpret these triumphs in a way that made them look like failures. Only the waiting, never the waves, had been real. And now it seemed that with the hot little girls he'd only engaged in repeated sorrowful transactions, trading their fake lust for his fake affection.

He wouldn't have bothered to suggest this woman here was any different, not essentially anyway. But she was more grown-up and felt much more real.

He didn't know what, besides that fact, had made him decide to follow this thing out. It had just been that kind of day, the wind making the ordinary sand harmful, filling the air with pain, and so on. This had the taste of a regular adventure. He takes on the woman and child forever maybe, or they rob him or he gives them all his money.

As he left the next morning, Clarence said to the kid: "You got a Social Security card? No. You're not a citizen of anywhere yet. You don't know how rare you are."

The boy crawled around on the floor looking for one of his new shoes. Meadows could see it under the couch but didn't feel like telling him where it was. Carrie sat all dressed up on the bed with her legs tucked under her and her feet, in those red pumps, sticking out sideways, her hands clasped before her, while she looked straight at him and wept. Not trying to make him pay; just honestly grieving.

He stood in the doorway feeling happy that he wasn't connected with these two. He could make any gesture he wanted to right now. He could piss on the floor. Start a fire in the wastebasket.

"Well," she said, "you fixed my car."

"I was born to mess with loose connections."

"Thank you. You saved us."

"Where do you get your religion?"

"From the road. From the radio. TV sometimes."

"You're not a member of a church?"

"The road is a church."

Denis Johnson ▪ *184*

"I guess it is," Meadows said.

Gassing up at the Big Chief a few minutes later, Meadows watched her across the distance of several hundred yards as she came out of the ground-floor suite and packed up little Clarence and drove her limping Dodge from the parking lot of the Super 8 Motel. Tumbleweed bounced along the pavement beside them. A buzzard's shadow zipped across their path. It was like that.

Not a half hour later, while the day widened over the interstate, he overtook them in the northbound lanes and thumbed the button on the wheel. But the horn didn't work. Some sort of short circuit, it wouldn't be much trouble to fix.

He reached the Montanan's clever cap from the passenger seat and put it on, pulled the brim down low, looked straight ahead as he passed them.

He took 580 when it forked off Route 5 and drove west and down among the Altamont windmills, hundreds of them turning fast, like white whirligigs, on either side of the highway.

The whole thing . . . he'd been right at the edge of seeing it. Sometimes it seemed as if the outlines, blurred by the activities of dust, suddenly went away. Then the true picture showed itself, utterly simple and vast.

The Mercedes wouldn't make it over the second bad rut— and a lot of new ones, some almost gullies, had him surmising it must have rained—so Clarence left the car at the head of the drive and came down through the woods walking and blowing his trumpet. He heard deer skittering through the brush, running from the trumpet's echo at their backs and then panicking to discover the sound suddenly forward of them. He was thinking maybe Billy would hear the horn and meet him halfway. He'd want to hike back up to see the car anyhow. But Billy hadn't showed by the time Clarence made the cabin.

On the porch Billy stooped above a bucket and splashed rain on his face, waking a little late this morning and still smiling at his dreams.

"Dude! Señor Clarencio! How many women did you soil?"

"Dude!—funny you should ask."

"I bet. I bet. Did you just hit the coast?"

"Yesterday afternoon."

"Welcome home."

"Your road's worse than ever. Did it storm much?"

"Inch and a half one night last week."

"I got a 190SL sitting up top of the hill."

"I'm right with you."

They took Billy's International. Clarence drove. "This shit will make you a believer," he said, plunging into and over the gouges in the track.

"Yeah. One of these days," Billy said, but he'd been saying so for years and the road just got worse. "Did you hear about the raids in Humboldt?"

"I think it's over."

"They spent two weeks tearing up people's gardens."

"Yeah. It doesn't bear on anything I'm into."

"Really?"

"Really. It was ordered in Washington. Just to show the coke countries we'll deal with it and no mercy."

"I felt that whole thing happening, man. I felt a burning sensation in my soul. I wouldn't want them here."

"If they were coming here at all, they'd have made it simultaneous."

"Those G-men are poisonous evil fuckers." Now, in sight of the convertible Mercedes, the tone of Billy's voice changed. "They don't know it, but they are."

As he walked around the car and looked it over, Billy was plainly so happy he couldn't discuss the feeling. "Does the top work okay? Any holes?"

"Have to wait for the next rain. She'll leak in a dust storm is all I know."

The vehicle was a 1957 with a white paint job over the original blue, faded right through in places, but showing no rust. Billy jacked the hood and held it aloft with one hand and politely refrained from mentioning the black oil sprayed all over the engine compartment.

"Must be some serious warpage there," Clarence acknowledged.

"It's not just a gasket thing?"

"I replaced the gasket. It'll take a whole new manifold."

"Oh well," Billy said.

"I figured what the heck."

"Damn right what the heck," Billy said, and screamed, "A ONE-NINETY ESS ELL!" and the region immediately surrounding them clenched, paused, then resumed its chattering and foraging. "Let's go," he said, and opened the driver's door.

"You go," Clarence said. "I gotta see your brother."

Your fifty-five wheels drive me crazy, Clarence thought: Nelson Fairchild had a sharp mind which he'd twisted, using pills and liquor, into an instrument of torture.

Out of this garden they'd shortly be rich, he and Fairchild. Anyway he himself would see out the year in style. Fairchild would go on sweltering in a self-dug hole. Nelson hadn't learned to live without— hadn't grasped the utter necessity of living outside the need of—the great slavers: money, women, euphoria.

Therefore every place was the wrong place.

"Do you know what I would like not to do? I would like not to hang around here," Nelson said.

"Relax. Hypnotize yourself. Be like them . . . " Buzzards floated lightly as ashes overhead.

"I'm trying to segue into a confession of what's happening."

The breezes through the canyon stoked the gray embers over which Meadows was baking up half a dozen buds in a pie pan. They'd had to move upwind of the plants, closer to the lip and over- looking a great, heady drop toward the creek—the treetops looked from here small and soft, almost like moss—because of the overpow- ering pungency of the marijuana flowers.

"Do you or do you not have your bong?"

Fairchild handed him the small portable water pipe from his pocket.

"Let's engage in a little quality control."

"Control? I wish."

"You do appear sort of messed-with."

The boo looked to be drying too quick. Meadows unsnapped the canteen from his belt and doused his hands with water and fluttered his fingers over the coals, steaming the buds a little. One of the buds had blackened on the griddle, and quickly he pinched it up into the pipe's bowl and held it out smoking to his companion, who hunched and moved sideways like an owl on a branch.

"No, thanks. Not in my present state of mind."

"You feeling psychotic?"

"Oh, I've been having a bad day."

"Here. Drugs make it all better."

"I think actually it's adding up to a bad life."

"Well, in that case, drugs won't help. You need a hobby."

"Can we be serious?"

"We're testing the *dope*, Nelson."

"Sorry."

"Let's smell the roses."

"When I was at school in Carmel there were guys who'd swagger into the bathroom and get you in a headlock while you were innocently standing there trying to pee."

"Hey, lemme ask you something—"

"Here, just grab my head. Hurt me."

"—I heard you were the student-body president back in high school. That true?"

"President of the Young Democrats. And my senior year I was editor of the Wharton School's newspaper."

"You need an engaging pastime."

"*The Crimson Handjob* or some such."

"You could buy my board and take up surfing."

"I think we should get out of here."

"The thing is if you start to understand a sport, you start to understand life."

"A philosopher of games!"

"Even a spectator sport. I watch wrestling on cable every Thursday night regular as I can."

"Are you kidding? That stuff is rigged."

"And everything else isn't?"

Fairchild laughed and swiftly darkened. "This camp smoke is visible to observers."

"You're thinking about the raids up there around Garberville."

"Just partly."

"It doesn't concern us."

"I agree."

"It's a foreign-policy thing."

"I agree."

"Nelson, you surprise me a little bit. I mean, a number-one chance to be paranoid."

"Paranoia is a fond memory now. I've got plenty more to scare me than a few thousand troops of the National Guard."

Meadows sighed and the usual slanted, half-angry pity for Nelson

Fairchild raked his brain. "Okay. I can't delay you. Confess."

"Only panic would drive me to, that's got to be obvious, only shit-pants motherfucking fear, Clarence. My life is at stake. I face them or I face you—I'm down to two options, and you're the less nauseating one."

"Who's them?"

"I don't know exactly."

"Oh. That them. One of those them."

"Anyone who followed me around for twelve hours would understand—you'd be convinced. Just shadow me."

"I'll shadow you if you go up to Fort Bragg."

"Okay."

"To the Redwood Lanes, okay?"

"The bowling alley."

"I'm into that. It's a new thing."

"It's very old. Since the Egyptians I think."

"I'm taking it up."

Meadows uncapped the canteen and tipped a dollop into the bong's water chamber.

"Please take this seriously. These are real live hit men."

"Hit men have to be paid."

"Shit yes, Clarence. A body has to eat."

"So who's paying?"

"Harry Lally's involved."

"Did you bone his wife?"

"We were partners on a coke thing. It didn't work."

"You wouldn't expect it to."

"This was an arrangement for several pounds."

"Uh-oh. How deep did it sink you, Nelson?"

"I owe him big bad money."

"Approximately what."

"Ninety-two."

"Sell your house."

"I don't *own* the stupid, son-of-a-bitching, cunt-fucking house!"

"Better not sell it then."

"You are impenetrably smug and deeply, deeply idiotic."

"Still—I'm not the desperate one."

"Profoundly! Radiantly! Do you think I'd admit all this if I saw *any* way out of this hole?"

"Oh no, are we gonna cry?"

"We're going to cry, yes. And we're going to beg. I'm begging you for help, Clarence."

"I'm not saying no right yet."

"For help secondarily. Primarily though I'm begging you for indulgence. I beg your forgiveness. Our own enterprise is threatened."

Clarence jumped up with a stick of kindling and laid it like a sword to Nelson's throat. "The plants better be growing right in this spot at harvest time."

"They will be. It's just that they've come into play in this ludicrous situation."

"And you think that puts *me* in play?"

"I didn't plan it like this."

"I refuse to be committed here. Shit. I'll just dump your body in Lally's pool."

"That would be something of a committed act, I think."

"The just punishment of a fuck-up."

Clarence loosed his weapon and dropped a bud in the bowl and set it going. Fairchild took a hit automatically, failing to savor, dragging it down where it wouldn't hold. He coughed and strangled and then looked weepy-eyed at Meadows out of his true face, the face of a naked sinner.

"Aah, Nelson. Nelson. Why don't you just clear out?"

"I live here."

"Maybe that's the problem. Is it time to leave?"

"I just can't make it anywhere else. I've never lived anywhere but here and down in Carmel. I've never *been* anywhere but Carmel and here and Italy."

"You've been around L.A., haven't you?"

"Okay. Yes. And I'm not going back. It's completely over for Southern California."

Clarence took a small hit and held the smoke down, and then an icy ridge seemed to congeal along his sinuses. He could hear and yet felt virtually deaf. "Well, I know what you mean." He decided he'd better not take another toke and then did so anyway and blew it out, saying, "Destiny's moving over this land. You just gotta ride it like a wave."

"Who made you the Surf City boddhisattva I'd like to know."

Meadows graced this one with no more than one-tenth of a shrug.

"I'd like to know who told you the rules."

"The rules for what?"

"For everything. How to get born and how to be cool."

Who knew what went on in that skull? Maybe a brain tumor beating like a jungle drum. Nelson was his brother's brother.

"Clarence, what are you going to do about all this?"

His head floated in a cloud of smoke and he heard it say, "I'm handling all this fine. All that you describe. I go bowling, I stay close to the sea, I suck down a lotta tequila. It's easy and short. It's a skate."

"How groovy for you."

"Thanks."

"Stay as groovy as you are."

"I'm doing that."

"Thanks."

They'd smoked too much. The stuff was almost immeasurably potent—uncured, half-dried, bitter. Meadows suddenly understood what it would be like to turn into his own tongue. Was he lying prone or draggling down from above? Only a breathtaking surrender of his soul kept him floating upward and pressed against the capsized ground. Any slight failure of this abject unwilled movement and he'd plummet into the sky.

He'd be thinking something and realize that this flotsam had been plying his mind untended for perhaps many minutes before cresting into view. He did not consist of his thoughts, did not even produce them, was just the nameless fact they drifted through.

In a while—a half hour or a thousand hours—Nelson roused him, stirring around in Clarence's own pack and putting on his blue enameled kettle for coffee and upending the canteen above the pot until it gurgled dry.

Nelson dumped in the ground coffee at the boil, let it steep a minute away from the fire, then looped his belt through the kettle's handle and, with shocking deftness and equilibrium, stood up and slung the brew in circles, driving the grounds to the kettle's floor.

"You've got moves to surprise a person, haven't you?"

"I was raised to this land. I can live off dirt. I can rope a tree, hunt the mugwump, all of that." He poured coffee for the both of them into Clarence's one big cup. Meadows breathed the steam and sipped. The day was already hot, and this made it hotter in a righteous and purifying way.

"This bud," Fairchild said. He couldn't quite get his belt restrung through the loops.

"This shit right here," Clarence agreed, "is the explanation why they make us outlaws."

"I'd hate to see it fall to the possession of corrupted souls. Moneygrubbers, hit men."

"Lally never seemed all that serious."

"I owe him close to a hundred grand. I'm worried."

"If you told me I owed him money, I wouldn't be worried."

"Clarence: if there were any action you could be persuaded to take, what would it be?"

"Me? I've been blown off the map. I'm way uncharted."

"Could you perhaps, you know, frag these mothers?"

"Don't think in extremes."

"Or maybe just talk to Harry Lally. Talk to him in a way that frightens him."

"He's frightened now. He leaves footprints of shit."

"And I'm no less a coward."

The tall coward plunged into a telling of some length and detail, reaching across the months and waters to Palermo a year ago July. At one point he jumped up and began weaving like a shaman and the soul of a wild boar entered his body. He snuffed and charged at breezes and shouted that false hunters had run him to bay in this secret garden of ecstatic herbs. Meadows was astonished by this primitive seizure. And made reverent. In silence he waited for the gusts of totem beings to cease storming through Nelson's eyes.

Later Meadows said of Harry Lally: "The guy's a silly cocaine dealer. Everything about him is pointless. After a while he'll get arrested or something."

"Arrested by whom? This is Mendocino County. People don't get arrested here."

"His scene will crumble. Wait him out."

They paused, both looking upward until it seemed they were doing just that, languishing in this sunstruck abyss until their enemies should fail.

"And your two buddies from Del Norte," Clarence said, "do they know about Billy?"

"What about him?"

"Like the location of his residence?"

"They'll get around to everybody eventually," Fairchild said.

The coffee had cooled and Meadows took a big gulp and found that he was thirsty and that it was good to drink. He watched the buzzards totter in the currents.

"Do you remember," he asked Fairchild, "where it was we met?"

"Everybody I've ever met I met in the Gualala Hotel bar."

"Well, that's right. That's where it was. We had a conversation, we sensed an opportunity, we struck an arrangement. Three years later it's still in effect. That's unusually lucky, when you think about it."

"Is this a farewell speech? Do I sense yet another divorce in my future?"

"No, man, no. In fact exactly the opposite. I'm seeing that we have a past here, and I want to value it. I will do what I can to maintain our partnership."

"Clarence! You're better than any shrink! What about the pig-men?"

"What can they do?"

"They'll staple my penis to something, I think."

"They'll leave. How long can they hang around? Didn't you say they left once already? I'll talk to them."

"Clarence, look: I'm happy!"

The night's heavens kept clear all the way to M-47, a galaxy lying some eighty billion light-years off and appearing over such unframeable distances no more impressive than an asteroid. In fact it would have swallowed the Milky Way and two others just as big. Meadows while at sea had learned to locate it. He and Billy lay now on a plastic tarp in a clear spot out front of the cabin raptly marking a pinpoint candescence's course toward M-47 and praying for a collision. A weather satellite, most likely.

"Oh lord, oh lord, so close," Billy said as the bright little mover failed to pierce the galaxy.

They'd put away a feast of venison sausage fried up with eggs and beans, and hard biscuits baked in a covered pan. Meadows lay there wedded to the deep basso pulse of all outer space and feeling only recently surfaced from total amnesia.

—No matter how untrustworthy his sensations, interpretations, conclusions, the bare unnameable fact remained. You couldn't know it. But you could be it. A relaxed but attentive attitude, nothing more was required. No need to push through to the next thing. It's already here.

As on the road that had taken him back this way. And he moving forward, blind and strangling, through the storm . . .

Billy said, "Did you ever imagine, like, a guy who keeps hearing something from way out, *way* out, but it won't reach down here where it's all twisted and full of vengeance, and it's like if he could get out *there*, he'd see—because he could look back down *here*—"

"Twelve now," Meadows said, counting yet another meteor's trace through the northwest quadrant.

"—and without all the boundaries cutting it up it would be made obvious—I mean like his unknown purpose, his not-to-be-revealed identity."

"His secret mission."

"Yeah. But don't laugh."

"I'm not. I was thinking those very things while I was driving up yesterday. Have you ever seen these trick hats that look like Greek writing until you get far enough back? And then they say, 'Fuck You'?"

Billy seemed to hold his breath in the dark a minute, and then said . . . "No."

In a while Billy asked after the garden, and Meadows told him how if a person only walked along the rows and breathed the plants' exhalations, he saw visions. "I got a couple crumbs, if you want a hit."

"I don't think I should touch anything even remotely psychedelic."

"That's what your brother said."

"*Some*times we agree. Not always."

"He's jammed up some way, he tells me."

"It's his buddy that he partnered with on a rotten deal."

"Lally."

"Harry Lally. He's slick."

"Slicker'n a wet bean."

"That's nothing. Nelson knows demons way past Harry Lally's level."

"I believe you."

"Why doesn't he try talking to a cop?"

"A cop?"

"Like the new guy. My instincts tell me he might be okay."

"Do you realize we're criminals, Billy? We don't think cops are okay."

"There are good ones and bad ones. Like any profession. The world is full of bad news. Anybody who's not an asshole—thanked be fortune. Thanked be fortune, cop or priest or I don't care who. The mayor."

"Thanked be fortune."

"Yes, you got it."

"Is this place getting crazier and crazier?"

"Very likely, yes. You referring to the North Coast?"

"Here. Here. Here, man. The entire western portion of the Milky Way."

Billy kept silent a minute and then said, "The whole age is turning."

"So they say."

"When you erase the lines, that's God. God is all."

"You're not gonna trip your wires now."

"Me? No."

"You haven't been doing coffee."

"No. But wow. The stars."

He asked Billy, "Did you one time tell me you had a Coleman stove? Could I borrow it? I think I better start sleeping out by the garden."

"It's in the Scout. Fuel's there too."

"Okay. Remind me."

"Remind you what?"

Clarence told Billy about the woman named Carrie, the woman with the kid named Clarence; of how he'd watched her calmly sleeping. ". . . but she's awake, she's penitent, suddenly wants to go chaste, all religiously deranged and messed up."

"Godliness isn't bad, Clarencio."

"Did I say it was bad?"

"Religion's okay. But those highways. Some people just get rolling."

"And their scene boils down to looking for the one thing that'll stop them. That's why she was out there in her defunct evening dress laughing and pretending to be normal." A thought came into Clarence's mind and he laughed: "I got me a bowling ball, dude. I got you a hat, too."

"It was probably just highway madness," Billy offered in defense of this godly woman he'd never seen.

*　　　*　　　*

The same constellations lit the clearing when he came awake that same night, disturbed by movements in the cabin where Billy must have turned in. Meadows lay by the cold coals where he'd drifted off, his bag wrapped around him but his feet sticking out and paralyzed by the chill. He kicked his boots off and jammed his toes into the down-filled folds while a flashlight beam jerked and floated the cabin from inside. With the moon so low it wouldn't yet be eleven; he'd only napped a little while.

The light moved outside and the cabin door clapped behind it.

"Something's wrong!"

"You sick or something?"

"Something's happening!"

"It's just a night on Earth, man."

"There's something happening, Clarence. I really—I gotta go."

"Are you about to disappear into the woods?"

"I'm going to Dad's."

"That don't seem too smart."

But Billy was moving. "Something's *happening*, brother."

The lantern swung west and Meadows could make out Billy's form occluding it. Billy headed out under the glittering galaxies through the trees and toward Carter's Landing Road, by which he'd find the coast.

Clarence was at a loss here, but judged that Billy would probably make his way and if he foundered would get his bearings easily by daylight. Meadows sat up in the bag and wrapped his arms about his shins and then saw the full moon break the treetops: dawn not five hours off.

He crawled from under his bag and pulled his boots on quickly, shivering against the breeze that stirred up around him that faint sweet fetid redwood smell like mystic yeast. He threw his things into Billy's Scout, made certain of its fuel level and gave the gallon Coleman tin a shake—plenty for the stove—before trying the road up to the ridge. The headlamps lit the ruts undependably, but he knew his way around the big ones, and before the moon had made ten degrees of arc he'd topped the drive and the ridge and was making east on Shipwreck Road, passing through pockets of varied airs that signalled, but not clearly, something noteworthy in the weather. By the time he'd reached the garden and hidden the Scout amid coils of manzanita, the wind was treading over the evergreens on the canyon's north, and he could smell the wet on it. He carried a flashlight but didn't use it descending, just checked any plunge with the jacks of his boots and went down in the dark hugging his sleeping bag with the plastic tarp and the Coleman stove wrapped within it. By the garden he made his camp quickly—braced the tarp with twine and made an A-frame and lay inside it. During a half-minute's eerie calm he breathed the pungency of the plants and also, with the higher air cooling quicker than the lower, a whiff of creosote just now rising from the valley. He could very nearly taste it in his throat.

As the storm broke it drove in under his protection. More wrack than rain, it didn't douse him badly. He sat with his knees drawn up and his head jammed between, heaving on personal seas, stunned and clinging, his life's tremendous wheel turning over. He looked up at it and howled out loud, *Who runs this scam?* The words went under in the medium gale—thankfully, as they conveyed nothing of how privileged he felt to find his inner maelstroms matched by outer ones, as if all the powers endorsed and had even orchestrated his journey. For years now the weather hadn't been typical. The drought through months that should have rained, and then the recent almost unprecedented August downpour, and now this one shooting tiny stinging drops that blew for three-quarters of an hour. Then it ceased, whisked itself away, bequeathing the calm of the morgue and a thin general mist. The silence rolled through him too, and he lay back to drift pleasantly down through his exhaustion. He'd brought nothing for breakfast, but he'd see to that briefly tomorrow, drop into the Anchor Bay Store and lay in some necessities and be back in an hour. He'd wake tomorrow and go down the hill and buy beans and eggs, bread and cheese, coffee and canned meat—and didn't know it yet but he'd also learn of Nelson senior's death and how everything was changed and how the sons, the brothers, owned ten thousand acres of California; and he wouldn't return here for many days.

and then, read the blood-marbled pages John Navarro held in his hands one year later—

and then in its every detail I envision it, how with the rain's letup Van Ness you came yourself into a spell of calm and leaned against the Volvo on the passenger side, draped your arms over the roof, laid down your head across your dripping khaki sleeves. Curious how the weather gusted out there in the seaward black, while right around you along the coast road everything wilted and scarcely sighed. You were drenched. You thought of yourself as glistening. Every few minutes as a vehicle passed from behind and rolled you through a bath of light it came to you afresh that these people didn't know in the least what they were looking at.

And me, the sucker, Nelson Fairchild, Jr.—he hadn't known. But now his eyes would be opened.

You got back inside the car, crossed the Gualala River onto the Sonoma County side and laid by again in sight of a bleached derelict cattle barn, its shape both looming and tentative at this lightless hour. You had another stop to make tonight, but not yet, a little time to kill before—and now you started laughing out loud, and the ocean laughed back. You wiped your mustache energetically, laid the white kerchief on the dash and turned to and cracked open with your dirty hands the Fairchild family's copy of *Thus Spake Zarathustra*, stolen earlier that night from Winona's living room.

And didn't you find this place in earshot of the sea's cachinnation and tolling completely in accord with your new understanding of Friedrich Wilhelm Nietzsche's words, of how Nietzsche's words rang hollow—kid scaring his elders to fend aside his own true terror, he'd never actually lived it all the way out, never tasted his own wares— and weren't you thinking about his words as you reversed direction three hours later and drove to the hill on the coast road's east side looking down at the hooded unintelligent eyes of the house where Nelson Fairchild, Sr., lay dead, as you watched the comings and goings of people with grim business in that place, and as you followed—at a great distance, but easily because it was the only other vehicle out that late—my, Nelson Junior's, sports car up onto the ridge road and into the iron moonless dark and nearly overtook him there; weren't you still thinking about Nietzsche as you pulled to the roadside a hundred feet back of the stranded Porsche and waited and listened while far, far away the Pacific rolled a marble down a tin groove of infinite turnings; thinking in particular of certain of Nietzsche's lines concerning evil, a subsistence with which it pained—or did it exult?—you to admit the philosopher had never really stained his fingers—

An image made this pale man pale. He was equal to his deed when he did it: but he could not endure its image after it was done.

—and thinking in special particular of one line you'd perhaps read over and over and felt you were probably enacting at this moment as you moved toward Nelson completely sightless but smelling him out by his fear—

In wickedness, the arrogant and the weak man meet. But they misunderstand one another.

—reviewing this line in great confidence having proven it wrong by experiment, by deeds, in fact knowing it wrong because we, you and I, the arrogant man and the weak, understood one another exactly to the degree necessary?

You heard the tenor of your footsteps alter, warped by the car's acoustic mass, you bumped your hand against the car's left rear quarter panel and dragged your fingers along the canvas top until they plumbed midair at the driver's open window, heard the driver's terrified breathing but couldn't find him in the drisky black except by reaching through the window until you touched his face. You could have put your fingers to your lips and tasted his tears. And you heard with a curious grieving apprehension the action of your own innards and thought to yourself that Nietzsche never experienced his own guts in his belly, not truly, not like this, and the other said:—I wasn't even sure you owned a car.

—You recognize me.

—Of course I do.

—You think you do.

—My father is dead.

Only the purity of this darkness kept you from laughing out loud.

—And my wife is still alive. As you know perfectly.

You kept quiet because the noise of words seemed to create this place by inhabiting it—nearness, farness, a space . . . The other coughed in the dark and you believed you heard him spit through the opposite window. He spoke again:

—This is the most absurd night in my experience. It's completely liberating.

—Don't bore me with lies. You don't get liberated by someone else's life or death.

—I mean the absurdity. The absurdity's liberating. Okay?

—Okay by me Jack.

—What happened?

—What happened when my friend?

—Don't piss me off, Van Ness! How do you know I'm not pointing a gun at you right now?

—Maybe a three-five-seven? Maybe for instance a Smith & Wesson? Maybe because I'm pointing it at you.

—What is that thing?

—I borrowed a book to read.

—The goddamn Nietzsche. The fucking *Zarathustra*.

—I borrowed it off Winona.

—What happened?

—Nothing happened.

—But you were there, right *there*.

—Nobody home it seemed.

—She was asleep, you son of a bitch, asleep as planned.

—I'm getting in.

You came around the car. The inside smelled of leather and gasoline and mildew. The other shrank and reared like a viper as you sat beside him.

—Do I gather my father being dead doesn't interest you very much?

—I knew about it.

—Who told you?

—Perhaps some asshole in the hotel bar.

—You *are* a mutated strain.

—I'm just one station farther down the way. I've shed just one more shape than you.

—Bullshit. You're crazy is all.

—Don't let a little earthquake shake you off. You're moving to a new stage of yourself. The caterpillar and the butterfly—they can't imagine each other. An intellectual like you, naturally your own metamorphosis is gonna scare you to the jams—it's a process beyond the grasp of your mind.

—And what am I metamorphosing in*to*, professor?

—The lion.

—Really? Which one?

—You know. The camel. The lion. The child.

—Oh . . . *Zarathustra*.

—First the spirit is a camel, taking on great tasks and reveling in its strength.

—*Alzo sprach Van Ness*. What a bore.

—Then it turns into a lion, fighting against the dragon of convention, rule, law, even morality—killing all that shit.

—And how does he turn into a child?

—How? According to Nietzsche it just happens, it's inevitable. The spirit breaks the rules and then experiences another birth. The child—(and you quoted now as if reading aloud)—is a new beginning, a sport, a self-propelling wheel, a first motion, a sacred Yes . . .

—Enough. Okay. I get it and it bores me. You bear the burdens as a camel, you break the bonds as a lion, you're born again as a child.

—Yeah. But Nietzsche's wrong.

—Of course he's wrong. How could anybody with five successive consonants in his name be right?

—There's no child stage. Why would there be? Child of whom? Nurtured and cared for by what?

—I don't know, boss.

—There's no child stage. Once you become a lion, a spirit acting from will and making its freedoms, that's the end of it.

—Your beliefs make you deranged. If you're a lion, your beliefs make you a rabid one.

—Relax. Isn't this better now that your father's gone? As soon as Winona's crossed off, you get all the money.

—Nothing I say can have any meaning to somebody as completely crazy as you.

—Let's give it another try.

—Nothing I've ever touched has ever been touched by you.

—Let's hit that little honey. Make her dead.

—I wish I could tell you, get through to you, one thing, the following thing: that you couldn't say anything like that right now unless you were the complete personification of evil.

—Evil? I thought we were way past that. Let's have another go.

—Just waltz on in.

—She'll fall asleep again.

—Fucking A. Probably does it nightly.

—One more time.

—Listen. Those Nembutals. It's not easy to make a switch. The capsules fall apart, the tweezers dent the little things, you have to be very gentle or they look plainly battered. Plus the powder gets all over them on the outside—enough to make a reasonable person wonder.

That's when you knew . . .

You struck a match and lit up the damnation in his eyes: the self-defeat, the foregone failure. A queazy self-righteousness translated through his face like oil. And you said:

—Here. Your book. Keep it.

(Carl Van Ness: I sixth-sense, telepathize and soothsay what you saw in my jutting ears and big gaze—the shocked naivete of a fawn picked up by the headlights. Oh yes my eyes had been opened. That everything would play as you wanted, that's what you saw. That this creature had worked out his own destiny at a table in a void with unthwartable agencies. You saw your own efforts like a spoon in a maelstrom and helping no more than that to stir it. You saw me. And I saw only Carl Van Ness with his nowhere face behind those thick specs, moving along our ridges like an empty wolf, preexisting and reexisting endlessly. As I see right now vividly and too late looking up out of the well of my own death with what fine velvet you played me. How you greased me along to stop me breaking to the cops. And what an idiot I was. I believed *I* was playing *you* until I'd have them trap you in some final way—catch you square by rights with your teeth in her neck and drag you down to dungeons, boy. I never should have tried to swap our roles. My mistake was thinking you the tempter. But it was I. All along you were Adam moon-naked and I was the baffled snake.)

—We'll give her another spin—you said.

—It would have to be after the funeral. My father's funeral.

You held the match till your fingers spasmed.

She leaned against the car a second and jumped back, swiping at her arm and squinting at where it burned.

Clare was weary and giving her the business. She put him down with a comic and went in to sit at a table near the videos the truckers played.

Eleven empty chairs before as many games—one farmer boy about sixteen dipping a quarter down into the cleft and the colored light changing over his face while a hand of poker snicked out across the screen—a waitress retying her apron while she watched the images from behind the boy's shoulder—the cook pressing meat down on the griddle so it spit—one old man and his old woman sunk to the bottom of marital silence in a vinyl booth.

"Any work?"

The waitress stared at the game and said, "A position you mean? Or just for a meal?"

"Position I guess."

"No, sorry."

"Swindling old monster," the farmhand said and fetched the machine an openhanded blow.

"Or maybe just for a meal, did you say?"

The waitress looked her over.

"I got a little boy travelling too."

She changed out of her dress to wash out empty lettuce crates by the Dumpster, spraying the asphalt to keep it cool beneath her bare feet. She drove the sad torn leaves against the wall and scooped them together into one big mess between her hands. She dumped them in . . . The tang of Dumpster rot . . . She rinsed and throttled her bandanna and scrubbed herself up to the fringes of her cutoffs.

Clarence came and joined her, though he should have been taking his nap. He seemed in a trance and broke down grieving when she sprayed him. "You got it *wet*."

"Well, you had to walk right at the hose, didn't you?"

"Shit anyway," he said.

"Don't foul your mouth over a goddamn comic book."

"I don't care what I do," he said.

She took him back to the car. He lay down and stared up at the comic until the drawings fell over his face, and later he seemed vague and content while they ate hamburgers by the cafe's big eastern window and watched the colors of the empty sky and ripe fields swiftly deepen and the building's shadow stretch out over the concrete-curbed row of walnut trees and the four parked cars. She listened to the farm boy and the waitress recite slowly, like bingo callers, lists of pregnancies and car wrecks. The Lord had banned her from smoking some months ago, and right now, with the day used and the coffee in front of her, she felt that old demon running just a feather along her throat. Clare caught up on his fingertips the last crumbs from his plate and fed them to his tongue. She said, "This is the most loveliest time of day."

She bedded him down up front and lay in the cargo space listening while the breeze felt around the cracks.

"Hey," she said. "Clarence . . . ?" and fell asleep.

"Yeah?" he said.

     The cook banged her up the next morning and handed her two boxed breakfasts through the car's window.

"For the road."

"Thank you very much."

"Can't let that little stomach get growly."

"Say thank you, Clare."

"Thank you."

The cook was a little woman with short arms and a flat face and a long-ago smile. "It's just the number three minus the gravy. You don't want gravy in a cardboard go-box."

"No ma'am."

"Where you heading?"

"Well, we're trying after a crop, if there is one."

"Sea urchins."

"Lemme get that open for you, Clare. Sit up straight. Put it straight, you're gonna spill it and have a mess all over you. Sea urchins?"

"Yeah, they're like a cross between a cucumber and a garden slug. The Japanese pay a shitload of money for things like that."

"Where do you pick 'em?"

"Near the sea, I guess. Or right down in it, for all I know."

"I'm no swimmer." She opened her box and fell to with the white plastic fork.

"Anyway the coast is just right this time of year. Summer's a bitch with a gun down along this stretch, I'm sure you noticed. Man. If I could cook gourmet I'd go to one of those little hamlets by the sea."

"This is good. Gourmet enough for me, eh."

"You ever been to Pacific Grove or any of those places?"

"Not as I believe."

"Anyway I think you'll find what you're looking for in the sea."

"Are you religious?"

"Fuck no. Not even close."

"I am."

"Your boy's got big beautiful eyes. What do you see with them eyes, sweetie?"

"I don't know."

"The girls are gonna eat you up. Did you know that?"

"No."

"Well, they are."

She drifted the Dodge past the Phillips 66 with the broken door on its john and the row of motel rooms with their red doors burning in the morning light, and gassed up as cheaply as she could at the other one, the Star Store and Fuel, figuring the distance to still cheaper prices at about four gallons' worth, or fifty-two miles. Back again on Interstate 5 with the driveline's regular shudder tunneling under her and the tires' intoxicated tremolo drilling her ears and the tightness starting in her nape, she begged for safe passage and unmitigated guidance and wiped the sweat from the wheel with a sour washcloth. They passed lengths of farmland separated increasingly by blonde hills. Buzzards explored the world far overhead, and beneath the buzzards a crop duster biplane switched back and forth over the highway, laying out a billowy white spoor. Mother and child drove right through it. "Hold your breath, Clare." The plane's image passed across the mirror. "Shit. That's him. That's the closest thing to Satan you'll see today. Remember how people got sick at the orchard?" She was coughing, dizzy, saw a giant foot planted in the sky with its bestial claws dripping venom. She needed a breather here but felt wary of turning off the car. Yesterday she believed she'd come to the desert to break down and lift her heart, felt the great promise in coming up against a storm—miraculous, unique type of storm—then her car gets fixed and she herself also, popped by the character from Los Angeles, and now the man gone and his smell all over her and the storm lifted, just the clear vista faintly messed with by agricultural chemicals.

So the dust storm wasn't the thing. And the desert wasn't the place. And the man was definitely not the man.

Carrie on Route 5 negotiated palpitating zones of heat alongside burn piles that cracked and rattled like the last two cars on the bone train, and then a whole acreage being burned away, the wind unrolling a black rug fringed with flames and thick mustard-tinted smoke across the open fields toward the anvil of the heavens . . . She made for the coast—up Route 5 as far as the town of Williams and then west over to Ukiah on California 20, past Ukiah along the Boonville road into rolling hills and oaks, and then among redwoods in Anderson Valley, on through Boonville to Mountain View Road, a skinny lonely zigzag alongside precipices made less nauseating by enclosing forestation, then down a long grade from whose halfway point she spied the open Pacific, where she had to get clean, even drown herself if necessary—made for the coast with something gigantic happening to her there to the west, and eastward, back of her, all death and Devil.

At the Coast Highway's T she observed the stop sign, waited in a pointless silence, in which she could smell the surf, while nobody and nothing came north or south, and then turned left only from a vague desire to have the Pacific at her right hand. The first town was Manchester, but it had no cafes, and they headed through it, passed a seaside Catholic cemetery in a cypress grove, stopped for supper in Point Arena, and south of there pulled into a lay-by with a public outhouse. Hours past dark she suddenly disliked the feeling here and sat up and drove off, deciding to keep on for Anchor Bay. "Eight miles," she told Clare when they passed a sign. Around 2 A.M. they arrived.

"Where are we?"

"Usually you don't ask."

He put his fingertips together before his face and lowered the joined hands slowly to his lap, watching the car's descent along a steep curve. She and Clarence rolled into Anchor Bay just as a storm broke—"Big thunder, little rain," she told him.

In the morning she shut the car door quietly so as to leave him sleeping and strolled among rows of trailers and motor homes to the toilet barn, carrying her kit bag and a change. The feathers of the redwoods had been washed and then torn by the storm and now rested, outlined with damp, on the dry patches of asphalt that remained from some paving operation many years back. The clock she kept on the dash had run down. She guessed the morning at eight. The campground lay mostly in shadow, but toward the beach the sun had found it, and she stood in the light to watch a few skinny wetsuited surfers who looked a lot like seals, slumped forward astride their boards and talking; she could hear their voices, the voices not yet changed of young boys. It swept over her, the feeling of having arrived and seeing no place further to go. She turned to the shack and went through the door marked LADIES and showered for some minutes, tromping her clothes clean beneath her on the stall's mildewed boards.

When she came out and wandered toward the stretch of beach to lay out her wash, she came upon a man, blond and bearded, the blue of whose eyes, like windows giving directly onto the water behind him, made his head seem like an empty quiet room.

The man was dry and fully clothed, but he appeared to have been borne here by a wave and now to be emerging cleansed and changed from the sea. "You know," he said, smiling at her, "something strange happened last night."

Something not just strange, but also bad. She could see that much. "Oh, no."

"He's dead."

"Oh, no. I'm sorry."

"I've just been walking up the shore all night. I never left the shore. Climbing over rocks and stuff like that. Cliffs. The radar's got me all screwed up."

She lowered her gaze and mutely prayed for him.

"What's your name?"

"Carrie. What about you?"

"Fairchild."

"That's a perfect name for you. Or I would have chosen Goodman or something like that."

"Thank you."

"You're welcome."

"What are you doing here, anyways?"

"This is where the Lord sent me."

"Yeah . . . A lot of people get sent to the coast."

"Or maybe I think Satan gave up chasing me here."

"Well, you could end up going up and down it. People get sent here but—highway madness. They just go up and down this coast forever."

"My car couldn't handle that."

"Yeah. Yeah . . . I just had to ask you what brought you here."

She jammed her hands in her pockets, stood there stiff-armed. Smiled, when she thought of it.

"He was way past due," Fairchild said, "but it hurts just as much."

"I believe it. I'll be praying for you."

"Do you go to church?"

"When I can."

"Have you been to West Point? There's a tiny little church there. They work miracles there all the time."

"I believe it if you say it."

"Get them to pray for my father," he said.

"I will."

Mo had located a spot near the cemetery's edge. Navarro let her go on and stood with the toes of his service shoes just touching the cut border of fresh sod over the terminal rest of Nelson Fairchild, Sr., who had lived on this earth from June 7, 1928, until just last week. *Californian*: so read his epitaph.

They spread a picnic among many such Californians, and Navarro popped the cork on a red wine while Mo worked open a can of smoked oysters and cut up some cheese. Before they got to the sandwiches they weren't hungry anymore and fell to kissing and talking. Navarro was happy with his decision, which he'd come to on their first night together, to let his heart run away with him. He lay next to her looking sideways at the headstones, feeling privileged to associate with these families, some of whom pre-dated even the building of the coast road, counting himself almost a participant in their blank-faced courage. Pre-dated even the pigs. They'd brought the pigs here, in fact. The pigs had gone wild and now flourished, hounded, lean, and gamy, inland among the hills. He lifted Mo's sweatshirt above her breasts and spilled wine onto her belly, which was hardly there. Her breasts were meager and her chest thin, frail, the rib cage very much a cage, her heart kept inside like something that would otherwise fly up out of her and get away. Navarro licked wine off her nipples. "Yep. That definitely gives the vintage a boost."

"Here." She kissed his lips, and he tasted more.

"Hey. Am I in heaven?"

"I guess in this neighborhood, you're getting close."

True enough. He crawled over to a patch of sunlight on a grave and lay back in grasses like voluptuous bedding.

"That ocean's got more sounds than a city," he said. He didn't know if she was listening or not.

She crawled over beside him and said, "The Indians used to believe the sea would kill you if you just waded in as far as up to your ankles."

"Oh, I didn't know that."

"Yeah. They did. They wouldn't go in it."

He shut his eyelids over a red pulsing warmth and felt beneath and all around him these many Californians floating in the dirt. Around quiet almost archeological places like this you started to think about the continents drifting for millions of years toward their present berths. Not ten miles north, a flatbed valley crossed the coastline and carried on down to the shore and then past it, out under the water. This was the famous San Andreas Fault. West of the road where the fault line, verdant and full of breezes, pitched toward the sea, a farm—an orchard, a white house, a red barn, a gray silo—waited, dealt out like a throw of dice on the floor of the trough while the earth held its breath.

"Listen," he told her, "this thing could work. It's already working."

With her chin on the backs of her hands, stretched out flat on her stomach, Mo stared over the surface of the grasses. "I don't fall in and out of love that quick."

"I never said I did either."

"You've got the moves, though. You're fast."

"Not really."

"Fast, boy."

"I can slow down."

"But your foot's still touching the pedal," she said, laughing.

"For the right person I can slow way down."

"Would that be somebody like me?"

"The feeling definitely has that quality."

"Yeah? What quality."

"The quality of I want those pretty tits to kill me."

She started to laugh. But her eyes stopped dead. "Man, I know what you mean." She undid the front of his pants, and he slid himself up inside the leg of her shorts, and onward. It felt just right, and then even better when she looked up over the edge of some huge late sorrow and said, "Man, we're so good together." He could hardly believe his luck, that it should come back again one more time after all those other women.

The sunset tossing the headstones up out of black shadows, and the green graves of all the dead strangers.

They lay quite still until he thought he'd come just from being inside her, or rather from her graciousness in permitting him there. Then they heard the sound of a small bothered engine nearby.

A rectilinear old-model black Saab came along among the headstones with its nose bobbing like a hound's over the trail. Parallel to them along the bluff it stopped, and a solitary man got out and started juggling maybe as many as half a dozen things, tennis balls or the like, his knees flexed and his head arced back slightly and his hands and head and shoulders moving a little and in a way that made him look, at first glance, as if he was only pretending to credit himself with the running of this system; as if though he turned away it would abide; his face making small circles linked as by the hub of a camshaft to the more majestic orbits of this flotilla he'd set before himself, in truth nothing about its flight escaping his concentration, its planets impelled and guided by his attentions. He stopped his head. The worlds descended and he gathered them out of the air to his breast.

"I think he's coming over," Mo said.

Navarro slipped himself out of her. Not what he'd have predicted. You're lying here screwing in the grass and a juggler comes and practices in the cemetery.

He adjusted himself and yanked surreptitiously at his zipper and wondered: should I arrest him? The guy stood on the bluff with his long shadow hitting a headstone and absorbed by it, and the headstone letting out its own shadow about the length of a grave.

"Salutations and prestidigitations!"

Navarro couldn't understand why so many coast people wanted to look like fairy-tale creatures. He'd have marked him for a reefer fiend but doubted any but the clearest synapses could have passed the necessary signals between those eyes and hands.

He wore a Jamaican beret and a brown beard divided at the chin into two braids, and was small with a stunted, vegetarian smallness. He'd clothed himself in patchwork burlap, not colorful, but of many origins. He began juggling again as he walked crab-legged toward them, feeling along the earth with his feet.

"I like it here this time of day. Can you guess why?—because the shadows make it look like every grave is open. As if our friends have gone wandering. If you came here at the right time of night on the right night of the year, you could see that same vision—only by full moonlight.

"Watch my eyes. Watch the eyes. W. C. Fields could read the label on a seventy-eight RPM record while it spun. The World's Greatest Juggler they called him. He was also the world's greatest comedian, and one of the great consumers of martinis. He didn't drink all that many. But they were big mothers. I am the most prestidigitous trigetour . . . in all of trolldom."

They were spongy multicolored spheres, his juggling materials. As many as six; Navarro couldn't quite count.

The trigetour plucked the balls from the air, cradled them in the crook of one arm, and turned to steal a blossom from a grave—a fresh grave—Nelson Fairchild's grave: a black-eyed Susan from the spray in a white pot of earth.

Meanwhile the red sun balanced briefly on the bluff and then rolled slowly backward. A squirrel skittered and paused and cursed on a branch. The whole grove turned a corner suddenly and stopped in a shady silence.

The trigetour stood above them in this silence, knelt long enough to hand Mo the flower, and walked to his Saab and drove away.

C larence ran into Carrie after crossing onto the Sonoma side of the Gualala River to visit the state-run campground there and look in on the two Lally'd hired. Ran first, in fact, into little Clarence.

The boy lay on a grasspatch in the sun with a red-haired dog, a bitch, the animal stretched out long on her side and chugging in the heat, the kid's arms and chin pillowed along the flank and his head bobbing, his eyes open and looking at thoughts. The river ran low, chirping on the juts and scrubbing along the bed.

Meadows said, "What's the skin, Daddy-o?" But maybe the kid didn't recognize him.

The door chopped shut on its spring. Carrie came out of the wooden Ladies' with wet hair, in a clean white Arrow shirt and cut-off jeans, the shirttails tied up under her breasts and her stuff evidently kitted in her damp towel.

"Whose dog?"

"What dog?"

"That your dog?"

"Oh—him," she said. "I hope not."

"Whose is it?"

"First I'd like to hear, Hey, Carrie, surprising to see you."

"Okay. I figured that goes without saying."

"Strange."

"You bet. Unexpected. Who does the dog belong to?"

"Two guys. The only other ones here. And I'll tell you why. Damn I'm in a fix. Fourteen bucks a night."

"Try Anchor Bay. They'll let you slide a couple days if it's for a good reason. Unless you're scurvy trash or something. And," he said, making his voice soft, "you're not."

"Thanks."

"They hunting?"

"Who, them?"

"Those guys."

Denis Johnson ▪ *212*

"Don't know."

"Just two of them?"

"Yeah, and a million dogs, it seems like. They jabber like a zoo."

"They going armed?"

"Now there's a strange question, don't you think?"

"Just answer it."

"I guess. They seem like nice guys, though."

"You see any guns right on their person like?"

She looked down at her navel with trouble on her face, untied the shirttails and tucked them down the waist of her shorts. "Actually, I stayed at Anchor Bay two-three nights ago."

"In holsters or some such?"

"Not as I recall."

The younger one swirled the coffeepot and tipped it toward a stone. "Make yourself easy."

Clarence said, "I guess you know your dog's loose."

"Yeah. She's okay. She won't hurt nobody."

"That's good. That's good. Because hurtin' is a hurtin' thing."

"No argument there."

"Good. Real good."

The two exchanged looks and the older one said, "I'm sure."

"Guy," the other said, "—why am I getting that feeling? That chilly feeling?"

"Shit, I don't know what I'm saying. Sometimes I just go apeshit. I get in an apeshit mode. Hey. I think you know a friend of mine."

"No, I don't." He shook his head.

"Harry."

"Harry. Nope. Don't ring a bell."

"This is just my opinion, okay? But he's all wrong. He gets people hurt."

The elder of the two said, "Oh. I see."

The younger said, "But we don't know him."

"People get around him, and they end up fucked up."

The older one smiled and said, "Am I supposed to be scared?"

Meadows smiled and said, "You're supposed to be rational."

Also carefully smiling, the younger one said, "Look, I'm into martial arts and I like to drop reds and drink shit and get rowdy. Do you know what I mean?"

"Enjoy our lovely coastline."

Everyone was smiling.

He left them with a wave and scuffed along the dirt through the trees, opting against the road, and back to the privies. Inside the Men's room he stood around with his pants unzipped and his penis in his hand, listening to the flies, unable because of emotion to pass water.

"Hey, Clarence," he said when he'd gone outside, "you remember me?"

"No sir," the boy said.

"Nobody does," his mother agreed.

Meadows lifted his BP cap and ran his hair back. "Can I get you to lend me a camp knife?"

"Here's a few things, yeah."

"What do you possess there? Lend me that bolo. Come on, sport," he said to the dog.

He took it over to the park entrance and rubbed its head as he looked westward over toward the empty highway. The animal looked part Ridgeback, auburn except in the hairs permanently raised along its spine, which ran a purer brown. Meadows cut its throat with a chopping stroke up through the larynx and major blood routes and then dragged it, blood vomiting from this second open mouth, around the circular park road the opposite way from Carrie's camp and then to the edge of its masters' campsite, where he laid it down in the shade of the yews to open the abdomen, first with the bolo and then wider with both his hands. Nobody in sight. The dogs in the camper went crazy when he walked around and knocked twice on its eastern side. The two men tumbled out the back door to investigate as Meadows walked through the cleared ground not twenty feet behind their backs with both the dog's ankles in his left hand's grip and its jaw scraping a track along through the sand toward the blue sleeping bags. He stretched the carcass out on one of the bags and made his exit, yanking at the entrails and unravelling them across the circle of stones, where they lay stinking and hissing in the coals.

From twenty yards back, among the stubby evergreens, he witnessed a fluid pantomime as the younger of them stood at the fire briefly paralyzed with fascination, ran about, heading toward the truck some several steps and then whirling to stagger over and look openmouthed at the dog again, shook his head, pointed accusingly at his friend, put his hands on his hips, found his breath, and said, "Fuck!" His friend watched all this somewhat warily. As the wild one rummaged under the driver's seat and stood up tall holding a gun, a long-barreled stainless-steel revolver mounted with a scope, Meadows departed.

He doused the blood away in the river and then returned the bolo to Carrie. She sat on a towel beside the car, combing out her wet hair.

"It's genuinely odd, you turning up here."

"Definitely outta wow."

"I believe you were sent again," she said, "by the Lord."

"I don't know. Is the Lord really that heavy into this kind of action?"

"I'm not a theologian."

They heard a shouted conversation from over across the campground.

"Those two. Don't tell them you know me."

"I don't."

They'd be right behind him. He should make Gualala before the crash. A familiar inner pressure stopped him. Not lust, not necessarily. Curiosity.

Time and drinking. With enough of each, anything could be accomplished between the sexes.

"Maybe I should return with some wine coolers."

"Maybe you should try down the road."

"I thought the Lord sent me."

"Well, I'm forwarding you on."

H ere we go. Gimme the Casull. Come here, baby."
  "Hey. Hey. That's exactly his game, right there."

"I can get him fifty yards out with this."

"He wants to get us crazy and running around the woods and shooting. Then we talk to the constable and—listen to me goddamn it, hey—that's that. We're gone."

"Fuck it."

"If you wanna drop thirteen hundred dollars of Casull in the creek, far out. There's the Casull, there's the creek. Because that's what's gonna happen if the Man comes around."

"I'll stash it."

"You'll *dump* it, man, because if he shakes the sheets and out it drops, man—"

"That fucker! That fucker! That *fucker*, man!"

Thompson pounded on the camper's walls with the meat of his hand and the gun butt, and the two live ones inside gouged at the door and vocalized like dozens.

"I want him *this* close when I blow him up. I want my tongue in his mouth. SHUT UP!" he told the animals.

"I advised you to don't bring no handgun. And no dogs, et cetera. In fact I pointed out from the beginning that this sucked. So anytime you wanna leave."

"A four-fifty-four Casull. Most powerful handgun ever made. This is a lifetime gun, man. Fuck you if I'd ever drop it down no hole."

Falls squatted on his heels before the poor bitch's carcass, dragged a brand from the fire, and touched it to a cigarette. "I'm ready to go back and bust up trees again."

"Stash this gun any fucking place. What are they gonna do, search the whole forest?"

"The bastard's gone anyways. He aced us."

"Who was he?"

"I don't know. But he was all business. Shit. Look at her."

"What's old Busk gonna say?"

Falls stood back up. "Let's get her bagged."

"I swear I'll kill him. That I swear to God."

"Let's just get her guts back inside her here."

"Jesus. This is tragic."

"And go get double shitfaced."

"It's tragic, brother. She was the only one of them worth a shit."

"We'll tell him a boar got her. He'll be proud."

They bent to the task.

He detected, under the colliding of the winds and the waters and the bluffs, a minor, solitary rhythm—somebody chopping wood out back of the place. Then as he followed Mo into the house and she turned to smile and give his hand a squeeze, almost a shake, as between strangers, and then let go, the sounds of the shoreline fell back, didn't trail them into the cathedral-ceilinged living room where one small woman stood, studying a ceramic ashtray on the bookshelf. Navarro heard a kettle signalling from the kitchen. Mo said, "Can I help?" and went that direction.

"Okay if I let down the blind?" the woman said. She wasn't talking to him. He sat on a footrest with his feet apart, forearms on his jutting knees in the room filled with almost horizontal light. The sun lit up faint roads of dust along the wooden floorboards at his feet. His Sears service shoes and his polyester pants. The woman stood with her hand on the cord, a blonde in jeans and a hooded pullover and spectacles that magnified her eyes and made the lashes prominent and whose rather thick lenses, when she faced him to speak, he saw were speckled with drops of paint. A short, ample type, still young enough that her plumpness was an attraction, though she wore a ponytail and Navarro generally didn't like that sort of thing. "I don't want to trap her on the balcony," she said. Yvonne, the medium, or channeler, or lesbo witch, stood out there with her hand on the rail. The house was cantilevered over the drop so that out beyond her only the sea and the sunset were visible, and she seemed to be standing at the bow of a ship and almost disappearing in the fiery illumination, miles from any earth. The sun had lolled into the space between horizon and cloud bank to shatter the Pacific into a lot of confusing colors, and she entered from the balcony with the light filling her loose shift and silhouetting her slenderness and sparking from the fork of her thighs. Navarro tasted some sort of sour thirst in his heart.

"Hel-*lo*—anywhere's good," she said, which he took to mean that sitting on this footrest was perhaps not good. He'd been waiting for an excuse to rise anyhow, having felt awkward, maybe even cowed. He did rise. "Have you introduced yourselves? Winona Fairchild, this is John Navarro."

"Hi, John."

"I came with Mo," he wanted them to understand.

Winona let down the blinds and a pastel silence opened around them.

Through the kitchen's entryway he saw a sweet-faced woman in stippled gray overalls laying out cups on an Oriental tray. Meanwhile a guy banged through the back door and then through the kitchen with firewood crooked in one arm up to his chin. He snicked the tennies from his feet deftly, getting them just side by side, and paddled like a duck across the living room in two thick orange socks. Navarro had never been introduced, but had seen him almost daily, attached to the side of a big Victorian right across the road from Navarro's own apartment in Point Arena. He was a carpenter, remodelling the old building. Navarro and Yvonne and Winona spectated with interest while he made a fire of shavings and loaded the stove with chunks of oak.

Yvonne said, "What's that I hear?" Everyone listened intently. "Nelson."

Now the motor's sound came up from under the breeze and stopped dead in midrevolution, dead so to speak in the middle of a thought, the way a good German engine will do when you cut it off.

Winona said, "Oh well," with a lot of world-weariness in her voice.

Through the living room window they watched two figures climb from Fairchild's old Porsche and come through the reddening light outside, past fir and cypresses swirled into human shapes.

Nelson Fairchild entered with a little hippie girl who turned out to be not a girl but a woman, a pale thin woman with a beautiful face, the face of a porcelain doll. She ripped from her head a kind of pillbox hat and uncovered a thick black braid coiled in a bun almost like the thing she'd just taken off. Glittering blue eyes. She smiled with her eyes but not with her mouth, and it made her seem frightened or sad, while Fairchild's eyes looked like somebody might have blackened them with a ball bat. He wasn't well. He'd dressed himself all in white right down to his crepe-soled shoes. He looked like a yacht-going lemur.

And now Navarro sat. And now the feeling was complete. He'd stepped quite definitely onto a stage where everybody held a script but himself. They had their passports and their tribal scars. Where was Mo? He heard her laughing in the kitchen. Somebody else had joined her, a squat female he hadn't seen come in. The carpenter joked with them inaudibly in there now, hovering in particular over the one in the railroad oversuit. A sweet young girl surely not yet twenty. Navarro wondered was the carpenter diddling her. Or either of them. Probably just diddling the fat one, he looked to have about that kind of luck.

Nobody said much. The young one came among them with the Japanese service. She paused before him and proffered the tray with the hint of a curtsy that made him smile and reach out and say, "Thanks." He put his cup to his face and inhaled some pleasant minty vapors. Gravitating toward the bookshelves and tilting his head as if reading the titles, he set the cup beside *Do What You Love and the Money Will Follow* and abandoned it there.

The young woman turned up again, smiling in a slightly apologetic way and shaking her head irrelevantly so that her long brown braid swiped along her spine. She was smiling at Navarro; she wanted him to move his ass. He and the others put themselves against the room's margins while she herded a miscellany of chairs into a semicircle.

Folks seemed to be taking up positions. He returned to the seat he'd just been prodded from while Yvonne put herself in a tall straight-backed kitchen stool facing them all in their various chairs, his own a deep-sinking type he'd probably be napping in soon, despite his alertness in these surroundings. What he'd at first believed to be distant chimes in the breeze he located now as low-volume New Age from a stereo, the speakers stashed up high in the corners.

Yvonne closed her eyes for ten seconds, opened them up wide, and smiled at each one of her guests in turn. "Everybody, let's introduce ourselves."

"Mo. Maureen."

"John Navarro."

"Melissa. But I want to change it."

"To . . . ?"

"Something, I don't know, but it should mean a word."

"Winona Fairchild."

The carpenter said, "Is that gonna be too hot?"

"I'm Ocean," said the young girl in overalls.

Yvonne said, "Ocean lives here."

"I'll fix the draft." The carpenter knelt beside the stove.

Nelson junior just sat there, staring at his wife, until Yvonne said, "And this is Nelson Fairchild."

Mrs. Fairchild didn't look back. Navarro dedicated himself to catching her at it, but she never glanced at her husband, not once. And generated thereby an impression of obsessive awareness of the guy, kind of a retina-burn threat, Fairchild's status that of hot spot or solar eclipse.

One more came in, the woman he'd seen in the kitchen with Mo, a flustered person with plain strong weathered hands but painted toe-nails, in sandals, and her meaty neck wrapped in a gypsy scarf.

"Sit. Sit. Everybody knows you but John."

Navarro nodded, and noticed as she sat across from him that she didn't shave her legs. When she crossed them, he glimpsed her yellow underpants.

"Hillary Lally."

"Like the nursery rhyme."

"What nursery rhyme?"

"Just kidding around."

She scowled and smiled and looked hurt. He'd meant Hickory Dickory Dock.

Suddenly Melissa let out a bright laugh, like change falling in the street. Gold bridgework in her mouth. She shrugged, and waved at everybody with her fingers. She'd chewed her nails down. She pulled her lips shut over a tilted smile and again she looked like a roughed-up, invalided child.

The carpenter hadn't introduced himself by name. "Where's Billy?"

"I wouldn't count on Billy getting here."

Yvonne smiled. "I'm a little surprised you turned up even, Nelson."

"Actually, honey, the entire world has been peeled away. Anything can happen now if you ask me."

"That's a tremendous juncture. You know the Chinese character for our word *crisis* is a combination of the characters for *danger* and *opportunity*, danger plus opportunity, did you know that?"

"I know I'd like a cigarette."

"I didn't know you smoked."

"Just to fuck you up."

She laughed in a charming way and then looked around the group, a long look that inaugurated a certain seriousness. She closed her eyes, breathed deeply several breaths in through her wide nostrils and out between her lips, and most of the others did the same, but Navarro didn't, and neither, he saw, did Fairchild. Yvonne opened her eyes and smiled at them both, as if recognizing without condemnation their resistance, and then addressed them all: "One of the things we've come together for is to celebrate the life and afterlife of Nelson Fairchild, Sr. He's between lives now, and we're here to thank him for his recent one and wish him well on his next.

"Something of great importance that we can do is just come together and let our perceptions of him smooth out. Let his deeds and personality, as we perceived them, sink back into the unruffled pool of time. Where he's without any earthly individuality. Beyond experience, beyond perception. He's not a villain. Not a bad guy. We'll do everything he's done and experience everything, maybe even work the kind of horror Hitler worked ourselves before this journey through a billion lives is over. Don't put anything past yourself. We let him go now. What we thought we saw is gone. None of that was real. What remains is pure. What remains is real. We say good-bye . . . we say hello."

They waited there in some sort of reverie for a while until Yvonne let out a long, pleased, somewhat phony sigh, and the group settled its attention on her again. She turned to Hillary Lally. "How was South America?"

"We were there three days and then we left."

"Oh."

"There was an accident."

"I heard."

"A young girl died."

"Was it when the car hit you? Hit your car?"

"Not then. Later. It was—she was a pedestrian."

"But was it the car that did it?"

"We didn't know. And then we left and—we'll never know."

"I think this is a good time to call Randall in."

This proclamation doused the house in silence. Yvonne put her chin on her chest and you could have counted no more than five before she lifted her face to them again.

"Hello. Good afternoon. I'm Randall MacNammara."

Her eyes weren't rolling in her head, her voice stayed exactly her voice, nothing about her had changed in any way. Nobody was playing spooky tapes or blowing fog. It showed taste and style, Navarro decided, to let the marks run their own grift.

Mo put her hand over his and something happened in his head, but nobody seemed to have noticed, so he wasn't sure. He was probably in love.

The witch had a true skill. This had to be one of the region's more elegant scams. But he'd showed, and something was working on him.

Yvonne was all touch. No push or pull. She'd slipped off her sandals and bared her feet, draped her shift's hem across her thighs. She had great legs; Navarro could see himself throwing cheap vodka on her and then licking it off.

"Let's look back," she said, or Randall did, "to our past lives . . . Relax completely. Start at the top of your head. Let the tension flow out into the void. Relax the muscles of your neck. Relax, let it all flow out . . . the shoulders . . . now the back . . . torso . . . hips . . . thighs . . . calves . . . Let every bit of tension drain now through the soles of your feet and into the grounding center of the earth beneath us . . . And as that energy drains away, the energy that we've taken in from all the daily influences outside us, what's left is a kind of very softly glowing pulse within, our true energy, the real, eternal, unchanging, unquenchable, quiet and irresistible truth that we are . . . Let's pause now and just be that truth."

Nothing happened for a while beyond the rearrangements of the wood burning in the stove. Navarro did his best, he believed, to envision this bit of swamp gas ignited inside him somewhere, either in his chest or his head, he couldn't quite determine which, and kept switching between the two.

"Now let this true self travel. It wants to take your vision somewhere, to share with you the sights and sounds of an incarnation you've forgotten. Keeping your eyes closed, become aware of the eyes within your eyes. Keeping your eyes closed, open the eyes within your eyes. Keeping your eyes closed, look around you with the eyes within."

Navarro engaged the game and envisioned a place, a kind of dormitory, the lowest floor in a honeycomb of indestructible lightweight cubicles, and he lived there. Lived as a cog, nothing more, with a sturdy suit and a weapon and no thinking past these limits, no desires. In another minute he became aware of Yvonne's voice again and realized he'd fallen briefly asleep.

". . . not to reveal any secrets about ourselves, but just to share where we've been, if that seems shareable. Any volunteers? Okay, Ocean. What did you see? Where'd you go?"

The young lady spoke. "I was by the sea, and I'm almost sure it was this coastline, I mean, Mendocino or right around here." Something just too beautiful seemed to be messing with her ability to breathe.

"And what were you doing?"

"I was washing clothes."

"What kind? Did you see what sort they were?"

"I think—Indian clothes? I don't know. I think I was an Indian."

Mo said, "A Miwok. Or some branch of the Pomos. That could be."

"What sort of clothes did the Miwoks wear?" Yvonne asked.

"I don't know," Mo said. "Skins, maybe, until they started trading with whites."

"You wouldn't wash skins, would you?"

Sadly the girl admitted it. "You wouldn't wash skins." The probability deflated her completely.

Navarro reflected she wouldn't have been signifying like this if she'd been one of the team. No partners, no promises, no gizmos. We're all marks.

The carpenter cleared his throat. "I—"

"Excuse me," Navarro said.

"Pardon?"

"What is your name?"

"Well, Philip—Phil."

"Hi, Phil."

He sensed a stiffening beside him. He turned to Mo and was just about to say, Fuck *you*, honey, when Yvonne cleared her throat. "Were you going to share a seeing, Phil?"

"Yeah. I don't think I was human this time."

"Oh?"

"Well, I was running across ice, and I had claws, big claws, I know that much. And I think it was dark. No trees or anything, or plants. I can't think if there was any wind. Just real barren. Wait . . . eight claws on each—they were like fingers. Real thick hairy arms. Well, legs, because I'm running on all fours."

Yvonne-Randall waited.

"What was that? Was I some kind of mythical beast?"

"You were on another planet. I'm not familiar with that one. Maybe I should tap in . . ." She closed her eyes. "Hm. You were out there. I'm not getting anything. Some of these planets have been destroyed, and there's word that some burned up when stars went nova very early along in the evolution of the inhabitants. They all scattered into various rebirths, widespread incarnations. They haven't made it up the chain yet to the afterworld."

"Nobody to tap into."

"Right, that's what I mean. Information is not forthcoming."

He'd looked for spooky stuff, but she was serving around a little sci-fi. "Question?"

She meant Winona Fairchild. "What?"

"You look like you have a question."

"I do," Winona said. "I was just—how'd you know I had a question?"

"Nothing mysterious. Just the look on your face. No telepathy here!"

"Oh. Well, I was wondering if anybody here of us, did we know each other in the past? In past lives?"

"Let me tap in . . ." She shut down again; a long pause; opened her eyes. "These two"—with two fingers scissoring and unscissoring, she indicated Mo and himself—"have been married four times."

Mo laughed with embarrassment. Navarro took it as a boost. Next time I pinch you, he thought, no ticket. But doubted anyway she'd ever failed to charm a cop.

"Three times you've been the wife," Randall-Yvonne said to him.

"Wish I could remember how to cook," he said, something affable being required now, in light of his tendency to look cross-eyed at and ridicule such geeks as these. Everybody chuckled, and a familiar fantasy came to him, one along the lines of seeing everybody stripped, suddenly, to their undies; but in his case, as he generally went armed and at the moment sheltered a Compact Officer's .45 ACP under his bulky sweater, in a holster clipped to his belt, the fantasy skewed toward multiple murder, as if he'd just whipped it down and opened up on everybody.

"I just wonder if you wouldn't mind," Yvonne-Randall said. "Can I ask you to put your weapon somewhere outside the room?"

He cleared his throat. Found no comeback.

"Something's creating a very low vibration. A distracting hum. Would it be your sidearm?"

"Uh—yeah, sure."

And why not? But what am I doing? he thought as he stepped from the room.

"Now you," she nodded in Hillary's direction as Navarro went out the front door, "have a tale to tell. I'd like to hear it."

He passed silently over the packed dead needles underfoot, looking back over his shoulder toward the driftwood-colored house and wondering what all that had been about. Okay, okay. Northward the bluff rounded to make an inlet and a strip of rocky beach no wider than a footpath, and then the shore tumbled upward to this property with its blunted evergreens crouching lower and lower as they approached the edge. The car was Mo's, her dinky Cadet. He disarmed himself and jammed the Colt under the driver's bucket, locked and checked the doors. Okay. You zinged me.

Nobody looked at him as he took his place again between Melissa and Mo. It was dark in here. Somebody had lit some candles on the bookshelves, creating shapes and shadows in a dimness. Hillary Lally sat with her head down and wept onto her knees.

"I guess he wanted to—he's not faithful. I mean he plays around. I'm used to it. I mean, not used to it but—you know. He plays around. I think he wanted something involving me. I might have done it. He knows me. I'm open to new things. So he, so we, she ended up overnight with us. In the hotel. It was a suite. But nothing happened. I mean she died. That certainly happened! She was in another room, just lying down. There was nobody there. She just wasn't alive the next thing anybody knew."

"Go on. It's fine. Go on."

"I went in and found her. Well, on cable you can get everything in English. No, I guess it's satellite. Well, who the hell cares? I don't know why I brought it up. We were just watching TV and Harry—we were doing, you know—cocaine is quite a casual thing in Rio. Harry said, let's go out, so I went to wake the girl up, Esperanza, they called her Perry, anyway she gave that as a nickname. Dead, like a lump of something. Like a great big fat fish, you could tell from across the room in the dark. I think it was a lack of vibration. Don't you? It was quite mystical right there, in fact at that point I left my body . . . and somebody else came in. Do you believe me?"

"Yes."

"Another soul."

"I believe you."

"Another soul entered my body." Hillary breathed rapidly several times. "A soul wandering for years and looking for—"

"Revenge against your husband."

"Oh! God!" Sobs burst out of her. She wiped at her face. "Who, who, who—was it?"

"Somebody born into a life of weakness. The weak lives are long ones, because they often continue in the void spaces between the afterworlds. They can involve a lot of wandering and confusion before the next birth. In his earth-time, out of weakness, he turned to pleasures and drugs. He blamed others for his weakness, your husband among them."

"I could feel his hate. I wanted to *kill* Harry."

"Shhh. It wasn't you," Yvonne-Randall said. "Maybe you felt the feelings, but they were his. Not yours. In your body he went in to stand over your husband for a long time. He almost killed him. Then he found forgiveness. He saw that this life is a punishment for your husband, at least in the terms of warfare and tribunal in which he sees things."

"I still hate him," Hillary said. "And there's nobody inside me now but me."

Was the woman claiming some evil spirit had entered her heart and made her want to kill her husband? An uncomfortable notion . . . Something Navarro didn't like known about himself was that stories of possession by dark forces, of people fallen under the control of enemy souls, felt to him quite believable. In East L.A. he'd arrested any number of sunk, baffled fathers or sons who only moments before had torn their houses down around their families, as if demons had come and gone in their hearts. And many times he'd seen a blurry happiness in the eyes of people just arrested for something inexplicable and ugly, as if demons had come and stayed.

"Goddamn Harry," Hillary said, still crying like a child. "Oh, Harry, I hate you . . ."

"Shhh. Shhh. Hush. You and I, we'll end up doing everything, tasting every fruit, whether good or evil. There can be no penalty, no purgatory, no hell. Only a relearning after error. There's no banishment, only wandering. No torture, no retribution for our deeds, no need for forgiveness except our own forgiveness of others. And of ourselves."

Hillary wept, drawing long jagged breaths and giving up her misery in short, interrogatory-sounding outbursts, and Yvonne said, not only to her, but to them all: "Shhhhh . . . It's Eurus . . ."

Shh. It's Eurus: Shhhh . . ." and her susurration blended with that of another flurrying past from offshore. "It's Eurus, god of the east winds." Out the window the runty bull pines and knotted cypresses hardly moved, they had built themselves against exactly such gods. Arboreal contortions, sculpted into agony. Topiary likenesses but likenesses of what? Some grotesque and lovely inner churning.

In the lull as the wind blew by and old Hillary whuffed as if foaling, Fairchild heard again Yvonne's Electronic Obvious in the air. Covering up her true music with this other.

Three days? Another reprieve rescinded, a sort of Easter parody, after three days down under, Lally jumps up whole. Lally back machinating after his glorious subequatorial whirlwind *thing.* The cop, Navarro, looked at Hillary. Crossed his arms over his chest. And then actually crossed his eyes in his face. Good for you. In his sharply creased Sta-Prest sports garb, his acrylic turtleneck from which dangled the black shooting-range wraparounds, you'd pick him out instantly at any political picnic as one of the Secret Service. A non-voter. He'd brought his moll. The waitress was all angles, cartoony, especially as she wore something on the silky side—or just as likely synthetic, what did he know?—a fakey Hindu pants suit, anyway it draped, looked tossed over wires. Fairchild glanced at her more and more often. And she was altogether pretty, the front of her head really just a location for her two immense eyes, quite blue and completely empty of harm. Only did later glances turn up anything else in the way of features, and the lips were full and small and the nose straight and deftly angled and poignantly disfigured by a tiny ring. She had a broad, quiet forehead. Her short haircut curled around forward beneath her ears, which were also lovely, shell-like and almost lobeless, not pierced, and their whorls, the routes to her brain, as he thought of them, not at all complicated. She had great hands, a bit knuckly and marked-up and on closer inspection actually tattooed, but all the better for that, shaped by days in a human life and promising to taste of the whole story. He wished he could lick them. And kiss her eyes. Miracles had blessed her with lids big enough to hide those eyes. When she closed them they came down covering a great dark peace.

He couldn't see Winona's face. She kept herself at an occluding angle, as if one look would audit and judge her. But he'd come for love, not judgment . . . The session, meanwhile, had become an embarrassment. Hillary went on her knees and rooted, at least in the bulging and shrinking candlelight it appeared she did, between Yvonne's delicious thighs. Amid the smoky amber shapes and green shadows. "Shhh. It doesn't involve you," Yvonne consoled her.

"But—"

"It doesn't involve you except by chance. You were there, and he used your body, came into you at a traumatic moment that left you vulnerable. He would have used you to kill your husband—would have made use of your resentments, your anger against him. We all have those feelings of rage and hate toward the ones we love most. But you found your own forgiveness. Thus did you thwart the demon."

A break for tea: the lights back up, another six pounds of hardwood fed frontways into the stove's blank face. "We have to pay the bills around here," Yvonne announced, tapping a wicker bowl on the bookshelf beside her. Despite her frankness, meant to disarm, the bowl skipped among them like a turd. Fairchild passed it on without touching his pockets. The others pitched in. Hillary deposited a check.

"What kind of tea have we got here, Yvonne?"

"Don't you recognize it, Nelson? That's Good Earth. Winona brought it."

"I thought I recognized the spices. I'd forgotten about its existence. Where is she?"

"Winona? She had to go."

He set it down and headed out through the kitchen.

"Winona! Winona!" he shouted in the dark.

The old Dodge. It wouldn't start but after six or seven tries. She'd parked off the drive, shoved right in amongst the scrub, where nobody blocked her exit. He clutched the door handle and looked up at her in the dark cab.

"I love you. Winona. I love you."

She tried again and the engine caught. The forward axle thunked as she engaged the automatic transmission.

"I meant to tell you, sounds like a U-joint going out up front," he said, "but that's not important now."

"Move!"

"I'm moving," he said. "There, I've moved, but let me talk. I love you."

She pulled onto the drive with her shock absorbers squawking. Gone on the highway, down the salt atmospheres. Hillary had parked her jeep behind the Porsche, or he might have chased after her.

By the windows' glow he found his way back to the house and went in again to sit next to Melissa, amid the other idiots and their Idiot Chief. "What are you going to change your name to?" he asked Melissa.

"I think maybe Music. I like folk music a lot."

"Am I interrupting?" he asked the others.

"We were just getting settled again," Yvonne told him.

"What about something more specific? How about Polka?"

Melissa laughed.

"I have thrilling news," he told the others, who'd assembled now as before. "Melissa has changed her name to Polka."

"I did not! He's drunk. But I'm not drunk," Melissa said.

"Have you seen me take one drink today?"

"Well," Yvonne said, "let's settle in and take—"

"Please assure these people of my sobriety."

"—take a few deep breaths, to settle in—"

"Sobriety! To you that's like Mars."

The cop smiled broadly at this until Mo ran a fingernail along his sleeve. He crossed his arms over his chest and shut his eyes as they all got quiet.

Yvonne held a pair of eyeglasses in her left hand. "I want to read you something from this book, just a short paragraph. *The Philosopher's Stone* by F. David Peat." She put the glasses on and bowed her head above the volume in the lap of her skirt, from which she'd probably had to wring, Fairchild wouldn't have doubted, a pint of Hillary Lally's teardrops.

"'Even the smallest region of space is filled with radiation from the extremely low frequencies of the Big Bang remnants, through the range of radio waves, from visible light and into ultraviolet, and so up to gamma rays of the highest energy. This radiation comes from stars, from supernovas, from quasars, from the event horizon of black holes, and from the twisting magnetic fields that stretch across vast regions of empty space. Moreover, all this light is carrying information—it conveys information about its origin in a nuclear process deep within the heart of a star or as matter hurtles into a black hole. Every volume of space is alive with electromagnetic radiation . . . '"

She closed the book, removed her glasses and handed both to Ocean, who rose from her chair and placed them on the bookshelf.

"That's beautiful," Phil said.

"Does it bring anything to mind? About our particular environment."

Ocean said, "The radar domes."

"Exactly."

"The Tibetan dome also," Melissa said.

"Well, that, too. But they're completely different. If everything is, at its heart and soul, electromagnetic radiation, then the radar in this area represents a serious environmental violation. And on a mystical level it violates us, too."

"And what about the Tibetan dome?" Melissa said. "It's big and fat and shiny. Like hell!"

"That dome calls to the soul," Yvonne insisted. "It's full of prayer and meditation. Clarity, not radiation. Emptiness. It's not a threat. But the white domes send out messages, in a sense. Calling to people, messing them up. This should be a place of healing, but instead a great deal of energy is concentrated on looking for, anticipating, destructive intercontinental missiles."

Phil said, "Russia's on our side now anyway. Haven't they heard?"

"Well, I suppose they help direct airline flights, too."

"What if whales could fly?" Phil said. "Wouldn't that play some games with their radar!"

"We should all hang a lot of crystals in every house," Melissa said.

"Crystals won't work."

"They work! I cured my appendix yesterday! With a crystal!"

"Crystals won't work for this."

"What will?" Mo asked.

"Well, some real countereffect might be achieved by burning their commanding officer's body and drinking his ashes in a potion. But it's hard to anticipate where you end up when you engage that kind of negative energy."

Hillary said, "Not *his* body."

"Pardon?"

"It's a woman. A she—the commanding officer."

Yvonne became quite still. "That would be most healing."

"That would work," Hillary said, "without getting too negative?"

"Yes. That kind of feminine sacrifice."

"I'd like to put a query to this policeman," Fairchild said. "Aren't sacrifices of either gender sort of kind of like illegal? Nowadays I mean Officer?"

"So is drunk driving."

Traitors on either hand . . . "Okay, Johnny Cop. I challenge you to a Breathalyzer test. Immediately, please."

"Nelson," Yvonne said. She was lighting a candle and turned from it. "What is this?"

"A matchbook."

"No. It's *this*." She tossed the matchbook at him and he batted it away beneath Melissa's chair. Yvonne pointed at the candle's flame. "And what are we seeing? This? No."

She sat back and regarded them all and smiled. "You know of course that what we're looking at is light. It strikes the eye, produces another impulse, which is also electromagnetic radiation, along a nerve. Cells receiving it discharge other impulses of light. And now we're told the self, the life field on which this makes an impression, is also light . . . The radar domes mess this up. That's why they cause cancer. The cancer is a result of effects on the life field. It stirs up negatives in our perception which we read as sickness. Sickness is anger expressing itself in our perceptions about our bodies."

Fairchild felt his face descending, and put up his hands to catch it. They smelled of Melissa and the Porsche's leather. Of course he was sober! But he was dizzy. The prickly sensation in his blood and the vertigo derived, he was sure, not from the ridiculousness of these cosmological assumptions, but from the fact that all his neighbors seemed to share them. At the same time an intense and accelerating episode of déjà vu, of having lived through this very moment, of being able to remember each frame of time in the process of its passing, seemed to narrow all perception, to focus it ruthlessly on the millisecond at hand. Yvonne's unintelligible voice sounded clearly against his soul, clearly: she was shamming for these people, all this talk of light and fields and dreams, but her voice was the voice of a witch, a vehicle of evil.

Seconds later he felt he may have fainted. The room had collapsed into the desolation of the candles' auras, and it looked like they hadn't got rid of this Randall person after all. She was at it again. The tip-off wasn't in her manner so much as her speech.

"The world may seem to cause you pain. And yet the world, as causeless, has no power to cause. As an effect, it cannot make effects. As an illusion, it is what you wish. Your idle wishes represent its pains. Your strange desires bring it evil dreams.

"Salvation does not lie in being asked to make unnatural responses which are inappropriate to what is real. Instead, it merely asks that you respond appropriately to what is not real—by *not* perceiving what hasn't occurred."

"Yvonne."

"Randall."

"Randall."

"Yes, Nelson?"

"Could you boil that down for us, please?"

"Sure: life is a dream, and to take it as anything else is a form of madness. What you call sanity is just insanity to a less noticeable degree."

"I've noticed much insanity in my life."

"In your waking dream."

"I didn't dream it."

"I'll say it again. All is illusion, therefore all is just as you wish."

"So I'm making the world up? That's an old hypothesis."

"An eternal fact. And when you see this fact, there are two possible responses: the first is to see that you're making it up, and make up something you like. The second is to let God make it up, let him give it a single meaning, his meaning, and cling to that meaning—"

"Which is?"

"Peace and love."

"That's two meanings, if I'm counting right."

"Peace and love, as opposed to war and fear."

"Look. If I'm dreaming, then why should I have any control over my perceptions? I can't control my sleeping dreams, can I? Otherwise they'd reflect my true corruption. Why should a bad man have happy dreams?"

"One day they'll be dialing up these vibes on various monitors. The doctors will adjust our auras and send us home. It'll all be quite nice, even the Christian fundamentalists will approve."

"Look—Yvonne."

"I'm not Yvonne."

"You sound like Yvonne."

"Why not? I'm speaking with her vocal chords."

"Still, some indication—you know—"

"You'd like me to roll up the whites of my eyes and blow smoke out my nostrils?"

"Up my ass is where I think you're blowing smoke, my dear."

"And grant you three wishes"—this in a basso voice that raised applaudatory laughter. "Spirit Guides, help from a higher realm—you don't believe these things," Yvonne-Randall said.

"Maybe I do. But I don't have to like them."

"What's the difference, if they're true?"

"Well, it's another world, dear. Don't I have trouble enough with this one?"

"You're saying you do believe in a spirit existence we can tap into?"

"Actually I find that I do—sometimes—in a very general way—but by ignoring it I find I live with a certain complexity and on several levels. If I participate in your cosmology, what am I left with? Rules. Explanations."

"Well, suggestions anyway. Even some answers, maybe."

"Recipes for magic antidotes. And cheat sheets for deciphering the cosmic codes."

"It doesn't matter what you do. We have time in which to experience everything, belief, nonbelief, and in between."

"Groovy."

"Nelson Fairchild. I want you to get serious. I have a message for you, Nelson."

He feared it concerned Winona. "Okay."

"It's important now that you take seriously what I'm going to say."

"Yes. I'm trying."

"Your father has recently died."

"Is that supposed to be big news?"

"No, it's not. But this is: your father's death is part of something that concerns you deeply, that concerns your soul. There's a term in use now in your world, in limited use—*holocoenosis*. It refers to the fact that each thing, everything, is affected by action on any *single* thing—kind of a cause-and-effect conduction throughout reality."

"Never heard of it."

"Would you by any chance be familiar with certain notions concerning bifurcations in dissipative structures?"

"I most certainly would not. In fact if I had to be I hope I'd kill myself."

"You have a parallel. A soul whose path parallels yours very closely. Kind of a doppelgänger."

"Holy smokes. Kind of a doppelgänger, did you say?"

Beside him, Navarro laughed and then tried to excuse himself with his eyes.

"He's out to devour you. He is a devourer . . . "

Nobody said anything now. Certainly not he himself.

"A soul twin. Many of us have them. In our more comfortable lives we don't meet them. In the lives where we do, the meeting creates cosmic fireworks. Legendary love affairs or strange hatreds . . . "

"For God's sake, spit it out, ghost!"

"Nelson Fairchild. Listen."

Her music had changed. Everybody's music had changed.

"You bitch."

"Are you listening?"

"What have you done with my wife?"

She spoke calmly, setting up no vibrations: "I think we should talk more privately, Nelson."

It made him weak with dread, though it was what he wanted, and he said immediately, "Maybe even in this lifetime. I'll pencil it in."

Later he stood with his keys in his hand, waiting for Hillary to get her rig backed out, and the cop stood next to him with his arm around the waitress's tiny shoulders. Melissa waited in the Porsche. "I'm not drunk," he told the cop.

"I realize that, man. I was just kidding."

"She got me shook. I hate her."

"She's got a rare gift, Nelson," the waitress said.

"Of one kind or another," the cop added.

"I guess so. I don't know. But I know she talks to the dead."

"What if she does?" the cop said. "So what? Why should I believe some asshole just because he doesn't have a body?"

". . . There. There is a man with a complete cranium," Fairchild told Melissa as they all drove off in two directions, "while the rest of us have these gauzy frayed places where bullshit keeps *getting in*."

"Could you drop me at the hotel?"

"If we weren't natural enemies, I'd want to befriend him and stay near him."

"He reminds me of a picture," Melissa said.

"What picture?"

"A *picture*. He's holding still."

"He's steady inside. But he's wrong about Yvonne. She's not a fake. She talks to demons. She works with evil. She can deal."

*   *   *

On his way to the apartment, having dropped Melissa at the hotel, Fairchild swung into the gas station. Nothing else in Gualala was open, nothing but the hotel bar, and that not visibly, stuck away on the building's north side. But here was the Phillips 66, effulgent, clarified, and lonely, like a stage before a darkened audience. It wasn't so much a need for fuel that drew him as the sight of it there, and of the attendant dumping out windshield water like a bucket of stars across the greasy pavement. The attendant stood still and watched with an air of uncertainty until the Porsche's arrival was complete.

"Are you open?"

"Yeah. Sure. Hi."

Fairchild got out of the car. "Should I fill it myself?"

"No, I'm happy to."

"Too late for the windshield, huh?"

"I'll get it. I've got some Windex."

"Let me unlock the cap for you. It locks."

He stood next to the attendant, looking right down on the top of his hatless head. A small young guy pumping gas on the weekdays, on the Sabbath he preached at the little church in West Point. He'd used to be a pitiful case, a drunken wreck and, it was generally assumed, an irremediable moron. Now here he stood, shepherd of a little pickup flock and purveyor of combustible oils. Holding the work of the Quality Nozzle Company in his grip.

"Tell me about demons."

"I'd rather talk about the Savior."

"What do you know about demons?"

"I don't know anything I haven't read in the Bible. You can read the same things, I guess you're aware of that."

"And what about spirit guides? You've heard of them. Do you believe in such guides?"

"Well, going by the Scripture, there'd only be two—the Holy Spirit, and the Devil Satan."

"Channeling—"

"You're only channeling Satan. Better cut it out."

"So you definitely believe in the Devil."

"Definitely. You want the Windex? You're all bugged up."

"Permit me to quote you something from Nietzsche: 'Whoever has theological blood in his veins is shifty and dishonorable in all things.'"

"I'll go along with that."

"I've heard you pitch quite a sermon at the chapel of a Sunday."

"You've heard it? Or heard about it?"

"Billy told me you've got the Spirit."

"You remember what I was like."

"I remember doing rum and coke with you one Fourth of July. Cocaine coke. Not the drink."

"I don't remember. So how could I deny it?"

"I remember you asking me if you could suck my dick, in fact."

"That could be. There's not an alky worthy of the name who hasn't had somebody's joint in his mouth some time or other." The preacher smiled. "So the question is: How did I get all the way here from all the way there?"

"I don't know. How?"

"Somebody prayed for me."

"Yeah . . . So would you do me a favor, please?"

"I won't blow you, no."

"I was going to ask you to pray for me."

"I do already. Every day."

"Thank you."

"You'd be welcome at the chapel tomorrow night. We have prayer meetings Thursdays, usually at somebody's house. But we're getting such a crowd we decided to use the chapel."

"Thank you."

"You're welcome, Nelson. Maybe we'll see you tomorrow night."

"I don't think you will."

"No, I won't count on it."

He turned north but drove past his fourplex building and pushed out of town, keeping the Porsche at a steady run, not slinging it around the curves, through the mute irrelevance of Anchor Bay, down the drop into the gully where the campground slept by the water, past Shipwreck Road and Shipwreck Rock and still northward, the double yellow lines wavering slowly ahead in a world denominated by his headlights. The landscape opened wide past Point Arena, and he continued through it in the general direction of Manchester, until the silvery pastures on his left ended in a grove of some dozen acres. Even in this hour of souls it looked like a friend. In the dark he couldn't make out the fence, only the massive cypress, eucalyptus, and oak—the wrought, asymmetrical varieties . . . His high beams lit up the white arch and the rickety birthday-party lettering suspended across its apex identifying this Catholic graveyard. The trees and graveheads jumped sideways and slid backward as the illumination crossed them. He drove in far enough that his headlights wouldn't draw the gaze of any late traveller, and got out leaving them on to see by and walked.

He left the pavement, started across the graves. Am I ashes? Have I come to scatter myself? The headstones like ruins, leavings. Past the older section and the names eaten up. Among the whiter crosses . . . *Californian.* So here we are. It's Wednesday, do they tell you things like that, down there in California? But I didn't pick up the *Barron's.* Anyway it's night and I can't read because it's almost as dark out here as it is in there. And is somebody praying for me?

Not likely.

But he said he was.

He pumps gas. He pumped you some.

I guess you know everything now.

I know more than I did.

You know—

I know you've walked your nose flat into a corner and you refuse to do the only thing.

Which is?

Turn around.

Excuse me, he said, walking across his father.

He knelt to the bucket of flowers by the gravestone and plucked from it a spongy toy, a ball. Standing upright he held it so as to catch what light he could. But its color was as indiscernible as its purport. He compressed it in his fist and shoved it into his back pocket. He touched his fingers to his father's stone.

He said aloud, "I love you."

September 13, 1990

Fairchild woke in an upstairs room of the Gualala Hotel in the afternoon. Melissa slept beside him: With your wings quivering . . . Around him the windows revolved, the white-hot windows. His grogginess gave everything the quality of extremely old films in which the static hums steadily and the voices move softly and almost inaudibly inside it.

"What did you dream?"

"I dreamed I was sad." Then she laughed. "But that's funny—because I'm not! I'm happy!"

"Are you?"

"But you—you're not. Nelson, why are you crying?"

"My brother. My brother is dead."

"Oh, my God, but you can't be serious! It was only dreaming."

"My brother is dead, and my father is dead."

"Oh, and it hurts—I know!"

"Tell me, baby, what were you sad about in your dream?"

"I was sad because I couldn't be ice. And I woke up now, and now I find out I'm melting."

"Oh! Melissa. Oh! I wish we were."

"Don't cry. Don't cry. It's one of those days."

H e was seeing things not in a decipherable, but in a perceivable, appreciable design—like snowflakes . . .

Van Ness left his car by the Pacific, on a bluff looking down toward the cove that had once, he assumed, harbored Carter's Landing, and he walked from there across the Coast Highway and up to the forested end of Carter's Landing Road. He passed through a neglected truck garden behind a neglected driftwood lean-to at the road's end, some bikey's hooch, some Deadhead's last burrow, and then entered the woods below William Fairchild's cabin, he didn't know how far below, carrying in a pillowcase thrown over his shoulder Nelson Fairchild, Jr.'s .357 Magnum. He turned back, left the path, and from the covering foliage satisfied himself that the lean-to he'd just passed was indeed unattended before going on. The grade steepened, the path narrowed. Probably only William Fairchild and wildlife ever made use of it.

In the deeper woods Van Ness came on a bear trap, corroded to the core and frosted with dry lichen along its jaws' northern edges. The teeth lay wide, and though he judged its springs to have set down long ago, still his groin tingled when he put his hand to the trap's tongue and pressed it.

The woods gave out on a gully to his right; the gully disappeared in vaporous eastward currents; in the currents he saw an entity fashioned of the vapor: an angel with great white wings uplifted from its shoulders, standing upright, an angel profoundly corrupted and profoundly feminine, drinking the blood of its young and turning to suckle strangers. Mother I have your diamonds. The prayers of the Inquisitors. She trailed them in her tresses as dew.

He moved around a broken cedar and lost sight of her, and she was gone, and the roiling mist was gone.

Farther on he entered the big grove. He felt its silence long before he came into the cool hush and sourceless dim light among the trees. They had a peculiar sweet musty smell. Most of the ground had the combed and fertile uniformity of a riding arena's floor. Nothing much grew between the widely separated house-sized trunks other than fern and fungus; no second generation competed with these ancients. Some of them lay fallen, suddenly occupying their astonishing dimensions, like downed airliners. The path divided to circumvent the base of one, the cake of its roots thirty feet in diameter. He walked around the butt and alongside the deteriorating length of it for two hundred paces. He'd come farther into the grove now than he needed, he was certain of that. Ahead he made out shafts of light where the younger forest resumed.

He turned directly to his right, found the edge of the grove, and threaded along this border between two eras until he spotted the creek. He followed the creek upstream to the cabin. Behind the house the grove maintained its immense twilight, though he himself stood amid a sunny thicket of sapling acacias, and in back of him the skyline opened all the way to the sea.

Through the cabin's north window he saw William Fairchild sitting with his feet up on his dining table and his hands locked behind his head.

Van Ness set the pillowcase at his feet, opened it and removed the gun, and then looped the pillowcase through his belt so as not to forget it here. For these simple movements he could hardly find the strength. The coursing of sugars unpent in his blood by adrenaline was turning him dizzy. His extremities fizzed and his ears rang. To decrease his intake of oxygen he opened his mouth and panted rapidly. Instantly as he thought he had the balance for it, he moved to the door and pushed it open. Though Fairchild's shape was at rest, he'd screwed his mouth to one side, one eye squinting, in an expression of puzzled thought; from between his lips a pencil jutted. He removed it and lowered his hands and put his feet on the floor, but he seemed to require some effort to get his attention back to the time and place.

"Can I help you? Excuse me. Can I help you?" When he saw the gun he turned away in flat rejection as he might have turned from a dirty photo or a wicked gesture.

Van Ness walked close, leveled the Smith & Wesson at the back of the head, and depressed the trigger—Fairchild hunched and winced and bits of blood and bone slung like slobber from his jaw as Van ushered him, with fanfare and fireworks, into a neighboring actuality.

For a few seconds the killer held the gun aloft exactly as the recoil had positioned it. He put it to his own head. One.

Two.

Three.

The pin smacked the cap. The cartridge whispered irresolutely. He could hardly hear it for the deafness created by the first shot. He tossed the weapon down beside the corpse's empty hands. It went on hissing.

Twenty seconds later the gun banged off, skipped across the table's surface, whirled around facing him with smoke issuing from its muzzle.

He walked out—he thought he noted a certain breath-held quality to the Pacific, and because he was standing on a grade the very sea seemed to tilt downward from the horizon as he turned himself toward Carter's Landing Road in yet another universe, laughing.

Taylor Merton noted that today even down by the water the weather felt almost tropical beneath the blue sky. Weather you could feel between your fingers. One big cloud had caught in the hills northeast of the Safeway parking lot, where the demonstration was under way; otherwise they had a moment too hot for a policeman's uniform. He wished he'd come undercover, in shorts and a baggy T-shirt.

All these people had stayed hidden since 1975, when they'd finally succeeded in getting America to lose in Vietnam. Not too many of them, about thirty dinosaur hipsters who appeared to have gathered in protest of the president's policies, policies of which they had no understanding whatsoever, as well as a couple dozen shoppers just pausing as they cruised by, and a bunch of kids smoking cigarettes and riding skateboards. Speakers croaking like frog after frog, speaking out against anything, now that a bullhorn was available. Everybody had a theory and nobody had a plan. Yelling now about the possibility of oil rigs going up offshore—well, he supposed that related, at least tangentially, as the Gulf trouble had started over oil.

A man in rags and a Rasta cap and a dozen yardlong blond braids with bells on the ends, his feet in slippers with the tips curling up, his eyes as empty and blue as outer space, danced heel and toe with his arms outstretched, danced like a Hindu god. He stopped still and smiled and pitched over directly backward, making a mysterious percussive sound on the pavement with his head. Merton was glad.

Two teenaged girls sang, "All we are saying—is give peace a chance," three times and then stopped.

A crowd had closed around the blond Rastafarian. Among them Merton spied his own wife, Kimberly.

Like a flagstaff they upraised him to the vertical. Your coma,

Merton thought, is now public and recognized. But the man hadn't stopped smiling. "That was a *thing*!"

Kimberly came over. "He's all right."

"I doubt if that's possible. What do you think you're doing?"

"Doing?"

He'd made her mad just like that. He looked away.

The litter can was full and letting out little kites of jetsam into the wind. A kid whose mother's boyfriend he'd once arrested skateboarded past, smiling at Merton and scratching the tip of his nose with his middle finger.

He linked arms with his wife. "So you came."

"They're going to make war over oil."

"Yeah. Well. Everybody's out here squawking, but your real vote goes in your tank. We vote with our dollars."

"You sound like a cop. I hate to say it, hon, but you do."

"What do you mean?"

"Above it. Aloof. Seen it all, no more passion for you. People are monkeys."

"Martians."

"Yeah."

"Yeah. They are. Let's get behind a bush and do it."

"You're on duty!"

"One Martian to another. I'd consider it an honor. I'm here to service the public."

A man he'd arrested last month for assault with a beer pitcher stood in the pickup's bed with the bullhorn dangling at his hip, speaking without benefit of its juice: "The president has one job. Lie. Lie like hell. The Joint Chiefs have one job. Kill. Kill 'em all. I did a tour in the marines, and that's what it's all about, it is not about anything else, folks, it's about killing. If we continue to let these assholes solve our problems then that's what we're gonna get for the rest of history—lying and killing, killing and lying. Away with government!" He raised the bullhorn to his fat beard. "ANARCHY! ANARCHY! ANARCHY! ANARCHY!" Nobody else took up the chant, and he smiled around and handed the device down to someone else—to Kimberly.

She stepped up to take the man's place. She'd gotten heavy, ungraceful, particularly in the hips and thighs. Merton didn't mind, not often, anyway, but now he minded. Kimberly raised the horn, spoke in a thin piping tone, examined the equipment, got the button right. "I JUST WANT TO ADD MY VOICE," she said. "LET'S NOT HAVE THIS WAR." She lowered the thing, looked around at expectant neighbors, lifted it to her mouth. "I DON'T KNOW WHAT ELSE TO SAY BUT THAT. THANK YOU."

A few old acidheads applauded. They'd gotten up out of their graves to attend this thing. Around them orbited two kids on bikes, shot forward stiff-legged over the handlebars like gargoyles or bowsprits, hopping the curbs. He drilled them with a glance and waved his finger and shook his head, and at that moment elected, forever in his soul, to quit the police before much longer and run against the mayor. Kimberly could go to work. She had a nursing license.

Fairchild zigzagged the small room in the Gualala Hotel, holding up his whites by the waist. "Where's my belt? Where's my belt?"

"You look like a monkey in his cage," Melissa said.

"I'm happy to amuse you."

"A chim*panzee*."

"Delighted you're delighted." He opted for getting his shirt on, snatched it from the floor, and uncovered the belt beneath it. Just these white socks—just these canvas shoes—these laces—these slow purgatorial tortures. "I believe we're way the hell past checkout," he said.

She pulled the sheet up taut over her head.

The intimations of her shape and the blindness and innocence of her intimated face; and suddenly he wasn't terrified anymore.

"I know everything."

"Oh! My God! Are you starting again?"

"I just want you to know I know."

"Then wonderful! Maybe you didn't realize that I realize that you realize!"

Leaning against the door frame, he put his face in the crook of his arm and laughed.

"Get out!"

"Take off your shroud and look at me."

"Get out!"

Downstairs he searched for someone at the desk whom he might inform that he wasn't paying for another day. But they were all out back gambling or in the john sniffing paint. Bills, requests, complaints might be dealt with also in the barroom; but he didn't want to cross its border. He'd ended up in there last night, and even at this moment, standing before a vase of richly colored flowers, he heard the strains of his own laughter still ricocheting among its walls. And somewhere outside, a robot's amplified voice crying, *Anarchy! Anarchy! Anarchy!*—Yesterday Yvonne in the middle of your phony seance the ground opened up. I saw the depth of my danger. I cried out my last words, I shouted my love to my wife. I went to the preacher. I went to my father's grave. And then to the hotel bar, the cathedral of parched souls with its big screen of heaven and in every hand a cigarette smoking like a nightsome, griefly thurible. I dived deep into the woman I no longer love. And all the time it tasted and sounded like any other day, I went to sleep terrified and woke up falling forever, and only the sight of her beneath the sheet like half a thought, like a tentative scribble, saved me—

But only, he sensed, momentarily. The wooden floorboards boomed under his steps, and he stood outside under a hot blue stratosphere squinting and trying to recognize his car. Something was happening out back, in the region that passed for Gualala's shopping mall. The fruit stand was trading briskly. Somebody was making a speech through a bullhorn from the back of a pickup truck. A crowd of several dozens had collected. People: shocks of straw, ready to break out in flames, disintegrate into ash. He was seeing too much. Before his eyes a kid on a bike ran over a quarter section of watermelon, turning it to bloody—There it is.

And how good its leather, and how it howls. All the way up to the ridge in second gear.

Off the ridge road he had to go carefully, passing two or three quiet, dusty homes before reaching his brother's land. He coasted to the side of the drive where it deteriorated into its ruts and little washes, and left the Porsche and set out walking, easily, as it was all downhill. He muddied his knees at the spring halfway along, and continued, wiping the water from his mouth and the sweat from his eyes. When he heard a motor somewhere behind him, he climbed a few yards up the bank to his right, realized he couldn't get out of sight quickly enough, clambered back down and across the road and huddled in back of a pungent bull pine as a jeep passed by: Billy's

International Scout, and it looked like Clarence Meadows at the wheel.

The vehicle blinked out around the next bend, and Fairchild resumed his own descent through its hovering exhaust. The sweetness of his exile, the shelter of these trees, their surrounding staunch idiocy, he took these things to his heart: he knew what Billy meant when he said the radar couldn't get him here. He'd give the Porsche to Clarence, give it to him free. If Billy wouldn't have him in the cabin then he'd camp right here for his lifetime, close by the clean trickling spring.

At the last bend Fairchild paused to watch Clarence, there below, where the path to the cabin joined the drive, walking backward out of the wood, and next standing still and looking at his own hands. He executed a series of dancelike, thwarted maneuvers, as if swarmed by stinging insects. He shouted, "Oh *no* you don't!" and turned facing the head of the path and cried, "Bull—*shit!*" and then feinted to his right, feinted to his left. He turned and looked up at Fairchild, waving both his hands and showing such agony that Fairchild thought he must have burned them.

Fairchild let himself slowly down the road.

Clarence hurried to meet him. "Don't go down there."

"I'm not climbing up that hill again. I'll get him to ride me."

"Nelson, he's gone. He's dead. He's face-flat on the table with his head shot in. Don't go down there."

"Billy?"

"I'm trying to figure out what to do."

"Wait a minute."

"No, there ain't no waiting on this one, he's dead."

"No. Just a second."

"Okay, yeah, I know."

"Yeah. Wow."

"Take a minute to get used to it. But get used to it."

"Wow. Billy. Killed himself!"

"He didn't kill himself. He wouldn't do that. He was fighting off those sons of bitches, those rats in his head."

"Fighting off? With a single-shot thirty-aught-six?"

"He went down with a three-fifty-seven in his hands."

"God."

"Either that or a thirty-eight, a revolver about that size, with about a four-inch barrel. That's all I saw. Maybe five inches."

"Maybe—you're sure he's dead? Maybe—"

"He's dead."

"Oh, my God. What a day for this world. The whole world."

"Come on with me."

"I can't. I'm gonna . . ." He gestured downhill, down the snaking road through the quiet wood toward his dead brother.

"I guess you have to."

"Oh yeah. I mean definitely."

He went down to the cabin and entered.

Fairchild scurried humpbacked through the brush carrying a great hollow region of storms inside him, in fact a dark where new gods must work vast horrors, the dark that should have been his brother's life. He had to keep shutting his jaw because his mouth hung open. He wasn't breathing. He was stopped against a tree's enormous muteness. A great hairy cedar with rot in its heart. He collapsed to sit at its feet and prayed to live forever in this anonymously peopled wordless place. He fell forward and threw his face against a root, wishing to break his teeth, and lay low as his blood drained downward and left his thoughts, white, skeletal and patterned, flaring before his mind's eye like sunlight on snow. From it issued the irresistible star-hot purity of his brother's and father's deaths and burned every trivial thing to ash and then burned the ashes. The sigh of wind grubbing in the treetops and moving the shadows of clouds and the ocean's far serrated thunder worked a swift metastasis over the land, and he suddenly experienced this dirt as the place of his life, and the outer world as something to be visited as with a ticket. That quickly his troubles divested themselves of his complicity.

He found his feet below him and watched them move, listened to the syncopation of his breaths and his steps. He shortened a dry stick of alder across his knee and hiked at a rapid march up the track toward the ridge road, and it began to seem as if he were turning the earth, dragging it toward and shoving it behind him with his staff. The more breathless and strengthless he felt as he climbed, the happier he became. He consciously desired for his eyeballs to burst from his efforts. He wanted his lungs to rupture. When he gained the ridge road he tossed aside his walking stick and broke into a trot. At the sounds of an approaching vehicle he changed course, left the road, and tore at a sprint into a thicket of manzanita that grappled with him until he went down, scratched and punctured in his flesh, and couldn't get himself up. He lay in this gnarled embrace with his left cheek in the dirt, inhaling and exhaling.

—That gun.

After a while, as much as half an hour, he turned onto his back and was surprised to identify his thoughts as his thoughts and to recognize himself as the same person he'd always been.

—Oh gun. I know you.

He sat up, located his shirttail, wiped at his face and neck. He wobbled to his feet and stood still, getting his balance on the earth.

—That was my gun.

Following his own course where he'd broken along through the chaparral, he took to the road again.

Some two miles north, at the intersection with Shipwreck Road, he turned left and commenced a mild curving decline toward the lowering sun, paralleling the panicked ascent he'd recently accomplished. Within twenty minutes he'd reached Wilhelm Frankheimer's driveway.

He crossed the yard beside an old VW van looking rather like the Sheep Queen's, with its purple peace and yin-yang logos and its bristle-textured sunburst-yellow paint job; passed among the stacks of scrap lumber, the two rusted MG sports cars and the mangled Ford Econoline, a pile of half-tools, a mountain of rebar and cables and chains; and would have knocked at the door had he not heard Melissa gasping in her characteristic way somewhere in the house. He stepped away from the stoop and looked through the window, across the living room and beyond, through an open doorway into Frankheimer's study, at the sight of them making love. And superimposed on it, his own reflection in the glass.

He brought himself into focus: translucent voyeur, like a ghost on his widow's wedding night. A thing removed to clarity.

In the living room someone talked: the TV was running: two scrupulously finished men in conversation, each leaning into the camera when speaking so that he appeared to be gazing into the study at the male and female joined there. Beautiful how huge he was and she how small. Reeling and rocking in the vampire light. They occupied the couch. Frankheimer kept his left hand flat on the floor to support his weight and with his right hand gripped the windowsill, jamming his loins repeatedly against hers so that her frail legs flapped like ropes and her little hands touched along his ribs as if seeking for something lost. Fairchild couldn't see her face. Frankheimer's head and shoulders stuck far beyond the arm of the divan, and she was somewhere under him, gasping, sobbing. Beyond them, past the end of the divan and Frankheimer's fantastically large feet, stood a set of shelves, and on it some sort of small engine, ribbed and greasy. Nearer to Fairchild, the living room looked in process, half-assembled in its walls and floor, and he noted also the grimy raised fireplace near the dining room's entrance, and on the dining room table a fat happy jar of peanut butter and a knife like a jaunty feather sticking out, and a plastic bag of bread, its ties loosed and the loaf unaccordioned onto the tabletop, a brand he surely recognized—"Ezekiel 4:9" it was called, after the biblical verse from which it took its recipe—wheat, barley, lentils, millet—a combination from which, Melissa was thus assured, emanated the finest nutrient powers. It was the prescription's exotic antiquity that convicted her, having reached her here across the many ages in her twentieth-century skinniness. It wouldn't have done to point out that her credulousness on this score unzipped the whole overstuffed question of the rightness of other biblical prescriptions—had they, or had they not, known what's good for us? How about the stoning of adulterers? Should I be fingering around my feet for a big old rock? But her thoughts ranged on the same brief leash as anybody else's anyway, such was the philosophizing of America, merely to survey its inconsistencies, its gaps and plunges, was to invite a bad dose of vertigo—*and* the man smothering her: he'd seen him just the other day, no more than a glimpse of looming strangeness as he, Fairchild, slowed for the curve before the gas station in Anchor Bay, and he, Frankheimer, had not looked well, looked like one to be shunned, untouchable even by the beauty of his surroundings, the sun piercing the moment, the fish-boats bobbing in a painful yellow glare, and the man's music, even, seemed to follow him at a distance, catching up reluctantly as he tottered beside the pumps and stared, chewing both his lips, over the sea: the Violent Femmes—"Hallowed Ground"— warped-amerika music, oh those nasty lyrics invoking patriarchal sacrifice, lamb's blood, weeks of psychotic purification in the desert, lonely murders at turnpike rest stops: *Don't you know nothing? You never tell no one, don't you know nothing? You never tell no one—*

Frankheimer rose up, covered his exquisite body with a ragged robe of brown cloth, headed toward the dining room, shutting behind him the door to the study and closing the robe's folds over the arc of his sesquipedalian dick. Now they were linked, Fairchild and this giant, Melissa the author of this union and in some sense its offspring. Now in this woman they were mixed. Fairchild had known him as a plumbing contractor, the kind you're sorry you hired, who sometimes had to be rousted out of this very house, where he sat surrounded by his weird books and theories, the kyrie eleison on his stereo, the cocaine and the channeling, the people inside his walls. Now they were married.

—I'm convinced of it, everybody's dead inside. Jerking, empty carcasses. Their souls have gone out like lights.

Fairchild knocked on the door. He watched through the window as Frankheimer went about lighting his fire. He knocked again. Drew back a foot to kick at the door and then his guts subsided and he tapped on the window. Frankheimer must have made him out, if vaguely, beyond the glass. He raised one finger and crossed to the door and opened it.

"Well. Here's somebody I don't owe money to."

"Can I come in?"

"That might be interesting. Sure."

He left Fairchild to shut the door after himself and reached to pull the cord at the window and shut the drapes. Now it was nearly dark in here. Frankheimer perched on the stone lip of the fireplace and picked up a hurricane lamp and occupied himself with the business of getting them some light.

"A little early for curtains," Fairchild said—"or a little late," and sat some feet away in an easy chair with his hands in his lap.

Without having to stand up to accomplish this, Frankheimer set the lantern on the mantel. The living room wasn't in process at all. It had served as ground for some manner of apocalyptic visitation. "Yeah. PG&E resents me. The power's off. I haven't been functioning."

"But didn't I just hear the TV? Among other things?"

"It's been off for two minutes. They don't turn you off till you're in the middle of a program."

"Not that you were watching."

From the study, no sound came. He might have confronted her then and there. But he had no curiosity about how she'd act.

Frankheimer said, "This is fun!"

He regarded Fairchild, smiling, and moved away from the fire, as it was quite hot now.

A curious trick of Fairchild's mind suddenly rendered the fireplace irrelevant, and he witnessed a man seated next to some burning wood. The man's eyebrows were arched in a fixed expression of curiosity, and when he leaned back into the shadows the sockets filled with darkness, making him look masked, giving his features the aloof inquisitiveness of a raccoon's.

"Is your father living?" Fairchild felt moved to ask him.

The giant reached up with thumb and forefinger and removed from his mouth two widely spaced artificial teeth wired to a plastic upper plate. He replaced them and shut his lips around them. "My father's alive. He's a Southern Californian. I owe him money."

"My father's dead. Three days ago I attended his funeral."

"Funeral for a snake."

"For Christ's sake, you're talking about my father."

"He was a snake before he was your father."

"I'll tell you something else."

"Will you."

"Billy blew his own head off. I just saw him with his brains coming out the back. Sitting at his own table. And I don't understand it." The sobs came up now. "I can tell you that much for goddamn sure."

Frankheimer scowled and coughed, but didn't speak. He used a sliver of redwood to drag something from the fire's edge. A cigarette butt. He skewered it and put its end into a flame.

"I want to find that friend of yours. And I know goddamn well he's your friend or at least well known to you, so just fuck any attempt to fucking mislead me, just fuck that."

"Okay. Consider it fucked."

"Carl Van Ness. Where is he."

"Unknown."

"Give him up. He's dead sooner or later."

"Sooner's fine with me."

"You think I'm *that* gullible." Fairchild raised his voice. "Hi, Melissa!" He stared at Frankheimer. "I know she's there."

"She won't come out."

"I know that too."

Frank brought his cigarette butt to his lips, puffed up a glow. "Did Billy really kill himself?"

"Billy. He really really did."

"You saw him."

"All messed up and completely dead, I mean it."

"Shot?"

"Yes."

"Did they say it was suicide?"

"They? The authorities? The authorities who authorize nothing? They don't even know he's dead."

"Maybe it wasn't him who pulled the trigger."

"Maybe it was Carl Van Ness."

"If that's what you really think, don't worry. I don't care, pal, I'd roll over on him in a heartbeat, but I don't know his whereabouts."

"Is Van capable of that in your opinion?"

"Oh yeah. He'll end up at Quentin. In the gas chamber."

"Yeah?"

"No question. He's all twisted up. He'll see. Van worked this strange trick on himself a long ways back. I'll tell you how to understand it. He's not psycho, not warped, wasn't brought up bad, no. He's not corrupted by this or that, like a politician, or a priest. But it's like this. Did you ever get a thing going with yourself where, let me make up an example, you start to feel that if you tie the left shoe first, something bad's gonna happen, so you tie the right shoe first? Then you're about to catch the doorknob with your right hand, but no, that's gonna fuck things up, so you have to"—he made a motion—"gotta use the left hand. Gotta pay with this dollar, leave this other dollar alone. Can't scratch my head till I count to five. Stuff like that all day long?"

"Some days. Many days. Quite often."

"So what do you do to keep from turning into one big neurotic knot?"

"Me? I resist."

"Exactly, man. You say fuck it. You override the impulse as a general thing. That's where Van is at, *right there*, but on another level, much further on down. He's turned that inside out. It's genius. He overrides any *override*, see boy? He actualizes every impulse. Years ago he started this—I knew him—we were comrades—I'm privy to this. Man. He's made himself into a knife. Just cuts right on through. Do it, don't think twice. That's his idea of freedom."

"You're absolutely right. I recognize him there. You're right."

"I don't admire it. Just on paper. No tragedies on paper. But life ain't paper."

"No, it's not."

"Yeah. He's not a crook—he's a demon. Transformed from the flesh."

"He's beyond good and evil."

"Right, how many's that—four words. He read four words of Nietzsche and ran out and built a life." Frankheimer laughed now. "I was the one who made the mistake of introducing him to Nietzsche."

"Nietzsche! I shit on Nietzsche. Have you ever tried to spell Nietzsche? Good luck!"

The door to the study opened. Melissa came out, looking at neither man, and sat by the fire staring into it. Fairchild leaned forward. He held out his hands for her to see. "I have been inauthentic. This isn't me."

She looked up at the ceiling and sang out, "Right now, it's impossible!"

Fairchild wept. "Nothing can hide it from me now: I loved my father. I love my wife. I know what love is. I see what it is—" Apologetically, with his dirty forearm, he wiped at his lips and nose.

Melissa and Frank were like two spectacularly unmatched andirons, he on the raised hearth and she on the floor.

"You don't know how tiny you are," Fairchild told her.

Frankheimer laughed. Melissa regarded her knees and very nearly smiled.

"Let's think about this," Frankheimer said. "You up for that?"

"Thinking?"

"About Van Ness. You really want him? All his life, he's worked the water. Water is his element."

At half past six, very near to sunset, Navarro turned onto the road down to Arena Pier with his stomach growling. Mo waited up at her place with two ribeye steaks, but he had to take care of this thing—because Merton had received the call, taken his own pulse, and diagnosed himself with a headache, putting Navarro's own status at on-call and unfed. Also pissed off. But as he rolled past the water-treatment facility and left behind its tainted atmosphere and felt himself dropping out of sight of the town itself, dropping into the twilight and into the quiet of an hour that truly felt like autumn, his irritation gave over, and he was surprised to find himself drifting with a sickly and fascinated heart in the big machine along the flanks of tattered homes. Where the hills on either side opened out toward the harbor, the haphazard rows of rootless dwellings, trailers founded on cinder blocks and unmatched rounds of timber, and the kennels with their wire fences bellied out or torn, and the trucks without tires or windshields, and the axles, engines, and appliances stashed under fraying plastic, and the wood smoke, and the bleary windows, all of it tugged at him as if he'd lived here once and missed it ever since. In this light it looked like somebody's idea of art, maybe his own. It all seemed all right—depressing, yet special—it all seemed out of reach. At the road's end the new pier, its wood still clean, strode out over the purple water. He drove down there and stood by the cruiser's open door studying the harbor's surface, but saw nothing floating on it other than dark quiet vessels, no more than a dozen of them. He got behind the wheel again.

The trailers had no numbers, but according to his directions it was only a matter of locating the one with an aluminum canoe out front. This he managed, and got out of the car and stood listening to small sounds which, by their separateness, made everything seem all the more quiet: a voice; a faucet; another voice; a refrigerator door; a TV hiccuping through the channels. A dog lived under the canoe, a small husky that didn't bark at him but just pulled at its chain, panting. Its bucket had toppled and rolled beyond its reach. Navarro set it right, and the animal plunged its head into the dark to chop at the inch of water remaining.

He knocked on the door in anticipation of the usual tableau, a couple of sad angry women, a couple of terrified kids, a couple of exhausted drunks with ripped shirts and rug burns. Only this time one of them would be wet from the sea.

But when a woman in a long quilted robe opened the door, the space behind her undisturbed and almost somber, he sensed he may have awakened her from a nap.

"Katrina Wells?"

"Mom."

"Okay. Mom. Who's fighting, Mom?"

"Mom called it in."

"Anybody requiring assistance inside your house?"

"Let me locate my slippers." The woman turned away, keeping the door open with her hand, and next came out wearing black rubber boots on her feet. "She's over here."

He made way for her and followed across the yard to the adjacent trailer, the door of which she slapped with the flat of her hand. "Mom! Your police have arrived!" She opened the door herself and went through. Navarro stood at the threshold and looked inside to find no recuperating combatants, only a teenaged boy on a kitchen stool, and a woman standing beside the gas range and saying, "Hah! Hah!"

"Katrina Wells?"

"Hah!" She gestured toward the youngster with her cigarette, which she held in the V of her thumb and index, the palm of her hand cupped beneath it. He'd seen monocled Nazis in the movies holding their cigarettes like that.

"I tell him fix his hair, his hair is silly. So he put on a hat. But the hat is silly, too! You see?"

"You're not my mother," the boy said.

"What is this about?" Navarro asked.

"You take your time, hah?"

"Previous shift took the call."

"Well, he left a long time. He go. He gone."

"She looks sillier than me," the boy said. His grandmother, if that was the relationship, wore baggy jeans and what Navarro guessed must be a Mexican vest, and those pug-nosed duck boots. She looked like anybody. And the boy's hat looked like anybody's hat.

"You reported a fight?"

"Fighting. Two men."

"Two people," her daughter said, "maybe two men."

"Two people! Men are people!"

"Wait, now. Who witnessed this?"

"I witness this. I."

"Just her," the daughter said.

"Did you recognize them?"

"They stand on the pier. Fighting."

"Were you on the pier at the time?"

"No. Just here, from the kitchen. He had a stick, a pipe, something."

"Okay, you think two men. Probably."

"He hit him like a baseball."

"Then what?"

"He fell in! Then he stand there waiting to see is he coming up or is he drown." She clamped her cigarette between her lips, hunched her spine, and raised her clasped hands to the level of her right ear. "Like this. Batter up!"

"What is your nationality, Mrs. Wells, may I ask you?"

She took a step closer, fixing him dead-on with a hooded gaze. "I—em—a—United States."

In order to keep from laughing, Navarro opened his mouth and breathed through it. His training had included this. "You a baseball fan?"

Mrs. Wells vigorously nodded, sucking at her cigarette, and spoke through her smoke. "Very much. Eighty-eight I saw Oakland sweep Boston. I was there in Candlestick. Game number four. "

"Are you Italian maybe?"

"She's not Italian," the boy said. "She's Slavic, and she's crazy."

"My dad married her about five years ago. He brought her from Yugoslavia."

"Yugoslavia! So what?" Mrs. Wells asked.

"So one guy knocked another guy off the pier with a pipe or a stick and waited to see if he came back up. Did he?"

"Who? What?"

"Did the man who fell in come back up?"

"What am I telling you? No! Please understand me—this description is a major crime. I witness a murder."

"And the guy with a stick—"

"Him? He throws it away. And I don't know after that. I called the telephone to report my findings."

"Did you see him leave the area?"

"I didn't see—no. But he left—yes. I heard a car."

"But you didn't see him get into the car, or see who was in the car that you heard, is that right?"

"God! I'm sorry, but how did they give you a job on the police? What am I saying to you? He's drown in there right now! Go get him out!"

"I already had a look. There's nobody floating in the immediate vicinity."

"Hah! But what about if he's far away?"

"Exactly. That's just the thing. So listen to me now, Mrs. Wells. I want to nail it down as to when this happened, because if there's a chance somebody's floating around out at sea who can still be rescued and revived, then I'm gonna have to call for an operation that's gonna keep a lot of people up working all night and run the county and state about fifteen thousand dollars. How long ago did you see this fight?"

"Thirty minutes. Nobody came!"

"Thirty minutes at least?"

"Even forty-five minutes. You didn't come! Then you came and had a nice long discussion! About Yugoslavia! About baseball!"

"Don't anybody leave, please. I'll take another look."

He drove back the hundred meters or so to the water's edge and sent the spotlight's shaft along the pier's pilings. The water sent it back. He left it lighting the pier, lifted the mike from its cradle. Cleared his throat. How would they be addressed? "Boats on the harbor"? He thumbed the button: *Boats on the harbor. Any occupants of boats in the harbor. Is there anyone on any boat out there?"* And then he added as if ashamed, *"This is the police."*

Among the trailers to his right he noticed doorways lighting up and one or two silhouettes in them; but the boats only floated in the dark. Taking his flash, he left the car and walked to the phone booth in front of the Cove Restaurant, a large building that had been closed for some weeks in anticipation of an overhaul. He squinted at the water as he dialed Merton at his home.

"Mrs. Merton?"

"No. It's me. Who's that? Navarro?"

"Yeah. Look—"

"Did I sound like a woman?"

"No. I don't know."

"What's going on? You get to the pier?"

"I'm at the pier right now. Look, can I get a boat out here with a good spot on it? Just a private boat, gimme a suggestion who to call. Somebody may or may not have witnessed a possible attack nearly an hour ago where a guy went in the drink, possibly unconscious."

"I thought it was a trailer-court beef."

"It is and it isn't."

"Man overboard, huh?"

"I wouldn't want to call in the Coast Guard or whoever. I guess he'd be ashore by now or drowned, one of the two, huh?"

"Unless he revived, and washed out past the easy water. So then he'd be swimming around out there."

"Shit."

"Oh yeah."

"Goddamn it."

"Did you check the shore?"

"I'm at the shore. I'm sweeping my flash around as we speak. A lot of rocks is all I see."

"You better get me a corpse, or we're gonna have a major production."

"Could he last an hour? I mean, it's pretty cold water."

"It's pretty cold, yeah."

"Could he last?"

"I'd say no."

Before he went back among the trailers he walked the pier, a solid and expensive structure some two hundred yards long, with a kiosk halfway down, and he burned the water with his light, but couldn't break its surface. No ghostly hand ascended. The rocks all looked like rocks. The tide's edge came not much closer than beneath the kiosk.

Katrina Wells stood on her doorstep when he drove up. He rolled down his window and motioned her over. "I'm gonna go right back down there," he said, "but let me just check this with you. The two guys fighting. They must have been this side of the cabin, am I right?"

"The cabin?"

"The hut there, I guess it's the harbormaster's office?"

"They were this way."

"Yeah, or you couldn't have seen them. Less than halfway down the pier."

"Close to the cabin. This side."

"Okay. Don't disappear on me, I'll be back." He left his window down and drove back to the pier with the varied aromas of dinnertime coming in to torture him, and he got back on the phone to Merton.

"You do sound like a woman."

"Who's this, please?"

"It's me again."

"What is it now?"

"What do you mean, what is it? It's the same damn thing."

"Are you loving it, John?"

"Listen. Which way is the tide going?"

"It's against us, as usual."

"I'm serious. If it's going out, I don't know. But if it's coming in, then the guy couldn't have hit the water because there's no water there. And if he didn't hit the water, then he must've boogied on his own steam, because he's for sure not down there now."

"John, all this is terribly confusing. Just call in the cavalry, will you?"

"Is that your decision?"

"Get them all out there. I want frogmen and airmen and everybody else. The fire volunteers and everybody."

"How much is this gonna cost the township?"

"Okay, don't call the volunteers. They're the only ones we have to reimburse in real money. Just call me back on the unit so they can pick it up on the scanner, and they'll turn up. They'll be all over the pier inside of thirty minutes. And better call the cafe."

"The cafe's closed."

"Not the restaurant. The cafe on Main. Tell them to stay open."

"Jesus, man."

"Folks gotta eat. And jot down your every thought, word, and deed, because the town council is gonna grill you."

"Me?"

"Yeah. Till you're crispy and tasty and just right."

"What about you?"

"They love me. They hate you."

"I've ascertained that he didn't hit the water."

"He didn't hit the water."

"Nobody hit the water. We do not have a water emergency."

"That's excellent. All I can say is I'm glad you didn't call me on the unit."

"I may be stupid, but I'm not insane."

"John, are you loving it?"

"I'm ejaculating quarts."

"Call me back on the unit. I wanna play with the druggies."

Merton took no small pleasure in discussing, for the benefit of growers he felt were scanning the police band, fictitious impending federal sweeps and searches.

This case was closed. Navarro wanted his supper and he wanted his lover. He determined that his best course was to call Mo on the pay phone and ask her to fire up the steaks. He thanked Mrs. Wells and assured her that everything had been taken in hand.

"You found somebody? I told you!"

"Well, if there's somebody out there waterborne, he's floated out of sight. We've alerted the Coast Guard."

"But you have to get out there, you must *look*."

"Mrs. Wells," he said, "my car don't float. We've alerted the Coast Guard."

About eight, just as they were sitting down with two steaks and two candles between them, he had to dress and leave Mo for a noise call. In a house not a hundred yards from the station, he found teenagers rioting happily among fumes of hashish and spilt liquor. The parents of the two brothers hosting this affair were in Missouri at a funeral. Finding for once a little justice in his job—they'd spoiled his evening, he'd spoil theirs—he delivered a speech, took down names, made the young girls cry. By the time he'd phoned all the homes and the children had bent low to sit in cars beside silent, angry fathers and be taken away to hell, it was past eleven. The chance to mistreat young idiots had snapped the day's grayness. He returned to Mo's place jovial. He felt too hungry to bother changing until he'd had some food. Mo put the steaks in her microwave and poured him a glass of wine, but before he could sip of it even once, the beeper blew. He had to go down to the Coast Highway for a vehicle-pedestrian accident not far north of Shipwreck Road.

CHP had it well in hand when he arrived, and in a dewfall that sparkled in the crimson billows of road flares two patrolmen and four EM techs were just raising a big man in the cradle of their arms onto a gurney.

Navarro pulled to the shoulder with the cars of stalled travellers and let the ambulance pass, then gave the cherry a spin and blinked his headlights. One of the patrolmen waved while the other stalked the pavement, letting out tape from a measure. Navarro chose to interpret these signs as his dismissal. He turned the cruiser around and drove back to Mo's, thinking to himself that he was almost certain the large victim had been Wilhelm Frankheimer.

In his sleep Fairchild turned over, and water poured into his mouth. He'd experienced dreams of such terrors. Yet this seemed like waking. Not sleep, but numbness. A vast stampeding liquid clucked about his head and dragged at his right sleeve, turning him over again and smothering him again. In order to wake himself he screamed: a distant sound, played back at reduced RPM, a slow-motion voice that suddenly he heard quite loudly as his head surfaced.

His eyes opened on the brilliant coast of Mendocino County a quarter-mile distant, brilliant for its springing up into view, but actually washed in the sunset. Bald-faced cliffs, and the flat scalp of trees raked over toward the ocean, and—as again the currents upended and released him—a sky without planets or stars, and the moon no more than a rind, all this too daylit to be a dream. Facing the empty horizon now. Any strength frozen out of him. Echoing off to his right, the sound of water sucking at rock. He willed to swim his way to the sound, but his hands stirred around his hips only by the action of the seething liquid. His ear raked against something painful, and an unaccountable spasm sent his left hand flying toward it. He draped his arm over an outcropping and thus kept his breath above the eddies. Let the motion lift him. Moving, it seemed, entirely by the power of a visceral desire. Virtually without the ability even to raise his foot. Slowly took himself aboard. Rested in the lee of the rock and the shadow of its brow. Spray coming around the corner made a rainbow. The sun slowly found him. He lay back on the rock and his flesh felt for any amount of warmth where the late light touched it. No other sensation reached him.

The left side of his head began to feel warmer than any other part of him, and before long it produced a pulse that became an unbearable black booming in his skull. His legs and back began hurting, and all this he took as a signal that some kind of life had been granted him. By rolling onto his left side and clutching at a knob of stone, he raised himself slightly and took his bearings, anxiously mindful of the sun's descent, of the coming darkness in which he'd be stranded. This rock lay not too far off Schooner Beach, south of Point Arena—he'd come half a mile along the water and hardly participated in the process. On the shore stood a palomino pony, bareback and free, alternately staring off toward the sunset and nodding at tufts of grass. From here three rocks made a line generally southeast toward it. He could flounder from one to the next and deliver himself back to the shallows. From there he didn't know. His legs might move him toward the land, or he might be carried back strengthless into the swells.

He put his face to the flat, glimmering debouchment and sucked until his lips were numb, then got upright and vomited weakly and went on climbing the steady rise alongside Schooner Creek to the Coast Highway. The exertion warmed him, but the hires of this incredible day came final as he reached the lay-by at the road, and he closed himself in a sturdy government outhouse, sitting on the cessbox, leaning sideways into the corner, pulling his feet up out of the ventilating draft across the floor, sleeping while the chill worked back into his bones and later waking aghast, baffled, in this chamber like an upright coffin. He fought to his feet, banged out into the blustery dark and oriented himself. Rather than use the facilities, he stood next to the cubicle working at the zipper of his damp whites, and urinated at length on the ground before setting out south along California 1. When he heard a vehicle approaching he stood still with his thumb raised, but as the lights topped the rise he took himself into the roadside trees and hid while it passed by. A half mile along, a raincloud caught him coming up the coast. It blew over in minutes.

Just north of the property he came on the site of a recent accident, long white painted lines intersecting with skid marks, designs of blood on the pavement, the scattered stub ends of high-way flares. A secret aftermath. None of it easily discernible in the night. The lights turned off on a party where everyone's been arrested. A party where the child has died. The birthday a deathday, the roman candles deranged by the wind and dribbling brimstone.

He veered from the path to the front door and stood in the slight illumination of the living room window, looking in; warm now from his hike of several miles, overly warm, and breathing hard. Still wet and stinking of the sea. Smelling of brine and spilt diesel. His reflection a mist-like darkness in the glass.—I'm the Coast Silky now. He put his face against this faceless other's. Saw nobody in the dim living room.

He heard her voice inside, talking low, and sensed by its tones the presence of an evil guest. Then he saw her pass the window, silhou-etted in the aura from a candle. Just a shadow. This was now absolutely the way of all.—I've made a world in which the men are sinister and the women completely opaque. In the shifting dark now shapes stir.

He tapped the glass with his fingertips. "Yvonne."

If she wasn't alone he would leave. Again he tapped, and the shape came close. "Yvonne. It's Nelson."

"Nelson?"

"Nelson Fairchild. I want to see you. Is anybody there?"

She turned and went to the front door. He sighed and tapped against the glass again, but she didn't hear.

He met her where she stood in the doorway looking right and left into the dark. "Nelson—"

"Who's with you?"

She backed away into the house as if she thought he'd do her violence. Stood in the center of an oval rug of Persian design in the center of the room, her legs silhouetted in billowy pantaloons and her midriff bare, like the denizen, the chief wife in fact, of some pampering seraglio. She looked strained, even woozy, to the point that his own condition went unmentioned now.

Ah, your true music: a tuneless keening in the woods.

He followed her in. "Who's here?"

As he shut the door against the night she sat on a hassock by the woodstove and hugged herself and sighed, averting her face.

"Where's Ocean?"

"Ocean."

"The young friend. I thought she lived here."

"Ocean is gone."

"There's something wrong here."

"It doesn't involve you."

"Maybe it does."

"No."

"I think it does."

She sighed once again, left off embracing herself and held her palms out toward the stove. She turned her face from it to gather in the sight of him at last.

"You're wet."

"I walked here from—from where I fell in. From where I got out."

She stood up, beckoning. "Sit here." He took her place on the hassock and understood none of this. He put the heels of his hands against the sockets of his eyes and lowered his elbows to his knees.

Thus he held his head up. He became aware of a cedary incense around him. Maybe sandalwood.

He heard her leaving. Heard drawers in the kitchen. He thought he heard her weeping in there and raised his head.

She came out with a white, flowered dishtowel and draped it gently over the back of his neck and raised its corner to press against his scalp. "You're bleeding. Or you were."

"God, that hurts."

"I'm just wiping away the blood. Your ear is terribly swollen."

"I was out, unconscious. I should have drowned."

She sat next to him and with tenderness applied the towel against his wound. "Did you by any chance see the kelpie?"

"Kelpie who?"

"The kelpie. A water sprite. Usually she takes the form of a horse. She comes to drowning sailors. "

"I saw a horse. Not a sprite. Just a horse. I'm cold."

"Move closer, then." She opened the stove's door a crack and a draft began thrumming up the chimney. She helped him scoot the hassock nearer the stove, and he hunched beside the steadily increasing heat while she draped about him a fancy saddle blanket, blue and purple and scarlet, and held it in place with an arm about his shoulders, a hand on his arm. "The fire has a voice," he said. He breathed deeply through open, quivering lips. "I'm going to cry." He tried to urge the sobs along, but his emotion expressed itself in a series of coughs and a fit of shivering.

"No, Nelson. It wasn't just a horse."

He was glad of her closeness. The minty currents of her breath.

"I was invited to a prayer meeting tonight."

"Perhaps that's where you should be then."

"Because nobody invited me here, you mean."

She deflected this with a gesture of her hand toward her face.

"Yvonne—what has happened?"

With a graceful turn of her form she left the hassock and lit on the chair it served. She curled her fingers around its arms, but forcefully, until her knuckles bumped up and her hands look gnarled. "What about you? Should I ask what's happened to you?"

"More than I can tell. That's why I'm here."

"I'm not understanding. Why *are* you here?"

"To make a deal. Any deal. Make a deal for me."

"With whom?"

"Well—your spiritual cohorts. Your angel friends, your demons, I don't care."

Apparently in weariness, maybe irritation, she shut her eyes, and at this moment his own sight widened to engulf their surroundings: the three candles in corner nooks giving them what light there was, beside each a brass snuff dish, the wall of bookshelves, the wide venetian blinds, on the facing wall a lamb's skin dyed red.

As if talking in her sleep she asked, "How did you get wet? Is it raining that hard?"

"I was wet before it rained."

"Where did you come from? Where's your car?"

"Nobody knows I'm here. Nobody must ever know I was here."

She opened her eyes on him. "Okay. However you want it."

"I'm the victim, the object, of not one but two quite separate plots to murder me."

"And you're thinking you can—what are you thinking you can do?"

"Whatever can be done."

"There's such a thing as karma, you know. You can't cheat the past."

"So the future is set, do you mean? I don't think so."

"Not the future. But fate."

"Einstein didn't think so."

"*Einstein*. Did you ever consider how contradictory you are? I mean self-contradictory in your whole system?"

"I'm confused, desperate and confused. I don't apologise for it."

"We live in a universe of space-time. Einstein mapped it to his partial satisfaction. But just like the rest of us, he lived his fate. We know our fate. On some level we know it perfectly. What we can't foresee is the way our fate conjoins with other fates."

"And our fate is terrible."

"Oh, no. It's beautiful. Only our illusions are terrible. And it's inevitable that they'll fall away. But first we have to pierce them. And be pierced by them"—Her voice was shaking, and her hands. "Why didn't you come to me sooner?"

"Because I don't like you."

"You don't like anyone." She clutched her hands together. "It's a mess now. You're not the only one doomed."

"You're scared. You've toyed with God, or Satan, or somebody like that—"

"*You've* toyed with them—"

"What can I do?"

"Shall I call Randall?"

"Look at me. I'm willing—I'm desperate, I said I was."

She settled back in her seat, shut her eyes and opened them. "Nelson Fairchild—hello. I am Randall MacNammara."

"Just like that."

Yvonne's face smiled. "It's easy once you know how." The trouble had left her. Her hands, resting on either arm of the chair, were beautiful again.

He began his dialogue with the void. "You indicated we might speak in private."

"And here we are."

"What have you done to my wife?"

"She's not your wife anymore."

"What have you done with Winona? Whatever she is to me."

"She's nothing to you. She's no one you've ever known."

"Well then, who is she?"

"Are you familiar with the term 'walk-in'? Do you know what a walk-in is?"

"A closet? A freezer? Come on, will you?"

"Your wife," Randall said, "is dead."

"My wife is dead."

"The person you've been dealing with is not your wife. Forget her."

"Not possible. She's trying to get me murdered, I think."

"She may be trying, but she hasn't contracted to be a killer this life around."

"And she's not the only one. I've got real hit men on my ass, Mr. Ghost. And I want you to understand I have no desire to get like you. Today I swam when I might have drowned. I drank water when I was thirsty. I slept when I was tired. Also I took a great piss. I wish I could go on doing things like that forever."

"Well, the vocation of hit men is to deny your wish."

"Can you help me? Can you operate somehow on these—types— these entities—"

"I wouldn't know."

"Look, can you or can't you work some changes in our little realm?"

"Nelson Fairchild, I don't know. It's never occurred to me. Do you care about changing the dream you had last night?"

"Oh, the *god*damn dream thing! Great!"

"When you've been caught in the world of perception you're caught in a dream. That's simple enough."

"Yesterday, you were talking to me about a doppelgänger."

"A soul twin. Your twin is in error. This error has led your twin into danger of a peculiar kind."

"Who is it? It's Carl Van Ness."

"Your twin makes a basic error in mistaking the self for the universe. We all use the self as the basic referent. He fails to use any other."

"You mean he's self-centered."

"As long as you don't mean merely selfish. We're talking about a failure of perception that amounts to total spiritual blindness and soul-sickness. This person compounds his basic error by believing that the universe started with his birth and ends with his death. If he believes in reincarnations, he believes in reincarnations of the whole universe. That eliminates karma, relearning, and the law of compensation—since each universe is a closed system, bounded by his lifetime. Through all these universes one after another, the only thread, the only continuity, is his identity. And the thread is endless. He has no destiny."

"And is that actually true?"

"It's as he makes it. He's condemned himself to an unimaginable interval on the current plane."

"To hell with him, then. But there are two others, two men, out to kill me."

"And so they will. But they're not important."

"I beg your fucking pardon?"

"They're merely completing a design you began—you yourself began—in an earlier existence. You killed in a previous era, in this one you experience the other side of that. The lesson begun in one life is finished in another."

"That's just—ugly! Justice should be rounded off in a single life, if you're going to have it at all. Otherwise it's so unfair, so unpoetic."

"It's a game, Nelson Fairchild. First you learn offense, now you learn defense."

"I'm not a gamesman. I look on things as serious."

"Well, things aren't serious. But this one thing is. This Devourer."

"Van Ness."

"The Devourer has possessed a body at the moment of death, and you took it home with you. You invited it in. Now it eats."

"And I'm lunch."

"At least you keep your sense of humor."

"Sure thing. Yes I do."

"He's the one to take seriously. The others are just figures in your waking dream."

"I take my waking experiences as facts. They have a certain logic, anyway. Meanwhile, dreams are jumbles. I know the difference."

"What you seem to wake up to is just another form of the same world you see in dreams. All your time is spent in dreaming. Your sleeping and your waking dreams have different forms, that's all . . . Nelson Fairchild: Do you believe in God?"

"When you get right down to it? Yes. Because I'm nuts."

"Then let me ask you this: Would God have left the meaning of the world to your interpretation?"

"I assume so. Of course he did. It's a stupid question, actually."

"If he did, then it has no meaning. Meaning can't change from person to person, and still be true. No. If God means something by all this, then only one set of interpretations will suffice. God looks upon the world as with one purpose, changelessly established. And no situation can affect its aim. Everything is in accord with it. Everything."

"Is there really a God, then?"

"Well, actually, I don't know. But I believe it more strongly than you possibly can in a chaos of perceptions like a funhouse."

"I call it reality. I'm stuck with it."

"Is it real? And are you stuck with it?"

"Randall MacNammara, Ghost Man, I'm ready to make a deal with you—offer you something. Just tell me what."

"I'll employ the same analogy again. What could somebody from last night's dream offer *you*? Riches and gold? Riches and gold in a dream aren't riches. They're just dreams. And the people, places, and things you fear are dreams too. Don't fear them."

"Easy for you to say. Couldn't you stop them?"

"Couldn't you face them?"

"No! Could you *stop* them."

"It's possible to work some effect."

"So do it. Hey—just for fun!"

"I'm sure you could locate a wandering bitter entity somewhere between the realms. They like mischief. Mischief and hurt."

"Then I will. I'll get me a spiritual vandal."

"I'm not interested in helping you."

"Why not? What's the difference—come on! You can't, can you? You're just a gig, a trick. Yvonne!" he shouted.

She closed her eyes. A minute of silence wore away in the room, which he realized had become unbearably warm. Fairchild shrugged away the blanket and wrapped a corner of it around the stove's porcelain door handle, and shut it tight. Yvonne said, "I'm tired."

"Don't fade on me just yet. What were you just talking about—about mischievous entities."

"There are such."

"Get me one on the line, then, how about. Whether I'm sure about all this working or not, I'm out to get these bastards done, okay? I'm out of options."

"But we don't know what bargains the two men have made. All their promises will be kept. All their mistakes will be corrected. Whatever they were sent here to fulfill will be fulfilled."

"Just cast a fucking spell, will you?"

"I don't cast spells. I can open a channel that leads to their guides. I can make a bargain with their guides—arrange to have them take a shortcut."

"Which means?"

"Help them reach their destination sooner."

"Destination?"

"Whatever their fate may be. Probably not a happy one this time around."

"You mean hire a cosmic hit man?"

"You have to understand. Whatever they're on this earth to do will be accomplished. If it's something you fear, then maybe we should leave it alone."

"Just make a deal. Any deal."

She put a hand to her forehead, let her touch fall to a gilded lamp-stand and fingered its intricacies—its cups, its capitals and its flowers. Her fingers found the switch and she turned it on with a spasm of her hand and let down an unflattering light over half her face. Her mouth worked in bewilderment. Then she gave him a tiny, angry smile.

He said, "Randall."

"The tap-in is not Randall."

"We gonna talk to Randall again?"

"No."

"No?"

The one he'd sensed from the first, the guest whose presence he'd felt all along, had come into the room with them.

"I am Miran."

"And who is Miran?" The question hovered unanswerable in the aether.

October 30, 1991

The blind people in prison. Suddenly I think about them, suddenly after all this life, the prisoners who are blind. How many are there? What's it like? Does my mother know some blind prisoners? At the facility she works in, they like to call it a facility, it amuses them to call it a detention center, at the ladies' pen a few dozen miles out of San Francisco, at the north edge of Marin County—at their prison, the gun towers are not the tallest things. They see pines climbing up mountains another nearly two thousand feet, ascending to the peaks and turning around and looking back at them. I'm not sure what I am getting at here but I think it must be important because I got out of bed just as I was at the verge of sleep to write to you about it, Winona.

There is something else. I know you made love to Glen Bolger, John Marks and at least one other person, I don't know which person, after we were married. You call me weak but if you in your lack of wisdom define strength as the ability to suffer worthless pain, well, all I have to say is oh, fuck you. I can see there's no real need here to finish sentences or pretend to be articulate. It's another one of those letters. You start out to do something sane and the next thing you know you're threatening the mayor's life or taking hostages in a supermarket.

Sometimes on these gray days the past just comes rolling armylike through the fields toward my naked heart. There was a certain person, one man in particular. I was that man. Now I'm not. I'm writing you only in order more terribly to feel

Officer Navarro set the pages aside and took a look at his wristwatch, an Omega designed to work underwater to a depth of several fathoms, though he wasn't a diver, and he wasn't pressed for time—had about sixteen hours, if anybody was counting, to burn until work tomorrow morning—but was just interested in how long the dryer might run. Another three minutes. Or four.

Impatient with the whole process, with repetitions in general, he opened the dryer's hatch in midcycle and watched the collapse of this galloping carousel. He took out his handkerchiefs and white jockeys. They'd dried, but his uniform and jeans had not. He let fall another dime and watched them go, his outer garments, these things of cloth all in a whirl and completely absurd.

He thought: I'm going up there. One of them sits two hundred yards from this spot.

He replaced the pages in their envelope and went out to his car, a muscular '76 Pontiac from whose hood he'd burnished away the gangster Firebird tattoo. Such signifiers he considered a little bit too glorious, a little bit too Mexican. But he liked the power, and he liked the handling. Tossing the white envelope into the child-sized backseat, he got behind the wheel and discovered on the floorboard on the passenger's side a small green plastic garbage bag containing, as he knew, his three bath towels and two washcloths. He yanked the bag up across his shoulder, and with a sense of struggle, with a sense these repetitions were overcoming him absolutely, with weakened steps, he went back into the Laundromat to start another washer before driving the short distance through the neutral dusk up the hill to the giant's home.

Wilhelm Frankheimer had recently moved, had rented a small house, a cedar-shake cottage quite familiar to Navarro, just up Anchor Bay's only east-west street. It looked pretty much the same, but had tipped detectably toward decline. The lawn was shaggy, the drive unswept. Somebody had broken the flagstones splitting wood out front.

Navarro picked up a headless axe handle and knocked it against the old ship's bell posted out by the path. He went on to the front door and knocked several times but had trouble getting Frankheimer to acknowledge. Yet he had to be there, the chimney was smoking and he almost never got out, and when he did he got no farther than the store or the cafe.

Somebody inside shouted, "Roll on in."

Navarro found Frankheimer stretched out near the fire on a plastic deck recliner, wearing an old brown bathrobe and drawing a blanket around his shoulders.

"Take a seat. Mind bringing me a glass of water first? In the fridge."

Navarro obliged him. On the refrigerator, held up by magnets, the school photos of two children fronted his gaze, a little blond girl and a smiling blond boy with a lot of tension in his face.

"Ignore the magic mushrooms in there."

"I wouldn't know what they look like."

"They look like mushrooms."

He brought Frankheimer the water jug, but Frankheimer only held it in the grip of his big hands. His legs went longer than the chair so that his shins draped down, scarred and lumpy and shiny, like worn wood, and his jaundiced feet rested at delicate angles on the floor. His metal crutches lay on either side of him.

Navarro sat himself in the bay window and, for no reason he could name, savored the ridiculousness of his presence here in this room where he'd lived some of his finest moments. This scene of some of his worst behavior. Mo had kept it beautiful; now the place felt cheap and close and smelled of stubbed-out cigarettes and dirty laundry—smelled as a matter of fact like his own place. He really didn't care about the psychedelic goddamn mushrooms or, when you got right down to it, any of this man's crimes.

"You here about the junk I left up there?"

"Not exactly," Navarro said. "But it was mentioned to me."

"I'll get around to it. It was a sudden move. I lost the house."

"Too bad."

"No. It's all for the best. I'm taken care of."

He flung a white gym sock into the fireplace and it started to smoke thickly and then burned.

"You'll see me dancing tomorrow," he said.

"At the big fun wedding? What makes you think I'm going?"

"Not you specifically. I was speaking to the whole world."

"Yeah. I'll be there. On duty though."

"Dancing on aluminum legs. Stay tuned for that."

"What caused this?"

"Wheels ran over me."

"I know. I meant what was the cause of the accident?"

"You didn't do the report?"

"CHP took care of it."

"The cause was I was fucked up. More or less sleeping when I was supposed to be awake. Can't do that, man. You end up in the road. Cars run you down. You spend nine months in plaster. You get six operations."

"Were drugs involved? Is that what—"

"What did the fucking? Well, ultimately, primarily, it was Yvonne. Principally it was her although a car is what apparently ran over me. You know Yvonne? Chiefly it was her."

Shame and sudden sweat shut Navarro up, and he changed around in his seat.

"So you got stoned. Didn't look both ways."

"You currently on duty?"

"No."

"Is this an official visit?"

"I don't know."

Frankheimer grimaced like an ape and put his finger back between his jaws. "I have a sore under my tongue."

"Well, no, I don't think it's really official."

"Okay. What is it? Social?"

"Maybe we could talk off the record."

"You're a cop. I'm a critter."

Navarro sighed, placed his hands over his knees. "I'm thinking I might resign the first of the month. I'm pretty sure."

"Gonna stick around? Maybe in some other capacity?"

Navarro realized he'd given it no thought—none.

"So what is the subject of our inquiry?" Frankheimer said.

"Carl Van Ness."

"There's a name."

"You guys pretty good friends?"

"Friends? Not by any means."

"Then what's the connection?"

"It's mystical."

"Yeah?"

"An energy thing."

"Yeah? How about aside from all that?"

"There's no connection on this level."

"What level?"

"The level of this which you call reality."

"Yeah?" Navarro said. "I don't call anything reality anymore."

"I don't know him."

Navarro raised his eyebrows at this nonsense.

"I'm telling you the truth, but in a language you don't understand."

"Try this. When did you meet him?"

"Oh, man. Lemme see, that's gotta be twenty-one, twenty-two years ago. We shipped together a couple years, three or four years. He kept in touch, maybe one letter per year, or just a card. Just a card addressed to Frankenstein. Then, when he showed up—that was it. It wasn't the same guy."

"You had a falling-out."

"It was not the same person. It was a walk-in."

"A walk-in what?"

"Sometimes a person dies, and before the soul's hardly out, another one walks in. A wandering soul. A sick soul, too weak to make it across the realms. A psychotic soul, referred to in most mythologies as a demon. It takes over completely. Sucks at the vital energy. It's Van Ness's body, and Van Ness's brain, even Van Ness's ideas. But it's not Van Ness. When people do evil things repeatedly without compunction, man, that ain't people. That's demons."

Navarro, who had crossed his arms over his chest during this dissertation, let them drop. He hung his head.

"Do you believe in such things?"

Navarro couldn't look him in the eye, but he found he could tell the truth.

"Yes," Navarro said.

This October had seen plenty of rain—a dozen inches since the first. And now a bit more along the cliffside pastures and over the highway, wisps of it stretched on intermittent gusts. He turned the Firebird's wipers on and set the timer for the longest interval. Passed along the wide fields where a yearling pinto stallion bucked and hopped by himself a quarter-mile distant from the rest of the string, who stood bunched under trees on dirt they'd trampled lifeless over the months. They'd rubbed up against and killed half the little bull pines back there too. He knew it was a yearling because he'd seen it last September as a rickety foal. The animal stopped still, looking out to sea, then lowered its head as the sky tore open, and Navarro saw the rain dripping from its curved neck as he passed, turning up the wipers full-speed—

Navarro disliked horses, and any species of animal of whom it was said, "They smell your fear."

Just five days ago, when he'd found the pages written in Fairchild's hand, the sun had blazed hot enough to burn away the puddles in a steam. Perhaps it had been the last clear day of Indian summer, the last beautiful day, as Navarro drove the coast alone, his heart reaching out toward the goodness of the world. A hot day, in fact. He had the windows closed. He had the climate control on and it blanketed him—cool air and thin warm sunlight and the ocean shredding itself silently on the rocks. He was supposedly on patrol but had kept on going, out of town, south, through Anchor Bay and then Gualala and past the green sign—SAN FRANCISCO 114—on the river's far side, and clear out of the county. If you just stay loose and cool and steady in your breath. Stay away from the spiral's edge. He'd kept them behind glass in L.A., but here he'd failed. He'd whirled right down into it with them, never even known he'd been in the soup till he was nine-tenths drowned. Slide along the coast. Keep these windows closed.

At the Stewart Point Store he decelerated, drawn by the vision of a soft-drink machine in the parking lot, and pulled in next to a Highway Patrol car and went inside to change a five. The customers in the quiet establishment were already getting plenty of the law, what with the active presence of the CHP: a patrolwoman in a white, visored helmet whom Navarro, if he hadn't seen the cruiser out front, would have taken for a fake, an impostor, nosing over everybody's shoulder in the place and giving one traveller the low-down on parking, or the placement of the registration sticker on the license plate or some such pettiness—Navarro didn't quite hear, didn't want to. There were such charlatans, he'd arrested one himself one day in Englewood, an LAPD-uniformed high school music teacher directing traffic skillfully, but without authority . . . Navarro thought, Lady, I don't wanna know you ever, as she came toward him nudging the brim of her helmet back with her baton, and he continued by thinking, You pompous bulldyke. He was embarrassed by, but nevertheless loyal to, such officers. We all started out okay. Citizens did this to us. "You from Mendocino County?" she asked.

"Point Arena. Just getting a Coke," he explained.

"I've got an abandoned vehicle reported on the west side of the West Point–Gualala road. Fifty yards north of Pepperwood Creek, about a hundred yards into the brush."

"You going up to check it out?"

"It's just your side of the Mendocino boundary."

"Well, I never did know where they put that line."

"Beg pardon."

"I don't know one county from another, Officer, except where you cross the river. Can you point me on a map?"

"Let's get out on the porch where I can spread her out," the patrolwoman said.

The Gualala River constituted the county line for a distance of some four miles, to where the river jogged south along the San Andreas Fault and the boundary hooked straight east, crossing Big Pepperwood Creek and continuing on into the hills. Several creeks, none of them marked by signs, descended over the north-south ridge. Navarro kept count of the culverts passing beneath the road and drove directly to the spot and found the Silverado as it had been reported, obviously intentionally hidden, driven deep into the tangled chaparral, the camper's aluminum roof just visible above the overgrowth. The low scrub it had broken through on the way to its parking place had grown back almost entirely; he locked up at the roadside and followed the ancient traces of entry beside the Pepperwood, finding it tough going along this way. The spot lay in the calm and the heat, several miles inland and a good half mile, he guessed, above the sea. The creek ran full and fresh. Just to be near it cooled him.

The fisherman who'd come across the vehicle had marked the way with shreds of his red bandanna, and with his last marker had unnecessarily draped the camper's latch itself. The truck hadn't been vandalized, but had waited here untouched for quite a while—peering into the driver's window Navarro saw a ball of twigs and grasses, mustered here by some rodent, he assumed, down among the pedals.

The camper too was full of such nests, and spiderwebs, and piles of grain collected by mice, and a military-style rucksack and a duffel and assorted gear for outdoor living, and many curled gray marijuana leaves, and the carcasses of two dogs. The animals had perished of thirst or exposure. The heat had baked and dried them. Critters had gone at their innards. Papier-mâché dogs, half-molded and abandoned, their muzzles shrunken and baring all their teeth back to the last dry brown molars.

He shut the camper's door and latched it. To get at the doors in the cab he had to break and trample down a lot of branches that had grown against them.

In the cab, on the passenger's side, he found the white California Board of Franchise envelope. The mice had gotten to one corner. He realized he shouldn't be handling it. Standing beside the open door, he used the bit of signifying bandanna to shield the dashboard from his own fingerprints as he supported himself by a hand on the dash and jabbed the glove box's button with his ballpoint pen. He took the documents there by the corners, one at a time and gingerly, between the tips of his thumb and finger, pushed the door shut with his pen, and went back through the brush to the road.

He intended merely to transfer these papers—the truck's registration and a mileage log of some sort—to his cruiser's front seat and then return to complete his investigation. But I'm no woodsman, he suddenly remembered, considering that an exploration of the whole scene was probably in order now. The vehicle had been hidden for a purpose. Whatever had developed for its occupants had been unforeseen, and maybe permanent. Dogs, live ones, would have to nose around now before the truck itself was again disturbed. They might turn up bloodstains or bullet casings or a grave scratched in the dirt. He didn't go back.

The camper had waited there for many months, and probably, judging by the way the manzanita had overgrown it, at least since the previous winter. Not much could come of a search for witnesses, not so long after the fact, whatever the fact might be. To his knowledge the small population of this area all lived in the Buddhist monastery up the road and never ventured out. But if only in the interest of covering his ass, he supposed he'd better talk to some of them.

Heading up that way he left his window down and breathed the heat of the day, which smelled of its stillness even as it drove in against his face. He wondered if he had his bearings right—he drove a quarter of an hour and saw no sign of habitation anywhere—and then the order's immaculate grounds opened wide, like a chasm in history, as he came around a curve. On his left a golden pagoda shone way back in a pasture, looking willowy in the thermals. Farther around the bend he found the entrance, and just behind it a temple with a tremendous copper dome, an almost extraterrestrial sight, a spectacle that wrenched him. He rolled to a stop before this vision. Barbed wire, a steel gate twenty feet tall, a quiet like a deep well into which poured all his childhood. He touched the key in the ignition. But he didn't turn it off.

Years ago on an ex-wife's street he'd paused like this, before the driveway of her new home. He in his cruiser with his twelve-gauge shotgun and gold-enameled badge.

Now, as then, he felt sadness even in his hands. He let it run and pushed the pedal down and blew out of there with his own smoke.

Since then, five days had passed. He'd mentioned none of this to anyone.

Navarro's Firebird possessed dual exhausts. Moving slowly along Main Street it chugged like a boat, and it splashed like one, its tires cutting three troughs along the flooded pavement as he executed, in violation of California statutes, a U-turn that put him in front of his building. He left his laundry in the car. The downpour wet him as he hot-footed across the sidewalk among small white explosions randomizing on a layer of rain, on the reflection of the cafe's neon logo like shattered candy, on the reflected light from its window filled with cutout happy-face jack-o-lanterns and the black silhouettes of hags riding thatch brooms. He dripped on the stairs going up. But under his crazy batik sport shirt the envelope had stayed dry. He tossed it flat on the table in the kitchen area and shed his clothing fast, trembling with the chill as he draped his shirt and pants across the only dining chair, but raising the window, because he liked the sound of the rain, before stretching himself out on the couch and dragging the blanket from the floor to cover himself . . . Then he guessed he'd been asleep. When he found his thoughts again the quiet had returned. Through the open window came the fresh breath of the world after a storm and the corrupt breath of the sea. Mo had slept here a time or two. He'd been smelling her perfume ever since.

He stood naked beside the sink and, raising a fifth gently by its neck, downed a couple shots of Cuervo, and then a third, before shutting the window, getting on his robe, lighting a burner under the cold coffee. He was off all day, but it wouldn't do to spend it whipping up a hangover. Double duty tomorrow—tomorrow was a big day in a cop's year. He'd arrest drunken women in hula garb, break up fights between men in bridal gowns, answer reports of shadows dancing in the graveyard and find nobody there. And the day after, too: the trees abloom with toilet-paper streamers, obscenities on the windows of the high school. Burst pumpkin rinds on the mayor's Nissan ZX and corky desiccated seeds and strings of pulp. All this would have to be written up. They always wanted fingerprinting done, and you had to illuminate for them the mysterious difference between Class One felonies and Halloween.

He'd go among them with his cheerless smile, his uniform right from the cleaners. And his badge hardly tarnished, as his first one had worn out suddenly. He'd tried a little target practice with it and had actually managed to hit the thing. The replacement, just about thirteen months old, he'd paid for from his own pocket.

And also, tomorrow afternoon, he'd be working in uniform as a kind of rent-a-cop, getting overtime for attending a wedding to which he'd received no invitation: the celebration of the marriage of Winona Andrews, formerly Winona Fairchild, to Carl Van Ness.

He sat at the table and held the white envelope in his hands. Maybe soon he'd confront them both. After all, this thing had their names on it. Deliver a copy to each and watch their faces and see—see what? No possible reaction could fool with the fact that he believed this story. Nothing could confirm it any harder. But nothing would give him hard evidence either—he worked at the clasp and took out the rubbishy pages—plus, he didn't really care. He'd changed. Before, he'd seen all decisions as simple: One thing was good and the other thing wasn't. The idea was to choose the good one. In times of confusion, follow the mood of the moment. Overall, count on the extremes, the clear choices, to navigate you in the right direction.

But the realm of confusion had expanded way past any horizons. The whole solar system now constituted one big gray area.

He could probably get samples of Nelson Fairchild's penmanship, could probably get a handwriting expert to call it a match. He could probably take soil samples from inside the rig and finish out the year trying to get analyses from forensics labs with higher priorities, driving to San Francisco on his days off and hanging around begging favors. And then finish out the century searching every spot the camper might have visited, including, probably, the Lost Coast—that region alone about thirty square miles in area, if his map read true—looking without anyone's help for the bones of Nelson Fairchild, or any sign of him. But the letter was sign enough. It satisfied Navarro.

He hadn't mentioned the letter to anyone because to be alone with it seemed the fair, the disciplined thing. The kindest thing. Unless he wanted right now to make a case against someone—and he could think of several likely people and numerous charges, including homicide—a case that would eventually be dropped, or so he would have guessed.

But he wasn't supposed to guess. He was supposed to take his thoughts to the county attorney, a guy named Ronniger—or a woman maybe, that's how little Navarro knew about things on the county level—and let Mr. or Ms. Ronniger be the one to anticipate the legal outcome.

But Navarro didn't want those Martians in Ukiah considering this case. He was convinced they'd proceed entirely out of a failure to understand the most important things about all this, which could hardly be spoken of or even thought about and had to do mainly with a gigantic silence at the center of everything—

fact I heard an automobile engine outside this very motel idling for quite some time that Christmas we vacationed here in the Trinities to get the snow. Then one car door made the sounds of opening and slamming. Your footsteps on the icy walk, key in the door—Oh, hello darling, asleep? No? Guess what? I walked back (you'd been at a film, or the library)—followed by several convincing details of your walk home, a piece of ice fell off a branch, how cold, are my lips purple, nearly slipped twice, et cetera, capped by a breezy explanation for extreme lateness of arrival in the clammy boudoir. You lied to me. This evidence wouldn't do in a court of law, but you know and I know, and now you know I know. That's the unidentified person. As for John Marks he foolishly confessed out of shame and asked me to forgive him. I am working on it. Glen Bolger I actually saw. I am ashamed to say I just followed you around for two days jealous and crazy. You went to Glen Bolger's house, you went in, I went back and forth at five-minute intervals between the bedroom window and the telephone pole at the corner and within twenty-five minutes I saw you with him crawling through the seas of passion in his bed, the Hawaiian-print silken seas. I went home feeling I had caused your adultery somehow by my own lack of faith—remember when I went to a couple of therapists and tried to make you feel responsible for it? That was just afterward, just after the night of the Glen Bolger Show.

(Yes, I invite adultery, I probably create it for myself, but that's an insight on a minor note because those betrayals were nothing, no, not even prototypes or the crudest sketches for your gigantic accomplishment. And if you'd planned all this you could never have made it work—no, I'm the one who did all the planning!)

Now for two or three minutes I've written nothing, staring at my face in the glass of this motel room (our old room in Weaverville, I can tell you that because you'll never read this), staring at my face which has always seemed too long, it's the face of a sad liar. And I was thinking about the dream last night, remembering the dream that woke me. Revising it to make it seem less pleasant. Wasn't it, rather than joyful, actually gruesome? In this dream I should have felt untimely, inadequate, resented. I should have had the terrible sense I get so often in this waking world that somebody important is about to burst through the door and denounce me. In this dream I find myself waiting tables in a really crowded fast-food sort of place, completely unable to keep up with the orders. Nobody seems angry about it however. We're all friends, no hurry here, we're all

Dear Win and Van,

"Win and Van"—how cute. First, congratulations for having killed all three of us and wiped out the Fairchild line. Billy and Dad are down, one to go. My blood's still ticking but I'm as good as finished too. I don't mind. I really don't. And now I'll open a liter of crummy sulphur-tasting Sonoma blanc and sit down (still standing at the moment) and put all my thoughts before you.—Wine, wine, wine—I'm not dead *yet*!

Incidentally, this is the only letter I'll send—don't think I'll turn you in, don't think for a second I'd alert the authorities, I mean, *fuck* them, and certainly, of course, fuck you, but above everything fuck *them*. I've always stood for that. Admittedly not much else.

Already Dead ▪ 281

Ah Win here's to California, the stuff pressed from its breasts—from one suckled on its grapes—in vino veritas—

The truth! It's actually quite relaxing. Once you've wrestled with it. When it's finally whipped you. Beyond that it's not so much like wine as water—clear and empty. Water, air, fire. You might compare it to anything elemental, always something concrete—never to some other abstraction because it's not like any other—never mind what Keats says, he had a meter to contend with, meters can make you say anything. "Truth is beauty, beauty truth"—it scans but it makes no sense. I feel all right, feel pretty good. I wish I could float indefinitely along on this intoxicated gratitude, but I get mad too. My little dirigible bumps up against big cliffs of hate.

I'm monstrous, okay. But so are your deeds. I mean it takes something like you to keep me from believing the world has some good in it.

My father! All right, that was practically a gift of mercy, you could rationalize that one while playing tennis. And maybe you didn't kill him. He'd sent you a note warning you you'd be cut out of the will—I saw the note in your kitchen—so you had what the detectives call a motive. But we all have motives, don't we, what we lack are the will and the blindness. Maybe his death just *occurred*, and presented you with an issue: the old man's dead, you inherit half his holdings, which, under California law, belong equally to your husband, whom you're divorcing; if your husband dies before the divorce, you get your half complete. If his brother dies, everything's yours.

Did the demon tell you he planned to kill my brother? I doubt it, not then. But he persuaded you eventually—or did you persuade him? Anyhow you knew. Whom else could he have asked for directions to the cabin? Van Ness I entered there just minutes after you—an hour, two hours after, not more. I went in there because I'd been told he was dead and I wanted to ascertain it, but—My brother . . . In films you shake your brother, you can't believe it, you shout, Billy! Billy! but not in life. Not with his blood jelled right over his open eyes. Not with his brains spilling out his mouth like he choked on them. There's no shaking and shouting in that case. There was nothing to ascertain. Do you understand? There was nothing to ascertain, nowhere to ascertain it, nobody to ascertain it about. Nothing. Nothing. Nothing. That's what I found in there. That's what you created.

May I tell you something? I fired that .357 Magnum only once and I found it difficult to hit anything.

Ah, Van: cutthroat, backstabber, unbelievable wondrous psychic betrayer—

Often I think, repeatedly I think, relentlessly I dream of you in my arms, my mouth on your mouth, the floodlit raindrops bursting the skin of the pond, the mud trickling out of your mustaches, your glasses sideways on your cheek, your eyelashes wet as if with weeping. And thinking it over I'm tempted by every sort of intellectual wildness—I'd like to bring to their safe harbors thoughts that are really feelings, and place a frame around images that are, in fact, fears: how I'd like to drag up by the hair something drowned, something classical and remote, like the Old Man of the Sea, who can be forced to read the future by anyone who holds him while he shape-shifts where he's risen above the waves at noon, and compare him helplessly to this man. But you, you're slicker than the sea's Old Man. You've activated everything. You haven't just predicted my future, but set it playing. And now you believe in fate. Now we all believe in fate.

I know what drives a man like me, I've felt it even if I've never had its name, but what produces a Van Ness, a man psychotically committed to his every fantasy, the inflicter of reality on dreams? She wouldn't have let you realize hers if I hadn't already let you realize mine. I wouldn't call you the Devil. Frankheimer called you that but I say no. We're the devils, she and I, tempting you with fantastic schemes while you, *you* are the attempter, the Adam, you're the *man*.

Like all men you have a religion—at least a way of looking at yourself and the universe both at once, which is all I'd hope a religion to be, for me, if I could only have one, if I were only a man . . . I'd call you a Zarathustrian.

But I mean, you know, *I'm* like Nietzsche. Aren't I? I feel deep suspicion of the mensch, of the reasonable, dutiful man. He knows what he's doing and it's identical to the doing of the other guy, the one who doesn't know. The mensch walks lockstep with the robots, in a long line of hooks hangs his soul on a hook next to theirs. But my father!

But my father was no mensch. He hated the reasonable, dutiful man. My father was the enemy of your enemy—can't you see my father was your friend?

Now, look here, you people. A man decides to kill his wife. What's so unusual? $E = MC^2$, now *that's* an unusual thought, and Newton's cogitations, et cetera, and Shakespeare never bothered a page with *them* therefore. But wishing to kill your wife, it's as basic as thought itself—"I want her dead; therefore I am"—it's why they invented divorce. But this man, our man—me—he can't get divorced. So he plots in detail. He'll find a Dying Person, enlist his services, let him take the blame—after the deed, the killer's a corpse anyway—it's a fantasy, and fantasies are harmless in a man without will or blindness. But then comes a man of will, a man blind to the border between the thought and the act. The bargain is sealed, but the Dying Person decides not to die. Determines to kill the plotter's father, kill the plotter's brother, make the wife the winner.

You left my wife alive, asleep. You turned from the place and went into the night. You went to my father's house. You walked right in through the kitchen, ascended the stairs in the darkness, put your ear to the doors in the hall, and behind one you heard my father hard at work breathing. You turned the knob and went in, and I wish I'd been there to witness the two of you: the one I conjured, and the one who conjured me.

Dad in purgatory exploding I imagine the balloons of little girls with your cigar-end: If you were here you'd know how to handle the sheriff, the cops, the judges, Harry Lally. By their tenderest parts you'd hoist up the pig-men and deliver a bitter lecture. You'd line up the lawyers on a spit like shish kebab, you'd drive Winona into the sea. They nourished you, those types. You could handle them all.

All but Van Ness, creeping up beside your bed.

Did my father fight? That I doubt, or he'd have bit your face off. They'd have found him with his fingers in your windpipe.

No. He stood up to meet you coming, but his legs gave way. He fell unconscious, pissed his pants, and dreamed. In his dream the forest stood still. The sky turned black. A funnel cloud tore down out of heaven and wrapped him down to the roots. Twisted the great tree slowly. And slowly the roots loosed their grip in the duff and my father for whom I am named, one of the giants of this earth, is dead.

And then you raised the window. And then you climbed into the dark. And then you hung by your fingers from the sill. And you wondered where your fall would take you. And then Van Ness, you dropped, and then in its every detail I envision it . . .

. . . You held the match till your fingers spasmed.

You two lovebirds! I'm sure you believe you've killed me, but I've survived. Probably to deepen my exile. Possibly to die at other hands—you're ignorant of the pig-men. The pig-men are my own fault.

Speaking of pigs, the huntsman in the fairy tale brought back the heart of a boar as proof that he'd murdered Snow White. Heart of a pig.

I keep waking in the middle of the night, around three o'clock. It looks as if a curtain of plastic has been laid over the moment to protect it. Neighborhood of kindness in the hour of moonlight . . . If ever I get back to you I'll touch your skin . . . listen in the holiness to your pink words . . . I'll wipe my feet, I'll never scream *I'm a genius* at you again. I don't believe I really killed you, that you lay dead and then rose up alive, the possession of a vagrant soul. In the scientific method there's much to trouble me, its smugness and myopia, its lofty forgetting of the fact that it's a method, not a model of the world, its upturned nose at roundnesses till they come back squares, but—what was I saying? Oh—that I shouldn't believe in ghosts, in walk-ins. You're you. I'm me. We're all of us *us*—not suits with souls zipped up inside. Yet I saw you, you looked dead. Then I saw you alive. I saw your face. It was yours but you weren't wearing it.

Neat! Okay! You bet! Wait—

Let me slow up, allow me to get a grip, "My fit is mastering me," as Whitman says. All right. Van Ness didn't kill you as we'd planned. But he came to the house, didn't he?

You were always one to take in odd animals—Winona, I'm talking to you. I know you invited him in, the mystery man.

And you, more mystery than man, was she The One? And did you pledge yourself silently without so much as a gesture? Follow and find her and float forward out of the pasture and put one foot up on the deck?

—Get out.

—First show me your pills. Your yellow pills.

—My what?

—Your bottle of Nembutal. Bring it here.

You brought him the bottle. He poured them into your palm. You touched the pills and tasted the dust of horse dope on your fingers.

. . . And you told her the plan and dried her tears and made love to her in your strange way and waited as it got dark for her to say it:

—*I* should kill *him*.

—Then do it.

—I *will*.

—You don't have to. Let me.

And letting him kill me wouldn't poison your conscience. After all, I started it, I deserved it, it was practically self-defense. Then after I'm dead Dad dies, and you get my share of California, the land of dreams and light and rippling and thundering mounts, the land of gold.

But it turned out, didn't it, that Father had to die first, before he crossed you off his one-woman list of heirs. And die he did.

I know full well now where my book of Nietzsche got to that night. Right there beside your bed, on the floor, am I right? And later Van Ness handed it to me in the dark.

Got it right here. I see the parts he marked. I hate people who make marks in books:

We do not wish to be spared by our best enemies, nor by those whom we love from the very heart.

You are not great enough not to know hatred and envy. So be great enough not to be ashamed of them!

You say it is the good cause that hallows even war? I tell you: it is the good war that hallows every cause.

The two of you! You read the *Zarathustra* together in bed and laughed.

I can surmise a few surmises. For one he got there in the sunset. Drove that car of his which I've never seen except in the dark down the drive with the redwoods taking on exactly that color in the late light and living into their names. The windless hush, the boards creaking as the stables cooled, old Red kicking up the dust in a slow circle and everything. The sun going down into the sea of clouds and turning their steel to wine, then to blood.

The man John who wrote the Bible's last book—on the isle of Patmos he envisioned just this, smoke flooding out of God's censer and a third of the moon and sun and stars darkened and a burning mountain cast into the sea and turning a third of the water to blood: envisioned coastal California in the evening . . . And you came into view. Ambled around the corner of the house, put one foot up on the deck.

—You don't belong here.

—Yes I do.

—How did you find me?

—It was no trick to find you here. The trick was finding you on the boardwalk that day.

No trick but one of fate. Fate along the scoured pier. Coming off the beach with your tennies grainy, whacking out the sand on a benchback and sticking them back on and he's watching the brown little simian feet with the blond hairs on the knuckles of your toes. And drifting from his eyes the smoke of stars.

She pulls her parka hood back and floats there like an ark in the deluge of the sun, this California with its fugitives and windmills and artichokes and clouds like thighs. Its vacancies at pink motels. Modesto in the dust. Walnuts shaken down early by quakes. Spanish razors. And here you come with your gypsy blood and your secret suit, feeling like fuck on fire. Straight out of Carmel. They couldn't touch you in Carmel. Not with their skin in shirts like skin. Their fingers in gloves like hands. And these others in Santa Cruz, they can't touch you either. Not in Santa Cruz this day. Dressed in your ragged bulletproof sweat suit or down-home beachside grubbies heading along the sandy asphalt past the stands followed a little ways and then abandoned by their chat, their jazz, their machine-sounds, jukebox whomp, nineties computer rock, fifties dead-teenager songs. I know how you moved. I know how you stared. How you smiled and failed to smile—smiled inappropriately, failed to when you should. Ran your finger around in the bits of spilt sugar on the dirty counter, couldn't resist licking at it, ordered your coffee among creaky robots with their faceless oval heads. I know what they told you—

—Hey. You look just like that guy who got shot last night.

—What?

—They had his picture on TV.

—No, that was the guy who shot him.

—Yeah.

—Yeah. You look like the guy who shot the guy.

—know how it runs for you generally in those places with their sensors clicking over you Mr. Roentgen and a series of Most Wanted pics fluttering past their minds. You stink. You fuck. You murder blandly. Everybody wants to ram you with a pitchfork. They just need a reason. But not you. You reach out and flip a switch. You burn up their innards. You do it without a thought.

She knew it a hundred miles away. She felt you click into place. She knew you made it happen. You had her by the cunt. She didn't even say hello. You didn't even look at her. The motel was pink.

She got on her knees by the toilet and held your penis for you while you pissed.

Ah, Winona . . . Long mustaches pale glassed-in eyes gritty cafe huge fans that stroke a wind like breath—naturally you had coffee in his eyes, in his hands in the park, in his room where the mirror was so small all you could see in it were your breasts. Your breasts saw your face.

Tired. Tired. Where am I? The two of you spent and sweaty and the odors of the Pacific in the pink motel. But what then?

Nothing comes to mind because I'm in pain. Lewd exotic California pain.

Marauders, have you turned back in the rain?

Sleep comes, roaring like a train. When it arrives it's going slow, slow, and the roaring isn't a sound anymore, but a sort of brown shadow in which you were about to find a thought . . . Then you're waking up. Lying in bed like a page torn in the middle of a word. Waiting for the fish to move, the fish on the wall. Waiting like a dog for the start of another broadcast day.

Okay Winona you stepped to the air conditioner and it chilled then dried your sweat. And as it evaporated from your skin, your skin evaporated too. You stood there immaterial and unaware. You slicked aside the curtains and in the dusk it was still out there sucking and stroking and worshiping the sand. Please if you see my friend

Clarence. Tell him something for me will you. Tell him I understand surfing. The sea wants to take shape. The wave promises some great birth, a monster's emersion, but it's only a flowing, only a flowing among many, and completely dies away. Changing sameness, change-less change. Our expectations fly to meet it and aren't jilted, but inexplicably satisfied. It's so right, it's so *right*.

And there you strolled, sockless in your tennis shoes, naked under your parka and your jeans. Watched the shabby surf finding and los-ing the shore. No: Immaterial and unaware, you walked out without clothing yourself. Stood on the vermillion beach stark naked and invisible, the boardwalk's clanks and whooshes and screams and tootly music blown near and far on the wind. They're paying in strange coins to ride the hurtling fever train, rolling up to heaven on the Ferris wheel, boys and girls released from life and dragged back down, G-force flattening their orange and purple Mohawks, mouths like wounds—it's terrible when somebody laughs, more obscene and revealing than anything they could say with words . . .

Past the boardwalk onto the street, the gauntlet of shops and beachside people, the quantum dregs, the never-ending pavement in their sighs, and always that music: dark rock. And you kept going, beyond the seaside part of town. Homes of stucco in the ashy twi-light, the street no longer dabbed with sand. Past the edges, way way past, out into the big place east of town, they call it America. Through the vandalized areas you wandered like a voice.

All the world is sleeping. The sea is sleeping. The sand is sleeping. One last form besides yourself invested with any waking. Fat black woman on a stool against a wall in a shadow with an accordion across her chest and a silhouetted, spiky 'do. Her skirt drapes empty below her thighs.

—Don't ask me to play. This thing don't play.

———

—I don't have any legs.

———

—You know where you are, don't you?

———

—California.

———

—You like where you are?

———

—You came a long way to get to California.

———

—You in California now.

———

Why couldn't you speak? Where in fact was your throat? Why did you have no hands? How could it be you saw right and left and backward—without turning? Had he killed you? He had killed you. Had he stopped your breath, your heart? He had. But you won't believe me because you I write to are gone. And you who replaced her: you don't love me.

Okay then Van Ness you murdered her. Strangled her for three minutes in the cool dim amber room while her face turned russet, purple, chalky blue, and the bewilderment evaporated from her eyes and her gaze went upward like a priest's, an ecstatic's. Unhooked your cramped fingers from her neck and thumbed wide her eyelids and shone a penlight at her pupils—no reaction—held a mirror to her nostrils—no pinpoints of mist—and pricked her flesh with a needle, and the hole didn't close—found no pulse in her wrists, none beneath her jaw . . .

And you sat by the bed in a chair until another demon tickled by you, entering Winona Fairchild's naked corpse.

Book Three

September 13, 1990

"B illy, Billy, Billy," Billy said a few minutes before his death at the hands of Carl Van Ness, "you my man Billy are something of a genius. No," he said, "I'm not—yes, you are," he said. "No," he said, "it's just inspiration." He cut the corner on a switch-back, raced to the crest of a bare knoll and stood still at half the height of the surrounding chinkapins, looking at their sickly branches and the tantalizing mist caught almost like confetti in the underlight, his hard breath the only sound until as it abated he heard the woods again, the birds and the currents and the leaves, and felt the noises almost as if they touched his flesh. Maybe they did. After all, these were vibrations. The laughter of the soul of this place. Maybe too in this way the vibrations of the Mercedes had communicated to his brain, shortcutting past his cogitations, the fact that not the manifold but the dipstick was the source of the runaway oil. The dipstick wasn't stock, but a changeling, an impostor, its cap just slightly too small for the aperture, and thus at high RPM's you get oil spraying so bad all through the compartment it drips down onto your head when you raise the hood.

"I have solved the problem."

He got back to the cabin with a desire to put on a little tea. Black tea, if he had any. Coffee, even. He had some coffee somewhere. Actually he had some Kenya coffee in the bean, in a bag, in the shed. He'd have to get after those beans with a hammer, though. As he thought about it he plucked a pencil from a knothole in the kitchen counterboard and dug in the wood box for some paper, an old *San Francisco Examiner* he could use the margins of. Sat at the table and forgot about the coffee, tearing the front page into quarters and beginning a note to Clarence. He got the first sentence down, across the top margin—the good news. He took off his new hat with its special message, adolescent, obscene, kind of funny, and set it aside and skimmed the sweat from his hairline with his hand. He sat back and put his pencil in his mouth, put his feet up on the table, locked his hands behind his head, and began to consider the list of things they'd need to get the Mercedes saleable, a short list of inexpensive things, now that he'd solved the oil problem. He heard the door behind him opening.

M eadows thought: What are you trying to do to me? Thinking thus he gassed the rocking Scout over the rise past the Gualala dump and onto the unpaved portion of Shipwreck Road, shortly afterward took a right onto the logging track of the Mendocino Redwoods Company and trespassed through their lands alongside the Gualala River's Little North Fork, in the bed of the San Andreas Fault, fording the stream several times and stopping finally in a wreck of dust and shade where the lumber corporation's holdings, and the road, gave out. He was now within two miles of the coast. He pulled the Scout onto the uphill side and fixed it with its rear to the descent, a position made necessary by its lack of any reverse, and made sure of his equipment: a memo pad and something to write with. The government-run Gualala Campground lay near enough by that he could smell a bit of cooking on the currents of the afternoon. Meadows left the jeep and made his way on foot along the river's western bank until he sighted camp smoke two hundred meters off, across the water, in the same spot where he'd last seen the Silverado and had talked with Harry Lally's delegation, the two piggers from Del Norte County. Walked downstream nearly to the bridge, just a few hundred meters above where the river jogged back west and widened, over the course of a mile or so, to make its marshy estuary on the Pacific. Crossed here at the last narrow place, wetting his boots to the cuffs of his jeans. With his back to the water he crouched for several minutes, listening but hearing nothing, and then reconnoitered warily above the embankment's edge. Smoke strung itself through the boughs, but nothing of the Silverado or its owners showed itself. Climbing over the bank and taking to the drive, he located Carrie's site; her yellow wagon wasn't around, but he gathered from the presence of a Styrofoam cooler and a gay plastic deck chair that she and her son still camped here.

The small voices of another party carried to him as he squatted with the notepad open on his right knee and scribbled the pen across its face to get a flow, and though he'd rehearsed and revised his thoughts all the way here and had imagined some kind of statement in full, the weeping of a child and the bursting laughter of several grown-ups slightly distracted him as he struggled with the elements of composition. He wrote only, *What are you trying to do to me. Signed Your Buddy from the Road. PS Hope its the same thing I'm trying to do to you,* and tore it off and put it on her deck chair, weighted by a smooth white stone.

Not at all sure what at this point to do with himself, Meadows loitered here a minute, taking the level of his failure. He'd intended to get across to her something about his soul, and her soul, and the certainty of the turnings that had brought them up against each other. The words to a Dead number hovered somewhere just out of memory's grasp . . . if he could quote them now, they'd put it over: *Till we all fall down/It'll do you fine/Don't think about/What you left behind/The way you came/Or the way you go/Let your tracks be lost/ In the dark and snow* . . . Possibly these lines had burned down through him when he'd lived with Cath. In fact of course they had. No, then: because echoes wouldn't do it. She'd sense any echoing quality in his program. She drove up as he stood there with his eyes closed. Her station wagon's right front tire growled and flapped and her little boy stared at him from the passenger seat. She herself got out and gave a little wave. He leaned low and squinted in at the kid and smiled and crossed his arms over his chest.

"You got a spare?"

"Believe it or not," she said.

"What about a jack?"

"Nope."

"Lug wrench?"

"I did have. It's under things, maybe."

"There's campers over that way. They'll have a jack."

"It just went," she said, and sat on the front bumper and turned her face to the sun.

"Hey, Clarence," he said. "What are you doing in there?"

"I don't know," the boy said, pulling up the handle on his door and getting out.

"Come with me, little dude," Meadows said. "Help me on this one."

When they came back with the jack she had his note in her hand.

"Who's camping over there?" she asked.

"A guy and two women. And a kid, a little girl."

"Did you say hi to the little girl, Clarence?"

"He did. But she didn't say anything back."

"Who said I was trying to do anything?"

"Aah—that's some kind of bullshit," he said. "I was trying to get a little deeper than that but I was worried did I have enough ink. So it came out bullshit. I'm sorry."

"Man, I don't know." She was teary-eyed. "It'd be easy to get myself hijacked emotionally right now, all things being in their current state."

"I understand."

"I'm trying to keep clear of any bullshit, isn't it pretty obvious?"

"The most obvious thing about you, yeah."

"Okay then."

"But what I'm saying is the note is bullshit, admittedly, but I'm not. That's why I'm copping to a lack of sincerity there. Because I'm sincere."

"Sincere about what, more or less?"

He cleared his throat and shook his head. "There's a Grateful Dead song."

"There generally is."

"'Make Yourself Easy.'"

"I made myself easy."

"Well," and he laughed—"do it again, okay?"

She wiped at her eyes. "Smooth gentlemen . . . slick gentlemen . . . Did you imply you were gonna change my flat, eh?"

"That's right."

"The spare is under the bedding. It's sort of part of the bed."

"We'll borrow some of this stuff," he said to the smaller Clarence, tossing out stones from around the fire pit. "We gotta block the front wheels."

She opened the tailgate door, and he dragged the spare from under their blankets and belongings and rolled it around front.

"My religious thing," she said.

He positioned the jack's nose under the front bumper and worked the handle till it came up snug.

"Okay, look," he told her. "I understand that better than you think. Anyhow I think I empathize, because I'm in a condition of religious turnaround myself."

"Have you come to the Lord?"

"That'd be going too far."

"Nothing works without the Lord."

Little Clarence brought him a four-prong tire iron from the back of the car and stood holding it in his two hands like a ship's helm.

"When two people see eye to eye in the Lord, then everything works," Carrie said.

"Look. Woman. I'm not gonna negotiate with you. I left you a note, and I'm getting your tire on, and I'm letting you know I'm serious. Stand back a ways, little dude." With swift motions he cranked the jack and raised the front end. "This is a good jack," he said. "These ratchet jacks."

"Just keep doing what you're doing. You're doing fine," Carrie said.

"I hope I'm taking that in the spirit you mean it."

She got her boy a soft drink from the cooler, and one for herself. "You want some of this?"

"In a minute I will."

"Soon as this thing rolls, we're moving up to West Point," she said. "The church is helping us. We'll have our own cabin. There's a Bible study tonight, if you'd like to drop around."

"Not likely, but possible."

Carrie sat in the deck chair. "There's a subject that has to be raised."

"Okay."

"Or maybe not. I don't know."

"Okay. Just don't tell me you're pregnant."

She sighed and got up, tossed her Pepsi into the fire pit.

"Look," he said.

But she wouldn't look. Or talk.

He let it stretch, most grateful to have this tire tool in his hands and this pentangle of lug nuts in front of his face. He loosened each, grunting, regretting even these small sounds on his part, as they seemed to signal a resumption. "I guess I don't have to ask if you're pro-life."

"It doesn't matter what I am. The Lord is pro-life, that's all that matters."

He wrestled the flat from side to side and free of the wheel, let it fall away and sashayed the spare into place. Twisted the nuts down with his fingers, tightened each with the lug wrench, laid it by, lowered the car with eight strokes of the jack's handle. His right hand leapt again to the tire tool—better get these things tighter, this is just the sort of moment for that—but they were tight. Now here, he thought, gripping the implement helplessly, are the hands of a coward. He dropped it and leaned against the car.

"It's nice of you not to ask me who the father is."

"Nice? Are you sticking a knife in me?"

"No. I mean I take it as a compliment that you don't ask."

"I guess you'll tell me when you're ready."

"Are *you* ready?"

"I guess that tells me, whether I'm ready or not."

"I thought you used something."

"Not the second time. I meant to."

"Did you or didn't you?"

"I guess not. Not the second time."

"Well, while you're guessing so flaming much, why don't you guess what I'm supposed to do next?"

He went over to the kid, who sat slump-backed on a chunk of firewood moving a stick around in the dirt and making noises like a boat. Man without a number. Little Clarence. Nice shoes.

Meadows stood up straight and sighed. "Does this feel like a fated thing to you?"

"Man, if it isn't, then nothing ever was."

The sun had just turned toward its decline and the light worked uniformly under the trees as he entered onto the track down to Billy's. The backwoods neighborhood appeared curiously upscale, what with the Mercedes wrapped in a clean beige tarp at the head of the drive, and Nelson's Junior's vintage Porsche blocking the right half of the road. Meadows in the Scout had to skirt the German cars carefully, putting his left wheels in the brush and dipping the right ones into a delve so that the differential's housing shrieked across a series of rocks.

He kept his eye out as he took the steep curve that straightened just where a spring trickled across the track a half mile in, lest he find Nelson bent there over the water, drinking, and maybe run him over. But he didn't come across the older brother.

At the track's end he parked the Scout as ever with its nose uphill so as to have the aid of the planet's gravitation in backing it up. Shouting for Billy several times, because Billy didn't care to be surprised, Meadows cut the corner through the trees along the creek and came at the cabin from its north side. The back of the dwelling looked out toward the sea; this time of day it got the sun, and the shadows of two old madrone trees fell across the small deck and the one straight-back chair and the set of weights that Billy never used. Grasshoppers somersaulted ticking in the clearing's warm air, and a garter snake quit the damp patch beneath the gray-water pipe and swiveled into the undergrowth. On the porch Meadows paused to take the black enamelware cup from its nail and dip from the plastic garbage pail, drink deeply of the creek water, and dip it full a second time. He walked with the brimming cup in his hand across the porch and knocked on the door and stood drinking a minute until he pushed through to find the shadows of the two madrones coming through the deck's glass doors and Billy sleeping facedown on his table. Meadows drained the cup and, moving to set it aside, saw that Billy was in fact injured and then that the news was really bad. His breath caught, and he choked on his mouthful of water, inhaling it so deeply that this was nearly an act of drowning, actually overshadowing, for a good minute, the discovery he'd just made. Completely off balance, coughing with such force he thought the veins in his eyes would burst, he dropped the cup and felt around with both hands for something to support him.

That Nelson and Melissa should have left his house together didn't surprise Wilhelm Frankheimer. Years back humans had ceased to astonish. He'd had his lights cut off before too.

A couple of cables and twelve volts and a will to find joy in austerity, that's all he needed. Lanterns worked but tended to make a closed room smell like the interstate. He believed he'd seen an auto battery in the shed, but tossing the place proved this recollection to be another phony. In the study he dressed in jeans and a sport shirt and before getting to the buttons suddenly remembered exactly where the battery was and went out to get it; it wasn't there.

When he got back to his living room, Carl Van Ness was sitting around in a most disturbing way.

Frank went to the window, drew aside the curtains. The Volvo was parked in the drive. "You must've coasted in," he said. "I didn't hear you."

Van Ness looked just as he had six weeks ago—even twenty years ago, when he'd first succeeded in cultivating his spectacular mustache.

"I'm real," he said.

Frank considered the assertion, patting himself down for a cigarette. "Believe what you want," he said.

"If anybody asks, I'm not here."

"Are those the same specs you were wearing the day we met?"

"You recognize me now." Rather as if testing it for the shakes Van Ness extended his left arm to full length. He meant to indicate three packs of Camels stacked on the mantel. "Matches are in the wood box."

"Did you know I was out back?"

"I thought you might be incapacitated. Like in need of help. So I came in."

"I hate to take these. All your gifts are tainted."

"No," Van insisted, and Frank was surprised to hear the pain in his voice. "Not my gifts to you."

Frank opened a pack by tearing away its entire top. "I might just smoke 'em all up at once. I was running low."

"Some days," Van suggested, "you just don't want to quit."

"Carl. What brings you around?"

"I wanted to see you."

Frank straightened himself and opened his arms slightly, the better to be seen.

"No. I wanted you to see me. To look at me on this day of all days. Do I look different?"

"You have no idea," Frank said.

"Do I?"

"I know you. You are the one in possession of Carl Van Ness."

His visitor sat back as if quite bored.

Frank said, "What have you done?"

His visitor scooted forward in his chair and reached amongst the kindling and tossed a book of matches onto the hearth. "This and that."

Frank sat on the hearth and leaned forward, animated now. "It's so amazing that you could be connected to me by this energy, and yet your actions don't touch me. The truth of karma is so devastating, man. Your karma is so totally your own."

"Buddy?"

Frank took out a cigarette. "Yeah."

"Get a brain."

Frank lit up.

"You've lost yours. Take out an ad."

Frank took several drags off his cigarette, nodding his head and puffing away and also tapping his foot. "Yeah?"

"I'm afraid so. You recollect taking any chemicals?"

"There's a percentage of pure sanity, whether or not I'm clean and sober."

"No. No sanity for you. None."

"Don't go away mad," Frank said as Van let himself out the door.

But immediately Van came back inside again, purple in his face and breathing hard as if he'd been gone a long time, running. "What did you think we were playing with?" he said.

"I don't believe I want you here, in the presence of no witnesses," Frank said.

"Did you think we were just thinking? Thinking forbidden thoughts? *Imagining* heresies? *Pretending* to recognize moral systems as instruments of oppression and control?"

"No, man."

"'No, man.' No. There's no thinking. There's movement, or there's death. You were dying, I was moving."

"Happily, I'm twice your size and strength . . . " Frank wished to be viewed now as unimpressed. But to his own ears he sounded frightened.

"I'm told you hang out with a woman named Melissa."

"What of it?"

"I'm looking for Nelson Fairchild."

"And he's looking for you. Little old Melissa took him up where his brother's just been killed. Took him to get his wheels so he could track you down because he thinks you did the murder. They left here a half hour ago."

"Where is he looking?"

"Try the water, that's where I told him you'd be. I'd say try the water nearest the alcohol. The Gualala Hotel, the Cove Restaurant and all that."

"The Cove is closed."

"Well, start at the hotel and hit the joints near the water and cruise the Arena Pier, and don't ever come back onto this property or you'll poison it with your ridiculously lowdown evil shit."

"You're terrified. I'm so ashamed for you."

"You are a demon."

"We were friends."

"You are a demon. We were never friends."

As the Volvo's sounds receded, in which direction Frank couldn't have judged, Frank himself left the house for the shed because there was something he'd noticed there and yet had overlooked.

The lines of the shed and the house blurred in the refracting moisture, the usual flossy graduating mist, but coming from the south this afternoon rather than up from the shore. He paused at the dirty threshold. Across the low room, in the shadows on a shelf: a rayon scarf folded over into thirds, as he recalled, and then sixths. He moved toward it in a dust-diffused, cinnamon light. Opened its portfolios and laid it on the shelf before him. There it was. Like a photograph. Disowned and beautiful.

As soon as he'd put it about his neck he recognized the depth of his error. The despair poured down through its touch and filled his throat, his chest.

What was coming was a voice, a word: his name. Building with the dark of the ocean's evening.

Frank.

Frank left the shed, violated what was perhaps once a hedge partitioning his and his neighbors' yards, and stood still beside their pine-log home, but heard nothing. He crossed to the rear entry and looked in through the screen to find a patio made into a hospital room, and in it his next-door neighbor, a long-bodied old woman in bed watching TV with a drip in her arm and many things in front of her on a bed tray. Water glass, medicines. Sewing stuff.

"Well!" Frank said. "Good afternoon!" A shadow on the sliding screen door.

"Is somebody—" She broke off in order to take in air. "Who's there?"

"Just me, out for a stroll. How are you doing this afternoon?"

"*You're* not Hank."

"Almost. I'm Frank."

"Oh! Frank. I almost didn't recognize you. How are you, Frank?"

"Just wonderful."

"Me too. Did you come to hear about my mastectomy?"

"No, ma'am."

"Good. There wasn't one."

"I'm glad."

"Me too. We're a little too far gone for surgery."

"I'm sorry."

"Me too."

"Good news, bad news," Frank said.

"*Oh* yeah." She took two breaths. "That's about the size of it, isn't it?"

"Are you taking real good care of yourself?"

"Hank's taking care of me."

"Is that your husband?"

"No, he's a nurse, he's not my husband." She breathed. "My husband's a fool." She breathed. "He's gambling in Las Vegas." She breathed. "I'm sorry—Lake Tahoe." She breathed. "He's gambling in five-day streaks." She breathed. "Then he sleeps. Probably upside down." She breathed. "In a trash can. Hank takes care of me." Much to his fascination, she kept breathing.

"Do you know what I think?" he said, opening the screen door and joining her. "I think I'll just join you."

"Well," she said.

He sat in the chair beside her bed. "May I?"

"Oh," she said. "I guess so. What's that around—?" she broke off gasping.

He put his hands up toward his neck.

"A crucifix?"

He fastened his shirt buttons, taking care not to touch the green Christ, the diseased, the defeated Christ at his throat.

"It's all dirty," she said.

"It's famous. And very powerful. The crucifix of Carla Frizelli."

She looked as if the name registered, as if she were about to recall, and then suddenly as if she didn't care.

"What are those people saying?" Frank asked.

"What people? On the TV?"

"What in God's name are they trying to say?"

"How should I know? I'll turn it up."

"No. Thank you."

With great authority she leveled the remote at the thing.

"No. Thank you. I'm not ready."

She set it down and looked at him.

"Would you happen to have any potions around here, potions for pain?"

"I get it from the bolus," she said. "Only so much so often. But I can push"—she paused for air—"the button as much as I want."

Her fingers leapt deftly to the cord and grasped the switch and squeezed. The digital readout blinked on the mechanical bolus and the bolus beeped happily.

"We all need our medicine," Frank said.

A voice far away called *Frank*, the free-drifting syllable foreign to his ears.

"Nobody—" She struggled to lift her head and stare at him and then fell back among the pillows, her face puffy and her lips clamped together. "Nobody gets it!"

"I do. I get it," he promised her.

Harry Lally grips the mirrored cabinet door and opens it on an array of medicines, but not before he's looked two seconds into his own face. Lally wears his hair swept back in the manner of a fifties hipster. He once upon a time wished to be one. He can feel its blondness leeching out to silver. Yes, there's bullshit in the medicine cabinet, chickenshit, fuck-all, and when he slams it shut the mirror broadcasts a rehabilitated TV preacher swing-band convict idol, back after prison, with a headache. Somebody around here is one hundred thousand in the hole. And he's the only one around here.

With his bathrobe slightly parted and a cigarette in one hand, in the other the remote, he sits on the divan in the den. With the lamps off, with the curtains closed. These facts he understands to be symptoms. Darkness at noon. Damn I'm a sad vampire.

Harry Lally watches a big dealer in cuffs and leg irons moving down the hall of a police station in Oakland on TV. You can see how tired the man's eyes look, as he tries at first to duck the cameras and hide his face, but then forgets and looks around at what's happening to him. For a long time he's been carrying this day of his arrest, this unbearable day, and now finally he's shrugged it from his shoulders to explode at his feet, surrounding him with hateful faces and a miraculous popping light. A long-haired Chicano, José Esperanza, alias Joe Hopeless, middle-aged and round-shouldered and hunched and sick of it, pitied by no one on this earth but Harry Lally.

Lally staggered shuffling out toward the pool with his own such day teetering overhead. The eastward view was all manzanita as far as the ridge. In back of the house the terrain dropped fast, and the landscape, mainly scrub, opened west into unreal vistas beyond a swimming pool that overlooked, or would have, the distant ocean. But somebody had built it wrong, placing the bathhouse and breezeway at the scenic end. He, as a matter of fact, had built it wrong. He dropped his robe and lay naked by the edge of the pool, shut his eyes, let the sunshine burn on his flesh. Almost immediately the shadow of his house found him.

"I've got goose bumps."

"What do you mean," Lally said.

"*Goose* bumps."

"How am I supposed to interpret that?" he said.

He kept his eyes shut until whoever it was went away. Some youngster.

He'd heard of Joe Hopeless, a creature high on the food chain. Joe had failed to pay up, or somebody had outpaid him. By a troubling coincidence the youngster in Rio had been named Esperanza also, the whore they'd picked up, hit by a car, just a glancing thing, she'd actually smiled, wincing and shrugging and forgetting about it right away. But then she woke up the next morning dead. The only corpse he'd ever touched.—And I felt how we're really made of clay . . . Lally had never actually seen a dead person before. You could tell immediately, although he'd assumed at first that she'd botched her makeup donning it drunk, and turned her face all white.

"Lally!"

Lally turned on his side to see.

"Harry Lally!" His name on the world's lips—somebody at the gate—on the lips of Parker, a retired Teamster with a slow, thick form, extremely short arms, narrow shoulders. An old long-hauler with a round beat-up slit-eyed Eskimo face. Hillary had left the gate open, and this person was simply strolling into their lives.

Lally sat up, put his feet into the water. He bunched the robe over his groin.

"I'm here for Sandy."

"You caught me napping."

"Sandy here?"

"Sandy."

"Yeah. My daughter."

"I don't know."

"You don't know."

"I'm just lying here. I don't know who's here."

"Sandy!" he yelled.

"She could be inside."

"She's fourteen years old."

"She just visits with Hillary."

"She's my youngest." Parker looked around himself. "Sandy Parker!" he shouted. He huffed and puffed. "I've got two others grown up. Her mother's dead. It's just us two."

The girl came out in her bikini.

Her father said, "Let's go."

"No."

"I said let's go."

She went over and sat on the diving board, mounting it straddle-legged.

Parker squatted on his heels and got his face too close to Lally's. "Lally. If she doesn't leave with me in thirty seconds I'm gonna go in your house and use the phone to call the police."

"I haven't done anything. Really, nothing."

"Not for you. For me. I'm gonna call the cops and then come back out here and get your head underwater and just hold you under, and hold you under, and hold you under."

He stretched forth his arms at the level of Lally's shoulders. He had unusually bulky, swollen-looking wrists. His fingers seemed to proceed right out of his forearms without any intervening hands.

"Look, hey—girl? Sandy?"

She reached her toes toward the water, swinging her legs.

"Visiting hours are over."

Harry Lally lay on his hip in his robe beside the swimming pool. He saw somebody out in the chaparral on the north side of the electric fence, a white form wavering above the manzanita and scrambling audibly among its branches and coming out in tatters and scrapes to stand still across the water.

"Don't touch that fence. It's hot."

Frankheimer reached out the flat of his hand.

"That's not a horse fence, man."

Frankheimer's face took on pallor and grimness as he held the wire down with his palm and stepped over.

"That's one-ten voltage," Lally said.

"I thought you meant like twelve," he said.

"No sir."

Frankheimer dove in, completely clothed, and headed this way underwater, Lally tracking his movements as he might those of a dorsal fin. The giant surfaced right under his nose, breathing hard and chewing his lips. Lally stayed motionless.

"Lying by the water?" Frank asked.

"Hell yes."

"Shooing the flies. Drinking drinks sideways."

Lally couldn't stop the laughter in his mouth.

"I would like some cocaine," Frank said. He turned his back and rested his arms out cruciform along the gutter of the pool and let his head fall forward. He extended his legs, and his bare feet floated up toward the surface some distance out beyond him.

"I could accommodate you," Lally said, sensing they were on the brink of a situation here, "to a small degree."

Hillary comes along on the edge of reality in her bright Hawaiian mumu, doing something. God knows what she's doing. More of the same.

"You left the gate open," he told her.

"_____"

"I'm not ending up on TV dragging down the hall in baggy jail-house jeans."

"_____"

"Harry to Hillary," he said.

"_____"

"The crack in my ass showing on TV. The whole world looking."

"_____"

"This does not end with me doing Youth Christian Fellowship in prison. I'll take a blaze of glory over that one."

"_____"

"Doesn't she talk?" Frank dipped his head and sucked, puffed his cheeks, spewed water like a fountain.

Hillary frowned at this display, and they lost sight of her, as she had a trick of becoming invisible.

"She knows I mean it," Lally said.

"She doesn't talk anymore?"

"She doesn't talk when my people are around. She's got her own people."

Suddenly Frankheimer ascended in a glitter, like a loose surfboard out of a wave. "Gotta go—"

"I'll get your package," Harry said.

They were moving out of the car and into their new home, formerly a saloon, now a sort of rectory for the West Point Holy Cross in the neighboring lot. Carrie took their things—mostly clothes—from green plastic trash bags, liberating dust and must, and laid them out in piles. "What's this!—Oh Lord—Oh, my!" she said frequently, discovering possessions she'd forgotten.

Little Clarence watched through steady almost sedated-looking eyes, rolling a gray golf ball back and forth between his hands along the wooden flooring and in and out of the dimples made by piano legs. The bar had been torn out—everything had been torn out, and in fact their quarters were very much as they'd been in the Dodge, only roomier.

"Don't go too far," she said.

He didn't answer. Outside he was surrounded as everywhere these days by big evergreens. He went to the lot's edge, by the narrow West Point Road, to bounce the golf ball on the pavement. As he understood it they wouldn't live in the Dodge anymore, and tonight they'd go to Bible study. The ball tricked wrong and rolled away down the hill with a henlike muttering sound. Something brattled from the woods behind the one-room church, a beast or a bird or a party horn. Around the corner of the building trotted a cube-headed dog, faintly brindled and jowly and muscled, like a boxer, but smaller, and with blood on its muzzle. It ducked its head and approached, obsequiously writhing. But when the voice called again the animal turned away and retraced its steps. Clarence followed. The dog had brought down a dappled fawn in the quiet wood and eaten most of its left hindquarter and was bent now, eager and friendly, gnawing at its hip. The fawn, laid out against a fallen log, looked elsewhere in abject repudiation of this circumstance. The dog turned to Clarence and said *yeah yeah yeah yeah*. The fawn stretched its neck and rounded its mouth and bleated. Clarence selected a soft clot of earth and tossed it underhanded to burst on the dog's flat forehead. The dog sneezed and stepped sideways. The boy tossed several others, a couple of which thumped against its ribs. It crabstepped backward diagonally and stopped and waited, waggling its tailless rump.

Clarence went back to his new home and said to his mother, "There's a deer that's hurt."

"Is that what I've been hearing?" she said.

"A dog is eating his leg."

"Okay," she said. She spent some minutes hunting for the machete before locating it finally under the car's front seat.

"Behind there," Clarence told her, and led her around back of the church.

"Oh, you poor thing," she told the fawn. "I oughtta kill you too," she warned the dog.

Clarence and the dog observed as she stood above the fawn and brought the blade down from high over her head with both hands.

"You'll be sick tonight," she told the dog. "Don't worry," she promised Clarence, "he's gonna get a beating. He'll diarrhea all over everything and his master's gonna"— she leaned over the dog—"beat you like a *dog*." The dog said *yeah yeah yeah yeah*.

"When will it be dead?"

"Don't worry. Once they get hurt like that they stop feeling anything. Look at its eyes. See they're all cloudy? It's dead."

For a little while Clarence traversed and circled the lot, striking at things on the ground with a short branch. The dog tagged along, curious to begin with, and then fascinated. It nipped at the boy's heels and then started biting harder and harder, as if it wouldn't stop at the flesh but might continue, happy and friendly, on through the skin and never flag in its thorough approval until it ate through his rump as it might any downed fawn's. Clarence threw the stick away and the dog went after it. Clarence escaped into the house. He found his mother seated on the floor under the window, crying for joy, with a stack of folded clothing in her lap. "We've been found," she explained, and began laying out miscellaneous garments for his pallet.

It occurred to him he must be somewhere in the midwestern U.S. He walked along the interstate in the middle of the fields.

A blue MG stopped for him and he got in. They drove toward a patch of sun about six miles off.

Frank watched two domes in the distance. Or rather, his own knees, drawn up to the level of his eyebrows. The driver of this blue MG was smoking a horrible-smelling French cigarette.

"How you doing man?" the driver said. "You used to live with me but right now all I can remember is you used to get up every morning and say to your dog, 'Don't die on me, buddy.'"

"I don't recognize you," Frank said. "I don't remember anything like that."

"Oh yeah." He pulled it around a tight curve and skirted the edge of a cliff high above the cymbal crash and slow, suspenseful grace of white spray over black crags: they'd reached California.

"I think you had a different name back then," the guy said.

"I gotta get out of this car," Frank said.

"You like the air. You feel like sleeping under the stars."

"That and more," Frank said, flinging himself from the little blue sportster while it was still rolling.

He walked through hot country full of long white grass and the flat shadows of oaks. He saw the fretwork of anything dead right through the scrub. Psychic radiology.

A woman let him into the only dwelling he came to. She was a hippie lady with her hair wrapped up in a scarf and a skirt so long it dragged on the floor. She hardly said a word, just let him walk into her place and sit down at the table by the sink. It was a double-wide mobile home in a time-chasm, with a nice paneled ceiling and picked-up furniture and stupid inexplicable stuff everywhere—crocheted HOME SWEET HOME next to a KEEP ON TRUCKIN' bumper sticker, diseased houseplants, fake flowers, toy rabbits, feathers and dried bones, a picture from a magazine taped up. Outside were the totally blank sky and the completely empty earth.

"Frank. It's me. Carleen."

"Old Carleen." A thought occurred to him. "Can Yvonne use your body?"

Carleen tried to laugh.

"She's trying to get in touch with me, and I want to talk to her."

"Shit, Frank," she said.

He asked if he could get some water. She said okay.

He stood at the sink looking out the window onto a weedy garden decorated with several gray cattle skulls. The blue MG was parked out there.

"I can't have another thought until this moment gets resolved," he said in a dry voice.

On the refrigerator somebody had written the words

Electric
Child
On
Bad Fun

"What right now is my location?" he asked.

"Are you looking for the ocean, or Route One-oh-one? Which are you looking for?"

"That depends."

"Frank. Are you okay?"

"Maybe."

"Do you know who I am?"

"Are we, like—big bad friends?"

"Shit," she said, "don't get all philosophical on me. I better take you next door."

She took him across the road, the both of them puffing up dust with their feet in the bright, silent daytime. They went through a door and everybody said, "It's Frank," and he sat on the couch.

"Frank's getting philosophical as hell," she explained. "Give him a beer or something."

Truman is getting worried, Frank fully intended to say, but perhaps said nothing.

In the kitchen somebody was pulling Cranky's hair while Cranky attempted to keep his bottle clear of the fray. "I'm gonna have to bussa *head*," Cranky advised. They banged up against the refrigerator in there.

"They're quarreling," the woman sitting next to him said.

He'd already had one era with her, and supposedly she'd died, but here she was again—somewhat changed, but you couldn't kill her. Not when the truest part of her hadn't even been born.

Yes, by secret procedures utterly changed.

He'd never been able to remember, conjure up, the day he'd first met Yvonne. That was because it hadn't happened yet. It was happening now.

"Hey."

"Hey, shit."

"That ain't no car I know."

"Damn!" somebody said as if having touched a flame.

"It's the man, it's the man, it's the man, it's the man."

One person went quietly toward the doorway and stood in it, but they pushed him aside. They looked like travelling salesmen, all alone and riding on good thoughts.

"Who we got here today?"

"You got a warrant?"

"I have several to serve, yes I do. Michael Edwards."

"Warrant for what?"

The man sighed. "Take a *guess*."

"Search warrants?"

"Arrest. Failure to appear. Yes, we got Edwards here, Sally Anne Kent. I see my personal favorite, Cranky Slaw. Maxwell Slaw— Maxwell? Will you put down that beer and come in here please?"

"I don't get it."

"Do you recall running an amphetamine factory on Faro Road? And getting busted, and being arraigned, and having a date set? I guess your calendar broke. And your map. You weren't supposed to set foot outside Ukiah. Failure to appear. Now everybody listen to me. I'm not about to do this four individual times. Are you Thomas James Anderson?"

"Nope."

"Yep. Yep. You sure are. Listen, you four: You have the right to remain silent, all of that. Give 'em the cards. You all sign these cards."

"What for?"

The other man put a gun to someone's head. "Goddamn you motherfucking piece of shit."

"Do you know your rights? Then sign the card. Turn around, gimme your hands. How do they look, Jim. Do they look rowdy? I don't want anybody scratching me, biting me, et cetera. You've all got AIDS. Don't think I haven't noticed you," he said to Frank.

The man stood them up all in a row with their hands cuffed behind them, all but Frank.

"What's the pooch's name?"

"Uh . . ." Frank said. "Truman."

"Yeah? Truman? Where's your bandanna around your neck, Truman? How come they didn't name you Kilo or Roach like all the other dogs? And who's that sitting on the couch with those big feet and no fucking shoes on, Truman? What's your name. You. You tall fucker. Identify."

Frank rubbed his palms vigorously across his knees. He cleared his throat and ran his tongue around his mouth and reached up and removed his bridge and two false teeth and looked at them. "I'm Frank," he said. He felt insulated by the fragilest membrane from a tragic ugliness.

"Listen, Frank . . ." The man thought about his next words for an extraordinary, a truly extraordinary interval.

Uh-oh, thought Frank, I've fallen down a time-chasm.

The car doors banged outside. The man looked out through the door frame, stepped sideways beyond the threshold as if to get a better view, and fell either into one of the numerous time-chasms around here or down a random gravitational well.

An hour after he'd left Frankenstein, as he drove north toward Point Arena, Van Ness noticed a figure on the grassy slope above the highway. Some ranchhand, hatless, walking away from the shadows where the horses were slowly killing the trees.

He now recognized the man as Frankenstein cutting a diagonal across the meadow, northeast, uphill. Mr. Natural himself. Very decidedly on the march. Van took his foot off the gas. And then immediately replaced it. Frankenstein faded from his focus.

Van Ness perused the oncoming traffic. His own alertness intrigued him. Entering Point Arena two miles later he found himself reacting with shock to the echo of his own car's engine off the buildings, as if it might be the sound of Fairchild's Porsche.

Now his strategy failed him. He'd started at the county's southern line and had intended to go north as far as Manchester, then double back. If Fairchild were anywhere between, they'd rendezvous. But a tour of Arena Cove, where Fairchild might as likely turn up, required a jog of nearly a mile off the Coast Highway; he had to choose.

He turned left toward the cove.

Here Van drove slowly. He didn't see Fairchild's car around; however, when he reached the pier and stopped, shifted to reverse, was backing up, Fairchild himself appeared, dancing toward him in the forward view with his hand doubled back at the level of one of his big ears, and, balanced on the palm of it, a large rock, which he launched in Van's direction so that it thundered on the Volvo's hood as the car lurched backward, Van jamming the gas; and now Fairchild went into reverse as Van Ness applied the brakes and levered into first and bore down on the attacker. Fairchild skitted left and right before turning his back and sprinting some twenty feet to the pier and up onto it, where the car, as it fishtailed on the sandy asphalt and its rubber caught and it shot forward almost catching and crushing him against a piling, couldn't follow, and slid to a stop. The fool had brought himself to bay. Van Ness tried backing up, giving him room in which to try for escape, but Fairchild only waited, catching at oxygen, slack-jawed, half-crouched, his hands on his knees. Van Ness, from the bottom of his spine and out through the pulse in his temples, the pulse in his fingers, in the pits of his eyes, felt something crimson and golden and filthy rolling. He inched the Volvo to the foot of the pier and parked sideways and opened the door, intending to sit there regarding and hating this entity for a while; but as soon as his hand felt the latch he was setting forth, leaping onto the boardwalk and chasing Fairchild down and aiming now to grapple with him and drag him off into the water and if necessary drown them both. Fairchild stumbled back, keeping the distance of a few yards between them, and caught up a length of two-by-four and stood waving it back and forth in an arc. Van stopped out of reach of the club. He circled to his left until each waited on the boardwalk almost opposite the other, and each with his back to the water.

Fairchild stretched his arms forth and sighted along his weapon at Van's face. "Let me ask you something, maestro. If you come back to life in a future universe after dying in this one, why should it be a universe you're accustomed to? Why this same one with the single difference being that you didn't die?"

"You thinking about dying? Good. It's time you did." Van Ness went into a crouch. To his left, out of arm's reach up the pier, the end of a length of one-inch metal pipe jutted from a pile of ropes and guys. Yet if he moved the necessary yard or two in its direction, he wouldn't be able to cut off Fairchild's escape down the pier.

Fairchild lowered the tip of his weapon to rest, like the head of a golfer's driver, between them.

Van said, "I feel hungry when I look at you. I wanna tear you up with my teeth and eat you. I really do."

"I make some people feel that way. It's my fate."

"You're being flip. But fate is. It is. It's vast—the pattern threads through the whole succession of universes. Take a swing at me, and see."

"You know what Wilhelm Frankheimer told me today? Not one hour ago? He described you as free."

"You're stalling."

"And when I first met you, you were full of talk—big talk about being a man of will."

Van stepped once to his left and Fairchild raised his cudgel and hexed him with it.

"A man of will," Fairchild said. "But now you go on about fate. Like it imprisons you."

"You have to see fate as a design, a pattern, and the will as the knife, the blade, the thing slicing through the fabric. If I like the design, then I follow the warp and the woof. When the pattern doesn't suit, I'm free to die."

"You don't come at these ideas in the context of world thought."

"You mean I didn't go to prep school."

Van leapt sideways atop the heap and grasped the pipe and pulled it free. Fairchild, rather than running, seemed to think it best to keep his weapon pointed at his foe and only pivoted, following the movement.

He faced Van and Van's metal pipe, a sturdy staff, shorter but heavier than his own, and more easily wielded.

Fairchild sighed. His lips trembled. "What now?" he asked.

"A fight to the death. One of us dispatches the other one to another realm."

Van shifted his feet for purchase amid the ropes and rubble. He bent at the waist and craned to present his jaw as if to a barber's razor. "Take your best shot."

"No, no, you didn't answer my question. If there's some future world in which you didn't die, then why isn't everything else different too?—in the future universe. A different president, a different population, different history altogether? Why not a universe where elephants rule the earth and all the trees are purple?"

"It usually is. Most realities differ vastly. You just don't know it. The one you resume in is the one you were born into. It's the only one you know, the only one you recognize."

"So the one you died in is gone."

"Surely."

"So a universe dies when you die."

"There's also a thread that is this universe, identically, changed only enough to account for your continuing presence, and no more changed than that. Eventually you get every conceivable universe and every conceivable variation of each, including the variation of the tiniest action of a single molecule. Listen, sport, we're talking about quite a few universes here. And in every one?—you're *miserable*."

Fairchild charged him. Had his sights on, was driving toward, the man's midriff when his leftward field of vision exploded in a great light. His feet rolled out from under him and the sea approached, touched, engulfed him, and he went blind. He said, "This is bullshit," but in somebody else's voice.

People wanted to get up close. They filled the front pew of the Holy Cross Chapel before any of the other pews, a sign, as Carrie interpreted it, of their enthusiastic belief. Carrie sat on the left aisle seat in the second row with little Clarence tucked against her ribs. Well before the designated hour the building had filled with fellowshippers of all sorts, in T-shirts and flannel shirts and long denim skirts like her own, with large Bibles prayerfully ruined and swollen with bookmarks like her own; old ladies and young women and big fat men in overalls with beards and men in ten-gallon hats lacking nothing to be cowboys except spurs on their boots; people who stank of sweat, some with whiskey-breath, some sorrowful, some perplexed, some suffused with self-congratulation and gratitude, others drunk on grace. Men carried in folding chairs and set them up in back, men in rubber boots and some in thick socks who'd left their spiked logging calks in the vestibule.

The preacher, Mike, was young and awkward and short but seemed to know, much less than Carrie knew of herself, how he'd got there exactly, in front of everyone and responsible now for guiding this medley as one body. He welcomed them and led them in a prayer of thanks with his hands clenched together and his eyelids fluttering.

"Psalm twenty-two sixteen," he said, and the Bibles whispered as everyone turned to the passage, "Dogs are round about me . . . twenty-two twenty. Deliver . . . Do you see it? Deliver my life," he read, his voice ascending to magisterial registers, "from the power of the dog!"

He set his Bible on the podium behind him and stood at the head of the aisle, almost between the two front pews. "Family that had a big, a great big dog," he said, and paused, put his left hand to his mouth and coughed, cleared his throat—"part Saint Bernard, part husky—not a Doberman, I don't want to bolster any prejudice. Not a pit bull. Big dumb friendly dog. Well, he was one of the family, romped with the children, had his own bed right inside the back door under the coathooks with everybody's name on 'em, Sally and Sam and Mom and Pop and little Joe. You get the picture? Friendly, friendly dog. But he took a tumor in that big old dumb happy head of his, a tumor nobody knew about until it put pressure on his cranium and his signals crossed all around and he—suddenly—turned—*mean*. He had that family, family that raised and loved and trusted that dog, cornered in a bedroom for an hour till the sheriff got out there and put that dog down. Shot him right in the house. Otherwise that beloved family member would have torn, them, *up*. Because a few cells went haywire, blitzed out—made PRESS-sure on his CRANE-ium and he ROSE UP AN ENEMY.

"This is the deal, you see, this is the absolute deal. That dog the psalmist is scared of is the same one that feels like a friend most days. Lot of you knew me just three years ago. Lot of you saw me sleeping on the beach with sand on my face, in my ears, in my hair, wandering around all the time with one shoe on looking for the other one. Boy, that booze was good to me! That bottle was my only friend. When my neighbors on Sunday morning were heading down the walk to church, I was alone in my living room scrambling around on the floor after that bottle, down on my knees, and I'd raise it up before my eyes and say—I, love, you. And down in the city while the church-bells rang on Sunday there were other guys, still are, walking into those X-rated movies and sitting all hushed and quiet in the pews. And when that screen lights up they find their only comfort. Oh yeah, you know—you know—I see by your face, Jim knows, don't you Jim? Jim: ever look around and notice that everybody was about three feet taller than you? Because you were down on your knees? Begging? Begging on your knees for a fix of heroin? Yeah, Jim knows. He knows. My buddy James knows. He knows too well—and when you got it, when you got that fix, you felt like Mommy just took you in her arms. Felt like your friend was beside you, that kindly old dog who's always there and always understands.

"When that dog took my throat in his teeth, it was the best thing that ever happened to me. Because it drove me to the arms of my one true friend, our Lord Jesus Christ who laid down his life for me. That's what it took, because I was lost, man—I! Was! Lost!"

Now the preacher looked worried, might have forgotten what he wanted to say, or thought no one liked him. His face took on a sheen, it glowed like the sun, and his tongue sounded thick in his mouth and he began drawling like an Okie. "We are deaf, dumb, blind, retarded, and crazy!" People in the congregation laughed and shouted Yes, Yes, Yes, or wept in silence, or shut their eyes and raised their right hands as if to touch some hovering thing delicately with their fingers. "We think up is down, black is white, true is false. No wonder we die!—something's abound to kill somebody like that sooner or later!

"Even when we mean to tell the truth there's only poison coming out of our faces. It's happening right now unless praise God I'm suf-fused, and I hope I am, with the Holy Spirit. Nothing on my own power. Nothing on my own power." Suddenly his face popped as if with shock and he shouted, "Praise God!" and then stood looking down at his feet and breathing. He looked up:

"You think action will save us? You really think there's anything we can do?

"Philosophy?—are we going to think our way out of this one? We've gotten ourselves in such a jam that this time God alone can help us.

"That's the position this world is *rigged* to put us *in* in the first place! This race is *fixed* so we come out *losers. Destitute. Flat* broke."

"Amen! *A*-men!" voices cried.

A great sadness bore down on him and bowed his neck and he swayed like a mourner. "Yes, I too am a fool, I turn to Jesus with these broken birds in my hands . . . "

"Amen! Yes God!"

"God's love, God's love . . ." Mike squinted, eyes closed, as if trying hard to hear something somewhere. "The Old Testament shows Him as almost a dragon, and we're dandelions gone to seed, and the best way He can love us is by not even breathing on us. By leaving us be. And that's love the hard way . . . "

"Praise God! Praise him!"—Carrie herself was shouting.

"He lets us—*lets* us—he lets us take on burdens we can't carry but maybe two-three steps and then boom! And we're just groaning under the weight of it. Groooaaning—Romans now," he said brightly, "Romans eight twenty-six and twenty-seven: 'Praying with groans that God understands.' You got it there? Groooaaaning. Groaning under the weight of sin. God leaves us grooooaaaning . . ." He stooped down low as if bent beneath some massive burden . . . as if completely crushed . . .

A small answering thunder emanated from somewhere in the pews, and two women stood up with concern on their faces and stumbled over one another, moving into the aisle as a big man slumped sideways on the bench. He moaned until the air was crushed from his lungs in a muttering gasp. The two women, sharp, well-turned-out ladies perhaps originally from L.A., fell both to their knees at the pew's end beside this collapsed logger, and one took his face in her hands.

Little Clare tried to stand up in his seat, grabbing at the back of it and squirming like a monkey. Carrie pushed him down by his shoulders and felt herself rising, standing, straightening up to ease a sudden burning in her solar plexus.

"God understands! God understands!" Mike shouted. "God knows!"

He doubled over, clutched at his belly, and let out a moan that ascended as he lifted himself up straight and then halfway over backward, until he wailed like an infant.

Then everyone began to groan. She'd never done this before but she was doing it now, letting it all go. If there was such a thing as the Holy Spirit, this had to be it, or the sound of it, or the Spirit tearing the voice of Satan from her heart, the music of his lies and nightmares flying out of her, and she didn't care where they went.

An hour passed in the time-chasm. The door, better than halfway ajar, feinted and stuttered on its hinges. Frank became aware too of physical changes, a silence, a cloud that disturbed the daylight. He understood at last; and would have laughed but his neck ached, his jaws were exhausted, he couldn't laugh:

Failure to Appear.

"Guilty," Frank said.

He rubbed at his face and stood up, moved quickly in an onslaught of disequilibrium to the door frame and its right angles. Its verticals and sensibles. He put his teeth back in his mouth. Stood massaging his groin through his pants. Nobody out there.

His body was all jags and angles. He took its cluttered assortment back to the couch and sat down and a long breath filled him almost to bursting before it racked out in a sigh. Bag of reefer right there on the floor, a red leather purse open on the couch beside him. Clouds took the daylight farther off.

The walls about him creaking and shrugging, he sat amid an arrangement of dark spaces on which he made out scattered hieroglyphics. I am in the deepest time-chasm ever, he thought. Thirst raked up and down his esophagus, or was it another craving? Maybe a cigarette—he couldn't remember whether he smoked or not.

The dog broke through it all, a dog of action, moving to the forefront and standing there in bleak nobility and communicating its desire for a can of soup.

Truman!

Frank rose up and made his way toward the kitchen, the world of soup, but heard the humming catch its breath around him, and he burst out of the place into the night.

New universe. Oxygen and fog. He'd exited that tomb and

regained the animal world. Things without thought but twitching. Heads closed around stuff like walnut meat that never bothered them.

"Your *rights*. Don't worry, I'll read them ten times to you in the car, okay? Let's go, the man here is hungry for his supper."

—This wasn't being said now, but hung out in the karmic aether to be bumped into much like the sappy mist. He didn't know where he was but he could hear the wheels of old carts laboring along the coast and the cries of scuttled fishers trying to find one another in the closing moments.

Yvonne was about to call him. She inhaled the last of the day, leaving the dark of eventide. She breathed out the word of his name. He heard it long before it reached him.

O n this side of the road the presence of a cherry-colored metal-flake Harley both moved and consoled Clarence Meadows as he entered the Full Sails.

He nodded to the leather-garbed bikey and his wife, who sat at a table with beers before them, also shiny black helmets.

"That your beautiful machine out front?"

"Yes it is," the man said.

"Best thing I've seen all day."

"Thank you."

Meadows wanted to correct himself when he saw the waitress, for she was another gift of the afternoon, almost as stunning as a Harley in the sun. Lovely in a way that made him feel like ordering something. He sat at the counter and said to her, "Wherefore."

"What?" she said.

"It's Shakespeare. It's all I know of *Romeo and Juliet*."

She didn't laugh. She stared at him until her evident concern prompted him: "Oh yeah," he confessed, "it's a deep down day."

"Are you feeling bad?"

"The worst in a long time."

"You need a friend."

"I lost a friend."

"You need another."

"Maybe we could"—he shrugged, sighed—"Go camping or something sometime."

The woman looked regretful. "I don't think I could."

"Why not?"

"I'm in love."

"Yeah. I guess . . . me too."

Outside he opened the driver's door of Billy's Scout. He guessed now it was his. He released the handbrake and pushed the vehicle backward into the road.

Clarence passed the Phillips 66 station, the mall, the offices of competing realtors strung together, gift shops, each with a philosophy, the Safeway's long glass windows. Citizens of the Empire stopped and went, blinded slaves, beautiful slaves, moving down the laser lines tuned to every electronic thing. With their tattooed pensions. Their chains and memberships. On the straightaway crossing the Gualala bridge he looked at the maniacs charging him in monstrous vehicles at better than a mile a minute: great, blimplike motor homes, and others parked by the sea, stuck among the driftwood sculptures of beachcombers. He had in him the power to lengthen his touch right through the walls and into their minds where they lay propped up with their TVs turning them to ghosts. Whatever else he himself might be accused of, at least he'd managed to stay out of their world. He couldn't truthfully be demonstrated even to be a citizen of this planet.

At the Stewart Point Store he turned left and followed the close, switching asphalt road upward. The weather clung but there was dust on the feathers of the redwoods. Rhododendrons bloomed in sunlit patches back among the trees. He crossed a tiny bridge over a gorge and thirty feet below a tributary of the Gualala compressed and bowed into white falls. Down there it was dark. The shadow of the planet's curve tracked him uphill as the sun went down.

At the ridgetop the road switched back south toward a bluff and a view and then north again alongside some properties and buildings. The name of this locale, West Point, referred not to some coastal spur, but to this promontory some miles inland.

Clarence rolled past the church and parked uphill of it at somebody's gated driveway and got out to hear, from the chapel, the sounds of a lamentation that he presumed to be very bad singing. Down the slope for miles. Out to sea. And the trees attending it with perfect concentration.

Twilight had caught him by now. He walked among a lot of cars and trucks past a couple of structures too darkened to be intelligible, cabins or sheds, and another possibly a workshop or garage. The chapel itself seemed to be howling out music, less like song than like the agonies in a hen coop at laying-time, two lit windows either side of its doorway making an astonished face.

He climbed the steps and stood in an entryway full of groans and the smell of old wood. In the vestibule he paused as he came against the cloud of their human warmth. He stumbled among miscellaneous footwear. Am I supposed to kick off my boots? Everyone was giving voice in a scary way. He saw netters and woodmen and professional poachers; lost beatniks, grandmothers, people who might have been in real estate, rocking forward and backward in the pews, not singing, all suffering terribly . . . Mike Rose, who worked at the Phillipps station in Gualala and was known formerly to Clarence as Shakey Mikey, a rehabilitated rumdum now, with some history also as a cocaine demon, stood at the head of the room shouting amid the uproar: "And the dawg! Shall rise up a human. And kiss! The lips! Of his master—

"Pray for the ones still out there. Pray for the ones still seeking but, Lord, they just don't know what. They don't know it's you, Lord, so help them, help them, help them."

In the crowded space the mob's colossal voice had a flat, concussive quality. It slapped against Clarence's head and he received rather than heard the preacher's desperate instructions: Psalm fifty-one! Psalm fifty-one! The sacrifice acceptable to God is a broken spirit! A broken and contrite heart, O God, thou wilt not despise!

The gales of misery came up out of their vitals and whirled around their heads. It drove over him the dense stifling vapours of their intimacy and stopped him there, sucked from him all the cursing and left only blankness, silence, a question mark.

He didn't see Carrie among them until she leapt into the aisle crying Jesus! Jesus! Her little boy clutched at her sweater's hem but she brushed his hand away. The assembly's roar diminished and broke into scattered urgent praise.

"Jesus save me! God forgive me! Please! Please!" she begged. She wobbled on her feet, feeling around with her fingertips like the blind.

Clarence moved toward her. Others tumbled from the aisle seats and converged on her. Mike began his groaning again and they all took it up along with Carrie's hysterical cries.

*   *   *

H e saw the blaze of Yvonne in the West.

Trees shorter than himself—hunched excited trees—muttering like monks as he approached the house. He looked in through a window at the quiet kitchen. Through the living room's glass he saw her stock-still inside, occupying a leather chair. Dead . . .

—Not dead, but emptied. Where had she gone, leaving this flesh? A suspicion—that same terrible feeling—as if he floated on a bubble's skin above a poisonous bath: Yes, she'd come around behind him. He felt on the hairs of his nape the fire-breath of her astral self. She'd outflanked him astrally, now large as a comet, making noises like a great jet engine, her light flooding and ebbing in the treetops. Bowed in fear, he turned around. She flared beyond the trees, orbited over the ocean, which had come around behind him in some cataclysmic shifting of the earth. He went forward toward the cliffs and surf. Breaking from under the treetops he knelt at her shores and raised his eyes toward the sun dawning behind her and her wings opening out and the heartrending beauty of her face and the blood-red darkness in her skull as her mouth opened. He didn't want to touch her. He only wanted to see her feet. He wanted to understand this vision in its details, to glory in it by transacting with its minutenesses. He shuffled forward on his knees . . .

Wheels ran over him.

L et this be the place, Lord. The start. Or the end. Or whatever. But the place," Mike prayed.

Others came to help. She looked up at the faces of love and joy, faces of welcome, and beyond them the face of the man whose child she would bear in sin, a stunned, confused, and violent man backing away. "Jesus save me! God forgive me! Please! Please!" she begged.

As Mike prayed, she wept entirely without control. A purple veil fell down over all things. She fell backward into the robes of Christ.

And the preacher stood over her with his arms parting the jungle of faces, his own mouth moving: The Lord just broke her heart. Stand back. Give her room. It's beautiful. The Lord has broken her heart. Let her heart pour out. It's beautiful, it's beautiful.

m eadows craned to see over their heads to the center of the throng. Carrie stood still among them, perceptibly vibrating, looking right at him. Then her eyes rolled upward to the whites. A spasm pitched her backward onto a soft buoying sea of worshippers. He would have got closer but a tremendous force, a great breath, propelled him out of the place and he found himself standing in the parking lot. The cabins next door stood mute, looked neutral. The wind spat rain on their siding.

He retraced his steps as far as the porch's gable and got under it.

The storm started out a scattered rain but blew harder by the minute. He sat on the porch with his back to the door and his arms around himself. This cold rain had him by the bones. From inside he heard one voice above the others, wilder than all the others.

Water fell on Frank's face. And then he stopped feeling its wet, stopped tasting it.

He floated out the top of his own head but didn't get more than his own height above his own body. Figures in complicated apparel knelt around him. It seemed they were bending his legs in mysterious ways.

He saw faces floating by. Police waving brilliant lights. A man pounding on his chest. Don't put me back in that thing. Please. Not in that one. It's broken.

But abruptly he was back behind his eyes in a general darkness, and he felt his heart like a fist grabbing at the life and pulling it back inside and closing over it hungrily and obscenely.

At this point he sensed the rain again. His vision returned.

Faces floated by, looking down at him from their windows. Police waving them past . . . Glories in the very air. Thunderous multicolored flashing.

H e started the day at Mo's, waking in the bed she'd left already and wandering out to find her. In the mornings the house was shaded; she'd made a fire. He sat at the table with his hands around a cup of coffee and watched her. She plucked at the stove latch and laid a chunk across the coals, bumped shut the loading door with the heel of her hand. Bending like that before the fire made her robe, unfastened, hang like Spanish moss from her bones. "Hey," Navarro said, "I gotta tell you."

"What."

Her eyes were so dark. But her face—no. Sometimes the light came from under her skin.

"I like your house."

She stood straight, spread wide the folds of her robe like a pair of wings. And such a sad sweet body, like it never grew.

He said, "Something hit me last night. After we were in bed."

"Yeah?"

"Yeah. Right in the middle of last night I got hit with, I don't know. Aloneness."

"I'll fix that shit," she said.

"I mean aloneness, I felt the true thing. Nobody fixes it."

"You can—" She broke off. Sat down across from him.

"Not that it scares me," he insisted, aware that he was insisting. "Once you feel it, it's like you don't need to feel it ever again."

"If you wanted to, you could move in."

"I practically live here now."

"Yeah, you do."

"Well, I like having my own place to fade to when it's time to fade."

She reached for his hand across the table. "Put it this way. You can turn up here when you want and you can stay as long as you want."

He stared at their hands, feeling a little uncomfortably that maybe this kind of thing was better said in the dark. "How long have we been at this?"

"This is our tenth anniversary."

"Ten days? It seems like longer. And shorter at the same time."

"I told you you were fast."

When Mo had left him for the noon-to-nine run at the Full Sails, he dressed in civies and presented himself to residential Anchor Bay, a dozen or so homes scattered up the hill behind the stores among many large pines and redwoods. The blue-and-white Caprice had collected a dusting of brown needles on its surfaces.

Navarro had taken calls the last two nights; Merton had worked the days. Navarro had lucked out completely there, sleeping soundly all last night while Merton, yesterday morning, had been forced to observe a kind of mini-demonstration at Gualala's shopping mall. Which would necessitate a written report—names and numbers, you never knew: the feds, the feds.

As long as he had the cruiser, he was on call, and so he took it up to Point Arena and parked it outside the shop between his own Firebird and Jenny's torpedo-style RX-7. Merton had evidently driven off somewhere in the county van, that is, the paddy wagon. Up into the quiet hills, maybe, where he could get a regular snooze.

Inside the shop, Navarro found Jenny down on one knee by the filing cabinets, her skirt hiked up prettily, two file drawers pulled all the way out and resting on the floor on either side of her. "It's history day," she said.

He sat at his desk looking at her thighs. She wore almost invisible stockings. Jenny was punctual, and more competent than they deserved. Mid-twenties, neatly appareled and nicely shaped with abundant auburn hair and a quite homely face. She cherished her small Mazda sports car and conversed fluently with Merton as to its idiosyncrasies. Navarro gathered it had a rotary engine. It was fast, but not that fast. According to Navarro's observations, homely women with trim figures got more dates than any others, but aside from her job and her car Jenny seemed to have nothing to interest her. He liked Jenny but he thought she'd probably be happier somewhere else in the world. Navarro wasn't at all sure what a rotary engine was.

"You gonna torch it all?"

"I'm weeding out everything over seven years old," she said. "It should be three, but Taylor says seven. That's a bureaucratic personality, right there."

"Bureaucratic? That doesn't sound like Merton."

"More of a pack rat, really. You give him eight-and-a-half by eleven inches of floor, he's gonna make a stack to the ceiling. It all started when we moved to this modular. Then he revealed himself."

"How old is the coffee?" he asked as a way of mentioning there wasn't any.

"Oh. I'm sorry," she said.

"No. That means I get the first cup of the day. I'm honored."

"I usually wait for Taylor."

Suddenly Navarro understood. "You're in love with him."

"He's good-*look*ing, but . . . "

"A crush."

"I wouldn't—what are you talking about?" she said. She slapped a stack of folders onto the floor and stood up smoothing her skirt.

"Any letters?"

"Letters?"

"Any letters for me?"

"Nope."

He left her the keys to the Caprice and drove away in the Firebird and headed north. Right outside of Point Arena he left the highway and lugged in high gear up Buckridge Road and, topping the rise, took the ridge road south, driving extremely fast and passing Shipwreck, which would have taken him down to Anchor Bay, and continuing south at a much slower pace—all on impulse, he wanted to suppose, though in truth he'd been planning this visit for some time—now watching for mailboxes on his right.

Navarro found the broken-off sign: HILD. He turned right, passed along a silent dirt drive to the ridge's drop-off, where a broken dirt track began, braked momentarily but kept going, skirted a car under a dust cover and then many other cars too, relics dragged aside and rusting away; and he came to believe, as he descended through the mute woods, that bringing the low-slung Pontiac onto this road ranked among his airiest plans. Apparently people drove here, he saw fresh tire tracks, but at the edge of more than one washed-out place he had to get out and ponder the depths and plot a hopeful trajectory across in order not to bust an axle. After a long mile, he checked his watch, worried that he'd waited till too late in the day for this visit—he didn't want to find his way out in the dark. But it wasn't yet two, though his solitude, his missing Mo, had made it feel longer.

Merton had more than once advised him, not about the road through the Fairchild property, but about the Fairchild brothers themselves. The younger one was a genuine curio—witness his file of letters—owing to experiments, decades of experiments, with psychedelic stuff and nonsense. Now even a couple cups of coffee drove him wild. If you ever saw him with so much as a cigarette in his hand, expect to be accomplishing his arrest. While the older one lives nefariously among us, anyway until his fate should nail him, the younger hides in the father's forest, where he's created a world strewn with junk and deadwood. His sister-in-law buys it piecemeal and makes it into, some claim, works of art.

The drive lost itself and dribbled away into a lot of trees, but where was the dwelling? He thought of retracing his route in search of it, and then spied a path to his left, got out and followed it into a clearing backed by a gully, and, overlooking it, a nice-looking cabin where he'd expected a hermit's shanty. He'd imagined a Stone Age life for W. Fairchild, and days and nights of personal chaos and visionary torture. Navarro respected the insane for living in a deep pit with their writhing ideas like somebody out of a barbarian folktale.

"Hello," he shouted as he walked toward the house, but got no answer. He guessed this porch to be the entry. The door stood open wide.

Inside, a man napped facedown on a black table in an extremely unusual physical attitude. Passed out? The paint looked—no. Blood. The vibrations of his approach snatched houseflies from the blackish coagulate into crazy orbits. Almost within reach across the table lay an old revolver, the bluing faded along its extrusions.

The chair had tipped forward, lifting its rear feet two inches off the floor; in rigor mortis the corpse had warped itself into a fetal curl; the tendons would have to be severed to unclamp the tabletop from between its chest and knees. The wound was conspicuous, and not indicative of suicide. Unless this puncture marked the exit, he'd been shot just above the nape. Navarro leaned over almost as if to whisper in the corpse's ear and determined that it was certainly not the exit—from what he could see it looked like a garden hoe had ripped out half the victim's face.

Not six inches from the gun, a baseball cap sat upside down. If the deceased had been wearing it, the hat would have ended up elsewhere in the room, and flies would be eating from it. Suicides generally removed their hats.

Navarro stabbed his pen through the weapon's trigger guard, letting it dangle before his gaze like a cart on a Ferris wheel. Somebody took somebody for a ride . . . Three of the four visible chambers housed bald copper heads; but the one left of the hammer was empty, as was the one, he could assume, directly under the firing pin—two cartridges had gone off. Either this guy, W. Fairchild, he was almost sure, had cranked off a practice round sometime before managing to shoot himself in the back of the head, or somebody else had done this.

On the other hand, he'd removed his hat. And a pencil lay nearby. And a square of newsprint rested under the shattered head, the paper soaked with blood and bearing, one corner not entirely covered in a puddle of jelly, two words in pencil. He couldn't make them out quite. But they appeared to be the tail end of a one-line communication.

Navarro had never before been the first one to a killing, or a suicide, or whatever this was, never the foremost to arrive at any death—only, someday, he thought, my own.

He'd given it to Merton, and now he was nearly home. From the window of the video store below his apartment his reflection greeted him, the reflection of a man without office, probably unemployed, and he realized he'd have to change into uniform and should probably shave: in an hour or so a few folks from the County Sheriff's Department would be meeting them at the station before they all headed back out there together in the dark. In the meantime, supper.

He wasn't hungry, but he knew the Sheriff's people would bring no extra takeout to the crime scene, and so he thought he'd better feed himself something quick in his own kitchen, something like corn-flakes.

In the vestibule, after he'd entered from the street, it caught him, his conscience—his right foot hit empty air and he tumbled to the bottom of shame. All those letters from W. Fairchild: maybe I could have helped the guy . . .

He stood still and waited . . .

Maybe I could have suckled every loser in Los Angeles at my teats.

He set his course upward and started climbing.

M eadows stopped in at Seaside Foreign Motors to talk to Frank Vinelli about getting a manifold. Vinelli wasn't any too helpful. "Not that many junk Mercedes languishing in the graveyards."

"Well, how about you punch away on your doodad anyhow?"

"Not much point, that's my main point."

When it came to foreign makes, Vinelli believed himself in posses- sion of all the answers and put himself squarely in the way of any- body's attempts to get them independently. He'd become a symbol, in Clarence's mind, of the proliferation of enslaving experts.

"Just check for manifolds, will you please?"

"The quickest and longest-term solution is to get one new. If it was some old Caddy I'd say look, it's junk, so go ahead and throw some more junk inside it. But you expect the one-ninety to appreciate. You want it around twenty years from now."

By squinting his face and looking upward and breathing deeply once, Clarence becalmed his inner atmospheres. He wouldn't have liked this man anyway. Vinelli kept himself back from a person, regarding the conversation as if it were a road map, keeping a careful watch for any turns that might lead to the subject of credit for his services.

"I guess you heard what happened to Billy Fairchild?"

"I heard about it. I heard he got killed last week and last week his brother disappeared."

"This car is Billy's and mine. It's a project I owe to him. Do I have to be any clearer about my attitude?"

"Maybe that's even more reason. I'm just suggesting the long-term solution. I'm saying do it right. New manifold, paint the engine, shiny new valve covers."

"Would you be about to tell me Hans and Fritz are waiting at my service? Just got in from Bavaria, hanging out in the garage?"

Vinelli had nothing to say. He put his hands on the countertop and rested his weight on them.

"Well, since you invested in the service, how about using it?"

Blackly Vinelli said, "I'll put out an APB for one junk exhaust manifold."

Clarence waited in silence for a minute.

"How can I help you now?" Vinelli asked.

"Yeah, we just went through how. I don't wanna push you, but time is of the essence."

Vinelli manipulated the buttons, and Vanelli's machine communicated to other machines its interest in Mercedes 190SL exhaust manifolds while Clarence left the place.

Outside he raised the Scout's hood and checked the oil. It showed a translucent amber on the dipstick, right at the Full line, and he gathered Billy must have changed it recently, but he drove over to Gualala and asked for two quarts of Castrol anyway at Haymaker's Hardware. While the clerk cruised the aisles in search of it, he stepped behind the counter and lifted a fifty-round box of Pro-Load .44 magnum, pinched it in the waist of his jeans against his belly, and buttoned his flannel shirt over the bulge. He wandered around with his purchased Castrol under his arm until another customer came in, then nicked a cleaning kit on his way out. He wasn't a thief—on the shelf next to other such gun paraphernalia he laid a twenty-dollar bill—but he wanted no record left of this transaction.

It had been eight days since the killing. He wasn't sure that people might not be busy at the cabin, so he left the Scout at the property line, beside the shrouded Mercedes, and walked the remainder and came around silently behind the place, not by the path. Nothing stirring but airs and spirits and ghosts . . . One good thing was being able to ascertain that the police had finished here. And though the scene had already taken on a grisly popularity among young couples, this afternoon teenagers were absent. The water bucket on the porch was nearly empty, the two inches of liquid at its bottom skeined with redwood needles. The kids had torn off and made away with all but microscopic remnants of the yellow crime-scene flagging across the cabin's entry. Meadows pushed through the door and in the red sunset glow took note of the brown blots intersected by the chalk outline of Billy's bust on the table, and of Billy's chair, which had been moved and the chalk half circle on the seat of it smeared and effaced by subsequent occupants. Billy had kept abreast of things with a twelve-volt automotive radio: the device and the battery had absconded. The cops or the kids had taken Billy's deer rifle. The trash bucket, and the woodstove's mouth, bristled with crunched takeout pizza boxes. Under the stove a rat had built and abandoned a bed of chinkapin leaves and pink fiberglass insulation.

Meadows wept and wiped at his eyes, traipsing among the blood-stains. Surely he'd heard of some sort of rite to be performed now for this departed earth dweller. In fact he had heard of just such a thing, and what he'd heard had been running in his blood, if not in his mind, and his blood had brought him here: in an article about the Dead Sea Scrolls, he read that the scrolls had been discovered first by three brothers who'd taken to a cave together with the extracted heart of an enemy, the murderer of another of their brothers. They'd killed and eviscerated this man, were preparing to eat his most vital part as a rite of vengeance when they stumped across the sacred texts. He knew the bastards who'd murdered Billy. And he determined at this moment that he'd be hungry when he crossed their path, that he'd eat nothing until that intersection should be accomplished.

Meadows went out the sliding glass doors onto the deck and down the steps into the gully back of the cabin, his resolve already slipping away beneath his feet. The door to Billy's shed was still padlocked, and he fingered the dust around the threshold for the key. On the one hand he wanted to avenge his grief. On the other he felt his grief tilting toward contempt for Billy's luck. They'd closed the zipper over his face, thereby expunged his right to compassion. The desire to eliminate these bastards seemed a combination of simple business prudence and human judgmentalism that struck Meadows as ultimately arrogant. But he was in motion now, and here was the key in the dirt.

He let himself in among shelves and barrels full of BMW motorcycle parts, nuts and bolts and gears and cams once greasy, now whiskered with dust, also his own surfboard laid lengthwise improperly on the floor below his black wetsuit spread-eagle on the wall. He located Billy's old lever-action Winchester, a weapon still manufactured in the style designed by Robert Moses Browning six years before this most terrible century. They came in various calibers. This one was a pretty rusty .44 magnum. Standing in the doorway he jacked the lever and peered down the barrel, holding the action open to the light. The barrel appeared to be full of something.

Shifting the rifle occasionally from hand to hand, he hiked back up off the property. At the Mercedes he untied its cover's stays on the driver's side so as to get at and collect the possessions of his life, his Brunswick bowling ball, his pool cue, the trumpet he'd never played.

At this final ridiculous thing, this moment with the rifle and cue stick in his embrace, the bowling bag between his feet, the trumpet dangling from his fingers by its tuning slide, his grief began to purge itself, he wept with these absurdities in his arms.

He left the Scout in the meadow overgrazed and spotted with dusty fern. When he approached the pen, the sheep moved in a small mob to the other end. It was late in the afternoon and she'd herded them back inside after their meager pasturing.

Himself, he didn't eat such meat. It smelled on a fire not much different than it did on the hoof. Lambs a few months along exclaimed bitterly amid the fold.

A split rail barred the property's gate, which he didn't disturb for fear other animals might be wandering free somewhere back of it. He gripped a post and scissored over the slats, and strolled across ground stamped bare and scattered with long peacock feathers in an airy silence. Then he heard the peacock's protest like a silly horn. As he passed nearby the bird suddenly pivoted and unfurled its shivering fan, eyes in the feathers looking right into his own. At the gate to the house yard a bushy white dog rose up from the shade of the Sheep Queen's banged-around van and walked over stiff-legged to snuff at his hands and crotch and lean against his thigh.

Next the Sheep Queen herself came around from behind the house in a long crinkled linen skirt and dusty laced boots and blue work shirt with her cuffs buttoned at the wrists, her eyes turning in her face like polished wheels, and accused him of being from the county.

He'd known her for years, mostly at one remove, and she'd always looked like this, her hair white as an albino's and radiating from her skull, the complexion of her face sun-cured, her attention groping in a way that made you wonder what was happening behind you. In Haight-Ashbury also she'd ranked as royalty, the Mescaline Queen. Since the sixties the Haight had been scoured of its psychotropic anarchy, slowly and almost completely, certainly much more so than this woman's synapses. "I'm not employed by the county," he told her.

"I thought you were the building inspector. The new guy. He's been tagging various places, so we're informed."

"No, I'm Clarence."

"Yeah . . . we've met a time or two."

"Where's your peacock at? He was here a minute ago."

"He gets all around the place. We think he roosts in a tree. We don't know who owns him."

"Building inspector hasn't been here yet?"

"Not unless you're him."

"Police?"

"Never happen."

"I thought I might visit in your trailer a minute. She home?"

"As far as we know," she said.

"What's your dog's name?"

"His name's Fucker."

How the Sheep Queen got money wasn't generally understood, but she made enough to get along on and also to have bought the Silver Stream parked by the creek down behind the stalls. The sheep were pets, family, not livestock. She bred several varieties and kept them segregated in pens, but if one was sick she brought it into the house. She kept Melissa on although she trashed things. Everybody kept Melissa on although she trashed things.

You couldn't hurt the aluminum shells of these rigs, but the window screens were in shreds, and both tires had gone flat. He slapped his hand on the side of it as he stepped up onto the cinder-block stoop and pushed the door open without waiting for any word.

Inside the trailer it was dark. Only the TV was happening. A fire burned on the screen, increasing with a series of whooshing explosions, crackling, flashing, and whirling, a cyclone of flame. Sitting there almost looking at it was Melissa, sweet little thing with her heart attacks and twisted tortures. The dwelling seemed unexpectedly somber and chaste.

"You must've cleaned her up."

"Why?"

"Nelson says you're a pig."

She got up and took him by the hands. She wore a half-cut T-shirt and white panties. "Come inside now. Come in and fuck me."

"There's probably two things I wouldn't do," he said. "One is fuck you."

"And the other?"

"I don't know. I just hope there's at least one more."

He entered, keeping her at arm's length. There was a peculiar feeling here. Her face seemed emptied of herself. "What is it?"

"Oh? What is it? It's Frank. Frank went in the hospital in Santa Rosa."

"Frankheimer? He's lucky he's breathing."

"And then they'll move him to San Francisco when he's more stabilized. They have to attach him together with screws. A lot of things like that."

"You deal with him frequently? I wasn't aware."

"Not so frequently. But we're strong together, very strong."

"Yeah. And what about Nelson?"

"Nelson is paranoid and schizophrenic. He's out of the picture."

"Where is he?"

"I dropped him off at Billy's road on Thursday to get his car."

"That was a bad day, Thursday, a big bad day."

"Nelson said he's running away from two guys. But I met them, they're not so bad."

"Two guys from nowhere, like? With a camper pickup?"

"Yeah. And barking dogs. They treated me politely both times when they visited."

"And when were those times, Melissa? Recently?"

"Oh. A while ago, once. And then just after Billy died. One or two days after."

"Shit. So they definitely know about Billy?"

"You mean that he's dead?"

"I mean *about* him, that he exists."

"Everybody's having accidents. Something's wrong."

"Hey. Melissa. Could we turn that thing down?"

She turned off the television and stood next to it with hunched shoulders, tightly clasped hands, toes working on the stained industrial carpeting. Lamentations carried down from the sheepfold. From the doorway he could see them in the corral mothering around the junk shell of some kind of sedan.

"I wanna make a strong recommendation now," he said, "for when the cops come around to see you."

"They didn't come."

"They will. And you better not mention the two men you just told me about. That's a serious request. It ain't no rif. You taking this in?"

"Yes. I'm not to mention the men with dogs."

"I repeat: Erase those two fuckers from your experience."

She sat on her Hide-A-Bed and wrung her hands, dropped them palms-up and dead-looking on her bare thighs. "It's supposed to be a place of healing. I don't know what happened. Somebody did something very dark."

At the top of Acorn Road, Merton recognized Billy Fairchild's roofless International Scout turning into his path. For a mile or so he hung back a dozen car lengths and tailed it. He was out of the fog. He closed up the cruiser's windows and turned on the climate control. At a straightaway he pushed the pedal. Pickup still impressive. This Caprice was four years old but had less than eighteen thousand miles on it.

He flipped the siren on and off and pulled it over.

Idling behind the old contraption, he unbuttoned his holster flap, cracked his door, and waited. The still inland heat came in at him. He cut the engine.

In a minute the driver showed his hands, making it look as if he were stretching and yawning, and kept his hands in sight by grasping the windshield's rim.

Merton got out then and came around on the driver's side. "Hey, Surf."

"Good afternoon. Top of the day to you." He removed his sunshades and set them on the dusty dash.

"You're on my list of appointments, Clarence," Merton told him. He fit the Doubtful profile: jeans, motorcycle boots, tank-top undershirt. This was the recent victim's brother's partner in illegal cultivation, and also the recent victim's partner in fixing up cars. The beach-boy partner, chasing young girls while selling shit down in Los Angeles. Tanned idiotic teenagers who don't realize he's almost thirty . . . "You visiting the Sheep Queen?"

"More or less. Why?"

"Can we step over to the shade? This isn't a traffic stop."

Meadows swivelled to put his feet up on the passenger's seat and jumped out over the door, and they walked under a tree. Merton snapped his holster shut. He unbuttoned his shirt pocket, took out his Skoal. Pried the lid loose. Offered it out.

Meadows shook his head and Merton put a pinch behind each of his jowls and tamped it down with his tongue. "I was just heading down there myself."

Meadows said, "Sorry to be delaying you."

"Melissa down there today?"

"She just might be."

"You hang with the hippies, Clarence? I thought you were a surfer."

Meadows showed him two fingers, crossed. "Hippies and surfers have always been like that. It's an age-old alliance."

"Where you from, Clarence?"

"I grew up in Bolinas."

"Ah."

"Yeah. I haven't been back since I don't know. Before 1980, probably."

"Bolinas."

"Yeah. The hippie-surfer thing, that was me, that was Bolinas. They're all old now, like fifty or more years old. Still going around saying 'Fer *sher*' and 'Righteous!'"

"And aren't you kind of old for a surfer? How old are you?"

"It's a sport, Officer. There's a physical limit but there's no age limit. Not yet anyhow."

Merton nodded at this and worked his mouth and spit on the ground between them.

"Where's Nelson Fairchild, Clarence?"

"*No se, Señor.* I was wondering myself."

"My sources tell me you and Nelson share a certain interest. Exotic horticulture."

"In the past once we hooked up on a deal, but it come up dead."

"And what of the future?"

"That too so far as I know."

"Can I trust you to come see me if he gets in touch?"

"Can you trust me?"

"Yeah."

"No."

"No? Then you can decide how hot do you like it, Clarence. Because I can make it very hot."

"Well, I'm just saying you can't trust me. I'm not saying I won't get in touch."

"Well spoken. All right then."

"Understand I'm willing to help you on this one. But you represent authority, and I'm mostly unauthorized. So, you know. It gets tricky."

"I've always said so. I said so the day I was born. Who killed Billy, Clarence?"

Meadows shrugged and looked off somewhere.

"Any idea?"

"Nope. What about you? Any idea?"

"Nope, not right now, not today. The Sheriff will sift the sands. My coworker had a look at the scene, and he doubts they'll call it suicide—he says the fatal wound doesn't look self-inflicted. So we're all suspects. At least until an arrest is made."

"I doubt that'll happen."

"Nelson's a suspect. You're a suspect."

The surfer scowled and appeared to be concentrating on images in his head.

"You've been a suspect in homicides before. I've done a little digging."

"Dig deeper. It was bullshit."

"You settled with a couple guys and then burned their bodies."

"That's bullshit all up and down it. It never got to the county attorney's desk."

"Clarence, I have you marked down in my mind as going in the Doubtful column. One of the people who didn't get born knowing right from wrong. Persons in the Doubtful category sometimes get the difference and suddenly straighten up. You know. When your feet get weary of the crooked path."

"Well," Clarence said, "I'll tell you what, Officer Law. I'm just a bit like the tomcat who made love to the skunk. I haven't had all I want. But I've damn sure had all I can stand."

He'd been as far as the door of the church. He'd made it just over the threshold and there felt the end of his chain, right there. She'd have to take him where he stood. He could go no farther.

Check and see does this thing work or do I junk it.

Clarence sat Indian-style by the cook fire shirtless, sipping coffee and examining the pages of a tattered 8½-by-11 *Firearms Assembly* this late morning. The Winchester lay across his thighs. Americans had used such rifles in Cuba in 1898, but they were no grunt-proof military item. Just to ram the barrel out he'd have to disassemble the thing. It wasn't entire in its parts—the finger lever pin stop screw had gotten away somewhere. He hadn't known it was called that; he'd thought a screw was just a screw. Using a key-chain screwdriver he removed the tang screw and separated the butt stock from the workings and set the butt stock aside. With a sixpenny nail he drifted out the finger lever pin and the link pins, using a flat stone as a hammer, and then held the buttless rifle upended between his knees and worked the link free of its trunnion. The machine squeaked and whispered, giving up its rusty inward pieces. He removed the screws on either side of the receiver and lifted the bolt carrier out.

Right about now they were dealing similarly with Billy at the morgue in Ukiah. Those buzzing circular bone blades. Talking softly into a tape recorder's microphone. Or maybe not, maybe they didn't work today, Saturday. By now they'd probably taken him apart and dropped the parts in a bag to be dropped in a hole. Meadows didn't think he'd make it to the funeral. Nelson was off-planet too. Arrangements would fall to Donna Winslow. She'd taken some hits the last few years.

He broke the action down and cleaned it, beginning with soapy water from a coffee can, laying the hammer and the locking and breech bolts and their carrier and pins and screws on a bandanna on a hot rock in the sun. He finished his coffee and then he scrubbed the parts down with Coleman fuel and a wire brush, rinsed them with the fuel, laid them out to dry again. In the navy they'd been forbidden to clean weapons with gasoline.

In less than a minute the parts had dried, and he swabbed them with gun oil from the cleaning kit. With the ramrod he ran a patch down the barrel, and out came a lot of crackly matter. Husks of beetles, as nearly as he could judge.

Billy had believed the radar was killing him. And if you cranked that down to the level of naked spirit, he had it right. Religion could be rough.

Religion wasn't dealing out wonders for Carrie. What—she barely had a roof and a ride. Now knocked up and only Jesus H. Christ to console her. Well, she was strong enough. Migratory sun-dried woman. He'd more than liked her from the start. But these irrevocable vibrations. He shouldn't have touched her. You pluck one strand and the whole net shakes, the whole catch riots.

He reversed his procedure, pausing to consult his firearms manual frequently, until he held a complete carbine in his hands. He cradled the weapon crosswise in his lap, pressed back the hammer with his index finger, and depressed the trigger slowly with his thumb. The hammer dropped. From his shirt pocket he took a Pro-Load round, slipped it into the magazine, lifted the weapon to his shoulder quickly, levered the round into the breech, and fired it into the hillside dirt twenty feet away. The machine worked; his hearing rang, but his head was still in its proper place. He wrestled the box of cartridges from his backpack and loaded nine into the magazine and commenced the deafening business of sighting in.

M any days back a rain had dragged its tail along the coast. Inland the drought persisted. Fires in Humboldt County some hundred miles off had produced an umber fog over all of central Northern California, and a certain smell which Mo thought of also as brown. John told her the fires in Humboldt had been started by hippie growers, maybe in retribution for recent raids, or else to occupy the helicopter crews with business other than ferrying around the officers of CAMP—the state's Campaign Against Marijuana Planting—to destroy what the National Guard had left of their herbal gardens.

As for Navarro, he considered only that there was fog in Gualala, and smoke over here in Boonville. It was a day off for both of them. He'd rather have spent this Sunday afternoon in bed with this woman than here at the county fair, or Mendocino Apple Festival, as it was billed. Driving there they avoided Mountain View Road, instead kept to the coast as far as 120 and went inland along the flat of a valley quilted with orchards and nurseries, and to get there they crossed, actually, the Navarro River. She asked, and he started to answer that it wasn't named after any of his relations, but suddenly told her it was. A great-grandfather. Why did he lie like that? It only kept them apart. And that was why. Gray-green hills and oaks like torches and the pale zigzag stripes cut into the steep hillsides: sheep paths. Maybe the precipices of his heart looked like that. Boonville might usually have been a pretty town, but under the smoggy conditions it seemed jobless and tapped-out and felt to Navarro like the kingdom of desperate childhoods. When they'd parked in the pasture outside the festival, he locked his Club antitheft device to the Firebird's steering wheel.

There wasn't a fence or even any boundary to speak of. Once you were out of your car, you were at the fair. T-shirts, fake tattoos, astrology, tarot readings, auras told, palm-telling. And apples and apples and apples. Huge carrots, huge apples, melons and gourds of an unreal size in the supermarket light of the big main building. Old logging equipment and daguerreotypes of bony men assembled around the butt ends of gigantic fallen redwoods. They passed through the antique and vegetable freak show and out again. People who'd paid money for this experience accelerated past them in the air, screaming. Mo sang phrases along with the stormy PA, Big Brother and Janis doing "Piece of My Heart." In the rests, the canned pipe organs of whirling rides. Then it was Hank Williams. Then the Beach Boys.

On a raised platform across the basketball court Mo saw somebody she recognized, definitely recognized, even with his hippie hair stashed under a tall stovepipe hat—in a coal-black suit, red lining on his black cape, rouge on his cheeks—barefoot, walking across a rubble patch of broken glass. He removed his cloak for the trick of escaping from a straitjacket. Country music ricocheted through the dry valley. Cowboys and lumberjacks strolled past with their small insignificant-looking women. They stopped in amazement to watch the trigetour. He passed a basket around and everybody gave him money.

Odors divided the day into rooms—meaty grease, hot caramel perfume, a little diesel breath from the rides, a certain amount of spilled alcohol and sickly gusts from the litter drums. Horseflesh, horseshit, poultry-stink, and a lot of other choking animal odors. But autumn. Mo tasted its breath in her own, quite clear, a little cold.

Navarro tasted spearmint as he observed the tossing games, shooting games, guessing games, one climbing game, a net thing you had to traverse without its spinning over to leave you clinging upside down, almost all of them murphies, gyps, and he stood back from the action, chewing his gum. In the suffocating barns, rows of cages full of bunnies and other rodents, different colors and sizes. Terrified chickens, their fear jabbed him such that he wanted to rip out his sidearm and shoot their heads off, pigs, each with a million big tits or else two enormous testicles, burros, goats, giant horses, also miniature ones, about the size of Great Danes. He didn't see any dogs on display. The local animal shelter presented a rehabilitated hawk, an eagle, two falcons standing, completely stoic, on a table staring right at you out of one eye and then the other, turning their heads. Two old guys in baggy overalls with a stepladder were stringing lights around the basketball court for the dance that evening.

Mo kept her eyes low passing macho carnie men in leather vests with cigarettes and sunglasses and elaborate pervading tattoos. And across there in a little smoke from a barbecue the trigetour lifted his tall black hat, releasing a trio of white doves. Hills on the west side were turning blue. She stopped being anyone but only saw these things. Was nothing but what was seen.

Mo kept him longer at every exhibit than was really necessary for taking in the sufferings and boredom of these prisoners. But she wanted to hang around for the country dance and let them try the two-step, she in her ankle-length peasant's shift and this man who looked like her bodyguard.

"I am the most prestidigitateous trigetour in all of trolldom. How does he do it?" Another show of juggling had started. The trigetour seemed not at all desperate, not doubtful, but hypnotized and almost lulled by the beautiful colored orbits. "Watch the eyes. There's no trick to this but psychotically obsessive practice and superhuman concentration. All featliness is learned . . . practiced . . . perfected over time. Let's put these away and let's pick up this bag. Let's fill it with bottles . . . Did that one break? Not a problem. I intend to break them all. What I need is a sledgehammer—well! Where did this come from? Let's smash this bagful of bottles into a bagful of broken . . . glass . . . sharp . . . sharp . . . piercing . . . deadly . . . lacerating . . .

fragments! Now, please note, I'm not littering here. I'm making myself a highway of pain . . . "

He dragged his clanking feed sack across the stage, laying out a wake of broken glass. "Stand back, please! If I open an artery, your cleaning bills will skyrocket. Lots of big veins pumping in the human foot. Silence, please!" Slowly lowered the bare sole of his right foot down on the shards and paused, looking upward in profile for such a number of moments that some of the crowd started looking up there too, at nothing but the sky. His foot at rest on the glass, he doffed his hat and shook out his—to Navarro somehow frightening, or disturbing—great brunette mane, and three doves. Turned to the assembled and said: "Yesterday was the equinox. Sun straight up and down from the equator. Happens every September twenty-first or twenty-second."

He looked directly at Navarro: "Do you know what selenography is?—Mapping the moon."

"Selenography."

"Mapping that old planet we can never get to—" and the glass skirled on the plywood scaffold as he walked across it, his lips jammed together and his gaze set.

Navarro counted back. It had been eight days since he'd found W. Fairchild's stiffened corpse, and still the County hadn't got back to him.

Mo promised herself she wouldn't push it—she shouldn't push and drive—but then she might, she generally seemed to. There were ways to be and ways definitely not to be. She'd already made herself clear. He knew the position. But she couldn't help saying right now, if only to doom it all—

"Just so it's a stated policy, you got a woman."

"Wo." He shook his head.

"If you want one."

"Yeah. I do if she's you."

"She better be."

—said this in a transparent attempt to drive the car.

She'd been in these things before, everybody had. He was moving at a hundred but he wasn't steering. Eventually he wakes up . . . but the walls have collapsed. Another buried-alive lover. He wouldn't move in with her. He'd turn up less often the more she bitched, until his attentions petered away into marauding, coming around half-drunk and ashamed late at night for thirty minutes in her bed until whenever she stopped letting him, until she'd sent him away often enough that he was satisfied she'd really turned the corner on him and would relent no more. But what could she do? The corner was out there, but it was a long way off. A deal was never over as long as the woman was willing to go to bed with the man . . . As she looked away down this road, the conversation crumbled and she realized they wouldn't hang around for the dance.

Navarro stared into a fifty-gallon drum chock-full of red-and-white striped food receptacles, and wilted napkins, and flies stuck whirring in coagulating clouds of pink spun sugar that irritated his mind by resembling the head of W. Fairchild's corpse. In the matter of W. Fairchild's death, nothing was moving. The Sheriff's Department hadn't interviewed anyone—they'd placed all their chips, you could say, on forensics. Merton had gone after Nelson Fairchild, Jr., and had put in a total of one hour on the search. He'd talked to the surfer who hung with the younger, the dead Fairchild brother, and he'd spoken with Nelson's hippie girlfriend, the one with the very white doll's face—Melissa. He'd chatted briefly on the phone with Donna Winslow; had put in a call to Winona Fairchild and expected she'd return it. Navarro would take it on himself to strike the last name from the list, not the least bit reluctant about it. It seemed there was just one person to be dealt with . . . These were the thoughts he entertained while his new girlfriend foresaw the end.

He asked her if she wouldn't mind skipping the country dance. She said all right. He told her he'd be visiting her buddy Yvonne tomorrow. She said, "You could learn a lot from Yvonne. You don't know her at all. You *should* talk to her one on one." He got the feeling she hoped he wouldn't. "You don't know what it's like."

"Well—what *is* it like?" he asked, but she seemed a little angry suddenly and turned herself off.

*I*t's like parking your car by the road someplace and just getting out of it. It's there, its yours, but you shut the door and walk away. You come down the path to this house. The woman opens the door. You come inside, you come in alone, carrying nothing, wearing no uniform, and you shut the door behind you. You've come here alone, you're alone in here with the woman.

"Come in." It was Yvonne. She says, "Come here."

He thought he was in, he thought he was here, but she brings him *slowly in, turning the lights down from someplace, narrowing the focus, blacking things down till there's just the two of them. She tuned them in, the two of them, until they were very sharp and nothing else was.*

"You are the holy Son of God himself. Say it."

Nonsense and incense. "Take a seat, John." She started to turn toward the kitchen and turned back and looked at him out of her iron-colored eyes. Said in a smoky way, "Is this a John call? Or an Officer call?" He guessed she was kidding him.

He shrugged. "I hadn't decided."

"Well, you're not all dressed up like a cop. I'll take that as a friendly indication."

She went into the kitchen, and he sat down in the living room's biggest chair and watched through the doorway as she prepared a tray of tea. "Why did you want me to say that?" he asked.

"Just a minute," she said, and he waited in silence, feeling exactly as he would have felt if there'd been a group gathered here and nobody knew how to begin, until she came back in and offered him tea and crackers and a grayish spread. He took his cup, and she set the tray on the hassock at his knees and sat on the floor on the other side of it. "You were asking me something," she said.

"That's kind of a strange thing to say when someone knocks on your door."

With a tiny silver butter knife she spread goo on a cracker and handed it over to him. "A visitor comes to the door," she said. "I know who he is. He's everyone. And everyone is the Holy Son. So I was just wanting us both to acknowledge who you are as you stand at my door."

Navarro ran another cracker through the dip. Not a vegetarian thing, but more on the order of fish. Spicy. Maybe chicken. He was hungry. With his mouth full: "It's said you're a witch."

"Said?"

"Yeah."

"Who says so?"

"The question is, do you say so too?"

"That I'm a witch?"

"Yeah."

"Yeah."

"Yeah?"

"I practice wycca. It's a form of work. Working with things not visible to us because of a mind-set. The inner world is generally invisible."

"Well, everybody's got their own. It's just not visible to the other guy, right?"

"You're talking about thoughts. I'm talking about the parts of us we never look at because we don't want to see them. But eventually we'd better look. Eventually we want to look, because nothing outside is working for us. It's simple, really. If you refuse to find out what goes on under the hood, pretty soon the car won't start and you find you're not getting anywhere."

"So you're kind of a mechanic of the dark side."

"You want to trivialize what I do by putting it that way. But that's exactly what I'm saying. It's a form of work. I'm the one who stands there pointing with the wrench and saying, 'That's your carburetor, ma'am. It's locking up on you in this hot weather. Just get somebody to hold a towel over the intake while you crank her, and she'll start.'" She smiled at him.

"So you round them up, grease them down, do a little shuffle." A ribbed wavering of smoke off a stick of incense on a bookshelf reminded him of her body, and the smoke's undulations even made him think of clutching her around the waist until something gave. "Maybe I'm being too cynical," he said.

"You're just being typical. People indifferent to the Spirit want to believe it's all a hoax. I'm not in it for the dough. If I wanted to make a profit by defrauding people of their hope, I'd offer something a lot more expensive. Phony real estate, maybe. Or I'd open a casino. Was I right? About the carburetor?"

"Vapor lock," he said.

"A mechanic showed me that trick just the other day."

He thought she knew exactly what he was feeling, that she felt it too, and that what they were saying didn't matter at all. "Can I ask you something?"

"Sure."

"Are we talking, or are you just running your shit?"

She touched the back of his left hand with one long, unpainted fingernail. "I think you know what we're doing."

That backed him up. He cleared his throat. "What's on these crackers?"

"A witch's potion."

"Tastes like salmon."

"It's trout paté."

"It's pretty good."

"Your tea's gone cold." Still seated on the floor, she opened the door of her woodstove, leaning out past him and shaping her posture like a dancer's with one leg outstretched and the other foot drawn in against her thigh. The ridges of her spine bumped up along the fabric of her shift. She tossed the liquid from his cup onto the coals so that it hissed, and poured him a cup from her teapot. She moved the tray onto the floor, rose and took its place on the hassock, leaning toward him with the cup cradled in her hands. "Wouldn't you like some witch's brew?"

Navarro relaxed and let her put the cup to his lips. It was warm but not hot. He'd had this stuff. "Miso soup."

"Witch's brew."

"Yech, lady. I like miso, but you can leave the tofu out of it."

"How about the bufo?"

"I guess tofu's healthy."

"I'm quite serious. Do you know what bufo is?"

This sass made him hate her. The inside of her ankle, the inside of her knee, her bunched thigh. The toes nestled under her other thigh as she sat there on the hassock destroying all casualness with her closeness, the innocent arch of her neck, chin raised, her other foot dangling, moving like a running-down pendulum.

She said, "The bufo's in the paté, not in the soup."

"This trout stuff? It's great. Is it smoked?"

"No, it's fresh. The smoky taste comes from the rest of it."

"There better not be any pot in this," he said.

"Henbane, datura—well, really, jimsonweed."

"What else? I'm getting a buzz, I think."

"Mandrake, ginseng, amanita mushroom—just a tiny bit—and lots of healthy vitamins. Morning glory seeds from Mexico. There's even a toad involved. Would you like to see?"

"If you just fed me a frog I don't think I wanna know about it."

She shifted and raised her thigh slightly higher and he thought she was opening her legs in a shocking gesture, but then she slipped her feet to the floor and stood up.

He got up too, enjoying all this, as a matter of fact remembering, here in midflight, how comfortable it made him feel to be seduced by a woman of the elevated, arty type, because eventually they let him walk on their masks, they owned up to their games. Not the really rich ones. But this one wasn't really rich. He let her lead him by his hand to the kitchen of oiled wood and lusty fragrances. From a basket atop the fridge she plucked a white knuckle. "Garlic."

"I didn't taste any," he said.

"It's not in the potion."

He followed her onto the enclosed back porch, or mudroom, a chilly space stacked along one wall with firewood. He shivered, and she said, "We have to keep him cold. Then he sweats better."

He ran the words back in his head, but that is what he thought she said.

"Look here, John."

On a white enamel table which he now got closer to, looking over her shoulder from behind, coming up softly against her, trying to restart the charge between them, he saw her mortar and pestle made of marble, several red mushrooms bearing white warts, a cardboard box with three frogs hunkered down in it stoically. Not big old reptiles. A bit smaller than fists. Two filthy white shoestrings, a metal bottle cap, an X-Acto knife, a matchbook. It all appeared more than curious. He was empowered by the sight of these little objects to toss the place, dismantle the whole building nail by board, and confiscate her cash and property. Articulable suspicion was the legal term.

She handed him the garlic over her shoulder and, without any sign of distaste, lifted up one of the frogs and stared at it eye to eye; meanwhile yanked from beside the box a length of stained flagging, torn maybe from a bedsheet. The frog jerked and swam nowhere, spreading its webbed toes wide. "You want garlic," she said to it. She held the ribbon of sheet between her lips while she pried the captive's jaws apart. "Put it in, John. Back in his throat—yes—"

He forced the clove between its jaws. The inside of its mouth felt cool, dry, smooth to his touch. She wrapped its muzzle tightly shut with several winds of her ragged ribbon. Over the lenses of its knobby eyes, small shutters dropped down.

"What's the difference between a toad and a frog?" he asked as she set it among its brothers or sisters. They'd taken up diagonal corners with their backs to one another. The other sat still with its eyes walled off and its mouth tied shut around the garlic.

"You know? I've never asked? And I don't think he'd tell me. Now he'll start to sweat. And in the sweat is the magic ingredient."

"Which is what, more or less?"

"Bufotenine. Five-hydroxydimethyltryptamine."

"Shit. I guess everybody's getting a mouthful." He looked out the door's glass window at the tips of evergreen branches. A psychedelic potion. "Boy, am I ever off the track," he said, miserable because he didn't feel allowed to show her how angry he was. He cleared his throat, trying to think. "Do they have names?"

"Yeah, they're all named Jeremiah. Do you know that song?"

"I don't know any songs."

Greenish beads hung by a shoestring from a tack pushed into the door frame. A lumpy charm or something. A cross. A crucifix.

"That belonged to a girl named Carla Frizelli," she said. "It's got quite a history."

He didn't touch it.

The frog hadn't moved, but now a vein beat on either side of its protruding closed eyes. "So, Yvonne. How much of your trout paté is Schedule Two?"

"None of it. It's all legal, Officer."

"Don't you think you should have told me?"

"John, John, am I with the FDA?"

He looked her in the eyes, but she didn't look away. "You want me to put my gun in the car?"

She did seem serious: "Not when it's just us two."

"I didn't bring it." He looked away first, only to have to observe thick beads of mucus weeping from the toad's warty hide. Yvonne scraped this product from it with a matchbook cover, set the animal aside, transferred the half-teaspoon or so to one of the bottle caps.

"And I just ate some of this," he said.

"That's what you came here for."

"I don't think so, no."

"Yes. And for information. And to be with me." She marked him with a bland stare and held him with it until the charge had started again, the silence between them humming, and he felt a thickness in his throat, then a dizzy thrill as he thought of snatching up a chunk of kindling and beating her senseless. "Between the male and the female everything is sadomasochistic," she said, perhaps very inappropriately, perhaps not. He would have taken her by the shoulders and put his mouth on hers, but his hands dangled like weights. He felt the warmth of her breath on his neck and then she turned away, caught at his hand, and released it as he started moving after her. In the living room he sat down quickly on the hassock by the stove and rested his elbows on his knees and his head in his hands, staring at the incomprehensible designs in the weaving of a throw rug. His blood flushed against his skin, as if it might burst out. The sensation ebbed away, and he realized he was breathing in rapid gasps and brought it under control. He was aware that she stood by the window, that she lowered the blinds, that she turned and sat across from him in the chair. He began to feel almost normal except for his eyes, which were teary and molten. "What are you going to say?" he whispered because he couldn't stand waiting any longer for her voice.

"Did you get a hot rush. Did your skin flush."

He tried to nod.

"That's only vitamin B-twelve. It passes. Is it past?"

"You gonna scrape off my sweat now?"

"You're okay," she said.

He nodded. "This was a mistake," he said.

She took his hands. "It's not a mistake. You and this woman have business."

"What woman?"

"The woman Yvonne."

"But you."

"I'm Randall MacNammara. You remember."

"I remember." His eyes were feeling better. Except for a slight distancing of events, he'd come around. The little lethargy didn't seem anything worth fighting. He might have drunk a strong martini.

"John, every moment of life has a lesson to teach. But most of us would rather just daydream our way past them."

"Ah, yeah. Potions." He sighed. "Witches and demons. I've put the cuffs on a few. I'm not interested in those lessons."

"This isn't school. It's life. What life teaches us is responsibility."

I'm all for that, he thought, but didn't bother saying it. He only said, "Snafu and tofu," and heard himself or remembered himself laughing.

"Sooner or later we take responsibility," she says, "for having created our world." Certainly, the demons were in his head. Gumdrops in a dream were not gumdrops, but a dream. But as long as you don't wake, they're candy. You can eat them. If they're poison they kill you. Then you wake, still alive. But in the dream you're dead.

"I had a purpose here," he reminded them both, or all three of them.

"What was your purpose?"

"I'm looking for Nelson Fairchild."

"He's dead."

"I . . . Why do you say that?"

"He died this morning."

"Uh," Navarro said. He looked around, but at nothing. "Was this on the news?"

"You're one of the few on earth who know."

"Well, but . . . where's the body?"

"That's irrelevant. The question is, where is his soul?"

"Okay . . . Hey, would there be any chance of—talking to him?"

"Not at the moment. Down the line there certainly would."

"Wow. Reserving the right to call Bullshit—how did he die?"

"I'm not in possession of that information, but it seems he was probably murdered. For some lifetimes now he's been caught in a drama that keeps turning out that way, I'm afraid. But it's over now. He's free."

She reaches her hand to his jaw and traces the line with her fingertip. Her own lips tremble as she breathes through her open mouth. He was hard. But the flesh of it felt tired, or cold. As did his lips and fingers.

"Do you like her?"

"Who?"

"Yvonne. The woman."

"Yeah," he said.

"Especially because you like danger, and trouble, and getting off the track. And that's why she likes you too. Because you enjoy defending yourself."

"Yeah."

"That's the kind of responsibility you believe in."

"Yeah," he said.

"But there's someone who wants to talk to you if only you'll put aside your defenses. Your moves, your programs, your John Navarro act. It's all out there waiting to resume, but none of it's here, in this house. Your certainties, your stock responses. It's like parking your car by the road someplace and just getting out of it. It's there, it's yours, but you shut the door and walk away. You come down the path to this house. The woman opens the door. You come inside, you come in alone, carrying nothing, you shut the door behind you. You've come here alone, you're alone in here with the woman.

"Come in." It was Yvonne again. "Come here."

He thought he was in, he thought he was here, but she brings him slowly in.

"You are the holy Son of God himself. Say it."

Turning the light down from someplace, narrowing the light, blacking things down till there's just the two of them.

"You are the holy Son of God himself."

She tuned them in, the two of them, until they were very sharp and nothing else was.

"I am the holy Son of God himself."

She let out a long breath and took in a long breath. A great warmth came off her, an easy welcoming sensual joy. Then she looked pained, her face swimming at him and a series of bad thoughts working on her loveliness. She covered her eyes with her hand and said, "Oh?" and it broke him like the song of an old love. She slumped back in her chair and her hand dropped away.

He remembered now. "'Jeremiah was a bullfrog.'" He spoke the words. He couldn't sing.

"I am Miran."

"And who is Miran?"

"There are deeper levels, or higher levels if you prefer. Or lower, if you like it like that."

"You're getting us into a different darker Babylon-type thing. I can feel it. I don't feel good," he said. In fact a prickly nausea overwhelmed him right along the blood in his veins.

"You've never felt good. Your suffering protects you. Pain is the ransom you have gladly paid not to be free."

She didn't appear to be looking at him, or anywhere else. But she rolled her shoulders slightly and seemed aware of him, electrically aware.

"Use her body."

With both hands delicately she raised her hem above her thighs. Beneath her shift she went naked.

"Feel between her legs."

It was like putting his hand into molten iron and finding it only pleasant.

"Isn't she wet? Take her."

Darkness all around them and particularly behind her almost like a light that put her in a gray silhouette.

"What are you?"

"I am Miran."

"Are you male or female?"

"Both. Neither. Both . . . Take her."

He couldn't see if her mouth was moving.

"Take her. Anything. She's ours."

He freed his fingers from the slick locks of auburn hair between her thighs. He took her by her forearm's flesh and then he was on his knees and pulling her forward.

"Throw her on the floor."

He's on top. He can almost see her eyes.

"Tear her up."

He was inside her but he was numb to any pleasure. He wrestled the shift up, covering her head, and raised himself stiff-armed and looked down at this white body in a light that was suddenly falling all over him. It was hotter than physical pleasure, more shivery, more melting. He raised his vision to where the walls had fallen away to reveal a sort of moving picture, a creature with a gargoyle's face, but it was her face, too—an angel, a cruel and glorified monster with Yvonne's iron-colored eyes, looking off, and a mist accompanying her. Great white powerful wings, but scaled, not feathery. Looking off, communicating with someone her satisfaction, the righteous, glutted quality of her contentment. Sharing it with someone he didn't want to see.

You want to, Miran said, you want to, it's hers, make it yours, take it in your hands. He dragged her clothing from her face. Put his fingers around her throat. Touched his thumbs together beneath the larynx and felt it buzz. A little harder, put her out, put her out. He pushed his thumbs against the beat. The lovely face began to fatten and suffuse with the colors of plums and the shut eyes slanted and looked like a happy baby's, who cooed and wheezed and gurgled. His own life filled him and spilled out of his pores and ears and nostrils, tore through the top of his head. It lit up the air, unbearably bright, burned rapidly all around him and went out. Only the glow of candles now, and it seemed veiled, remembered. He loosened his hands on her throat, and instantly the face blanched and almost disappeared, as if its shadows were sketched on the rug. Give the woman her breath, give it back, keep it. He moved his hands to her jawline and it divided slackly at his touch. He kissed her open mouth. Yours now, keep it, give it back, something said.

Lying out in the garden patch watching the stars, Meadows swam in the wasted confusion and panic he'd felt during childhood illnesses—the true understanding of the scene: no doctor, no medicine, nobody's mom or dad can help you.

He tried to tune in to its physical sensations, tried to stay still inside and wait for things in there to come right. It got down as usual to discipline: be with this. It was an art. Like surfing, it wedded the mind to the muscles.

He concentrated his mind on the heavens. There was Orion's tri-star belt, and the stiff dangling sword. This far from any artificial light source the Milky Way's rim stood prominent, snaking among the suns. One day he'd see one of those things go nova. He just had to live long enough and watch. Many of the ancients had believed that a nova, no matter how far-off, signaled God the Dragon's most intimate incinerating touch on the feathers of history. The magic man called Takinsata, or Doctor Snake, had witnessed such a thing in the sky two thousand years ago from this coast—the same herald-star of Christ in the unimaginable East—and been fixed with such power that afterward he melted rocks with his breath and with his claws raked scars in the surfaces of the lakes. He strode the coastal forests tearing and scattering the red hairs from his head and they grew into the redwoods. Where he sprinkled his urine rhododendrons grew up. His eyes were so strong and so beautiful that fish from the sea swam up into the fresh streams to find them, and the steelhead and salmon and cutthroat still do so to this day, and there they find his eyes, which look to us like their births, spawning, and deaths. Doctor Snake gave the coast people their language, their skills, their legends. Eventually a god of the White Darkness, one of the Athabascan progenitors from five mountain ranges north, came and gave him a red mushroom with shiny speckles and he ate it and flew away.

But Doctor Snake had witnessed the very moment of a nova's birth. Thus his power.

Meadows watched the constellations wheel above. A probing visitant illumination edged his sight: silent heat lightning stuttering up from too deep a place to be audible, the hills around flickering and failing as if trying to kindle themselves out of the empty dark. He wept. He fell asleep.

Later something shocked him awake. A gigantic voice. An agony at the foundries of the real. The slap of it drove down his flesh, but then it was only thunder, small and lowing, rolling down and gone away. He sat up; the hair tickled all over him. A wind had been working, and he tasted dirt. Bright veins scintillated to the east, real lightning, though he didn't smell a bit of rain. He watched the dry storm. It struck just across the canyon once, twice, an election designated by crippled-looking talons—the flash, the black catch between, and then thunder to tear your skull away, first an incomprehensible fact, then a sound, then a voice, rushed and elderly, fading at the brink of intelligibility. The lightning started a fire in the hills. For hours it seemed covert and unlikely, signaling at great intervals as a struck log, he guessed, was fanned intermittently. But eventual gusts drove it into the brush, and then it woke up and raced around with the breezes until on the tindery hillside a riot of flames was under way.

He crouched beside his sleeping bag over the lantern and got it lit, pulled on his boots, broke down his A-frame and weighted the tarp, flattened on the ground, at its corners—with his bag, his rifle, a rock, a chunk of firewood—but he set the lamp aside and worked beyond the perimeter of its light, because he needed both hands. He walked the garden, tore out each plant and beat it viciously against the earth, clearing the rootwork of clots, and lay each across the plastic. The tarp, ten by twenty feet, barely accommodated this premature harvest. He rolled the tarp up from one end as tightly as he could, appreciating sadly that he was producing, in fact, one gigantic mother of a joint. Ten feet long and two yards in diameter and weighing above a hundred pounds, laced around with yellow nylon rope. He cached it behind the spring box and sprinkled its blue bulk with bits of manzanita and rhododendron. By now it was well past dawn, by now the atmosphere to the east was full of brown smoke and carried a noise like a distant locomotive. Two spotter planes, small Cessnas, plied the sky like fish in a tank.

S hortly after ten o'clock in the morning, Meadows stood
finishing a can of Colt .45 in the grave site behind the
Gualala Lutheran Church. The chapel and its residence were fifties-
era buildings, both of them, though out back on a bluff which, but
for evergreens, would have looked down a short drop onto the
Gualala Safeway, lay this little inexplicable fenced plot of graves from
the turn of the century. One of the saddest and most satisfying places
he'd ever stood in.

That it probably belonged to the Lutheran churchyard was news to
him. He'd come on it from below, climbing up here one day to
watch—was it fireworks?—something out over the sea. He couldn't
remember. Now he'd stumbled onto them again, these seven wooden
markers, not crosses, but listing and reeling blades of cedar too
weathered to be legible.

Today his awareness fixed itself toward the upward slope, toward
the two Lutheran buildings. The daughter would be at school. But
Mrs. Connor ran a bookshop that didn't open till eleven or so. He
waited among the graves until he heard her car fire up and get away,
and then walked around the church's left side, the side farthest from
the residence.

None of the churches had any size to them in these parts. This one was no larger than the one he'd blundered into and out of in West Point. He tried the front doors. Locked tight. He went to the building's corner and saw no cars in the open garage.

The door to the residence opened, and the reverend called, "I'm over here! Hi!"

Clarence lifted his hand in a tentative greeting as he hiked the long porch.

"Good morning!"

"I'm Clarence Meadows."

"Of course, of course—Clarence. Come in." Reverend Connor, though at home, looked dressed for business in a western shirt and string necktie and dark slacks, his paunch divided by a wide rawhide belt and buckled fiercely with a Stetson buckle. Meadows knew him to have come from Buffalo, or maybe Albany. "I'm afraid we've got fire in the county," he said.

"I'd say so."

"It's a shame." For a few seconds he studied Clarence's face. "Is that LP land over there? It's due east, isn't it?"

"Georgia Pacific."

The minister shut the door behind them and led the way to the living room. "What a waste. And it's mostly blowing east?"

"I haven't heard."

"I heard it was. I guess we're spared, but what a terrible, terrible shame. But it was lightning. What can you say to that? Sit. Sit. Would you like some tea?"

Clarence sat on the couch and said. "You know me. Of me."

The Reverend Connor seated himself in a leather easy chair and continued looking Meadows over, openly puzzled. "Well, of course I know you, did you expect me to forget? You helped Cassandra when she hit that poor sheep." The minister had a teenage daughter, unlucky behind the wheel more often than just the once, and a beautiful dark-haired wife who seemed entirely nice but to whom Meadows, on nothing but a hunch, attributed the Reverend's secret apostasy.

"I guess you know what kind of sinner I am."

"Now, wait a minute, Clarence. I don't know what kind of sinner you are. How could I know? It's between you and your conscience. All I can say is—and I'm not supposed to, they told us in the seminary not to act surprised—but I was surprised to see you coming up the walk. Well." He smiled, lifted his hands. "It's God's world. Anything can happen."

"You deal with sinners of my type."

The Reverend nodded and shrugged, both smiling and attempting to smile.

Meadows added nothing.

"Did you say you'd like some tea?" the Reverend asked, and stood up.

Clarence shook his head. The Reverend sat back down.

"With all types," the Reverend said, proceeding with a studious frown. "Nobody is so lost, so . . . *lost*—"

"With my particular type."

"Well—" The Reverend stopped and thought about this. "I don't get it."

"I don't know. Maybe you don't."

Meadows added no more. The Reverend seemed to accept this silence as significant. He joined his fingertips together across his belly and then lifted them to probe gently at his double chins. He had delicate hands and a very white face and thick red lips and was, to Clarence's eye, a man created very much in the image of his childhood, a good boy, a pudgy boy. "I don't like that kind of rumor floating around."

Clarence leaned forward. He couldn't read the whole inscription tooled into the Reverend's belt, but he saw enough to understand that it said, THEY CAN HAVE MY GUN WHEN THEY PRY IT FROM MY COLD DEAD FINGERS.

The Reverend said, "Is it floating around?"

"Not around here. But I know Herman Hayes in Long Beach."

"Oh, shit."

"And this guy, Tony, I can't remember his last name, dude used to roadie for the Byrds. He seems to know you. Some of those guys down there."

Connor drummed his fingers on the arm of his chair and blew out a long breath. "Well, we have these mutual acquaintances. Maybe you'd better come right to the point."

"It's kind of a salvage opportunity."

"That's what we're here for." The Reverend laughed and immediately looked worried again. "This isn't about a loan. Because I really—"

"No sir."

"I just can't. That's absolutely out."

"I've got seven pounds of female tops picked too early. They're going cheap."

Connor raised his eyebrows and relaxed. "Well, cheap had better be damned cheap."

"Ten even."

"What are my people going to want with trash?"

"You dry it till it's crisp and powder it up real fine in a blender. Bind it in little wafers, like two by three inches in size."

"Bind it?"

"Bind it with a little varnish. Call it kief. Little green squares about a half inch thick."

"And what is the return?"

"Retail? Seventy per unit, minimum. You'll get four gross out of the plants. They'll bring ninety apiece if you just don't push. Exotic inventory. Just say, 'Oh, incidentally,' to your more sophisticated customers."

"Varnish."

"Or whatever works."

"But varnish works, you're saying."

"If you want to move it, ask five grand per gross. It's off your hands, and you double your outlay."

"And if somebody comes back about, well . . . varnish."

"If they do—tut tut. Those fucking Arabs. They actually do bind hash with varnish anyhow. Some of it."

Connor hitched forward and half stood and looked out the living room window toward the church. "I'm wondering now about your vehicle."

"Down by the Safeway. I came up the hill."

"We're unobserved."

"I'm not a fuck-up. Check with Long Beach."

"And why me?"

"Because you can move. You can talk to the bank if you have to. The thing is," Clarence said, and he leaned forward now, aware that he was pushing, "it's the fire. The plants are up, and I've got no home for them. Now's the time."

"A victim of the drought?"

"I was in the wrong place. Let's say this: You take the night to think about it. Check with the folks in Long Beach. They'll tell you I only make bargains to the benefit of both parties."

"Have you actually ever cooked up this kief yourself?"

"I've seen it done. A buddy of mine in the service, in the navy, and this was light-years back. He got home from Lebanon totally empty after making some serious promises, so he came up with this inspiration, these wafer things. Everybody went away happy."

"Surely. But. Clarence . . ." Connor waved a hand and shook his head. He sat back in his easy chair and looked Meadows up and down, long and carefully, in a plain attempt to make him uneasy.

So close to the sea Meadows wore an open flannel shirt over his tank top. He raised the undergarment to his neck by its hem and bared his middle and also, evidently to the surprise of the Reverend, unzipped his fly. "No wires, no mikes. Nobody's hot, I'm not up a tree. And we're structured here so it would constitute entrapment anyhow."

"I'm not interested in legal constructions. The first time somebody narks me even to the neighbors, there goes my program. No, no, no," the Reverend said—and now, by a certain shift in the Reverend's manner, Clarence felt his instincts in coming here exonerated—"this is really unorthodox. The way you've arranged this, I can't help but feel intimidated. I think maybe it's completely unacceptable."

"I guess I'm giving you a jolt," Clarence agreed as he rearranged his clothing, "but I'm forced to improvise."

"I'd expect you to offer some adjustment in the price, considering the nuisance of it all."

"I've adjusted the price already. It's killer shit. The only problem is the bitter taste. So you change the packaging and make that a selling point."

"At the very least, it's a form of harassment."

"No way. If you pass, I was never here."

"I pass."

"Why not have a look? You can always pass later."

"I pass."

"Eight-five."

"Pass."

Clarence stood up. "I can't go lower. I'll take the hill back down. Don't sweat it, I was never here."

The minister didn't rise. He waved a hand between them, whisking away any shreds of unpleasantness from this encounter. "In that case, I'll take a look. Eight-five is good. I just wanted to know where you were coming from."

"Good enough."

"We'll see," Connor promised, "we'll see if we can't get you straightened out in some manner. I'd like to help."

"Check with Long Beach."

"I'll make some calls. If Herman likes you, I like you."

"He'll put you at ease."

"If it's primo, we're on. If not, no hard feelings?"

"Not a one. It's your call."

"Yes, Clarence, it is."

"I'll give you a few hours in the morning to get the lay of things and do what you need to do. I'll turn up after lunch. You expect to be around?"

"Of course." The Reverend Connor nodded. "Here is where we do our work."

Late that afternoon Clarence made a crest on Shipwreck that opened onto the distant east and watched a modified DC-3 floating above the fire. As it banked away and vectored low over the hills of smoke, too far off for the sound of the engine to reach him, an orange spoor of chemical retardant exploded from its belly. In the next instant he was forced to run the Scout's tin hide against the rocky road-bank as a pickup came at him too fast around a curve and they entered each other's dust clouds. A black Silverado with a camper shell.

Immediately around the bend and out of sight, Meadows cranked the steering a half turn to the left, depressed the clutch, and yanked up the emergency brake hard. Headed now directly at the bluff's edge, he dropped the brake, straightened the wheel, popped the clutch, jammed the gas, and accomplished a sliding bootlegger's U-turn and went into pursuit.

Falls dreams often of the moment he killed his father, put one in his heart during an argument. The killing had been completely unexpected, a shock to everybody, although one had been going to shoot the other for a long time. Only, and he was more and more certain of it the older he got, only his father hadn't quite realized this until the slug split his breastbone. Then his eyes had clouded out, turned to little bright stones in the sockets. Falls goes over this moment when he wakes from dreams of it, holding it carefully in his mind, pressing his fingers to his temples, staring at the face he's just dreamed, intensely curious to find in those eyes a beat of light—shit, the light would say, I get it: We've been fucking with the ultimate . . . But the dream had been fading out over the years, the decades. He woke remembering, but you couldn't say the dream had actually run itself through. It only signaled itself by scattered half-images, like stations ticked over as you spin the dream-dial.

Meanwhile Tommy gave up and turned off the radio. Falls said, "Good. That activity irritates the shit out of me."

"Nothing comes in."

"Garberville's got a station."

"Not on this piece of equipment."

Thompson managed to contain himself for a while, looking out at 101 and the tracks running in a ravine alongside it.

Falls tried to distract him by bringing up the Mexican girl again: "Hey, you know that Mexican girl?"

"What about her?"

"She wasn't half bad. What's your opinion?"

But Tommy gave out with something that combined a sigh and a laugh. They'd met the Mexican girl two days ago, and both had agreed at the time that she was an ugly dog. "Okay, Bart, back to the thing. Straight, no bullshit. *Mano a mano.*"

"*Mano a mano?* You mean *hombre* to *hombre.*"

"Goddamn! Fine!"

"Okay—"

"No. Way to go, man."

"All right—"

"Way to go."

"Can I answer your question?"

"Yeah . . ."

"It'd be best in a war."

"Were you in a war?"

"No, I'm really just guessing is all."

"Okay."

"But it'd be easier to lay it down later. You take off the uniform, and you lay it all down."

"Yeah, okay," Tommy said, "I gotta lay it down."

"That's the message."

"I just didn't know how I'd feel afterward. Now it's afterward and I still don't know."

"Man. I'll never understand you."

"You don't have to." Thompson watched things go by out in the world. "In fact I don't want you to." He wrinkled his nose. "It stinks around here." A brown atmospheric haze had followed them down from the fires in Humboldt County.

They ate cold sandwiches at a picnic stop north of the Leggett turnoff. "We going to eat in a restaurant one of these days?"

"It wouldn't be smart. I don't wanna be remembered," Falls said.

Thompson stood up and attempted a jump shot with his wrappings toward the rubbish can. "Two points," he announced, although it hit the rim and went wrong. He sat down backward at the table and reached for his Michelob and told Falls, "We should be bringing back an ear or a finger."

"He's got a private swimming pool from which he looks down on the ocean. He don't wanna see nobody's ear."

"Shit, man. Why are you keeping that thing?"

Falls had taken out the pages again and begun shuffling them around in his lap. "This is like a hundred pages long," he said in wonder.

"Why'd you keep it in the first place?"

"You can't leave it to fly out all over the world like when they let down leaflets out of a plane, man."

Thompson said, "You're in a mood."

"I knew that before you did."

"I don't feel nothin'."

"Look. It's not about that." Falls bent close over the pages in his lap. "I think it's in a foreign language. Or I think it's in code."

"I'm gonna get a fire going."

"Be my guest."

"Gimme some of that diary to get her lit, please."

Falls said, "Here's some good shit. This bark is dry."

He was putting it back in its envelope in the morning when Thompson woke up and said, "So. Breakfast is not served, I guess?"

"This thing," Falls said, "is as good as a finger or ear or whatever."

"I think this conversation started before I joined in," Thompson said.

"You can get an ear just about anyplace."

"Excuse me? Did you say something stupid again? Did you say you could get an ear just about anyplace?"

"It would take me a year to write this much," Falls said.

"You can't even read it, man."

"Good. Because I looked at it, and I *could* read it."

"You gonna read it?"

"I don't wanna see it or even know about it. No, I'm not gonna read it."

"Just don't go giving it to Lally. We need genuine proof of completion."

"After we dig in the garden, we'll have proof."

"*If* we find it," Tommy said. "That guy was delirious. He was meat anyway, and he knew it. He could've given us a totally false location."

"He didn't lie. He wouldn't."

"He might've lied about it just to be funny."

"That's why he told the truth. Just to be funny."

After they'd finished their business in Fairchild's garden and washed up at a gas station, the men and the dogs celebrated with pizza, canned all-meat Alpo, imported Dos Equis beer. Well past the supper hour they parked in the pullout in front of the client's gate and killed the engine. No lights showed in the house. The wind moved little floating toys around in the swimming pool. Tommy started chewing on a cuticle. It looked like he was sucking his thumb.

"Wish he'd take a bleeding phone call. I mean we could've said something neutral like, hi, your order's ready."

"He's paranoid. Probably keeps him outta jail. We should be paranoid too."

They heard quarreling in the camper. The truck rocked slightly.

"Damn their shit."

Thompson whapped the back windshield. "SETTLE DOWN!"

"If those two get into that bundle, they'll have a hell of a party."

"Can dogs get stoned?"

"Sure. They're animals. All animals can get stoned."

"Crayfish? Salmon?"

"Can I say something, please? I'm enjoying our success, and you seem to wanna mess with me. It ain't fun. You're bringing me down."

"I'm just prodding you, man, to be a little more accurate in your statements."

"Hey, you asked, I answered."

"Really I'm just trying to think. I feel like some sort of other plan is coming out of left field."

"That's a powerful shitload of dope, man," said Falls.

"I see. Great minds think alike."

"Unfortunately it ain't drying right."

"Sure. And it's picked too early. But still."

"It might not be quick. You might have to practically retail it. Meanwhile Lally hires somebody to come after *us*."

"That one car was on us for a while."

"That jeep, yeah."

"Bullshit."

"Probably bullshit—but. I wouldn't put it past him to have us tailed, see if we stick to business."

"This whole entire thing," Tommy said.

They napped awhile, waking whenever somebody's headlights swept through the cab. Lally hadn't shown by midnight.

Hadn't shown by 1 A.M. They'd slept more than they could be expected to, all folded up like this. The dogs were kidding around in back, but in a stealthy way. Before too much longer somebody would have to set them loose to do their business. Falls wondered if they missed Sarah, the dead one. They hadn't exhibited any particular signs of it.

"Okay," Falls said, "open that glove box there. No, man, no. The notebook. Gimme that, please." Falls opened his notebook on his lap. "I got a sequel for you. Part Two of the Ballad of Tommy Thompson."

"Oh, brother," Thompson said.

"You remember about loving the waitress and—"

"Desperado in the parking lot, yeah. You should make that the title. Not the Ballad of Tommy Thompson."

"Here's the part that's really like you'd do it, if this would be you," said Falls.

"Did you hear me?"

"Of course."

"I wish to remain anonymous."

"Desperado in the Parking Lot," Falls agreed. "Second verse."

> *Later down the road it's midnight,*
> *people sleeping in their beds.*
> *You'd like to come up soft on tiptoe,*
> *put a bullet in their heads.*
> *Go downstairs and get a sandwich,*
> *pop a beer and turn on the news,*
> *put your feet up, get the phone book,*
> *call her and say, You got the blues?*
> *I got 'em too, hey, come on over,*
> *no one home but me these days,*
> *just like you, let's burn their albums,*
> *warm our hearts around the blaze.*

Thompson sighed, cleared his throat, jerked up the handle of his door, and spat out onto the ground. "Well, what that is," he said, "is sick."

"It's not sick if it's from the heart."

"That's not like me. I'd never cap some poor family asleep in their beds at midnight just to use the phone, man."

"Well, I just launch it and let her drift."

"I hate to tell you, but you drifted way the hell past me. I have no beef whatsoever with regular folks. Just assholes. I know who that's about. And what it's about. I know."

Falls closed his book.

"Aaah," he said.

"What."

"I can't talk to you when you start running tickets."

"I'm just responding," Tommy said.

"You're just repeating shit that you heard."

"I'm giving you an honest response."

"No," Falls said. "You're just running tickets."

Tommy rested his head against the seat back and jammed his knees against the dash. A car passed and lit them up briefly, but it was just nobody again.

"Look," Falls said after a silence. "I'm feeling responsible about the various shit-disturbances, man. Like maybe not all of them, but too many of them."

"Aah. It's been tense. All these unexpected variables."

"We been ragged-out by this deal, understandably. It's been seven ways from Sunday and every bit of it wrong. But you've hung on every inch of the way, man. You hung on, you made one. You done good."

"Wo. Wo. *I* had to keep *you* on. Or you would've booked two days in."

"Yeah. Yeah. This is my acknowledgment of that."

"I had to knot the end of your everlovin' rope and put it in your teeth for you, man."

"Acknowledged. You done good."

"Apology accepted."

Then Tommy laughed, and Bart also laughed, and both said together, "'It's a *growth experience.*'"

"Ah, man. Ah, shit," Tommy said. "I should've fucked her."

"You told me you did fuck her. You told everyone."

"And you believed me? Educated bitch like that always wears flat shoes and glasses? The only one of us who could've fucked her was Yates. And Yates did fuck her."

"Yates? Yates is a ridiculous wimp."

"He's a deeply sensitive mass murderer."

"Yeah. I can see the attraction. From her point of view. From her semiclinical but still cuntly point of view."

"Well, I never touched her. But when she transferred, Yates lost his mud and he confessed to a few people. I mean, the way it came out, you had to buy it."

"How come all this got by me?"

"You were gone."

"She took him out of group. They went to one-on-one, I remember that."

"You were already out when she transferred."

"'Please, you can just call me Doc'. . . You could've fucked her if you wanted to. You just don't have the confidence," Falls said. "You don't understand your own . . . you know. What about the Mexican girl?"

"Who?"

"You know."

"With the baby?"

"Why do they always wear T-shirts with American words all over them? It's kind of pitiful."

"I wonder if I'll ever meet her little baby again," Tommy said, "like later. When he's all grown up."

Neither said anything else until Bart said, "Anyway . . . "

Tommy said, "Yeah . . . "

Thompson settled back, breathed once, sat forward, ran his fingers over his scalp. He reached under his seat for the Casull. "I'm going in."

"What are you doing?"

"I'm gonna climb that gate and sit by that pool in one of those poolside-type chairs and relax." He got out. "I might take a dip, man." He slammed the truck shut.

Falls watched him shake the gate in the dark like the door to his own personal cage. "It ain't locked. Come on," Thompson called.

Falls followed him in and they stood there beside the pool.

"Where are the chairs?" Thompson asked. "He doesn't have any chairs."

"I don't know," Falls said.

"Well, I'm going for a little moonlight swim, only there ain't no moonlight."

Thompson shed his T-shirt, his shoes, his pants and briefs, and weighted down the pile of them with his Casull. He mounted the diving board and stood on it and spread his arms and said, "Ah!"

"Kind of breezy for such a number," Falls pointed out.

"Ah!"

"Bullshit," Falls said.

But Tommy launched himself and went in cleanly without much of a splash.

Falls watches him swim, this almost undiscernible thing in the dark water cutting toward the shallow end and standing upright with a seething liquid sound and saying, though out of breath, "You coming in?"

"Okay."

His hands shaking, he strips himself down. He can hardly manipulate the buttons on his shirt.

Thompson says, "Your teeth are chattering, man."

"Yeah."

"Mine too, huh."

"Yeah, I guess!"

"Come on in, it's heated, man."

Falls sits naked at the pool's edge and let his left leg in up to the knee. "Heated? Fuck you!"

Thompson turns and kicks off and out into the deeper water, spins in a balletic somersault, the words coming up with his face from under water: "Fuck *you!*"

Falls lets down both his legs, shivering, his throat pumping in his neck. He slips forward and stands in the shock of it up to his waist. "Not as bad as a trout stream!" he cries, and sets out into the cold dark toward his friend, and swims past, and Thompson grabs his ankle. He spins around, grabs at Thompson's crotch. Thompson heads to the side in the deep end, clutching the ladder one-handed, laughing, saying, "Hey!" as Falls passes his fingertips over his groin again very lightly. "Hey. Don't do that, man."

"What?" Falls grips his thigh and squeezes hard.

"Just wait, just wait, just wait. Hang on. What's the story on Lally, man?"

"He ain't here. End of story."

"He's in the wrong place, if he ain't here. Because I just came to a decision concerning a shitload of stinky green sinsemilla."

"We keep it."

"He can send somebody after us if he wants."

"Anybody he sends—we'll send back the bastard's pecker in a FedEx pack."

"We been killing people lately anyway!"

"Oh, yeah." Falls runs his hand along Tommy's belly and crotch, and Tommy swims off leaving Falls alone standing in water up to his chest. With the plunging sounds of water Falls strides toward the shallow end. He can't tell what's going on here. Is he supposed to be angry or happy?

Thompson faces him, but Falls can't see his face. "We're moving now, man, we've stirred the waters. It's kind of a lustful thrill."

"Let's go see some people."

"Why not?"

"Why not?"

"Let's do it."

"Piss on that," he says as Tommy makes to get his pants on. He walks away toward the gate without touching his own stuff. "I'm breaking out, I wanna feel it all."

"Wo. Do it."

"Super-sensitized all over. Not even shoes," he hears himself saying, "are in style this particular evening."

"Oh. Oh. I like it. I mean—"

"I mean it's like this marauder bonzai *fuck*."

"It's a party," Tommy says. "This is all I'm wearing," he says, picking up the Casull. "It's so delightful."

"It's so delightful," Tommy said. He spat out the open window and said, "What happens to your spit in a wind like that? Does it disintegrate?"

"I don't know. Who knows?"

"My skin should feel freezing, but it don't."

"Past a certain boundary, freezing equals hot."

"I like it."

"It just lifts you up and sails you, don't it? How we doing?"

"One set of lights about a million miles back there. Otherwise the world is ours. Unless we're walking into a scene full of armed security."

"If they had security they'd be stationed at the gate."

Falls killed the engine and they looked at the temple's dome like a storm cloud blacking out the constellations.

"You got them cutters?" Tommy said.

"They're electrician's cutters, man. That's number-one chain link."

"We gotta scale it and cut the bob-wire."

"No we don't. We just climb that spiky gate."

"One slip and you're castrated."

"Probably the best thing for me," Falls said.

Any front entry to the building itself was impossible. These Buddhists had barred the big, medieval castle doors from within. Thompson stooped and panted for breath, still tired from the climb over the gate, one hand on his knee and the other dangling his Casull. "Right or left?" he asked.

"The least-resistance thing," Falls said, walking a ramp off the side of the vast porch down to the ground and feeling along the wooden siding.

"We need a moon," Thompson said.

"This is the place," Falls said.

"Where?"

"We're standing on it. It's a root cellar. Maybe it's connected."

"It don't open."

"Get *off* it."

The door pried upward as they felt along it edge by edge and heaved. "The question is, are there steps. And how deep is it. Other shit like that," Tommy said, but Falls just lowered himself into the hole and dropped and slid backward and went down in blackness amid a multitude of dirty spherical things he guessed were potatoes.

"Bart, Bart," Tommy called.

"I'm swimming in food."

Thompson thumped down and stumbled against him and laughed in fear.

"Keep your weapon outta my face," Falls said. "Keep your finger off the trigger."

"It isn't cocked."

"Nevertheless," Falls said.

"I don't cock it till I know my target."

"I found stairs," Falls said.

"Look up—that's the stairs back up. We could've walked down," Thompson said.

They'd descended maybe eight feet below ground level into this bin.

"I'm measuring off with my hands about like . . . ten feet from wall to wall"—Thompson thumped and swore—"and now I'm on my ass again."

"It keeps going," Falls said.

Where would it go?—a sort of tunnel, completely dark, Falls feeling with one hand along the wooden wall and the left hand wavering before him. He didn't even know if he had a body.

Tommy shuffling along behind him—brief rapid scraping gasps— he touched Falls's spine with the flat of his palm.

Falls couldn't help himself, and said: "Do you feel like we're way over the top here?"

"Way over, yeah, I do, a long way."

"Do you feel like cancelling out?"

"I'm scared shit if you are."

This drove Falls two more steps into the thing.

Thompson followed, touching his back. "Why do you do that? You just get me to admit I'm scared so then you can fucking ignore me."

"At least you're honest."

He caught at Falls's neck in the dark, caught at his shoulder, spun him around. "No, man. Don't flatter. I gave up my insides. Now I want the same from you."

Falls drew him close, groin to groin.

"Look, we been in this thing a long time," Tommy said. "I mean it's happening. It's happening like you want it to."

"Oh, now you're gonna say you love me. Tommy loves Barty . . . Does Tommy love Barty?"

"That's it." Thompson pushed him aside and moved on despite his own blindness. "You get nothing from me now." His gun struck against something in the dark. Falls came up close behind him and a fissure opened in the boundless black as Thompson pushed backward against him, pulling open a door.

They mounted a dozen wooden stairsteps and walked naked into a chamber almost like a public school gymnasium in its dimensions, its motionless atmosphere fogged with sweet incense. The light was meager but quite bright to their eyes. Small statues, many hundreds of them, overwhelmed the walls—icons, looking like gold. The quiet was vast, but seemed to fit itself around Falls's head. Breathing it in gave him a hopeless feeling. When he moved, the smoke moved right through him. He wanted to mention that he'd dematerialized, but he just couldn't put a crack in this silence.

Thompson looked all around them at the colors—gold, blue, winking bits of red. The light came from thousands of candles burning next to little Buddhas in a vast honeycomb of cubbyholes. "This whole scene's on fire and it's making me feel cold."

"Don't whisper, man."

"What."

"It's ridiculous. Don't do it."

Thompson cleared his throat. "Yeah, I'm losing my authority."

Falls looked everywhere at this world, its horizons miraged with reduplicated icons, and moved forward with the machinery of grief suddenly grinding inside him.

"What is it?" Thompson said.

"These things are wood. They're just wood painted gold."

"It's a scam. Like religion in general."

"There's gold here somewhere."

"Maybe it's gold paint. Like real gold, gold leaf."

"Don't be a hole."

"Jesus," Thompson said irritably, following him through a little door into a tiny room where a man sat meditating on a pillow with an army blanket around his shoulders. A youthful-looking guy with wisps of hair sticking out. Baby hair. His legs crossed in a knot.

He looked at them as if they were people he'd forgotten but was now forced to remember as Thompson put his gun hand on his hip and jutted his groin.

"Excuse me," the man said.

"It's so delightful. Do you have any spiders to eat?"

"Can I help you?"

Falls said, "Marauder bonzai fuck, sir. Veins in my teeth. I am not a slave."

"Let me put it this way. What are you doing here?"

"I don't know," Thompson said. "What do you want done?"

Falls said, "He's just kidding. We're here to rob your ass if you don't mind too bad. You don't mind, do you, sir?"

The guy looked quizzical and amazed and almost happy in his shiny eyes. "Yes, I do mind."

"Aah," Falls said, "we're just doodling around."

Falls reconnoitered, finding nothing but this sorry victim and one lit candle over which he moved the palm of his hand to set the flame wavering as he said, "Wish I had a Marlboro. Got a smoke on you?"

"No smoking."

"You got incense all over here. Incense causes cancer."

"You're trespassing on private property."

Thompson said, "You're ruining my moves. You've got clangy vibes. You should be dead." Thompson raised the Casull before his own eyes and did a double take at the sight of it. "Hey!" he said. He peeked over the gun at the little baby-haired enlightened one.

"You're deceased, sir," Falls assured him.

The meditator hitched his blanket close and stared at a point between them, trying to smile or else smiling against his will.

"The Little Monk!" Falls said.

"Monkey-man." Thompson stepped close enough that his shrivelled organ floated not twelve inches from the monk's face. "What do I look like?"

"You look like . . . Japanese demons."

"We're gonna require a shitload of valuables," Falls said. "And something to lug them home in."

"Nothing here belongs to me. Nothing here belongs to you."

"Well, that's why it's a robbery, sir. Therefore that's why I'm applying that word to this transaction."

"So where is it, Monkey-breath?"

"What?"

"Gold, jewels, mystic treasure."

"That's gold," he said, turning his gaze to the shadows in a nook.

Falls peered into the corner and lifted out a statuette like all the others, only smaller, a bare-bellied greasy depraved fat Gypsy Buddha with earrings and a pointed hat or something over its curly hair and its eyes squeezed shut in mirth, quite heavy for its size. "Seems like gold," he said.

Thompson lowered himself to sit cross-legged before the little monk, the gun at rest on his ankle. "So . . . where do you come from originally?"

The man said nothing.

"Come on. Where are you from?"

"Connecticut."

"That's a shitty state," Thompson said.

"No," the man said. "One place is as good as another."

Falls set the Buddha down on the floor, the beginnings of a pile. "Nobody around?"

"Not too many. A few. In fact," the man said, "things are still under construction."

"I need that blanket."

With an outstretching of his right arm the man drew the blanket away and laid it to the side. He wore a gray sweat suit.

"What about that tower out there? Is that real gold?"

"It's covered with gold leaf, yeah."

"*Told* you, damnit," Thompson said. "Incidentally, just for that I've decided not to kill you."

"We have sacred texts etched into the panels. You want the gold but the truth in the texts would give you much more. Still," the man said, and sighed as though it pained him to say it, "you have the truth already."

"I've decided to kill you. Do you have a few last words for the cameras?"

This Buddhist guy was just some skinny little veg-head, astonished that his life needed this death. Jogging shoes next to him on the floor; and they were too clean and too white. For that alone Thompson put the gun to his forehead.

"You know what I'm doing?" Thompson asked him, truly curious as to whether the man understood.

"No."

"This is one big gun. This weapon will make a wound that medical science cannot repair. I'm putting my hand up like this so I don't get bone fragments in my face."

"Don't," the man said.

"Don't put my hand up? Or what?"

"Don't make a wound," the man said.

Falls said, "Tommy?—The valuables. Can we get a location first?"

"None of this belongs to me," the man said, staring at the gun and at the gunman shielding his face with his free hand. "The idea that you can steal it is an illusion. Listen to me. There's a penalty to be paid if you fail to separate truth from illusion. Illusion is the penalty."

Falls said, "Bullshit."

"Yes. All right, that's a better word. The penalty for bullshit is bull-shit."

Tommy lowered his hand. "Here's what I've decided. If we get some good old-fashioned loot, I don't kill you. That's my latest decision."

"None of it's mine or yours. Nothing we do can change that. Shoot me."

"Wow," Tommy said. "You are insane."

"We all are," the man agreed. "Some more than others."

"Well, I score you right up there, way up," Tommy said. "How'd you get so stone-fuck silly?"

Falls was getting impatient. "Can I see your one big gun please?"

Tommy handed it on, and Falls stood over them holding it. "So where's everybody else?"

"Praying in the sanctuary."

Tommy asked Falls, "You think they know we're here?"

"Of course they know," the meditator said. "They're praying for you."

"No! What's your name?" Tommy said.

The man seemed not to want to do it, but he answered. "Bill."

"I really want to fix this person up," Falls said.

"Me and Bill were just talking here," Tommy said.

"I never shot anybody for nothing before. But this one—*man*, he's a stinky little unit. I mean basically a cunt. A human vagina."

"I think he's funny and silly, man."

"Listen to me, he . . . is . . . evil."

The man closed his eyes.

"You are the proto-original motherfucker. Do you think you're so terrifically enlightened you can handle a bullet in the head?"

"No sir. I'm all confused. I'm scared."

"Then what's the use of sitting around for years with your dick in the dirt?"

"I can't handle the bullet. But I can handle the fear."

Tommy said, "Excuse, gents," and abruptly went out through the small door.

"What's he up to?" Falls said.

The little monk failed to respond. He kept his eyes closed.

Falls felt he'd maintained possession of himself, but now he couldn't help breathing hard and feeling completely terrible about getting into this situation. He cocked back the hammer with his thumb. The click sounded luxuriant, precise, like a tongue against the palate. The pistol was the work of much craft. But still. The target ten inches away, and a weapon you could hit Mars with.

He leaned closer and put the gun barrel under the man's chin. He thought he'd have to pinch him to get his attention, but the man opened his eyes. He looked willing to speak, but unwilling to say the wrong thing.

"Are you ready, cunt?"

"Not exactly, no . . . "

Thompson crept back into the room and said something under his breath.

"What?"

Thompson said softly, "There's vehicle activity outside."

"Where?"

"In the road. I heard wheels and doors but no voices."

"Who is it?" Falls asked the monk.

The monk shook his head and raised his hands and went on shaking his head.

"Okay," Falls said, "Let's see, uh—shit." He couldn't think.

"They were shutting doors too damn quietly," Thompson said. He pushed the palm of his right hand forward and clicked his jaws.

"Okay," Falls said again. "Everybody shut up. We're just gonna ride this out."

Thompson sat down carefully on the carpet. The monk straightened his spine and closed his eyes and began breathing slowly and regularly. Falls leaned against the wall, which was rough to his skin, textured Sheetrock. He cocked his left knee and rested his left forearm across it. He'd spent weeks, months, maybe years if you added it all together, in variations of this posture in rooms about this size.

Thompson said very low, "How long we gonna do this?"

"Until whenever. Whenever the last ding has dung, buddy."

After a long time, even an hour, Falls was thinking of the Mexican girl. He thought Thompson was thinking of her too, and of many other things, his head driving all over California and up and down his life. This is what made these small rooms so small. In the end you didn't mind. But it took three or four months for the games to fade, for the streets to dry up and blow away. Then you were settled. Home free. Just stay off the telephone.

They'd been inside the place long enough that the things that had happened in there might have taken forever, but it was just now dawn.

The two naked men came around the back side of the temple in confusion, along the fence line, through pastures and pairs and trios of oaks standing beside their great shadows, came shivering and doubtful to within sight of the gold pagoda.

"We weren't turned around," Falls said, "I don't think."

"Where *is* it?"

The chill wasn't off, and yet here and there a warm dry pocket drifted over the pasture, almost like the scent of baking through a house. The early light seemed hazy and smelled of smoke from distant forest conflagrations.

"Where's the rig?"

"This is gold."

Tommy swallowed away his understanding that the truck just wasn't anywhere and said, "Is it gold?"

"It's heavy enough."

"It could be lead just painted."

"It's gold. Weighs about a pound."

"How much is that worth? What's the price of gold?"

"I don't care. I'm not gonna sell it."

"He was surprised you didn't kill him."

"I got him to pee though."

"I'm not so sure about that."

"I think he peed. You should've let me zap him."

"Did I stop you? It was a thing, man."

"Aah," Falls said, "I wouldn't just zap him, I know the rules."

Thompson said, "Whoops."

Somebody, his long shadow ruled out imperfectly over the dewy grasses, was coming toward them.

"Hey. Guess who," Falls said.

"Is that our old buddy?"

"It's the guy. The dude who gutted Busk's little dog. Isn't it?"

"I'm gonna waste him."

"It might not be him."

"Too damn unfortunate."

"He's got a rifle."

"He don't see us."

"We better get back to the dogs."

"He don't see us."

"If he don't see us, then what is he aiming at?"

Falls was teaching words to the Mexican girl . . . She touched Falls's blue scars. Falls said, "Scars."

Scars across his chest where he'd been stabbed with a large nail, about the largest you could get, a number-twenty galvanized—under what circumstances? He remembered a man in a parking lot and somebody locking his elbows together from behind. He was drunk and he'd spilled something on the pool table—they'd paid him off for that clumsiness.

He carried such a nail with him now, and had since that night.

"*Estrellas.*"

"No, not stars," he said, and then the little dream stopped.

The two disciples came ten yards into the leaf-floored copse of hardwood before slowing their march and standing still and taking cover, each respectively, to the right and left behind a couple of madrones.

Meadows, on his knees before a fire pit and tending two fistlike chunks of meat on a spit above the coals, did not look up.

After some period of scrutiny, the two men let themselves into view and approached where Meadows studied over his fire like a primitive.

Both had dressed warmly in overalls and flannel shirts this slightly chilly morning. It was breezeless, the whiff of the fire still permeating, though the coals were long past smoking.

One said, "I'd say no."

The taller of the two regarded the primitive.

"If you're reasonably sure," he told the other.

The other approached a snapped-off trunk and looked at the object set out crazily on its incline. "This is ours," he said. "It's stolen property." He put it in the pocket of his very blue overalls.

He came closer but Meadows remained on his knees, unimpressed or oblivious.

"You have to know you're trespassing. You wouldn't have climbed over a ten-foot fence unawares."

Meadows looked off deeper into the little wood, a light-dappled scattering of leaning madrones with their papery tattered red hide and green wood beneath.

"Are you connected with the two men who broke into our temple last night?"

This primitive pulled at his mustache, worked his lips, perplexed and short of words.

"We've got to have you off the grounds," the man said. "Right now."

The primitive breathed rapidly, blowing through his nose. Cleared his throat. Looked at them finally from far away.

"I guess I can finish what I started here."

The men would insist, but think better of it.

"This game you're cooking—were those the shots we heard earlier on?"

Meadows lifted and unskewered his meal from its spit and set it on a dusty plate of oaken bark. "I guess you wouldn't join me."

"We don't eat flesh," one said.

"I guess you don't."

"You killed it. You eat it," he said. "It's yours."

*   *   *

W here have you been?" Mo said.

Where? At the edge of a cliff, in the wind above the sea, like an advertisement for happy Pontiac touring—

"Getting drunk," he said.

—until he'd bruised his arm against the window frame, tossing an empty pint-jug of Cuervo way out there into the foamy crashes.

"Merton called," she said, standing there with her hands knotted before her breasts. "I didn't know what to tell him. I mean, yesterday he called. Your uniform's in the closet."

"Uniform!"

Let's get right to it.

Tearing his sweater off over his hair, he floated toward the back room headless and pinballing along the hallway. She entered behind him as far as the bedroom doorway while he stood before the closet with his shirt and sweater bunched around his right shoulder, his right arm still ensleeved and his palms against the closet door as if he had to scale it. He let his arms fall to his sides, stepped backward, gripped the knob.

She was done talking now.

When he turned around, clutching the deflated suit by its neck like some culprit's, she wasn't there. He stepped on his upper garments and pulled free his arm.

He frisked his uniform and got the thing out and threw the rest aside.

In the kitchen Mo stood with her head down, her eyes closed, her left hand resting on the table, maybe for balance. He took hold of a chair by its back and drew it out with brief, experimental movements and sat down across from her with his elbows on the table, turning his badge in his hands.

"I've been married to an infinite number of women like you."

She didn't move.

"It'd be a shitty cowardly thing for me to beat on a woman."

He pinched up the flesh of his left nipple and clipped on his badge.

"Just one more shitty cowardly thing," he said.

He sits down across from her with the badge clipped to his bare chest.

He says, "The punk look." Stares with his mouth open and his eyes like an old dog's and says, "The punk look. Huh?"

"I guess."

"Huh?"

"Yeah."

"The punk look."

"Right."

"Damn right."

He took the clip-on holster from his belt and placed it in front of him on the table. After a couple of deep breaths he removed the blue .45 from its holster and held it loosely in a two-handed grip, his elbows on the table again and the barrel nodding more or less her way.

She's white, shit-pants afraid: "Man, I'm not happy about this."

He looked at her standing still with one hand on the table and one knee turned slightly inward and her eyes on him careful and steadily seeking.

He said, "You have true grace."

He held his gold badge in his hand while Jenny talked about her car. The Wankle rotary engine possessed a limited life, and a rebuild presented only problems, insurmountable problems, considering the types of mechanics in this area—

"I like a big V-8. Wouldn't own anything else," he said.

She stopped talking and crossed her legs and sat there looking at the phone. Until Merton created another mess, she had nothing else to do.

The badge wasn't responsible. It wasn't the badge's fault. The badge caused nothing. It didn't give you the disease, it only warned the others that you had it.

He clipped it to his uniform pocket and got on the phone to the coroner's office in Ukiah. It had been eleven days now. He explained this to the administrative assistant on the other end and told her he couldn't understand it. "I'm waiting eleven days and nowhere around here is there any letter calling me to the inquest. William Fairchild, the inquest, I assume you'll need me to testify. I found the body— first on the scene," he said. "I found the body."

"William Fairchild? Nothing's scheduled. Was that an alias?"

"No, ma'am."

"Give me another name."

"Ma'am. His name was William Fairchild. Shot in the head."

"Oh, the Point *Arena* thing. Oh yeah. Nothing's scheduled yet."

"I don't get all this, not entirely," he told the voice. "Do you have the final report there? One-page thing, Sheriff's letterhead, addressed to the county coroner?"

"I do not, sir."

"What about the inquest?"

"I'm not sure. I don't think there'll be one. The Sheriff's people did their report, and the coroner's ruling it self-inflicted."

"Based on their report? What about the position of the wound?"

"I don't know about a position, sir."

"He got it from behind, in the back of the skull. Doesn't seem likely he blew his own head off, does it?"

"You can tell the coroner that. I don't know, maybe I have it wrong. Maybe he'll want an inquest. Mainly it was because of the note. Oh, right. It says here they want the inquest deferred pending verification of his hand on the suicide note."

"It says that where?"

"Right here, the letter from the Sheriff—September twenty-first?"

"I thought you didn't have it."

"I thought so too. Sorry."

"Well Jesus, friend, the earthquake hasn't happened yet. Point Arena's still on the map, you know? Could you fax us a copy please? And fax us everything you get about this from now on?"

"Keep your tone civil, please, Officer."

"Aaah—pretty please," he said.

"We're all on the same side, remember?"

"Advise us of all developments please."

"Everything's on its way."

When the fax came through, Navarro held the one-paragraph communication in his grip, his head beating with rage. Maybe the coroner had seen an autopsy report, but these three small sentences made no reference to one, only to a lab report, which was not attached. He called the lab in San Francisco. They'd transmitted a report to somebody, somewhere; it was listed in their document file, a technician told him.

"Fax me that mother."

"To be faxed it has to be printed."

He kept a civil tone. "How long?"

"Requests are normally processed within forty-eight hours."

"Who do I talk to to get it read over the phone?"

"You talk to me, and hang on while I get clearance to put it on my screen. Or I can call you back in a minute, but it's better to leave it off the hook, so I don't take ten other calls."

"I'll hold."

In a minute the lab tech rang on. "I remember this one," he said.

"Okay. The victim's communication."

"Right."

"Did you get what the writing said?"

"Yeah. Eat More Pussy."

"Beg pardon, now?"

"Yeah. You have to get a few feet away. One of the forensics guys noticed it. Then I think he stole it. One of them did."

"Wait a minute. What are you doing to me?"

"What."

"You're jerking my head."

"No."

"Yes. Are we talking about the same thing?"

"The hat?"

"What hat?"

"The baseball cap."

"Look. Are you looking at the lab report? Would you read me the name, please?"

"William Fairchild?"

"That's it. What does it more or less say?"

"Yeah . . . Blood is O positive like the majority of people, brain, bone fragments, powder, copper, steel, et cetera consistent with a bullet wound. Graphite on his fingers. I have solved the problem."

"Who? You? What about the writing. There was pencil writing."

"That's the graphite, the writing, his last words: I have solved the problem."

He takes the badge out and nails it at the level of his chest to the scabrous bark of some kind of oak tree, the hammer coming at it: pring!—pring!—pring! like the big maul stamping out badge 714 in the original *Dragnet* shows.

They all said it, fat old cops who ended up retired in their trailers scattered with fishing lures and empties. Sorry about the crap. Nobody to clean up around here. It was par. It was rote. It was standard to the core. He felt like a loser in this shipwreck of bullshit . . . Busted by the badge. He stepped backward several yards.

I get you thinking it'll work. Love you in a storm. Vanish like a magic light.

He stands looking over the series of idiot ridges toward their vanishing, then wanders toward the Firebird toed in from the dirt road with its engine idling and one door wide open. He pitches the hammer into the back, drags the plastic carrier over the gearshift from the passenger seat and thumbs the latches and takes out the Colt .357—stainless steel, the finish they call "Ultimate"—and three speed loaders. And there you have it. The cylinder out, loader in, the chambers full and the cylinder closed.

He let the empty loader drop anywhere, put the others in the right and left shirt pockets of his uniform, and turned and fired. A bit of bark jumped onto the ground, and he stood there dumbstruck while the gun blast travelled the valleys like a wheel on a track.

Smoke hangs in the air a second, and then a puff of wind sucks it away.

He sent another and then several more down after it, squeezing the trigger regularly until the badge disappeared. He'd blown it from the spectrum. But he saw it off to his right, winking in the grass. Retrieved it, fixed it to the oak again—ran its new bull's-eye down onto a shag—and fell back five paces to reload.

He approaches the badge with his arm straight out, firing after each step forward till it flies from its tree and spins over into the grass, and then he reloads and stands over it shooting, follows it where it takes a hop and shoots again, stalks it among the shadows of the oaks, shooting, shooting, shooting till there's nothing left.

He parked the car off the Coast Highway and went quietly in the blackness of his uniform along dwarf forestation to the bluff. Dogs' voices whipped away on the gusts: this was private property. He was dizzy; his bloodstream seemed to flutter. The moon was invisible, but it was around here somewhere, light from the clouds showed him his hands in front of his face. He rested at this shifting height above the imploding surf, then descended, almost squatting, the seat of his slacks dragging over the knobs of bared roots and stones, his arms out either way, catching at others, until the earth leveled and he felt the shore like muscle under his tread and heard the water licking and breathing.

He'd climbed down to the north end of a small, almost beachless cove. On the bluff above the southern end was her house. He didn't know why he couldn't just walk down her drive and knock. He listened for his explanation and heard nothing. Stood there ashamed and beautiful. Offshore the ocean appeared to pulverize itself against the great rocks, but he understood this to be completely illusory; the rocks were the ones disintegrating. Right now, she felt him. This was the place for them. She would come. Right now, she was watching.

Crazy. But the way, afterward, she'd wept in terror. To see her busted like that. Even if it wasn't himself who broke her down.

He made his way in the darkness along the waterline until he found the path up to her and climbed it fast, not pausing until he could make out, from some ways below, the house jutting over the bluff and the big glass doors onto its balcony reflecting the night-clouds offshore.

She might let him back in one more time. She wouldn't let him come again after that. She'd call the cops on him. Merton would have to drag him out of here.

The back rooms of the house were unlit. He walked around front and it was the same. The house was thick with a special darkness. She waited inside it . . . He stood still, not making a sound, surely less than twenty feet from her door.

He'd be arrested if he insisted on coming around—he understood his worth to her, he knew it wasn't anything, he realized he'd spent it. But perhaps this one time more. He stood paralyzed in the gantlet of small tormented trees, and how many had once been lonely men, how many of them had been her lovers? And now he was in motion toward her door. He didn't know what he would find. He didn't know what he would do. But he knew what he would find. He knew what he would do.

September 14–25, 1990

F our days before Clarence Meadows shot them both
dead, as they headed north on Route 101 to reenter the
logging industry and sleep once again in sheets, Falls spat out at the
rushing world and told Thompson—

"You're doing it. You're doing it. You're doing it right now."

"Wonderful," Thompson said. "Everything I say."

"I admit it's not even a conscious thing," Falls said.

"Then I don't talk? I stay totally mute?"

"Would you put your shirt back on, please?"

"You're just bummed."

Falls is silent. Ruminating on a seed of hate.

"So we saw the world," Thompson said, "and at least broke even."

"We lost old Sarah."

"That's Busk's loss, not mine."

"She was a good dog. He'll want restitution."

"My credit's good with Busk. How old is that dude? He must be in
his eighties. And he still practices every habit that's supposed to cut
you down."

"Hey," Falls said. "Look at that."

"Pull in! Well. It just could be."

In order to negotiate the exit, Falls had to stop on the interstate and back up along the shoulder slowly, staring at the extended side-view mirror. "Very few little ragtop hummers like that around, man."

"I believe we're under a sign," Thompson announced.

They made slowly toward the Porsche.

"All of a sudden I like it. This is fun."

"It is. It's like we're detectives."

"Hunters, but on a new level, a higher level."

They'd run across Fairchild in Point Arena nearly a week ago, and at first sight of them the grower had bolted north, along the coast. Somewhere before the town of Mendocino, they'd lost him.

They'd doubled back and tried the road up to the Albion Ridge, but it was just an empty upward quietness in which the motor started overheating while their energies drained away. "Great view," Thompson said when he'd turned the Silverado around and they sat looking at the Pacific in the light of a cloud-eaten moon . . . They'd returned to Gualala, hung around town till Tuesday, just in case; in case nothing. Lally had paid them two hundred each and begrudged them something extra for gas and had dismissed them—with his eyes, with his shoulders, with his little drink, he'd dismissed them.

This morning they'd broken camp and slunk away before daylight, deferring payment of the fee. And now, parked all by itself at a rest stop one hundred miles north, here's the Porsche convertible.

At the cool, still general store in Whiskeytown, Fairchild bought a packet of a hundred typesheets, two ballpens and a fountain pen and many liters of wine. They had shelves of California vineyard labels but not one large-size envelope. In the car he found an old one, creased but not torn, from the tax harpies in Sacramento, an envelope once the vessel of extensive really penetrating—burrowing—irritations, but he felt nostalgic for regular civic troubles now. Though in love with the name of this town, he pressed on for greater altitudes. For Weaverville.

"Dear Win and Van"—Win and Van, he thought, how cute—and wrote that thought down too and, still standing, wrote for several minutes more before uncorking the wine and sitting down at the desk by the window of a room in the Trinity Alpine Lodge: above

a pond sprinkled with leaves and twigs like fingernails and bones, a low-rent swannery where waterfowl drew arrow-feathers in the surface. At so high an elevation, snow would soon be descending on these ducks. He didn't know what would become of them then.

After he'd half-filled a second page he got up, went into the bathroom, and turned on the shower. He sat down again at the desk and dangled one hand toward his shoes to unwork the laces, his eyes on the words he'd written, and started adding to these words, forgetting his feet, and wrote until the sound of water invaded his focus he didn't know how much later. He got up and turned the shower off.

He ate supper the first night at a cafe down the street, but thereafter took no more food, and spent the following four days writing, napping occasionally, wandering sometimes—finding himself sometimes inexplicably, without any recollection of having moved—downstairs, where Ames, the proprietor, this cockeyed bastard, Fairchild had forgotten he was cockeyed, kept abreast of things on an astonishingly tiny Sony TV despite his left eye's divigations, in a parlor of hand-peeled pine—the furniture, the wall logs stippled with brown cambium and wavering in Fairchild's sight, as upstairs too, in the room, where a single big rainbow trout floated on a plaque above the bed and a yellow-toothed agate-eyed black bear struggled across the floor.

The fourth, the fifth—which?—dawn found him still piling his thoughts onto pages, disembarrassing himself of certain burdens, clearing his brain and vision of the rubble of all this mania he'd brought down, interrupted only once by Ames as he made the rounds with kindling for the rooms. It reached the eighties in the daytime, and Fairchild hadn't used any kindling. Ames refused to greet him. The wheezy old moron. He disliked Fairchild because Fairchild suggested that by the look of the pelt maybe his bear rug had been hunted down with ack-ack . . . Fairchild wrote this description down, sorry to have offended the old character—but this was his special talent—with a single anemic

joke. Anyway wherever I am it doesn't matter, I'm already dead. But how have I ascended to this alpine autumn, to the Trinity Alpine Lodge? Leave it at this: I crawled from the sea and next day retrieved my car (if only you'd known, Van Ness: it sat just back of the Cove Restaurant, you could have pushed it into the ocean after me) and beat it out of town with Harry Lally's pig-men right behind. Heigh! ho!

they're a couple of reasy blokes, I'd love to throw you all in a bear pit together and watch. But those boys don't know the coastal ins and outs the way I do, and they don't have a Porsche, and I'm afraid I rather goofed them. Took 20 east out of Fort Bragg, slept in the car in the mountains, came in the height of noon thru the inland town of Willits, through the xeric mystery of its baking Mexico silence, all the little shutters swung to, the main street cherishing the parade of identical summers, the summers of ugly young girls who kiss the ice cream from their fingers, the innumerable virgin mothers of God, the bigamist wives of flesh and doubt. Hey—

How did you know I went to prep school? Anybody around Gualala could have told you, I suppose. But I think my wife told you.

And you, Van Ness, graduate of nothing, uncomprehending memorizer of F. W. Nietzsche—one passage you didn't underscore with your dull pencil:

There are the dreadful creatures who carry a beast of prey around within them, and have no choices except lusts or self-mortification. And even their lusts are self-mortification

and then Route 20 to Interstate 5 and around to Redding and up and over and down to this room made of logs, every inch of it a personality, knots and grains and adjustments, with the trophy trout and the bear emerging from its floor, to study the facts about you two, but it comes down, really, to the facts about me:

I tore up Harry Lally's packets of coke.

I have consumed what was intended for sacrifice. Hell to pay.

Then I made an arrangement with a demon. Why did I do that?

And to the inane, null, phatic, garbled question "why?"—the answer "why not?" will do just as nicely.

You know I don't believe I ever mentioned to you young lady that when we visited Palermo I made something along the lines of a coke deal. Me and Harry. I muled it as far as Rome but no farther.

I flushed Harry Lally's philtres of powders. I attacked him in his substance. Old Harry. He couldn't forgive me.

That's what it's about now, attacks against the substance, the calling down of the Fates. The facts are spiritual facts now, that's what this letter is telling you, it's all about gigantic crimes and gigantic forgiveness.

Nietzsche-boy, you framed me good. I suppose I can never go back to Gualala, nothing lined up for me in the village of my birth but a short shrift and a taut cord. But you who read this, you confess me, you give me shrift.

Then you will soon forget me who am a wretch.

The most horrible things we've done feel the best because they were things we absolutely had to do. The best things, the good things, have a richness the horrible things don't have—but a difficulty and an alienness and at times even a wearying absurdity.

I don't dare speak of God. But let me point to a glacial patience overarching everything. I join with it, ally myself. You Are Loved—Home Sweet Home—Expect A Miracle—have you seen those bumper signs and badges? I embrace them all. It's all I can do. I can't revolutionize myself. But I'm out of the loop, I reject your desperation. Whatever happens now, I stand aside from evil. This beautiful planet of violence and love. At last I'm a citizen. Love and violence—not to conquer one with the other but to live with both, that's what I've learned. Each pulling me a different way. If I relax my struggles they don't tear me in two, but lift me up. Here I am in some mountain motel, tears behind my venetian blinds, man in a wood room. Me I live in this chamber with the clean torture of the truth. Exemplar to dark acolytes. Come poke the creature's cage.

So many demons! And I'm happy to see them, and speechless with gratitude for the others I've met along the way. Surely if we have these demons we have the rest of it.

I've been here for days, can't remember what I was saying, but I think—So you see, when you two met each other in Santa Cruz I was actually not so far away, in the city. San Francisco and its cascading streets. I ate some popcorn and watched a woman raised from the dead. Meanwhile you pressed against Winona sweating, your heart a black hole. The reverberation of your touch: funeral in flames. And that motel. I bet it was a pink one. With or without the sunset a torturing pastel.

If I'd had any real, any little bit of slightly real contact with my life I would, at that moment on that street, Army Street, have seen that I'm fucked by forgiveness. Fated to achieve it.

All these tragedies. What do they spell, these threads that cut us, in the great tapestry?

Ah Winona let me stop now for reasons having mainly to do with our sighs.

PS, (Next Morning) Man I just got happy. I'm thinking for some reason of lucky Clarence—Clarence waking up in a friendly warmth with a woman who smells like Italy. I wouldn't mind a brief vacation in his simple universe. A world wherein all that might eat me is extinct. I like Clarence. I like simple men.

Can't say how many days I've hid out here now but it's getting to be a few. I have to go back to the coast, to the ocean, I must. I'm developing a sense right now of the hugeness of the neighbor Pacific as another universe of space with its own laws of light and dark but also as very much a universe of time, and transience (the ocean washing its terrible histories toward us, always its terrible histories, because the happy ones, the stories of safe arrivals, briefly hesitate then unroll onward, inland, while at the shoreline nothing stays but the wrecks and deaths. So I belong there: I envision it: the Lost Coast: extra green the shallows this morning, like county jails), anyway a sense of these legends overtaking and enfolding us, the old stories backgrounding and enveloping the new ones. Yes, like waves. The Lost Coast.

The clouds are low today in these mountains, and the window is just a gray blank. I don't see the trees or the pale lakes. There's nothing left of the sky. Nothing. Why is that so beautiful? I don't know. I don't know.

He paid his bill in cash, and then stood before the counter with his wallet cupped in his hands like a prayer and gouged at it with his thumbs. Down to forty-three dollars and a credit card. The card hadn't cleared for months. He needed a gas-up without a computer link, maybe in Redway or one of these hamlets well back from the lanes of commerce. He smiled at Ames. Ames hadn't uttered a word beyond those desperately necessary for checkout. Fairchild said, "You think I sneer at you."

This startled the man. He shaped himself to deny it; but then said matter-of-factly, "It's because I'm short." He turned his face toward the television.

On Route 36 down out of the mountains, Fairchild met with a piggyback logging truck, empty, rushing upward. The pavement seemed hardly wide enough for the Porsche alone, but when this collision was suddenly on him something stretched in the weft of physical reality itself, and they were past each other, apparently having occupied the same point in space-time. It happened again not fifteen minutes later, and by the time the mountain road had come down out of its turbulent hunting back-and-forth and found the easier slope, he'd passed through several such ghost trucks harmlessly.

The road straightened out. But it got harder to go on. Outside Mad River he stopped in a seafood restaurant's parking lot and put the Porsche's top up, sat in the car with his typesheets and fountain pen, making an entry: I'm looking for the Lost Coast, he wrote invisibly. He much preferred the ballpoint pens; they worked. *I'm looking for the Lost Coast* . . . He produced three lines, looked at his maps, and kept going.

His route met with 101. He turned south. Not many roads reached the Pacific from here. He aimed for one at Redway that would put him in the area of the King Range Forest and the Lost Coast.

Past Phillipsville he slowed at a sign for a rest stop and followed the exit ramp. He would have imagined a long-haul oasis, rows and rows of big trucks with diesels gurgling, a happy little town. This was not one of those. One rig in the place, apparently abandoned, a rusty pickup with a big plywood camper built onto it and only three wheels. It was lonely here. The drinking fountain by the bathrooms didn't work.

He'd just put his lips to the metal teat to suck out of it whatever drops of moisture he could when in the course of his flight across the state he reached a most amazing crossroads. The black pickup truck with the camper cargo, the Chevy Silverado he'd hoped never to see again, pulled up beside his Porsche some twenty yards away. The top-heavy vehicle stopped and appeared to be still rocking on its springs as the two men jumped from it. There were terrible noises. Momentarily he mistook the whining and yelping as coming from the men, but it was of course their dogs scrabbling in the camper as the men moved toward him without words. And now in a tender moment of dreaming or magic he was going to be shot. One man suddenly went down on one knee, pointing his pistol with two hands. Released an orange flower into outer space. Stood upright holding a flag of smoke. The head flew off the drinking fountain.

Still holding the gun straight-arm, the gunman tilted a glance around the monstrous thing to check his target. He lowered the weapon and considered its great errancy. But Fairchild was on his knees, keeping his face above the grass by one outstretched arm, the other moving to his right side, his breath stuck fast in his throat while five feet away the drinking fountain pissed water leftward drunkenly. He rolled his head and chopped his mouth. At last he drew a breath that buoyed him powerfully aloft, and he began travelling with the passive sense that the current of his own revulsion was carrying him toward a *place*. He bumped against a door frame, batted away a beige sink bathed in yellow light as it floated up against his chest. The flood he rode on drove him backward, and he sat on a toilet. He fainted with his head against a partition.

B efore Falls was halfway back to the truck, Thompson climbed aboard and slammed the door. He fired the ignition, and the truck sat there jiggling. The dogs had gotten very quiet.

Falls reached him and leaned against the driver's door. "You didn't miss by *exactly* a mile, did you?"

"I'd like to know who's been messing with my gun."

"You think you're Joe the Sniper. It don't work that way."

"A Casull. I'm dumbfounded."

"And what were you planning to do now? Just leave?"

"What. I thought we should split, because of the noise."

"Ain't nobody here but us, chief. And him."

Thompson nodded, and coughed, and matted away the sweat from his face with his shirtsleeve. He turned off the engine. "Okay—I blinked. Nolo contendere. What do you advise? I'll go in and do his ass."

"No, no, no. We gotta talk to this guy about his pot plants."

"I thought that was over."

"No, Tommy, it ain't over anymore."

"Okay. Don't talk down to me."

"Sorry. I'm sorry." Falls took note of his own emotions, which seemed acceptably matched to the level of decision-making required now. The flat outrageous luck in turning over this number, finding Fairchild underneath. This smelled like the kind of bait laid too often by life. But there was nothing to obstruct their business that he could see. "Okay. I'm gonna join our buddy in there. Our policy is take him alive. But if he comes out, bust his tripes."

"Will do. But he won't come out. He's all boxed up."

"Unless there's a window." He jabbed his finger repeatedly in the direction of the rest rooms. "So your job is to circle the building."

"How can I circle it? There's only one of me."

"I mean walk *around* it, in a damn *circle*. Can I ask you to do that, please?"

Falls went inside. Two sinks with mirrors, a hand-dryer, three toilets: and the pot-grower wilted against the partition of one of the doorless stalls like a heartbroken teenage girl. In this yellowy rest-stop gloom nothing had its regular hue, and the faucets were of the rest-stop water-saving design: Falls turned one on and it turned itself off. He held the button down and bent to scoop water up into his face. As he stood in the dryer's warm electronic breeze, waiting for this contraption to accomplish something, the grower came to. He sat there on the john and stared at the floor with his hands hanging, but when Falls stepped over close to him he jumped up to attention, put his thumb in Falls's left eye and gouged.

Falls banged at him with his left hand, yanking with his right and stretching the neck of the man's T-shirt to an enormous oblong while the man's thumb only burrowed. Falls swiped at him again but slipped on the wet floor, really only flailing at the air half a foot from any part of Fairchild. Falls's head felt shot through with a burning brand. Am I stabbed? Falls backed away and turned toward his own image in the mirror. Yes—it's got to be—it's blood. He felt for the faucet, got the water flowing, bent and doused his face with one hand, looked up to see Fairchild standing there in the mirror rapidly throbbing and radiating veins of neon light. "What did you do?" Falls asked him. But Fairchild wasn't there.

Falls hurried as far as the doorway and stopped. Across a field of quivering X rays Fairchild executed a strange half-crouching run to his Porsche, struggled into it and drove away. And where was Tommy?

"Tommy?" he called. He couldn't see.

Falls turned back toward the men's room with the sensation of stepping out into a chasm, tearing at his buttons as he went. He threw his shirt at the sink and kept the water running over it while he crouched, resting his upper weight on his other forearm across the bowl, and dropped his jaw and winked each eye repeatedly open and shut, breathing hoarsely through his open mouth. He took his shirt in both his hands, laid his face to its wet folds and stood up bending backward, and let the water finger along his neck and shoulders. He uncovered his face and bent toward the floor and studied the slick muck in which he'd lost his footing, and thus the grower.

Tommy expected he'd be forced to put him down. The stupid nonchalance with which Falls disappeared into the men's room just didn't seem in-charge enough, considering they'd run this Mr. Nelson to ground and erased his choices. In a crazy situation like this he might hop right over Falls's head and come ripping out of there like a cougar off a rock. The cinder-block hatbox housing the rest rooms was windowless on the two faces visible to him. Tommy circled the structure, going right, this next face also a blank, and now the back, too, nothing but four slatted vents a small snake couldn't breach. The only other vehicle at the rest stop today sat in knee-high grass at the ladies' end, a pickup with a plywood camper, a self-propelled shack, missing a left rear wheel and supported at that corner by a punky round of oak. The boulder and bough that must have been used to lever it up onto the round lay beside it, however, and its owners would be coming back sooner or later with a patched-up tire. In fact he heard somebody talking in there right now. And now sobbing, and now howling in Spanish.

Shame clutched at his stomach, and he hoped sincerely that he hadn't caught someone with a stray. But it sounded like a woman more alarmed than wounded, a woman in panic. Terrified no doubt by the gunshot. With certain vague reassurances on his lips he tapped at the door, a regular interior house-door cut down to fit this home-carpentered camper with colorful stickers of various kinds all over it. As he knocked once more the woman inside screamed the louder, and he heard a little child crying. He turned the knob and drew the door open just two or three inches. He couldn't see any child, but just inside was Mom on her knees in their plywood home licking her lips and tasting her tears. Howling over a naked baby that lay across her thighs, touching the baby strangely and quickly, all over. A baby painted blue—touching it with the palms of her hands and taking them away as if making sure the paint was dry.

"Okay," he said to the woman," what do you need?"

She pushed the baby from her thighs and screamed EEEEEE. EEEEEE.

"Jesus, will you shut up?" he said. No savvy, right. "SHUT UP," he translated. "Okay?"

Already Dead ■ *397*

He felt sick, had to swallow his saliva repeatedly while he tried to think. There was nothing in here but a lot of stuff all balled up in plastic rags. And an older child, the one crying, also balled up over in a corner. The baby lay on the floor. Couldn't have been more than eighteen inches long. Oh, shit . . . he'd shot a baby, a Mexican baby.

"Where's the old man? *Su esposo.*"

She just kept screeching. Tommy set his gun in the grass between his feet and rose up straight.

He put his hand through the doorway and touched one finger to the infant's blue face. It felt hot—fevered. The eyes had rolled up glimmering and fishy. Flickering like little faulty bulbs. This is not from bullets. It's a disease. Some weird tropical thing, a deadly plague. Just the same he bent low, his head in the doorway, and put his mouth down over the child's face and puffed. The breath squeaked out from between his lips and the baby's hot cheeks. He stuck his finger in its throat and dug out a plug of food or phlegm. Put his mouth over the baby's, but as he blew into it, snot exploded from the baby's nose and spattered the whiskers at the corner of his own mouth. He shifted the cradling of the baby's head to his left hand and held its slick nostrils shut with the other and blew again into the baby's mouth, working up his left-hand fingers around the head and trying to keep the jaws spread as he did so. He didn't think this was helping. "Don't seem like it's breathing no more," he explained. EEEEEEE. EEEEEEE. EEEEEEE, the mother screamed. He tried everything, shook it brutally, whomped it on its back, jammed his finger down its throat looking for more obstructions. This critter is DOA. But no, it was drawing breaths, turning red. It was bawling. Not loudly, but making a wet, whirring noise with its voice and holding up two fists beside its crumpled face. The mother quit screaming.

She held her baby by its head and rump in both her hands, staring at it and saying, "Ah? Ah? Ah?" with some considerable confusion and amazement.

Thompson nodded in an exaggerated way, nodded with his whole torso, repeating, "*Si! Si! Si!*" and making gestures signifying the greatness of this rush. This baby had been dead. And who was this child? Thompson suddenly felt the connection. This kid might grow up to—any connecting thing at all. Run him down in the street one day.

"*Momentito,*" he said, wagging his head up and down, and picked up his gun from between his feet and backed off.

Falls came around the corner of the building naked above the waist, holding his shirt bunched up against his face. "Where were you?"

Where in the world had he been? "I was over there. I was in back."

"Well, he came out the front. That's where the door is."

"What happened to you?"

"Don't, man. The Porsche is gone, the guy is gone. I thought you were gone."

Thompson opened his hands before him and squinted, breathing through his teeth. Gave up trying to speak and just shook his head.

"Let's go."

"Shit, I'm sorry."

"We gotta go."

"That Porsche is gonna ace us on this highway." Thompson was still shaking his head. "Flat-out or curving, the Porsche can't be caught."

"Well, can we at least make a semiprofessional attempt?"

"Bart— if he's gone, he's gone."

"My eye hurts. The fucker stuck me." Falls turned away. The eye was tearing badly, possibly bleeding. "I think he had something in his hand."

Thompson said, "Hey, I saved a baby's life over there."

Falls looked at him with his mouth shaped strangely, as if it held a word but he didn't quite know which one. "You did?" was all he could say.

"Yeah," Thompson told him, "I did. He wasn't breathing at all. Come here. Come here. I gotta show you this."

The young mother had left the camper door open, and she sat on the tailgate in her jeans and T-shirt with the baby in her arms and her stick legs dangling.

"*Días,*" she said.

She'd wrapped the baby in a towel. She was extremely dark-skinned, as much as any black person. But her face came to a point like a rat's.

"*Días,*" Tommy said. "This critter was DOA. There was crud stuck in his windpipe and I got it out. She has another kid stashed in there," he told Falls.

Falls looked them over with a growing, heavy sadness, and it leapt into his mind that there should be a sort of dog pound where you could take people like this and leave them in the hands of experts.

Then Falls said, "Jazzbo, you are a fluke of fucking nature, man."

"I am. I'm under a sign."

Falls surmised they'd traded for the rig with North American wanderers: it was pasted all over with bumper stickers in a language this woman could never have translated. He smelled the Southwest in the plywood's creases, the dust and the Mexicans and conveyances broken-down and the earth just soaking all this shit up.

"You ever been to Mexico?" he asked Tommy.

"No, I haven't."

"Me neither. Now can we be about our business?"

A vehicle dodging here and there and blaring a song came directly at him and he braked, saying, "Pardon *me*," and bore right onto sunken grassy ground, the median, he gathered, as the Porsche swapped ends and climbed backward onto pavement again. He thought he understood: apparently he'd been southbound in the northbound lanes. He'd landed now in the southbound, pointed north. He mashed the clutch, the gas, worked the gearshift like a pump handle. Excuse me. I have got to deal with this wound.

At the gas station in Redway he parked around back of the building and found himself able to move, more than able, strangely unencumbered by his own weight, and he got out of his car like anybody. But all of him above the waist felt both numb and terribly painful, and his head began to crash as he stood by the garbage cans and raised his T-shirt's hem to check his injury. He couldn't quite see for all the blood.

He tried the bathroom, perhaps it was the ladies', whose lock was engaged though the door itself wasn't closed, and he shut it softly behind him and found the lightswitch. The bit of man in the tiny mirror wore a slick patch of jellied blood below his right armpit and down out of the frame. He got the neckline of his T-shirt in his teeth and tore it down lengthwise, peeled it from him and sopped with it at the area of the wound. He'd been gashed along the belly, exposing a brief pallid streak of what he believed to be a rib. He filled and patched over this hole in his flesh with brown paper towels and tied his T-shirt around him, knotting it along the opposite ribs, sucking air through his teeth and singing, "Oh man! Oh man! Oh man!" continuously. One of his deck shoes and the right leg of his white pants were soaked with blood. He sat on the toilet and kicked off the shoes for the first time since—he didn't know; he'd forgotten they weren't his feet; he'd been fighting and swimming and hiking and driving in them since birth. A proper lodge would have had a tub! A proper lodge would have had its own restaurant!

He took several minutes getting his pants off. He didn't think it was physical shock, but only doubt and disgust, that had turned everything to molasses. He rinsed his trousers in the sink and twisted the pink water out of them, pausing at intervals to breathe and allow himself to whimper, then bathed away the blood on his hips and leg with wet paper towels and donned the wet pants—a good cool clean feeling that woke him.

He sat in the car out back of the Texaco until after sundown, listening to the radio so low he couldn't actually hear it, quite dazed and only imagining the music.

In the latter moments of dusk he collected himself and began driving west through Redway and out toward the coast on the asphalt two-lane, and soon it was night. He kept to the second gear, took it slow so as not to disturb his injury, steering one-handed, the road bodying forth into his low beams and a crouching, wolflike blackness on either side. Past occasional homes, or hovels, with implements and woodpiles presented under electric lights, little tableaux of repairs undone.

Then he found himself moving slowly over a rough main street with his headlights jactitating. With some difficulty and a reawakening of his pain he managed a right-angle turn into a wide alley. Or was it a street. And parked beside a tavern. Or was it a cafe. He shut off the engine and lights. He fell asleep, and woke with dawn pale over the town of Whitehorn.

They left the Mexican girl and her Mexican baby to be toyed with forever by their luck and went south on 101. Thompson drove. Falls sat with his head back, lecturing through the wet handkerchief he held against his face. "You gotta think about what works. What works? A twenty-two target pistol."

"And when it slips out of your waistband at the policemen's ball, everybody knows what business you're in."

"I'm not here to debate with you."

"Then don't."

"In real life you gotta walk right up and do 'em. A twenty-two magnum to the back of the skull. That's universal knowledge." Falls took the rag from his face and doused it afresh with iced tea from the Thermos.

"How is it?"

"I'm completely blind is how it is."

"No, but for real, man, is it getting better or worse?"

"Better. But on the left side of things there's still this continuing wavy electric line."

"That guy."

"People will surprise you."

"Okay, I'm him," Falls said as they peed together in the men's room of the Texaco near Redway.

"Okay," Thompson said, "you're him."

"Either I turn back north and shoot up the big road all the way to Canada, or I pull off and hide."

"The smartest thing would be a steady straight run in that little Nazi smoker. We'd never catch his ass."

"He might not be driving too good," Falls said. "He was dripping all over the john, and I don't mean this stuff." He zipped himself and started washing his hands.

"I hit him?"

"Something injured the man."

"You said I missed!"

"You took one shot and slaughtered the drinking fountain is all I know."

"Hey, man. Don't be twisting with me. Did I or didn't I?"

"Maybe the fountain was a secondary hit."

"No maybe about it. You get the scope up. You put the red dot where you're aiming. I told you and told you."

"Another magic bullet."

"It's common as houseflies, Bart, it's called ballistics."

"We gotta try every side route."

"Oh, man. What do you think that'll accomplish? Aside from wasting eternity?"

"That's the viable option. The other is he's a hundred miles up the road already. The world isn't complicated if you stay with the viable options."

"You know what? You talk like a lifer."

He woke up paralyzed. It was the cold. He'd slept uncovered, bare-chested except for his big bandage. For the next couple of hours, while the rising sun warmed the car, he tracked the return of his energies through his limbs, a pleasure that slowly intensified until it was glory and trumpets blew that he hadn't been killed. He unknotted his T-shirt and unstuck his loosest paper bandages from the others. . . . The jetting debris, he assumed it was, had clipped an inch of flesh from between his sixth and seventh ribs on the right side. Not a colossal violation of his unity—on a fatter man, a scratch. It had bled during the night and clotted thickly, but he feared setting it bleeding again. He rested in his body until something else, not pleasure, strummed along his nerves. He thought he'd better try his legs.

A touch of the Scary Electric. Just a breath. A little lick of the jim-jams. There were taverns in this town.

The Blue Deads the Purple People the Yellow Fellow. He had to move.

The tavern he'd parked beside looked just the one, obviously open soon and certain locals already creaking in their tattoos and wickers along the front of it in motorcycle senectitude. Toothless Wild Ones lined out and tilted back like courthouse louts, with flies clustered on their hats. His body was functioning persuasively, breaking its inertia and putting itself out in the street. He found nothing to cover him but Melissa's white terrycloth. He stood next to the car and donned it, cinched it only quite loosely because of the discomfort. Tied the belt in an unbreakable square knot and went among his people. For want of entertainment they watched him come on, squinting at his image against the morning sun.

"He ain't open."

But the door stood open. Fairchild went inside and climbed onto a stool holding his wallet in his hand. He stared at the bartender's back. "Open at nine." At his stationmaster face. "I'm just airing out."

"And what's the time?"

"Seven minutes."

A guy slighted outside, Fairchild couldn't hear the insult, continued on into the place with a kind of blunted ebullience and sat on the stool beside Fairchild's. The others were coming in too to take their places.

"A man in a bathrobe."

"The dress code has been temporarily suspended."

"If that ain't country you can kiss my ass."

"If that ain't evil you can kiss my ass."

"If that ain't sociopathic you can kiss my ass."

"You can kiss my ass. You can pucker up and smooch my rosy red pimply butt. Charles. A shot and a beer. Charles."

"Open at nine."

"Time marches on."

"Time marches, rolls, and flows. It's got more metaphors than God." This remark had the air of something rehearsed.

Whitehorn . . . surely these wrecks and ringoes had a purpose. Fairchild and the man beside him exchanged the look of dogs on chains. No, no purpose. We've all been consigned to this by accidents of cowardice. Fairchild watched the guy hand-rolling a cigarette out of a pouch, licking up the length of it to keep it closed.

"Where's the amusement?"

"I'm laughing," Fairchild said, "to see such sport."

The barman said, "One at a *time*," as they were open now.

"Shot and a beer," the man said. "I'm owed some money in this town, and that should be enough to say. Instead I'm in here killing off my appetite for breakfast because I'm owed, but I ain't paid. You can't do your work if they don't pay you. Ever heard of expenses?" As he spoke he searched his environs for someplace to strike his match, and this became rather the focus of his world—snapping the white cap with his thumbnail, sliding it longways up his boot, jamming it against a nailhead in the wood and ripping it off. "Ever heard of gas? Food? Rent? Goddamn it, gimme a light."

The barman tossed down a pink disposable, and the man paused while he set the butane feather against the cigarette depending like a bit of root from his lips and got it smoking. Dragged deep. Stared significantly at Fairchild. "Ever heard of overhead?"

"Have you got another little stogie, partner?"

"You? You don't smoke." The man turned away looking sad.

The barman raised his eyebrows at Fairchild.

"Something about halfway fatal. An ounce."

"Tequila? Rum?"

"Tequila, please, and please," he added as the barman nudged open with his knee the little icebox, reached within and turned to him holding in one hand a gleaming blade and in the other a yellow, a quite yellow, a solar-yellow lemon, "no food."

The barman set it out. Fairchild tipped the shot to his life and relaxed the craving. The man sitting next to him did the same for himself and waited with his hands in front him on the bar, the black penitentiary futharks on them blurred by trembling. Others joined them, other hands at the shot glasses like shivering newborn puppies—the randomly incised and greasy hands of bikers—carpenters' hands with their discompleted fingers—sawyers' hands epoxied with pitch and dirt—and they all got right with shots and watched the images on the tube.

"There he is."

"He do look dead."

"Shot him right through the tattoo. The heart on his tattoo. Rock of Ages tattoo."

"Yeah?"

"Yeah, you know the tattoo with the drowning lady hugging a big old motherfucking cross."

"She been in a shipwreck."

"Yeah. Right through her own chest."

"Shot 'em both."

"Him and her."

"That's too beautiful to laugh about."

The barman pointed his remote and hit the same murder on another station.

"Guess there's a dope scare on in Oakland."

"Hey."

"Hey there."

"Hey. Somebody capped Joe Hopeless."

"No."

"Yep. Assassinated him at the driving range. They just showed him laid out with a bucket of golf balls spilled all around him."

"Who did it?"

"Unknown assailant."

"Lee Harvey Oswald."

Not bad people, not evil people, but actually storms of innocence. Deadheads telling their tears. The town where Jesus got his swastika removed . . . Fairchild wondered about the possibility of living here forever.

A second tequila went down in Whitehorn. The Thing melted away and Fairchild turned to his right. A face: cuneiform features. "How you doing?"

"My muscles up my back are all kinked up. Back trouble."

"Would you be Mr. Harley?" Fairchild asked. "Or would you be Davidson."

"I am who I am. What brings you to our parts? You look like an escapee."

"I'm exactly that."

"Escaped from what?"

"Some incredibly boring people."

"Charles. Same again, Charles. On the tab."

"The tab? Tabs do not exist here."

"You stingy shit. Ghosta Joe Hopeless gonna get you bad."

"I don't believe in ghosts," the barkeep said.

"I seen a million. In the war I probably wasted more ghosts than gooks."

"Let God," one man quoted for them, his face blank and staring, "sort 'em out."

"Oh, yeah, *ghosts*, yeah," the barman said. "I hate to inform you. When you see a ghost walking around a battle zone, that is not a spirit. It's all electromagnetic transactions on a series of fields. I mean, for instance. Have you read Whitehead?"

"Stop right there," Fairchild interrupted.

"Drop a little acid sometime. Then read Whitehead."

"A *Whiteheadian* tavern-keep."

"Whitehead must've dabbled a little."

"How do you know? Hey. Charles. How do you know?"

"I wish I didn't work in a bar where intelligent conversation gets impossible after nine-fifteen A.M." The tavern-keep stooped down and rose up with a burning cigarette, dragged on it with half-shut eyes. "This is a lonely business." He crouched and snuffed it and turned away.

"Boudreau."

"Boudreau. Get in here, Boudreau."

"News of the hour: they killed Joe Hopeless."

"Who?"

"About fifty thousand suspects. Take your pick."

"Lord God," one man said, turning directly to Fairchild, "I was on the golf course with my bookie when they nuked my street." Goofy dude, he assumed so anyway because he was smiling with his jaw doddering open and brown tobacco juice strung through his chin

whiskers. "Wow. You are the dead spit of Normal Bates. Hey brother."
He choked on his plug. Tears filled his eyes and he drank down his
beer. "Did you realize you're bleeding like raw steak?"

The barman peered over and down into Fairchild's lap. "You having one of them days, boy."

"Normal Bates is bleeding. Must've stabbed himself in the shower."

"Pay no attention," the barman advised Fairchild. "He was fricas-
seed by a power wire a few years back."

They both studied the man for a moment.

"Oh yeah," he said as if suddenly remembering. "I got a metal plate
in my head."

"*Getch*er ass in here, you snake."

"You hear about Joe Hopeless experiencing a little difficulty?"

"Broke his neck stepping out a cigarette."

"Killed trying to get to the phone too quick."

"We all die. Whose thrifty-six is that setting out there?"

"Mine, sir. Let me buy you a drink."

"Beautiful. Shot of Black Velvet, Charlie."

"Black Velvet. Outta five. My name is not Charlie."

"'Scuse me. Charles, Charles."

"Outta five. And sir?"

"Tequila. No food."

Fairchild, grown strong and optimistic, heads for the Lost
Coast. He passes between high forested hills and lowland chaparrals
of manzanita, mobs of near-leafless crones, but still hung with bear-
berries, and he gets near but can't quite locate one or two small
towns in the back country, nothing but a schoolhouse or a tiny
grange hall and a sense that somebody must live here—the creeks of
intrigue burbling through square dances, and tall gone columbine
leaning over into the road—and one tiny kid waving, just holding up
his hand as if to prove it. Out ahead of him a small dog trots lop-
sided, fetching its tongue down through California.

A road not hardly a road," Thompson said. The worst he'd
seen. An African footpath. He'd bought a pint, by now a
half-pint, in Whitehorn, a settlement of dinosaur bikeys too dried-
down to get it kicked over; and not by any means drunk, still he'd
lost interest in worldly things, had melted halfway into the seat cush-

ion, his head rolling with the terrain. "We are lost . . . We are scrotally alone in this universe . . . "

Falls drove, as his sight had come back. But it showed him nothing but ruts and trees, too deep and too close. Whenever branches knocked against the truck he said, "Come in? Come in?" Even the ocean found a place to hide behind these trees. In gaps the country fell away over cliffs topped by wind-flattened grass, the emptiness hung with gulls. Then boom—the jungle. "This ain't no coast," Falls said, "not to me. To me a coast is where you can touch the water."

"'Lost Coast.'"

"I didn't see it on the map."

"Lost Coast. That's what the sign said. Ranger Station, big white arrow."

"That was pointing right. We went straight."

It said 'Lost Coast.' And we're sure as shit lost."

"We ain't lost." Foliage whacked at the windows. "Come in? Come in?"

"Well all I know is one of us is lost. And the other one is with that one."

"Bear must've ate a tourist," Falls said. "Tommy, wake up. There's a vehicle in the road."

Thompson stared up ahead and then said, "I do, Lord. I do . . . I do believe."

When they were close, Falls stopped the car. For a minute both were speechless until Thompson said—

"You realize what's happening, man."

"He's everywhere. There's fifty of him."

"We're under a sign, guy." Thompson got out to check the Porsche. "This is more than coincidence."

Falls could only say, "People are scary."

When Falls cut the truck's engine, Tommy raised up from around front of the Porsche and cupped one ear. "It's still humming. And I can smell the exhaust. Can you smell it?" He came around to the rear and put his hands over the vents of the engine compartment like a healer in the throes and arched back his head. "Warm as a young woman!" He dug his penknife from his front pocket and stabbed through the two rear tires near the hubcaps, going from one to the next and then pausing to look up.

He put a finger to his lips and whispered: "*I'm about to make my bones.*"

Falls got out of the truck while Tommy urged him, with clenched teeth and a rictus face and quelling motions of his hands, to do it silently. But Falls had already heard the brush snapping somewhere off the road.

Tommy tiptoed over to the truck and opened the passenger door quietly and disappeared into the interior.

Falls drew his knees up, sitting on the Porsche's rear bonnet. "Make my bones? Did somebody turn on a Mafia flick? Is the TV on?" he said.

Then the door opened to its full extension and Falls looked right into the barrel and scope of Tommy's Casull.

Falls leapt like a spider from his perch and out of the picture, shaking his head.

The grower, wrapped in a white terrycloth bathrobe and scratching his scalp vigorously with both hands, stepped into the road at quite some distance beyond the Porsche, nearly a hundred feet. He carried a kit pack over one shoulder and made altogether a confusing picture.

Tommy rested the gun on the doorsill and got one off at an actual target while the man still constituted a target, then stepped aside and emptied the cylinder after him, pausing to recover himself and cock the hammer again behind each enormous report.

Falls said, "Boy, that thing is big."

"Shut up. I can't hear you anyway."

"I rest my case."

"Let's see if we can chase him down."

"I'll give it an hour or so. Till I'm tired. Then let's try the dogs."

Tommy had his ammo on the truck's hood, plucking rounds from the little box and reloading. His pride and joy was no fighting gun—he had to pry out the empties with his knife. He put each in his pocket as he extracted it from the chamber. Had four new ones in when he slapped the cylinder shut—"I hear him!"—and raced off the road and leapt like a ballet dancer over the downhill crest, one arm back and his gun hand out and his legs spried forward and back, firing. Bart was yelling, "TOMMY! TOMMY! TOMMY!" and kept yelling it over and over as Thompson clambered up onto the road and came back toward him, "TOMMY TOMMY TOMMY TOMMY TOMMY," mechanically and quite loudly, even into Tommy's face.

"WHAT WHAT WHAT WHAT WHAT, ASSHOLE?"

"Do I have your attention?"

"Let's get him."

Falls sat on the truck's front bumper and looked as if he was think-ing.

"What. You're pissed."

"You know, the thing is, Tommy, we've agreed and agreed."

"What. Not to shoot him. I know. He was a million miles away. I just got off a few."

"Nine. You got off about nine here in the last two minutes."

"Well, I won't get off no more till we talk to him. Here." Tommy dangled the revolver by its trigger-guard, offering the handle.

Falls took it and stood up and tried putting it in his waistband, but the ridiculous telescopic sight hung it up. The barrel was hot and it was far too heavy anyway, nearly as heavy as some rifles he'd carried. The thing would yank your pants right off you. He'd have to lug it by the grip.

"Remind me don't never go hunting with you, Tommy."

In his crepe-soled canvas shoes, his celestial terror, Fairchild skied downhill over the duff, slapping at trunks just wider than his grasp. He put his hand to the left side of his neck, which bled, but he thought not seriously, not from the majors. A carotid wouldn't have given him time to consider the matter. The jugular would have spat streamers of his life higher than his head. Just leaking steady like a spring in a draw. But where do you put a tourniquet for such a thing? With his palm he applied pressure. It was the best he could do. They'd snicked by all around him like flies, like thoughts. One had hit a rock or such and screamed past like an airborne dentist's drill. Maybe a fragment from that one. He didn't know. Anyway they'd hurt him again.

This forest ended at the sea. He would descend to the shore, fol-low along it to the ranger's shack, communicate with that person in any way necessary to stop all this.

At this point in his thoughts he realized that he was lying on his back with his left shoulder nailed to the ground. Thunder rolled away above his head. Gunshots. He felt intensely cold down that side of him, the shoulder freezing.

Pilloried thus he looked up at the boughs. A breeze turned the leaves in equivocating gestures. He sensed he was not where he thought he was, nowhere near the place. He'd tumbled downhill, and there was dirt in his mouth. He spat it out. It rained down in his eyes.

Convulsively he sat up and wiped at them, smirching his face with loam, and collided with a tree before he understood he'd come upright, his legs were running, he was terrified of everything behind him and was getting away from it. But he was falling, and now he was stopped again in a shocking embrace. Two fat thighs crushing the breath from his mouth. He saw himself cradled horizontally in the crotch of a forked alder. His face wavered and the bark's blemishes throbbed. These images were reflected ones: He looked down on a slow creek. In an attempt at righting himself he struggled backward and the steep woods dropped dizzily from his view and he saw the ocean, and several rainbows between shore and horizon, half a dozen of them, double ones, intersecting even, moving strangely as the clouds moved, disappearing, reappearing, working along his nerves a spasm of dislocation and alarm because he assumed them to be evidence he was losing the dependability of his senses. Then he understood them to be real. He wriggled backward from the tree's scary avuncular lap, his toes found the earth, he leaned against a branch.

The creek's gully widened into a rocky arroyo, a fissure in the obscuring vegetation that cracked open the view uphill, to his right, where one multicolored arc descended like a blade into the sunny hillside. Down through the light came a small intricate rain, and through its twinkling shreds came the pig-men. Over this distance their minute progress along the hillside seemed involuntary, they seemed dumb as tiny insects. The pig-men moved through a rainbow and didn't know it. The two figures entered another rainbow and didn't come out.

From his right shoulder by one strap his rucksack dangled. He pinched at the strap with his fingers and tried to shrug it away. Ice exploded through his left shoulder, as if he'd been struck there by a miraculously penetrating blizzard—pain, and of a probably undiscovered category. He turned to take a step, to walk away from it, to continue, but sat down with his legs splayed. As if on wheels he proceeded downward until his feet had sunk in the brook, where a long riffle drubbed over them. Still sitting, he worked toward the little pool at its head, but now he was wading out into the creek. His rucksack slipped along his arm, and he paused until he had its strap in his hand and slung it toward the opposite bank, a distance of four or five feet. Down nearer the water's level it seemed much wider, a placid river whose other side was lost to his eyes. But it was swift, and getting deeper. Wading and floating, he lost the bottom and the rushing water cartwheeled him—pebbles, bubbles, pebbles, bubbles—

He was looking up at leaves again . . . The forked alder leaned down close above him. His rucksack lay beside his head.

He entered a tentative communion with the person watching all this, through which he formed a vague understanding that the person watching had been unconscious, and that he was the person. One of them jerked upright now like a marionette, and the other sent him downhill, dangling near the edge where the gully plunged deep and he felt himself also plunging. By refusing to think about the gully he began to lessen its pull. He began to go another direction simply by thinking about it. Water clucked in his shoes with every step. Rain fell heavily. He heard the gusts and the cannonading surf. This thing had to be dealt with, this thing that had happened.

Each time he looked up he saw the pig-men in the distance—in the lightning, in the rainbows, in the sunset, in the dark woods—always silhouetted, like some sort of monument to nothing. To themselves.

Again he found himself among trees, and he rested, leaning downhill, astride the trunk of a eucalyptus. Reached up with his functioning arm and grappled down a lot of long dry leaves. Plucked like a flower, hauled into the sky, the tree began to slip upward away from him. He went down on his side, waited for strength, crawled on two knees and one forearm toward a small slow-running wash. Lay with his face in the water and sucked at it. Turned his head sideways in three inches of clear water that drifted in and out of his open mouth. His right hand crawled up toward his ear and dislodged a length of shale from beneath his cheek. Lying there with half his head in the little flow he scraped away the pebbles before his eyes and pried with the shale in the layer of clay beneath them. He pushed to a sitting position and let himself backward against a rock and once again rested, watching the misty crimson tresses lengthen from his pants leg down the rivulet, over a six-foot drop and out of sight.

The nasty pimpled alder stood above him. Beside the water lay his rucksack. He began to understand that he'd accomplished these innumerable journeys, so many and so involved he could hardly remember them, in a radius of three or four feet.

A path, too wide to have been delved by animals, a path for human traffic, passed along among the trees quite near to where he sat against this small boulder with his lap full of mulch and muck. Sleep pushed itself against him, gigantic and soft, but he was certain if he drifted sideways and lay along the ground he'd never get up.

Like a one-handed baker at his bread he rigged two poultices of clay and wrapped them in long eucalyptus leaves and paused a while, looking around him at things he didn't quite recognize.

The roving dilated apertures of him zoomed down to pinpoints. He was looking at a broken stump.

A buzzard alighted, slowing its descent by clapping its wings together before its chest, and then stood there on the stump with its wings outspread and uplifted gingerly to dry—drops pending from its pale liverish under-feathers and the light behind it streaked with its silhouette—a raindrop on the tip of every feather. Everything else was wet too. Smooth nuggets plummeted from the forest's upper stories.

"Hey man."

Did I say that or did you?

"You are the Thunderbird." That's me. I'm the one speaking.

By kicking at it he loosened a stone from its nook, a flat rock the circumference of his head, four inches thick. Moving along on his knees, he pushed it into the middle of the path. He set the poultice beside it. He lay himself on his side and stretched his right arm out to drag toward him his second cake of clay and eucalyptus.

He positioned his materials, the poultices, the flat stone, next to a knee of rock about the span of his hand cropping up beside the path. Slapped a poultice across his back, across his shattered left shoulderblade, and lay back with the poultice between the rock and the wound and screamed, putting the pressure of his weight against this point. The buzzard's dark shape crossed his face. He breathed hard and fast for a minute, then gradually slower. With his right hand he pushed apart the lapels of his white robe, reached for the second poultice and placed it over the entrance wound, and wrestled up onto it the flat rock. His outcries gave over again to rapid breathing, which didn't slow, but instead accelerated until his features relaxed and he lost consciousness.

Though he woke with a storm and red fog in his head, certain thoughts came clearly. The bleeding had abated, or he'd never have wakened. The Thunderbird had crossed him with good luck. His remedies had saved him, and he had to move. He did so instantly, sitting up, pushing his good hand against the ground, and by the device of placing his feet downhill from him on the steep ground, managed to get them under himself and managed to stand. He clung to a trunk and rested, then began to let himself down the hillside from tree to tree. In such dampness the fitful light can't be heat lightning. And not some synaptic arc-welding as his consciousness burned up inside his head, because its silent bursts complicated the foliage with shadows.

Where the gully's sides had collapsed and the trees had fallen over, a hole opened in the prospect all the way to the horizon of the sea. Out there a pall of cloud rose precariously from the flecked water, branched with brief emanations and flickering inside as if it had swallowed TNT. A thing without a face, maybe without a head, it executed a lewd tyrannosauric hootchycoo and it thundered. Wrenching, pitiable. Behind it a second bank of clouds luffed and darkened, then a storm gathered down onto and devoured it. Here the leaves dripped quietly, hardly moving, but out at sea the sunset had been erased from the blackboard, replaced by a gorged darkness. All of this sent a wave of violent air over the water and against the land with the force of a detonated bomb.

Had he touched something, set something off in his face?—his robe puffing up like a balloon, his hair nearly dragged from its follicles with a pain that made him angry, the trees flattened, stripped like bones in a boil, leaves blowing at and over him. Lightning, a hag's hand ripping out, pointed at his destination down there. An interval of brown retinal shock, and everything drowned in thunder. More flashes denominated certain milliseconds: uphill from him, a man here. A man there. Turned toward each other in poignant stopped confusion. Then again—floundering up the hillside. Fairchild floated, the balls of his feet touching earth once, twice, down the hill and again under branches.

The ground leveled. The forest fell away. The storm was over, the cloud bank wadded along the horizon and the episode already forgotten, the whole ocean fallen flat, conked out like a baby animal. The sky overhead appeared a vacuum, without weather or stars, and he came down through moist ground-clinging perfumes into the uniformity of twilight.

The creek fanned open, two inches of water slid over flat sand through a dale that must have been cleared by settlers. An untended orchard. A rusty hayrick, some isolated fenceposts teetering like ashes. Uplifted, freshened by the changes in atmosphere, breathable changes, he kept on alongside what must once have been a road, not down to the sea, but up out of the sea, a little quarter-mile track letting cargo from the ships to the logging town that wasn't here anymore, past the cabins and the schoolhouse that had gone and around and through the orchard that hadn't. The apple trees were ancient, unpruned and extravagantly branched, the later growth curling around like tusks. You can see where one year the apples grew so fat they cracked the boughs. Most of the fruit had been nipped by deer and elk. In the highest branches a few green knuckly fortunate ones. He passed the crumbled vestiges of a wagon, its hubs and axles outflung as if to keep from going under.

Through the trees at a tangent drifted a steamy canescence like the cloud he'd seen earlier, not flickering now, but still engaged in a deep feminine writhing, also a small absentminded humming, almost intelligible.

He shut and opened his eyes, now witnessed a woman who quivered in a faint, personal glamour that shouldn't have been visible, really, not even in such a weak light, a woman in a dark gray dress. Others behind her. The pig-men coming through the shadows. No, not the pig-men, but two presences.

Fairchild thought she was downcast, her head perhaps bent forward and hidden against her chest, but when she turned and this was definitely the front of her, the upper fasts on her gray dress torn open, it was the same. She was headless.

He heard the singing and knew it to be hers, but it came from elsewhere, as if she hid in a tree and only remembered this tableau, singing, while the body, or embodiment, drifted like a lantern in its own light. She sensed her pursuers and took a sprout over the apple boughs. The dim light from her was real, it liquefied the branches below her in its passing and spooked a shadow from under a campsite picnic table. The two presences darkened his view of her briefly, and the dimness of her drifted out toward the water. It sashayed out past the shore; over the water its to-and-fro accelerated, until it wobbled like a drop on a hot ember and suffocated in the dark.

Fairchild had only a little way to go—this probably green but currently indiscernibly colored State Forest Service picnic table. He sat down, facing out, sitting straight, his heart kicking in his throat.

Fairchild leaned his back carefully against the table, thinking that if he'd been going to stop anywhere at all before his feet shuffled into the waves, it could just as easily have been sooner. He'd thought he was being harried out past the shore to drown, but it was only the hill, only gravity, that had driven him.

He felt other presences, fleeting and distant, mostly, except for his father with his ferocious, unabating eyes. He'd been aware of his father's presence for some time now, as clearly and sensorily aware as if he'd heard his father bushwhacking down the draw behind him.

Out on a hunt, boy?

More or less perhaps.

Out catching bullets. You'll end up trephined like a slice of Swiss cheese.

They're working on it.

If only you could've sassed the world like you sass me.

His maculation altered when he spoke. The old man looked patched together out of areas of light and dark, sitting on the other bench across the table and watching things, while Fairchild watched his father.

You're not the only ghost around here.

I never claimed to be.

There's a woman out there.

Her? That's the schoolmarm.

What about her head?

Gone.

Man, me too. I gotta go, I gotta groove.

Whatever for?

The dogs.

The dead dogs. The ghost dogs. We're all ghosts in these parts.

What about me?

Oh yeah. You, me, them. The old schoolmarm and her two buddies. Look who else is here.

Winona? Winona?

Oh yeah. Ever since her boyfriend choked her dead . . . That's the old Winona. The new one's somebody else.

I knew it, Fairchild said.

We don't speak.

They turned to watch Winona suffer past in a mist of confusion, touching the fingers of both hands to her neck.

Father, did you know I was coming?

Hell yes. You were here when I got here. Always have been.

Fairchild thought about this remark but steered around any understanding of it.

Hell, Fairchild said, that sure was a storm.

His father just stared at him.

Hell, Fairchild repeated, that was a storm on loco-weed.

Father went on staring.

Was there a storm perhaps you saw?

Never was any storm but you.

Other demons loitered here in their nakedness and neediness and strangerness, other wraiths, including Indians crucified on the trees and cowboys with their scalped, decorticated craniums. All seemed the sources of little illuminations. Including himself: a man of dreams and failure.

Don't talk to him. When the time comes you'll know everything he has to say anyhow.

Fairchild watched his own ghost wander far down the beach, carrying an air that didn't seem particularly unhappy.

All appeared very much alive. When his father yawned he produced a mistral breath.

What say we all get a little sleep?

I can't.

Why not?

The dogs. The dogs.

The dogs are sleeping, his father said.

His preparation for sleep was like that of the animals. He found a place away from light and noises, where his body wouldn't be threatened by predators or thieves and he could relax without moving or falling. He lay still under the table and yielded, for once, to no ambush of embarrassing moments—old moments that beset you just before sleep, moments that rise up on their hind legs and walk like dinosaurs. His eyelids fluttered. The little pond between waking and sleeping is bewitched . . . no one floats across with open eyes. He renounced control over his train of thought, he said farewell to concerns, to any capacity at all for concern, he let his will fall into a bottomless pit of passivity and nihilism . . . Then there began to appear to him those first messages of a new world—hypnagogic phenomena. He was shaken by truths, electrified, soothed.

On the day of his death Nelson Fairchild received numerous grants of peace and grief, proofs of the beauty of the world, clarifications, deep consolations, and happiness. Descending from clear dark spaces, he came first into a kind of translucence. He woke with a warm easy feeling and didn't hurry into the state of waking. Faint, unfriendly messages arrived from that territory, regions of discomfort, aches. Now he was on the shores of awareness, rolled up onto the sands in his own body, sleep a particular to be grasped at, an outer garment he tried to stay wrapped in. But something about the darkness under its baggy folds . . . It seemed bigger than any darkness he'd ever visited, and scared him further awake.

Dreamed I was real.

Lying on his right side with a bump of sand-grown switchgrass under his cheek, his rucksack cuddled against his belly, he watched what appeared to be the shores of an ocean from his near-sleep. He caught himself caressing his groin with his good hand; realized he didn't want to stop; understood that he took comfort from it. The other hand had evidently been taken away, erased, and the arm and shoulder too, expunged from his experience and all mirrors and all old photographs of himself. A generalized suffering stole over but didn't entirely smother his sense of the rightness of things—the shadow of his situation, a little distant, troubling but accepted. He smelled something like the faint rancid signature of a tomcat—eucalyptus. Heard the fustigating breakers—he would write that down.

Oh well. Why not?

He got up and sat at the table he'd slept under. He considered, for a while, how that might have been accomplished, went over the operations he must have performed on the physical plane, the crawling, standing, balancing, lowering, and gathered that he'd just now been heroic. This crazy immense nausea. From now on he promised to be a coward.

It was morning, but with an evening light. The shadow of the mountains worked far out onto the sea and stopped there: here was the gray-green water, there were the clouds, and between them a cupreous molten interlude ate its way toward California. Way back in the highlands the buzzards walked precariously on nothing. The seals calling, the gulls calling, but he couldn't see them. He worked one-handed at the buckles on his rucksack—his papers, his pen.

Although entirely alone he was embarrassed at the literalness with which he'd taken it all lately, allowed almost a whole afternoon and evening to swim through him uninterpreted. His was not a mind to permit such things. No unsupervised swimming. His soul never took its clothes off—Melissa said it ruined him in bed. Winona might have said it too if she'd been granted the sensitivity ever to have figured it out.

Then he heard the schoolmarm, the humming of almost intelligible words. A song and a voice reminiscent, decidedly so, of an Indian flute. And now the low strangled death moan of a man, these sounds more frightening, for their being daylit, than they'd seemed last night.

He moved again, jolted along by his alarm but swiftly powerless, and sat down right beside the sea. The Ocean, the source of life, the place of death, he intended to write, the Ocean behaving like a deity, but he forgot. Sitting in the wet sand he apprenticed himself to the sea's infinite pitiable preoccupation with the shoreline.

As I write this this morning in a camp in coastal Humboldt County, the sun touches the canyon and absolutely ignites the path leading out of here. But I doubt very much I'll be walking that path.

I feel in fact as if I live here, on the main thoroughfare of ghosts, in a traffic of nonentities. I hear their shuffling steps in the grass—

And the moans of the man. He could make out a couple of animals, seals—maybe some kind of bird—or otter perhaps—rummaging after gull eggs—scrambling over the rocks with oologic obsessiveness. Ah, here were the seals offshore, balneating with their snouts up like French intellectuals.

The shuffling feet went past. Fairchild kept his eyes down and saw only the man's waterlogged shoes and the laces' aglets licking at the sand. But had to look up. The rapist priest of Schoolmarm Cove—clutching his rat-gnawed Holy Bible.

He'd written, he saw, nothing at all. He wrote:

I am dying in Wheeler, California, a village by the Pacific around forty miles straight up the coast from Fort Bragg. I'm the only person in town. In fact, to call it a town or a village, or anything like that, is misleading. There are three or four walls standing around here in a little dell the old maps call "School Marm's Cove," and two or three big rusty pieces of last century's logging machinery turned out lop-sided under the oaks; otherwise this place is just a place—a creek, a grove, a meadow. The thing is, it's still called Wheeler. There are two or three campsites in the grove maintained by the Forest Service. I'm the only person within miles. Except for the pig-men.

I'm here to decide whether to let my life go, or fight to stay inside it. To face the music, or stay dead.

Or—I've come here to be alone for the rest of my life with the tension, the beautiful tension, between those two alternatives. I may decide nothing. May stay here forever with my alternatives. May take them both out of here with me.

I just want to let myself be guided, in this solitude, by my truth.

He wrote some lines, trying to remember the whole paragraph, but failing, lines from Hermann Hesse's *Demian*—"*. . . because of my evil and misfortune I stood higher than my father and the pious, the righteous . . .*"

I almost wrote "eveil"—I wrote "eveil" and crossed it out—as if evil veils something that is not evil as we understand it—a gift—live—evil—veil—

He rested, looking out at the flotsam and haughty seal-snouts in the water. Looked down at the page. He could find only three words: *I am dying*

Though he sat in a shadow, a darker shadow fell across him, and he leapt up. The schoolmarm in her pale torn dress with its empty neck-line. She left no footprints, but the priest's shoes dragged shallow troughs in the sand as he followed. The Moor followed the priest.

Fairchild came last with his pen behind his ear, clutching his papers. The four kept to the water's edge with a good distance between each of them, paralleling the brazen horizon, the populous cloudscape. Offshore the gulls dove upward against sudden atmo-spheric walls, the wind sawing and gusting, the sea jagged but unflecked. His hair felt greasy, and the skin of his face. He tasted salt on his lips.

They drifted into the creek's wide flat mouth and he followed. His strength gave out as the water narrowed. He sat down beside it at a second campsite table scattered with leaves and watched the water's movement. A sense of passing and staying.

I want to die like this river. I want to drift away and I want to be clear and cold. And underneath my passing I want a cruel bed of stones.

Where was Father?

He called "Father?" but his throat let out only a breath shaped like Father.

The Old Man wouldn't show. No phantasms visited him other than the schoolmarm passing headless by. She was surprised by smugglers or, some said, Pomo Indian renegades, but Fairchild liked the version in which she was surprised by the priest, a Spaniard ruined by mescal or syphilis. The priest and his Moorish boatman had escorted her here from San Francisco to take up her duties, and when they discovered nobody around, the three had hiked four miles north to pick blackberries, known to them as roundberries, beside Bear Harbor, where the priest and the Moorish boatman fell upon and raped her, then chased her all the way back to this town of Wheeler. She was young and frail, it was said of her she looked hardly strong enough to carry her auburn hair's beautiful abundance, but she fought back against them, disemboweling the Moor with a scythe, which the priest wrestled away and used to behead her, and then he hung himself. And now the two rapers live here as ghosts, in earshot of her singing in heaven.

I can't remember, he wrote, *if I'm remembering this or learning it just now.*

He looked up because he heard the dogs, the dogs.

Some people we glimpse as chasms, briefly but deeply, even to the death of us. Others are shallow places you never seem to get across.

He examined the page. Still only three words had appeared.

The wonderful fountain pen. The pen had run out of ink. To get its halves uncoupled one-handed, he took its butt end in his teeth. He filled it from the dark red puddle of himself he was sitting in on the bench.

Up in the forest, the dogs bayed. The wind in and out of boughs like the suspiration of organs, *I am no longer passionate for Melissa who lit up my bones, but for solitude, more and more in love with solitude.* His left arm laid his blood all over the margin of the pages.

Oh, but he understood now: I am the schoolmarm of School Marm's Cove.

The demons roiled in her belly and exited through her heart as sobs and sighs. Worst were the slow stirrings of frozen emotions waking up, astonishingly delayed responses, the putrid dregs of childhood traumas, old griefs clawing their way up out of her, bursting from her throat, nothing connected with any memories at all, only the feelings themselves.

The dogs. The dogs. She heard them baying. Saw them come like leaves blown down the hill among the trees. Then again, lower down the hill. Their music was the song of dogs, full of joy, tamped down and flowing over. And offshore the seals, some yipping like pups and others saying, Heart? Heart heart? Heart? When she saw the men she felt explosive incommunicable gratitude.

I'll probably never leave, the schoolmarm wrote in her own blood. *Is this strange? Yes, wonderful and strange. The blades of the pasture stopped in the sun have had all the life cooked out of them by the drought—all the hope, the strength to grow, to suffer—and now*

and now they are God. I'm standing barefoot on the grass, writing these words. And I must keep it a secret. I can show this only to the people I've failed, and to those I've had the privilege of betraying.

Clarence Meadows entered the Gualala Hotel and walked sharply left, into the bar, where the drinkers of the forenoon listened to the jukebox. Meadows took a table quite near the large-screen TV and faced the window onto the highway. Out there across the road in his church minivan the Reverend Connor would be pausing for a minute, long enough to be recognized, before he travelled on to the rendezvous. The Scout, parked just there, did not look conspicuous. He'd transferred the plants to three silvery space-age trash bags and jammed them in back with the bunched tarpaulin; it all looked like so much what-all, the usual stuff. But it reeked like baking spinach.

Meadows shook his head at the barmaid before she'd made the crossing, and she leaned herself on the bar again and put her face close to another woman's and went on with the conversation. The TV played, but not its sound; only the jukebox's furry music.

The blue Lutheran minivan pulled up across the empty highway, idled there for sixty seconds, and departed.

The image of the man on the big screen, in his weariness and his handcuffs, with his fingers working continually for circulation, was as large as Meadows himself, sitting beside it. It was old footage. Then the videotape of yet another bad day in the history of Joe Hopeless: José Esperanza murdered, face down in a galaxy of multicolored golf balls with his shirt up and his big tattoo bleeding. They'd been showing this stuff all week. The station was infatuated with this amateur video taken minutes, even seconds, after the shooting.

Meadows went to the bar and out of a big glass bowl gathered a whole lot of stale pretzels in his hands. He took them back to his seat and spread them out on the tabletop and started eating them.

Meadows had no training in civilian murder, but he gathered keeping the weapon afterward was no good. Yet he'd wrapped the Winchester in a ratty blanket and rested it at a haphazard angle in the scout's camper, and had driven off still in possession of this evidence against him. It was down on the floorboards under the dope even this minute.

He'd broken his fast and kept down his meal of vengeance. The two had been dressed for death just as they'd been at birth. The mystery of their nakedness he took as a signal of his justification.

Inside of an hour he'd come back here with a lot of money. Rent a room and take a very long, very hot shower, get under the sheets with his hair still wet and resign the office. Leave it to the younger wolves. Sleep for twelve hours absolutely without moving. He intended then to get married, at least informally, to the mother of his future child.

He'd opened the camper door and rousted the pair of dogs, and they'd made like bullets for the creek and sunk their tongues in it. The plants had been wrapped still in Meadows's own blue tarpaulin, and covered with a blanket. The dogs had been sleeping on them.

It had occurred to him as he reached the culvert, and then the road, that he probably should have shut the camper door after the dogs had exited, lest they shelter inside it and the wind blow it to, and trap them.

Anne asked, "Are you going somewhere? Going far? I mean I need the van this afternoon."

Not far, he said, or maybe he didn't say. Some days you just can't hear the sound of your own voice.

"I've got books, seven boxes I think."

The Reverend Connor changed his plans and let his wife have the van for the morning. He sat around in his living room, fully dressed down to his loafers, watching TV and refusing to answer the telephone.

Just before noon he pulled a turtleneck sweater over his head and walked by the road, avoiding the hill and the plot of graves behind his home, down to the Gualala mall, where Anne sold books.

As he got near the post office he spied a woman whose name escaped him, one of his congregation, holding her new baby, a daughter, if he recalled. "Hi!" the mother shouted. Dad was just going through the door with his letters and cards, and he turned and picked out Connor across the parking lot and smiled and waved.

How's the new baby, he called and went over to pat the baby's head, or actually not. Not in this kind of mood. Actually he brushed on along the buildings and hoped they thought they'd mistaken him.

The church's van needed new wiper blades. To purchase them he went over to the Phillips station where the young preacher from West Point tended the pumps, because whenever he came down the hill he always approached this citizen, entered into some little exchange, the way he imagined a very rich man would stop and give money to a beggar, just to feel himself going to hell.

With the wipers tucked under his arm he went through the mall's glass doors and into the heady smell of grinding coffee and stopped in at the bookstore. Anne sat, as she always did, in a tall chair, wearing somewhat unattractive spectacles and chatting with whoever came and went. He didn't think she sold many books.

"You need the van?" she asked. "I'm done."

The register binged, the drawer came open. She dropped the keys into his open hand.

"Cassandra?" she said, and he recalled: Cassandra played this evening with the orchestra, the school band. Everyone would be embarrassed, but nevertheless. "You didn't make any plans, did you?" his wife asked.

In fact his plans included going to see Harry Lally, selling him a crop, a near-worthless crop. Which actually meant telling him a story, a beautiful story. A story about sailors, fires, and varnish.

"I'm vague," he made sure he said aloud.

U nsigned, unexplained, unclassified—confession or con-
jecture? Murder plot or movie plot? Notes of a conspirator or notes of a suicide or ravings of a madman or—

I'll probably never leave, he believed they said. *Is this strange? Yes,*
they seemed to say, *wonderful and strange. The blades of the pasture
stopped in the sun have had all the life cooked out of them by the
drought—all the hope, the strength to grow, to suffer—and now*

The rest was just not possible. The man had written his last words
in blood. And nobody would ever know what they were though you
could hold them in your hands.

He let the letter fall to the tabletop and looked for his own reflection in his kitchen window. Nobody there. Outside, gray light delivering another day. He reassembled the pages in their envelope.

Navarro put on his cap, fastened above his heart the badge of his
office—the replacement, it had cost him eighty-eight dollars—and
descended, taking the envelope. The breeze blew a bit sticky, not at
all cruel, and the sky was lightly overcast but nothing much threatened. Good weather for the wedding. Urchins went in and out of the
grocery across the street from his apartment with cigarettes clenched
in their teeth, hugging armloads of spray-paint cans.

Before he went down to the wedding at the pier, Navarro stopped off at the station, or office, or, if it was honesty you wanted, the hut. Jenny had drawn the blinds and was consolidating things in near-darkness, mostly on all fours, shaping the files and stacks and ridiculous trash generated by their endeavors. Navarro switched on his desk lamp and sat down.

The fax from Criminal Records had come, the report on the Silverado's owner. He'd seen it on the screen, but he wanted a print-out, something he could ball up and toss in the trash when the time came. The vehicle was registered to a John Falls, Jr., middle name Bartholomew, who'd served sentences amounting to half his life in various joints, the first stretch for murder, second-degree, charged as a juvenile but tried as an adult, a ten-year sentence, and he'd done the flat dime, nothing indicated in the way of good behavior. The last one in San Quentin for battery plus conspiracy—that meant he'd been hired. The state's big computer had him listed as a goner, his parole violated as of last October, no trace of him since.

Navarro pitched it in his wastebasket and nudged the receptacle out toward Jenny. "The round file, ma'am."

"I've been working here forever, and I was supposed to help. I *did* help. But it's just piling up again."

"How about tossing everything that hasn't been filed yet?"

"Good idea. Much easier. But I'm supposed to *un*file everything over seven years old, to make room in the files for all the new stuff."

"I bet some of the alleged new stuff is more than seven years old."

"Probably. But he won't let me file anything until he puts it in the To File box. Do you appreciate the paradox?"

He turned back to his desk and arranged a pen and paper and started to prepare, in longhand, his letter of resignation. Jenny could put it together in typed sentences. He just had to supply a few reasons. In his mind the reasons swept up everything around him, this place, these people, and himself, and carried them out to sea and over the horizon. What was needed was a letter like the one he'd been reading the last few days. Eighty, ninety pages in a hand that varied from line to line, growing and shrinking, standing up and leaning one way and then the other, like revelers, and the whole thing stained all over with his own blood.

"Why do people choose Halloween to get married?"

"There's quite a good explanation," he said.

"Well, what is it?"

He found he couldn't even start. "Yeah. It's a terrible thing."

Last Halloween he'd pulled sick leave and gone to Ukiah with Mo and watched videos at the Doubletree Inn, formerly the Luanne Motel. They'd asked specifically for the Green Room, so nicknamed because in 1988, toward the close of the Luanne era, the orange carpet under the bed had been stained by a wet olive duffel bag stuffed with five million dollars in cash and hurriedly stashed there, along with two M-16s, by two of the perpetrators of history's biggest cash rip-off. Other partners, all members of an offshoot of the Aryan Brotherhood who called themselves The Order, had taken off north with the rest of the ten million they'd heisted without bloodshed from a Wells Fargo vehicle on a long hill outside town, but these two had rented a room at the Luanne and taken a well-earned rest and awakened to find the parking lot full of federal license plates winking in the morning sun, and the rooms around them rented by gruesome feebs and marshals. The thieves had abandoned the evidence and tiptoed away. The stuff under the bed was found months later by a maid named Constance, still, as of last Halloween, cleaning rooms there, possibly with inspired vigilance. More months passed before most of The Order died in a shoot-out with every known manner of fed, at The Order's hideout in rural Washington. The place had burned, the corpses too, and half the money . . .

Between him and Mo scenes had been enacted, he'd be the first to confess it, scenes in monster-light from lamps knocked over, and afterward cheap repentance in the form of expensive gifts, like maybe a new lamp, a better lamp. But they'd loved each other, and really nothing more than the usual troubles had developed along the way. He'd grown tired, increasingly absent, and hadn't she waited long enough to put her foot down? One day he'd seen clearly she wouldn't go to bed with him anymore. Women, in general . . .

Jenny wore slacks today, really good ones, of a loose violet material that draped and followed when she bent over, tracked the curve of her belly when she stood, caressed her thighs, stretched over the faces of her knees when she crossed her legs. She leaned backward in her swivel chair, arched and sighed.

He'd known her better than a year, but never socially. He caught her watching his eyes as he looked her over, thinking he should have tried dating her a long time ago, but in any case should try now, definitely, now that he intended to quit. But definitely.

Denis Johnson ▪ 428

"You know what I'm thinking?"

Jenny regarded him. "Yeah. I do," she said.

"Okay. And what do you think about it?"

"I think definitely not, John."

A minute ago Navarro had seen the groom around some-where, but the groom had disappeared, maybe into the kitchen of the Cove Restaurant.

There stood the bride in white, chatting, patting her hair. Lacy and antique, her gown. Really a secondhand dress, but not inelegant. Blushing and sparkling, she raised her gown's hem to polish her glasses, dropped it to wave hello. Not necessarily at Navarro.

The letter waited in his cruiser, on the passenger seat, beside the riot gun, the bullhorn mike. The letter that told you none of it, but said it all. The letter explaining everything about nothing.

He stood in the middle of the parking lanes, publicizing his big authority. Somebody tried to hand him their keys, thinking he was here to park cars. "I'm just security," he said.

The bride and groom would get the bill for this festival. Nickels and dimes—Winona owned property and houses now, possibly this very land, this restaurant, and half the Pacific. She stood here not as a rich widow, but as a rich divorcée. You couldn't credit every rumor, but it sounded like she'd get rich all over again come '97 by claiming half a million in life insurance. Navarro didn't know how these things worked, whether she might have to keep up the premiums for six more years, until lawyers declared Fairchild dead.

Everyone got invited to everything on the Mendocino coast, Navarro had surmised that much in his time here. All classes and types banged into, slid amongst each other, intermeshed happily, lin-ing up, filing past aluminum kegs and paper-covered tables. The restaurant provided potato salad and hummus and unpeeled apples and bananas. They went at it like beggars, twitchy with pot-induced hunger. Small intoxicating currents of dope smoke wafted past. Merton had told them, All right, in a car or out back of the restau-rant. Anything more flagrant—off to the cages in Ukiah. Red-eyed hilarious Cowboys and Indians and Mexicans. Tree-killers, pig-hunters, Deadheads, the horsey set from Sea Ranch and the skeletal neo-hillbillies out of burnt-up communes, well-to-do escapees from the entertainment industry, denizens of Low-Income Housing.

Only a minute ago he'd seen the trigetour, looking perfectly straight, his hair tied back and hidden down his collar, just walking around in a beige suit.

Others had disguised themselves: around him, he knew, were witches and demons beyond the stories and fears of any child, lovers of evil to make even a cop afraid and childlike. He knew this, but he no longer knew what evil was. It rarely got arrested. People liked it. The human heart was only one of its homes. Beyond these few ideas, words couldn't follow. Yet they were doing Halloween in the ordinary sense: jack-o-lanterns, paper silhouettes, and all the costumes, phony witches in warty masks, hoboes, that is, men who looked pretty much as they usually did except for baggy pants held up by suspenders of string, ogres in scary masks, warriors in primitive masks, one woman in a Nixon mask, Nixon going braless in black high heels, President Bush masks, Ronald Reagan masks, and dancing girls wearing beautiful masks of thickly applied cosmetics. Nell Taylor, whom he'd dated once, the regional Jazzercise and aerobics queen, performed the Dance of the Seven Veils while a dark, portly man charmed her like a snake with exotic sounds from his clarinet. Navarro thought he'd better date her again.

This, and other more or less formal feats of entertainment, took place next to the restaurant in a train of half-built motel rooms serving nicely as stages. People danced to a band, a revolving pool of local musicians, some recognizable as fallen stars. Navarro was sure at least one of them was supposed to be dead a long time ago. The trigetour hopped up into another of the three-walled motel rooms and created his multicolored system of planets. He escaped from a straitjacket and walked barefoot across broken glass, his spiel inaudible, thanks to the music. Navarro liked rock and roll, but these people hadn't practiced together much, they banged away relentlessly at the standards, and he believed he was hearing "Louie Louie" for the third or fourth time. Between numbers it was all laughter and water. People making frolic, and tiny waves.

Navarro supposed he should stand aside, on the alert, but he let himself be drawn into sassy conversations and drank two beers quickly beside the kegs. Waved to Mo, a dancing girl. She lifted her hand and passed along the edges of his own irrelevance like a figure on a carousel.

The husband of the lady who ran the tack-and-feed store in

Manchester had killed a wild pig, a boar, and he and his brothers had submerged it in a pit overnight with stones and hot coals after wrapping it in corn husks. The three hairy men raised it slowly out of the ground on ropes, unveiled it, and handed it out on paper plates to those who ate flesh, including Navarro. The pork fell away from the bones in wet steaming shreds and tasted like smoke. Meanwhile a logger who looked just like Paul Bunyan pulled the trigetour's Saab around at the end of a rope, the other end clenched in his teeth. Two men pushed the small car from behind at first, to break its inertia, then he dragged it across the parking lot while everybody clapped and yelled.

The ceremony itself came late in the afternoon and was really just one of the things going on at that particular moment. He would have expected Yvonne to be standing over them on a boulder with her scaled wings outspread, blotting out the sunset and putting them in the dark. Instead, they grouped themselves on a bit of sand, away from the stage scattered with instruments and tangled cords, just the three of them. Yvonne faced the couple, but seemed to shrink back. This impression came not from anything about her posture, exactly, but from her hands. Her slender arms fell loose at her sides, but she bent her hands upward behind her, palms down, just as she might if she'd been leaning back against a low railing—thumbs clenched and curved and the fingers straightening with tension and just slightly parted. Carl Van Ness, in a long dressy box-cut Polynesian-looking formal blouse, stood much taller than Yvonne, Winona much shorter. Too many people were talking, and he couldn't hear the vows. Yvonne said words, and the betrothed echoed after. It looked like another anticonventional Northern California sacrament, except for the terrified way she held her hands. It took about a minute.

This out of the way, things got even merrier, a bit debauched, nondancers suddenly dancing, nonmusicians sitting in with the pickup group, nonsingers singing at the microphone, not singing, braying, people trading masks and convening in a rhythmic throng full of ogres with the faces of presidents, hoboes with the faces of witches.

Wilhelm Frankheimer danced with his canes, jutted from the melee with his huge jaw hanging down in a grimace, or smile—yes, dancing on aluminum legs with tiny small Melissa. They'd come dressed as themselves.

Another tall fellow, though not nearly so tall as Frankheimer, began manhandling his wife instead of dancing, and Navarro had to arrest him, inviting the guy over to the squad car with a toss of his head and cuffing his wrists behind his back. "You're not gonna get sick in my ride, are you?"

"I feel okay. I'm sorry. I'm an asshole."

"Watch the head."

"I'm an asshole." Suddenly he bucked backward, rage coloring his face. With the heel of his hand Navarro whacked him on the skull. "Don't make me choke you out."

"Okay. Sorry."

"Choke's illegal in L.A., but not up here."

"*She's* the asshole. FUCK!" he screamed at the top of his voice. Then he folded into a zigzag shape, seized by a moment's meekness, and got in the caged backseat.

Navarro had accomplished what turned out to be, because he soon quit this work, his last act of law enforcement.

A young girl wandered by and stared and said, "Look, it's Kenmore. Kenmore—what'd you do?"

Kenmore said, "I broke their strange laws."

Navarro left Kenmore to cool his heels in the cruiser. Took the letter in its messy white envelope and buttoned it up inside his shirt.

He danced in his uniform, pretending it was rented, though he suspected everybody knew him. His cap flew off and people sailed it around like a Frisbee. He felt he'd made a mistake. Sweat prickled his skin. But the cap came sailing his way and the person next to him caught it and handed it back, and everyone laughed.

The crowd disassembled before the groom, who made his way to a white limousine and opened the door and waited for his wife.

As Winona said good-bye to grotesque well-wishers, taking kisses on her cheeks under raised masks, Navarro made his way toward her. When she was free of them he stood in her path, fingering the envelope through the gaps in his blouse.

"Ma'am, are you a murderer?"

She looked confused, laughed, the moment quickly passed out of her eyes, her attention altogether—

She was gone.

The restaurant's kitchen was open. He went in and sat down in a chair beside a steamy vat of potatoes rolling over and over. The torching humidity was enough to drive him out, but he desperately wanted to be obscure and forgotten for a while; however, the cook came through the door in his whites and apron, nodded, put on his padded mittens, and lugged the big pot to the sinks.

Next Yvonne came in with an empty platter in one hand, white flowers in the other. She didn't say hello, only stared at him. Close up he could see she'd put on makeup for her performance. Still she looked haggard, hounded, as if everybody she loved was cheating her. Her eyes got watery. Her looks went soft for a second. If it wasn't for this letter—

"Is she coming back to me?"

"Mo? . . . Many times. In many lives."

"And you too. You too."

She raised a hand as if to wave, and smiled a very small smile and touched her fingertips to her throat.

"My wife," he said. "My beautiful wife."

And then she, too, was gone.

"Come here," the cook said. An older man, he watched out the window from his craggy profile. "See this."

Fairchild was gone. Mo was gone, though you could look right at her. And he himself was gone, to tell the truth. He just hadn't quite left town. Suddenly he knew he would. He had come here to prove one thing and one thing only about himself and then leave: that he didn't own this loneliness. He dangled down into it and so did innumerable others. It's not ours. It was here before we came.

"Goddamn," the cook said.

Navarro and the cook, each man at his own deep stainless-steel stink, stood looking out the window at a man alone down on the beach with his head tilted way back, exhaling balls of fire. It was the trigetour, in a scene lit up by the thoughts Navarro had just been thinking. Dusk fell and he stood by the sea with his neck arched, face uplifted to the dark sky, clouds of flame rushing up out of him as he touched a brand to the gases in his open mouth. Navarro and the cook observed this process blandly, completely equal to this mystery. Each fiery gust evaporated instantly above the juggler's face. No audience. It seemed a solitary pleasure.

Navarro left the kitchen and crossed through all the voices to sit in the car with Kenmore, who didn't speak. He'd have to take Kenmore back up to the station, and Merton would have to drive him in the county van to the Ukiah jail. But there was room for another back there in the cage, and Navarro thought he'd better wait for that one. Maybe Nell Taylor in a cloud of veils.

In the backseat, Kenmore breathed in and out of his mouth loudly, indicating wrath. Together they watched the party, the prisoner leaning sideways with his wrists cuffed behind him, Navarro hoping for the chance to cudgel another near-innocent for no good reason. He unbuttoned his shirt and took the letter out. If it wasn't for what he was holding in his hands—

"Here she comes."

Mrs. Kenmore, or her legal equivalent, headed their way in a tall peaked witch's cap. With her mask off she looked about Kenmore's age, late thirties, and they'd probably been together a long time.

"She won't jail me."

Navarro didn't think so either. He got out of the car and met her some yards off. "You can come to the station tomorrow if you want him charged."

"Can't you get him out of here?"

"I can send him home. But unless I have your word you'll go through with pressing charges, I can't keep him."

"Can I talk to him?"

"Sure, for the rest of your life. But for now? I'd say give it a break."

"Well . . . I don't think he needs to be locked up."

"Tomorrow's soon enough to change your mind."

Back in the car with the prisoner, Navarro told him his wife would come to the station tomorrow with a decision as to his short-term future.

"She'll never jail me."

"I can take you up to the end of the straightaway there, and let you go."

"Sounds like a plan."

"But if you turn up here at any time later tonight, I will produce my weapon and empty it into you. Are we clear?"

Kenmore's eyes widened and his ears moved back and his scalp jumped. "Jesus," he said. "I guess I better agree to your terms."

"And you come to the station tomorrow at one P.M. sharp."

"You bet. Whether you shoot me or not."

Navarro drove along the flat of the empty vale. All the trailers of the former shantytown had been removed to make room for plans and schemes, for some faintly rumored or only imagined luxury resort. Where the curves began, he put Kenmore on the road and watched as he moved off with a studied lack of bitterness, swiveling his wrists and working his hands, taking it on the heel and toe.

In a few minutes Navarro drove up near the water-treatment facility and turned the car around. He parked by the road at the head of the straightaway, upwind of the imperceptibly boiling green cess. Here he could turn on his dome light and discourage drunk driving among those who'd be heading home soon, just by the sobering sight of him. And he could read.

He knew these to be the final three pages, because the one in blood had to be the very last, and the other two had been stuck to it. The second-to-the-last bore a single line in ink:

I am dying

and the one before that only a small entry:

> *I'm looking for the Lost Coast. Run up against the moment*
> *I can't go into this new thing, I can't pass the V's of the valleys*
> *divulging bits of Pacific like the throats of silver girls, or this*
> *seafood joint with its amber windows and poised above a*
> *crimson neon martini a crimson neon fish of sorts. The clefts of*
> *the valleys. The décolletage of the valleys.*

He thought he could make out the first words of the bloody entry, but the rest were completely illegible. The blood hadn't behaved like ink, had worked a microscopic dispersion through the fibers and had averaged out into blots, mainly, with occasional stems, so that it looked as if for his last words Nelson Fairchild had composed a piece of musical notation, a song, a melody, an air.

Maybe he'd take it to a musician. Maybe it was, in fact, a bit of music. But he wouldn't take it anywhere. He really didn't want to give it up, give it away. It was his. It spoke the language.

Navarro tried the page at varying distances from his face, seeking just one more word. If it wasn't for what he held in his hands he'd be lost.

Author's Note

This creation is not my own. I owe the deepest thanks to the genius of Bill Knott, whose "Poeme Noire" provides the plot of this tale, and to his wonderful kindness in letting me elaborate on it as I've done.

The terrain where this story is enacted is not entirely as it exists on the maps. Landmarks have been moved and whole small regions created out of thin air. As for the area's population, the portraits presented here are portraits of no one.

In some passages, the dialog is sprinkled with quotes from the text of *A Course in Miracles* in a way that distorts their intent. To anybody wanting a truer understanding of some of the notions touched on by the character Yvonne in her discourses, I recommend *A Course in Miracles*, the Text, Workbook, and Manual for Teachers, available from the Foundation for Inner Peace, P.O. Box 635, Tiburon, CA 94920.